P9-EDF-040

Praise for *Dark Ambitions*

"A rip-roaring crime thriller . . . electrifying."

Publishers Weekly

"An intriguing blend of faith, romance, and suspense."

Booklist

"Fans of high-octane romantic suspense will enjoy every bend and twist of this riveting conclusion to the Code of Honor series. A strength of this story is in its ending, which the author spins perfectly out of control."

Interviews and Reviews

"A ride with so many twists and turns, even the most experienced readers will need to hang on at some point. From the opening pages to the last, *Dark Ambitions* will leave you white-knuckled."

Remembrancy.com

"With the perfect blend of romance and mystery, this book was unputdownable."

Write-Read-Life

Praise for *Hidden Peril*

"Hannon combines intrigue and restrained romance to create a story layered with multiple intertwining mysteries."

Publishers Weekly

"Top-notch and probably one of Hannon's best to date. If you like mysteries or thrillers, what are you waiting for? This one is a real winner and one I am happy to recommend to all ages."

Bookworm Banquet

Praise for *Dangerous Illusions*

"The suspenseful conclusion and believable romantic element will leave readers eager for the next installment."

Publishers Weekly

"Hannon delivers a new romantic suspense series that starts off slowly but then races full speed ahead, spinning out a twisty plot. The author's many fans will devour this work."

Library Journal

POINT
OF
DANGER

Books by Irene Hannon

Heroes of Quantico

Against All Odds

An Eye for an Eye

In Harm's Way

Guardians of Justice

Fatal Judgment

Deadly Pursuit

Lethal Legacy

Private Justice

Vanished

Trapped

Deceived

Men of Valor

Buried Secrets

Thin Ice

Tangled Webs

Code of Honor

Dangerous Illusions

Hidden Peril

Dark Ambitions

Triple Threat

Point of Danger

Standalone Novels

That Certain Summer

One Perfect Spring

Hope Harbor Novels

Hope Harbor

Sea Rose Lane

Sandpiper Cove

Pelican Point

Driftwood Bay

Starfish Pier

POINT OF DANGER

IRENE HANNON

Revell

a division of Baker Publishing Group
Grand Rapids, Michigan

© 2020 by Irene Hannon

Published by Revell
a division of Baker Publishing Group
PO Box 6287, Grand Rapids, MI 49516-6287
www.revellbooks.com

Printed in the United States of America

Library of Congress Cataloging-in-Publication Data
Names: Hannon, Irene, author.
Title: Point of danger / Irene Hannon.
Description: Grand Rapids, Michigan : Revell, a division of Baker Publishing
    Group, [2020] | Series: Triple threat ; 1
Identifiers: LCCN 2020003702 | ISBN 9780800736170 (paperback) | ISBN
    9780800739058 (library binding)
Subjects: GSAFD: Romantic suspense fiction. | Christian fiction.
Classification: LCC PS3558.A4793 P65 2020 | DDC 813/.54—dc23
LC record available at https://lccn.loc.gov/2020003702

20 21 22 23 24 25 26   7 6 5 4 3 2 1

To JoAnn Case—
My one-hundred-year-young friend.

Thank you for enriching my life beyond measure.

We may not be bound by blood . . .
but you will always be family in my heart.

1

THE PACKAGE WAS TICKING.

Eve Reilly froze . . . sucked in a breath . . . and gaped at the FedEx box propped beside her front door.

Tick.

Tick.

Tick.

Tick.

The sound was faint—but distinctive.

And was that . . . was that a *wire* sticking out through the tape?

She squinted.

Yeah.

It was.

Heart stuttering, she eased the door closed, snatched up the cell she'd dropped on the hall table, and jabbed in 911 as she bolted toward the back of the house.

The box definitely didn't contain anything as prosaic as the new water filters she'd ordered for her fridge.

"911. What is the nature of your emergency?"

"There's a package on my front porch that's t-ticking—and a wire is hanging out of it." Eve dug through the drawer next

9

to the kitchen sink until her shaky fingers closed over the back-door key for her neighbor's house.

"I'm dispatching as we speak." The woman's voice was calm. Like she dealt with bombs every day. "I want you to vacate the premises and find cover a safe distance away until officers arrive."

"Got it." She pulled open the back door and clattered down the deck steps while she answered the woman's questions, trying to wrap her mind around this surreal turn of events.

Hate mail was one thing. An occupational hazard you learned to live with in her type of job.

But a bomb?

Way out of bounds.

She skipped the last step and leapt to the ground.

Maybe her sisters were right.

Maybe hosting a controversial talk radio show *was* a dangerous job.

And maybe, in the future, she wouldn't cavalierly dismiss the venom that was sometimes spewed at her by listeners who didn't agree with her opinions.

For now, though, she had to focus on keeping her neighbors safe. Willing as she was to put *herself* in the line of fire as part of her job, it wasn't fair to endanger the innocent residents of this bucolic St. Louis suburb she called home.

The 911 operator finished her questions as Eve sprinted next door.

"I'll stay on the line until officers arrive. Are you moving to a safe location?"

"Uh-huh." Or she would be soon. After detouring to Olivia Macie's. The eighty-one-year-old widow would either be watching TV with the volume sky-high or napping without her hearing aid. She wouldn't hear her phone—and she might not even notice the noise from the emergency vehicles that would soon descend on the quiet cul-de-sac.

After bounding up the steps to the woman's back porch, she skidded to a stop, set the phone beside the pot of geraniums on the patio table, and pounded on the door.

"Come on, Olivia. Open up. Please!" As she squeezed her other neighbor's key, the first faint wail of a siren keened through the muggy August air.

She continued to pummel the door until the spry, white-haired woman at last pulled it open.

"Gracious, Eve." Olivia adjusted her glasses and blinked. "I thought I was being raided."

"Sorry. You need to go down into the basement ASAP." She gave the woman a choppy three-sentence explanation. "Until the police get here and tell us what to do, that's the most secure place."

She hoped.

After all, if subterranean walls of concrete offered protection from tornados, they ought to shield a person from a bomb that was a hundred feet away . . . right?

And it had to be safer than fleeing in the open air. What if the package exploded while Olivia was outside?

Her skin grew clammy as a stream of stomach-turning images strobed through her mind.

"There's a bomb on your front porch?" Her neighbor stared at her as if she'd just said aliens had landed in the yard.

"I don't know for sure—but it's ticking, and I'm not taking any chances. Can you get downstairs by yourself while I stash Ernie in the basement?" Her neighbors to the north would be devastated if anything happened to the coddled bichon frise they'd left in her charge while they attended a wedding in Chicago.

"Of course—but you should take cover too."

"I will." She tossed the promise over her shoulder as she hurtled down the steps and dashed across her backyard to her other neighbor's house, the wail of the sirens louder now.

Please don't let that package blow up while I'm out here, Lord!

With that desperate plea looping through her mind, she zoomed to her neighbor's back porch, breaking every personal speed record.

Once she slipped through the door, Ernie pranced around her feet with a happy yip, then charged toward his food dish and gave her a hopeful tail wag.

"Sorry, buddy." She snagged his leash off a hook and swept him up. "You can chow down later. In the meantime, you and I are going to the basement."

The white fluff ball began to squirm as if he'd been attacked by a band of marauding fleas.

Clearly the word *basement* did not conjure up positive vibes.

She set her cell on the counter and tightened her grip. "Sorry again, but that's the best place for us until this is over."

Negotiating the stairs with a wriggling fur ball in her arms was a challenge—but self-preservation was a powerful stabilizer.

At the bottom of the steps, she snapped on his leash, secured it to the rail, and set him on the floor.

"Chill, Ernie. We won't be down here for—"

Bam! Bam! Bam!

She jerked, hand flying to her chest as the pounding on the back door reverberated through the quiet house.

Ernie whined, and she gave him a quick pat before starting back up to the main level. "Stay."

Instead of following her order, the pup clambered up on her heels as far as the leash allowed, almost knocking her off balance in his frenzy to avoid banishment.

Tuning out his plaintive howls, she hightailed it to the back door. A police officer in tactical vest and helmet with the visor down was visible through the window, fist raised as if he was preparing to bang again.

He spoke the instant she pulled the door open. "Ma'am, you need to leave the house. We have a possible bomb next door, and we're evacuating the adjacent homes."

"I know about the bomb. I called it in. I live there." As she flapped a hand toward her modest Cape Cod house, his eyebrows rose. "I came over to take care of my neighbor's dog, okay? They're gone for the weekend. I have their key." She held it up. "The basement's safe, isn't it? Because that's where I told my neighbor on the other side to go too."

The man pulled his radio off his belt. "I'll give the officer who's working those houses her location." He took her arm and urged her out the door. "We'll get a statement once we're out of range."

"Should I bring Ernie?"

He frowned. "Who?"

"My neighbor's dog." She motioned toward the basement door. "I wouldn't want—"

"He'll be fine. Let's go."

Without giving her a chance to respond, he hustled her across the yard, keeping the houses lining the street between them and the package on her porch.

While the 911 dispatcher had treated her call as routine, the officer from this quiet, local suburb seemed a bit rattled.

At the end of the cul-de-sac, he handed her off to a County officer inside the yellow police tape that cordoned off the neighborhood.

The uniformed woman introduced herself, but the name didn't penetrate the fog that had begun to swirl through Eve's brain.

"Ma'am?" The officer peered at her. "Are you all right?"

The question registered at a peripheral level, and she forced herself to concentrate. "Um . . . sure. I think so." She tightened her grasp on the key in her hand as police officers swarmed the area, sweat glistening on their brows.

But the hot sun couldn't dispel the cold chill that rippled through her.

"Let me get you a bottle of water." The officer kept tabs on her as she strode toward the emergency vehicles that were multiplying like mosquitoes in a stagnant pond.

Eve suppressed another shiver and tried to tune out the controlled frenzy around her.

Weird how she could pontificate for six hours a week to a quarter of a million listeners around the country about the violence, vulgarity, and vice besetting society, yet when serious nastiness hit close to home, her stomach morphed into a blender.

It wasn't a good feeling.

But she was *not* going to succumb to pressure. Or threats. Or intimidation.

No way.

She'd honor the promise she'd made to herself the day she'd launched this venture—to seek and stand up for the truth, whatever the cost.

Still . . . a bomb?

Seriously?

Yet if someone was determined to undermine her resolve, an explosive device did have more punch than a nasty letter.

Except the scare tactic wasn't going to work.

She mashed her lips together and lifted her chin.

Whatever the motivation for today's incident, she was sticking with her principles. She would *not* back down from her point of view, no matter the danger. Tomorrow would be business as usual.

In the meantime, though, she needed to rein in her galloping pulse, get her shakes under control—and try not to lose her lunch.

So much for any hopes of a quiet end to his first week in the Crimes Against Persons Bureau.

Expelling a breath, St. Louis County detective Brent Lange shoved his cell back into its holster, executed a U-turn, and pointed his Taurus east.

A possible bomb hadn't been in his Friday afternoon plans, but if you were the detective closest to the action, you got the call.

And even if it ended up being a false alarm—as most such calls were—he'd be on the job long after the bomb and arson crew called it quits. Someone had to dig in and get all the details, make certain there wasn't more to the story than a silly prank or a simple mistake.

Despite his rookie detective status, after ten years as a street cop he knew how the system worked.

Flipping on his lights and siren, he pressed harder on the unmarked vehicle's gas pedal. It would be much easier to get questions answered before the news crews descended and added to the chaos.

Ten minutes later, as he approached his destination in a neighborhood of older but well-kept middle-class homes, he gave the area a sweep.

In the distance, yellow tape blocked the entrance to the cul-de-sac where the possible bomb was located. A second perimeter had been staked out beyond that to create a working zone for law enforcement and emergency crews.

Standard protocol for a situation like this.

He flashed his creds at the local officer who was monitoring the flow of traffic into the restricted area, and the man waved him past.

Brent wedged his vehicle behind a County patrol car, slid out of the driver's seat, and surveyed the scene in the outer perimeter.

It took mere moments to locate the 911 caller. Eve Reilly,

according to Sarge. As the only civilian inside the yellow tape, she wasn't difficult to spot.

Pausing near the front of his vehicle, he studied her. The slender thirtysomething woman was clutching a water bottle, every toned muscle of her five-foot-sixish frame taut, her free hand clenched. Gray leggings extended a few inches below her knees, delineating a pair of notable legs, and a moss-green tank top outlined generous curves. Her copper-colored hair was pulled back into a stretchy band, but the elastic loop was losing its grip, leaving her short ponytail askew. While the strong tilt of her chin hinted at fortitude, her pallor suggested her stamina had taken a major hit.

As if sensing his scrutiny, she angled toward him.

His cue to approach.

Resuming his trek, he took in a few more details as he drew close.

Gold-flecked irises the same hue as her tank top were fringed by lush lashes. A faint sprinkling of freckles arched over her nose. Her full lips bore no trace of artificial color.

Even makeup free, Eve Reilly was a beauty. The typical girl next door, with a hint of exotic glamour.

An intriguing combination.

But nothing in her appearance offered a clue about why she would be the victim of a bomb scare.

Determining that was his next order of business.

He nodded to the female officer who was sticking close. "I've got this, D'Amico. Thanks."

"No problem." She moved off.

"Detective Brent Lange." He turned his attention to the redhead and extended his hand. "Eve Reilly?"

"Yes." She attempted to transfer the bottle of water to her left hand but appeared stymied by the key she held—as if she couldn't recall why it was there or what it was for.

"Your house key?"

She inspected the ridges in her fingers. Shook her head. "No. Uh . . . my neighbors'. I grabbed it as I left. I wanted to put their dog in a safe place." She set the water bottle on the ground and held out her right hand.

Her grip was firm—but her hand was cold despite the late-afternoon heat, and subtle tremors vibrated through it.

"Let's move over to the side." He indicated a bench near a mailbox that was out of the line of traffic, bending to retrieve her water.

He let her lead as they wound through the crush of emergency personnel and vehicles, then took a seat beside her and handed over the bottle.

"Thanks." She tipped her head back and took a long swallow, the plastic crinkling beneath her fingers.

Brent pulled his gaze away from her long, graceful neck and retrieved a notebook from his pocket. "Why don't you walk me through what happened with the package?"

She recapped the bottle and gripped it with both hands. "It was there when I got home from spinning class. About three-thirty. I saw it as I pulled into the driveway, so after I parked in the garage and dropped my gear in the kitchen, I went to retrieve it. I opened the door, started to bend down—and heard ticking. After I spotted a wire sticking out, I called 911."

"Keep going."

"I left the house and went next door to warn my elderly neighbor. Then I ran over to my other neighbors' house to stow their dog in the basement and take cover. One of the local officers met up with me there and brought me here."

He frowned. "Didn't the 911 operator instruct you to vacate the area?"

"Yes—but I didn't want Olivia or Ernie to get hurt."

"You were taking a chance." True as that was, it was hard to fault a woman who put the safety of others above her own.

"I couldn't live with myself if anyone was injured because of me. This mess isn't their fault."

"You think it's yours?"

"The suspicious package was left on my doorstep."

"Any theories about who did it, or why?"

"Nothing specific—but I'm on quite a few people's black-list."

Not what he'd expected to hear.

"Explain that."

A wry smile touched the corners of her mouth. "I take it you don't keep up with local talk radio."

"No."

"I host a syndicated current-events show three mornings a week. While I try to present all sides, I make no secret about my personal conservative leanings. That doesn't sit well with everyone."

"Does that mean you've been targeted before?"

"Never like this—and never at home." She watched the bomb crew in the distance prepare the robot for deployment, faint creases marring her forehead. "Until today, the attacks have been confined to words and an occasional harmless package."

"Define harmless."

"A box of manure was delivered to the studio once. Also the back end of a two-person donkey costume. And a few months ago someone sent a voodoo doll that resembled me, with pins stuck in it."

Powerful statements—but not dangerous.

"Any serious threats?"

"None that keep me awake at night."

That didn't answer his question.

"How about any that would keep the average person awake at night?"

"Maybe." She shrugged and took another swig of water.

"After a while in this business, you develop a thick skin. But that"—she pointed her bottle toward the cul-de-sac—"is disturbing."

At the very least.

"Did you see anyone unfamiliar in the area as you drove in?"

"I didn't see anyone, period. Most of the residents are young couples. The neighborhood's deserted during working hours."

Great.

That diminished the odds of finding someone who could have witnessed the drop-off.

And except in high-end neighborhoods, most residents didn't have a video component in their home security systems.

But they'd canvass the area anyway. Just in case.

"What are the odds the package is a real bomb?"

At Eve's question, he shifted his attention back to her. "Low. A homemade bomb *could* be triggered by an alarm clock, but digital timers are more common these days."

"What happens if it's a fake? A prank?"

"We investigate. Planting a hoax bomb isn't a prank. It's a felony. Let's talk about any recent troubling communication you've received."

"It's all been the usual kind of garbage. None of the comments raised serious red flags."

"Have you ever contacted law enforcement about any of these hostile messages?"

She rolled her eyes. "If I reported all the nasty notes I got, I'd be on the phone with the police every day. The left preaches tolerance—but only as long as you agree with them. If you don't, they consider you unenlightened and fair game for their wrath. Sorry to offend if you happen to be of a liberal bent, but that's how I see it."

The lady wasn't shy about speaking her mind.

No wonder she ticked off some of her listeners.

"I'm not offended. Depending on how this plays out, we may want to see any recent malicious communication you've received."

"I'll give you the contact information for the program director at the station. He and one of the admin people monitor my snail mail and social media accounts. The volume got away from me months ago. Now they just send me any notes they think merit a direct response. They'll be happy to provide anything you need."

"Are there any disgruntled listeners you hear from on a regular basis?"

"Some." She rubbed her thumb over the almost-empty bottle. "Near as I can tell, though, they prefer verbal sparring to bombs."

"One of them could have decided actions would speak louder than words."

She flicked a glance at the first responders in the restricted area, faint furrows denting her brow. "I suppose that's possible."

"Any particularly controversial programs in the past couple of weeks?"

She huffed out a small snort. "Every program is controversial to some people."

His phone began to vibrate, and he pulled it off his belt. Sarge—wanting an update, no doubt.

"I have to take this."

"No worries. I'm not going anywhere. But if I could borrow your cell after you finish your call, I'd appreciate it. I want to tell the station what's going on, and I left my phone at my neighbor's house."

"Give me two minutes."

He scanned the crowd for a small pocket of quiet. Spotted one behind an ambulance that was pulled up to the curb.

As he walked toward it, he gave Eve Reilly another once-over.

20

She was watching the activity inside the inner perimeter, clasping the empty water bottle in one hand, her neighbor's key in the other. Given her calm demeanor, no one would suspect she'd found a possible bomb on her doorstep less than an hour ago.

But he'd felt the tremors in her fingers. Seen the taut cords in her neck when she swigged her water. Heard the slight breathlessness in her voice. Felt the waves of tension rolling off her.

She was putting up a brave front, but she was spooked.

Big time.

As she should be.

Maybe she was used to negative feedback, given the rancor she roused on her show.

But someone had risked a felony charge by putting that package on her porch.

And anyone who was willing to take that kind of chance wanted to do far more damage to Eve Reilly than best her in a verbal sparring match.

2

I APPRECIATE YOUR CONCERN, Doug, but I'm fine."
Eve repositioned the phone against her ear, keeping Brent
in sight as she talked to the station's program director.

"I still can't believe someone left a bomb at your home."
Shock dulled Doug Whitney's usual upbeat tone.

"It's probably a fake." Shifting away from the reporters
massed behind the yellow tape who were calling out questions to every first responder within ten feet, she took a quick
inventory of the tall detective.

Athletic physique. Neatly trimmed dark brown hair. Coffee-
colored eyes. Powerful shoulders and broad chest beneath
a tailored jacket. Authoritative posture that gave him a
commanding—and reassuring—presence.

He looked like the kind of guy who would be comfortable
wearing a white hat and riding into town to—

". . . is real?"

Whoops.

She'd lost the thread of her conversation with Doug.

"Sorry." She turned away from the distracting detective.
"It's noisy here. What did you say?"

"When will they know if the bomb is real?"

"Soon, I hope. But the detective said the odds were low."

"A major hassle—and scare—nonetheless." He exhaled. "I'm sorry about this, Eve."

"Don't apologize. I'm the one who throws out all those incendiary topics to the masses. Pardon the pun."

"I'm glad you're able to joke about this."

"Joke may be a tad strong . . . but I *am* trying to take it in stride."

"You think you'll be up to doing your show on Monday?"

"Count on it. If whoever pulled this stunt is hoping to shut me down, they're going to be disappointed. Unless *you're* getting cold feet."

"No. Sorry for the clichés, but intimidation raises my hackles and makes me dig in my heels."

"I knew there was a reason I liked you." Brent began weaving toward her through the crowd. "I have to go. By the way, the detective said he may be in touch with you to review any recent nasty communication that's come in."

"He better set aside a whole afternoon."

"I already warned him."

"I'll alert Meg to begin putting a file together."

"Perfect. She's a dynamo."

"I agree. She wasn't the best candidate on paper, but I'm glad you convinced me to hire her. Keep me in the loop on the bomb situation."

"You got it." She pressed the end button.

Brent dropped back onto the bench beside her. "You didn't have to cut your conversation short. I just wanted to let you know the press has picked up that you were the recipient of the package."

"It was only a matter of time."

"I'm assuming you'd prefer not to talk to them."

"Correct. I'll confine all public statements to my own show and social media." She lifted the cell. "Do you mind if I make one more call? I don't want my sister a couple of hours from here to find out about this on the news. She worries too much about me as it is."

"Help yourself."

"I'd also like my other sister brought up to speed . . . but it may be safer if you initiate that contact."

His eyebrows rose. "How so?"

"She's a County detective—on her first undercover assignment as we speak. She said she'd be unavailable for the duration, barring an emergency. I don't want to put her at any risk, but I'd like to reassure her I'm fine and that the situation is under control."

"What's her name?"

"Cate. Same last name as mine. Do you know her?"

He gave a slow nod. "I've run into her on a few occasions, but we've never worked together. I can ask her handler to communicate your message." He tipped his head. "You two don't resemble each other at all."

"Nope. I got my dad's Irish blood, and she got my mom's Greek DNA."

He studied her for a moment. "You have a touch of your mom's Greek heritage too." Without giving her a chance to respond, he rose. "Let me get an update on the situation while you phone your other sister."

As he left her to join the bomb crew that was watching the feed from the robot, she punched in Grace's number.

The phone rang once . . . twice . . . three times . . . then rolled.

Naturally.

She blew out a breath. When had she last connected with her younger sister on a first attempt?

But she didn't want to hear any excuses for the detour to voicemail—especially if they involved the gruesome details of an autopsy.

Eve shuddered as she left a brief message. Her sister's clients didn't send nasty letters or leave bombs on her doorstep, but cutting up dead people for a living had its own downsides.

Not that you'd know it talking to Grace, though. The woman loved forensic pathology. Claimed it was like living a mystery novel every day.

Go figure.

But if it made her happy . . . hey. To each his own.

"Good news." Brent rejoined her. "Your bomb appears to be a fake. One of the crew is going in to verify that." He motioned toward a guy who was donning what looked like an overinflated space suit.

She handed him back his phone, and as their fingers brushed, a spark zipped through her nerve endings.

Oh, for pity's sake.

She was a mature thirty-one-year-old, not a teen with unruly hormones. She needed to get a grip.

"Does, uh, that mean I'll be able to sleep in my own bed tonight?" She tried for a casual, conversational manner—and came close to pulling it off.

"I don't see why not. We'll be around the area for a few hours talking to neighbors, searching for any evidence the delivery person left behind—but you can go back to your usual routine."

Usual routine? After finding a pseudo bomb on her front porch?

Ha.

The chances of a routine Friday night were zero to none.

"Or not."

She blinked at his postscript. "What?"

One corner of his mouth twitched. "Reading people's expressions is a handy skill in my business. You're thinking *normal* won't be in your vocabulary for a while."

"I guess a poker-playing career isn't in my future."

"Let's just say winning a fortune at blackjack in Vegas probably shouldn't be on your bucket list."

"Never was, never will be. Cycling through Tuscany, however—different story."

"Now that sounds appealing." His gaze locked on hers, warming for an instant before he stood abruptly. "Will you be okay here by yourself?"

"Uh . . . sure. I'm used to going solo."

He hesitated, as if debating whether to respond—but in the end walked away.

Easing back against the wooden slats of the bench, Eve watched him until he disappeared behind a fire truck.

Interesting man.

Intriguing, even.

The kind of man who could be an enjoyable companion on her wish-list cycling trip to Italy.

Perhaps even the kind of man who could be an enjoyable companion period.

Now wouldn't that be fun to explore?

Except Brent Lange was here in an official capacity, and she was just one of many victims he dealt with every day. The odds of their paths crossing again after this incident was put to rest were about as low as the odds had been that her bomb was real.

She sighed.

Too bad.

Because confident as she was in her ability to stand up to intimidation, it would be comforting to have someone like Brent in her corner if by chance today's prank morphed into a much more ominous threat.

———

"Honey, I'm home." Meg Jackson dropped her purse on the kitchen table and continued toward the booming TV in the living room.

Steve glared at her from his overstuffed chair as she entered. "Why didn't you call and tell me about this?" Muting the sound, he waved a hand toward the screen, where video footage of Eve's scary afternoon was front and center on the evening news.

"Doug didn't tell me until five—and I was anxious to get home." Summoning up a smile, she continued toward her husband of eighteen months, trying to settle the flutter in her stomach. She *should* have called. Given how negative he was about her job, it was a no-brainer he'd be upset about today's incident.

But it was easier to deal with his agitation, calm the waters, in person.

At least that was how she justified the delay.

"You could have called from the car."

She perched on the arm of the chair and bent to kiss his forehead. "I thought this merited a face-to-face conversation."

The twin crevices above his nose deepened. "That doesn't change the reality of what happened. You know how I feel about your job. Now I have to worry about you being in danger *and* overworked."

"I'm not overworked—and Eve's the one in danger, not me."

"What if the bomb had been left at the station?"

"It wasn't—and the building has excellent security. Besides, Eve told Doug the bomb was probably a fake. Did they say anything about that on the news?" If she deflected his focus, it was possible they could avoid another row about her job.

"Yeah. It was a hoax."

"See? Everything's fine. *I'm* fine." She rose. "Let me get dinner started. You must be hungry."

He grabbed her hand as she began to move away. "Meg."

She braced and angled back. "Let's not argue about this, Steve. Please. I like my job. This was a fluke. I'm not in any danger."

"I don't want anything to happen to you. I couldn't go through that again."

She gently wiggled her fingers to loosen his taut grip and sank back onto the arm of the chair.

Cut him some slack, Meg. Losing a young wife to cancer had to be devastating. If he's a bit overprotective, live with it. You might feel the same if the situation was reversed.

"You're not going to lose me, I promise." She brushed back the lock of hair that liked to fall forward, onto his brow. "I'm safe at work, and what I do there doesn't take away from our relationship. You're gone all day too. And sitting around here moping after the miscarriage wasn't healthy for me. We agreed a job could help me get back on my feet emotionally."

Well . . . that wasn't quite true.

She'd pushed hard for the job, and after tons of cajoling he'd given in—with clear reservations.

But framing it as a mutual decision could help keep this discussion from escalating to an argument.

"You seem to be doing fine now. The job was never intended to be permanent. We also agreed on that."

"Yes . . . but I've only been there six months. After how Eve went to bat for me, I don't want to walk out and leave everyone in the lurch—or cause an issue for her."

His jaw hardened. "I don't care about Eve Reilly. I care about you."

"I know, but she did pull strings to get me hired. If she and I hadn't been high school classmates, I doubt I would have gotten the job. There were better-qualified candidates."

"I wish one of them had been hired. You don't have to work. My salary can support both of us."

"It was never about the money."

His nostrils flared. "I don't know why you can't be satisfied running the house and being my wife."

"I am." She bent again and touched her mouth to his stiff lips. "But being here alone all day while you were at work was hard. The job was a godsend after I lost the baby."

"I can think of other ways to describe it." Anger scored his words—and twisted the knot in her stomach.

"Oh, come on, Steve." She forced a lightness she didn't feel into her tone. "I'm here tonight—and I'm all yours for the whole weekend."

"I thought you had a church thing tomorrow."

Yes, she did.

But if giving up the annual ladies' luncheon would placate him, it was a small price to pay for a peaceful weekend.

"I'll cancel that. We'll have the whole day together."

The tight lines in his face relaxed a hair. "I like that idea. We can sleep in and go to Bob Evans for a late breakfast."

She did her best to mask her dismay.

He knew she didn't like heavy, calorie-laden breakfasts. Knew she was working hard to lose weight after her late-term miscarriage.

And Bob Evans wasn't the place to follow a diet.

Worse yet, he'd insist she join him in the high-carb, high-fat splurge he could afford, given the physical nature of his construction job.

"What's wrong?" His frown was back.

She realigned her features. Balking at his idea would only create more tension. "Nothing. I'll get dinner going."

"What are we having?"

"Pork chops and mashed potatoes."

"One of my favorites." He smiled at her.

Finally.

"I know. It won't take long." She stood.

Once more he caught her hand, the tender expression she loved softening his features. "You're a good wife, Meg."

Her throat tightened. "Thanks."

"You're not sorry we got married after such a quick court-ship, are you?"

"No." Her response was immediate. It had to be, or Steve would mope for days.

And it was true. Really, it was.

After battling weight and self-esteem issues her whole life, how could she not have fallen in love with a smooth-talking, charming, attractive man like Steve who'd made her feel like a femme fatale for once in her life?

If—in hindsight—she sometimes wished they'd taken the relationship slower, learned more about each other before committing for life . . . if she was sad that her parents had judged her hasty nuptials as a foolish mistake and written her marriage off as another one of her dim-witted blunders . . . well, everyone harbored a regret or two.

Besides, fretting over history was pointless. The deed was done.

He released her hand, unmuted the TV, and turned his attention back to the screen. "That's what I like to hear."

Meg rose, kissed his forehead again, and returned to the kitchen to prepare dinner.

Rubbing her temple, where the first hint of a headache was beginning to throb, she crossed to the fridge.

It would be nice once in a while if Steve kept her company while she cooked—or lent a hand with cleanup.

But after living with a gourmet chef who'd banished him from the kitchen until the food was ready, he would never think to offer assistance. He was used to how his first wife had prepared meals.

And since she wasn't anywhere close to Le Cordon Bleu caliber—as Steve often reminded her—the least she could do was let him wind down from the day in front of the TV.

Marriage was all about accommodation, after all.

He doesn't accommodate you very much, though.

She clenched the handle of the fridge and yanked the door open.

That wasn't true. Letting her take the job at the station had been a big concession for a man who'd told her up-front he wanted a stay-at-home wife and mother—terms to which she'd agreed.

Yeah . . . but he only relented after you almost died from the miscarriage.

Meg pulled out the pork chops and slapped the package on the counter.

Enough.

Steve was a fine man.

So what if he was a bit overprotective and controlling?

Grief—and fear—could do that to a person.

After his experience with his first wife, he'd naturally be terrified about losing her too. That's why he always wanted her close by, kept tabs on her activities and friendships.

Stifling the dissenting voice in her head, she pulled two potatoes from the cabinet and began peeling them.

Her husband's behavior was perfectly reasonable, given his history. She should be flattered he hovered and wanted to keep her safe, not resent his attention.

And it wasn't as if this pattern would last forever. Once they settled into their marriage and he felt more secure, he'd ease off, badger her less.

She began quartering the potatoes . . . but stopped as a putrid smell assailed her nostrils.

It didn't take her long to find the source. There was a rotten spot in the middle of one, hidden under skin that had appeared normal.

Wrinkling her nose, she tossed the potato in the trash—and quashed a niggle of unease.

Hopefully the bad spud wasn't an omen about the meal she was preparing. Steve wouldn't be happy about an unpalatable dinner.

So in case the chops were dry or the potatoes were lumpy or the green beans weren't cooked to his liking, she'd serve his favorite dessert tonight instead of keeping the sundaes until tomorrow.

That should earn her a smile.

And life was so much more pleasant when Steve smiled.

They were still at it.

Eve propped a hand on her hip and peered through the blinds in her spare bedroom. Brent's Taurus and the car that belonged to the detective who'd joined him remained parked in front of her house, although the Crime Scene Unit van was gone.

She rubbed her fingertips together, still gritty after the elimination prints she'd provided. The house-to-house canvass Brent had said they were going to do must be taking a while.

She let the slat fall back into place.

It was possible one of her neighbors had noticed the person who'd dropped off her ticking package, but she wasn't holding her breath. Most of the residents had arrived home from work after the police descended.

Wandering toward the kitchen, she detoured around the cans of light gray paint destined for the walls in her living room and hall. One of the many chores on her weekend to-do list.

Maybe she'd get a jump on it tonight. After today's excitement, it would take hours for her vital signs to—

She jerked to a stop as the driving beat of "I Won't Back Down" pulsed from her cell in the quiet house.

Lungs jamming, she rolled her eyes. Just what she needed—another adrenaline spike.

This did not bode well for a restful night's sleep.

In fact, if her nerves didn't settle down soon, she could end up painting until dawn.

As the ringtone filled the house with music, she jogged toward the kitchen. Thank goodness she'd remembered to stop and retrieve her cell when Brent escorted her back to the house after the all clear.

She snatched the phone off the counter and skimmed the screen.

Grace.

Shoving back a few errant strands of hair, she tapped talk. "Hi. I take it you got my message."

"Yes. I was in the middle of an autopsy for a farm accident. It wasn't as grisly as the one I did early in my tenure for a guy who got caught in a combine and lost both—"

"Stop! I do *not* want to hear the details." Eve pressed a hand to her stomach, which was already flipping around like a beached fish.

"Fine. I didn't call to discuss my job anyway. What's going on? Why didn't you respond to my texts?"

She checked the screen again.

Oh.

Grace had texted six times in the past hour.

"Sorry. I've been a little distracted."

"Under the circumstances, you're forgiven. Now fill me in."

She gave her sister a quick recap, pulling a soda out of the fridge as she wound down. "Law enforcement is talking with my neighbors as we speak, but I'm not expecting any breakthroughs. Unless the person who left the package also left behind a piece of evidence or two—a long shot—we may have to chalk this up to a disgruntled listener who was more creative than most of my critics."

"I don't like this, Eve."

Neither did she—but if she admitted that, Grace would toss all night too. No sense both of them missing out on their beauty sleep.

"I'm used to negative feedback." Eve released the tab on

33

the soda, and the CO_2 hissed out. "This was nothing more than a prank. If the person had wanted to hurt me, the bomb would have been real."

"Maybe next time it will be."

"Gee, thanks for that cheery thought."

"I'm being a realist."

"More like a pessimist. You're overreacting."

"You always say that—and you're too blasé about the risks of your job. Cate agrees."

Eve snorted. "Like she has such a safe occupation."

"She's trained to deal with unsavory people—and she carries a gun. You ought to think about doing the same."

"Get real, Grace."

Her sister exhaled. "Fine. Scratch that idea. A gun would be useless to a woman who puts life and limb at risk to rescue a turtle stranded in the middle of a busy street. You can't even kill a fly."

"Not all of the Reillys were wired with a penchant for blood and guts, okay?" She sipped her soda.

"You are so like Dad."

"I'll take that as a compliment. He's the kindest, gentlest man I know."

"I agree. And that's fine for someone in his profession. Archaeologists don't tend to find ticking bombs on their doorstep."

"Tell that to the ones in Syria and the Middle East who are trying to preserve antiquities. ISIS is *not* their friend."

"Dad's in Cambridge at the moment. Not exactly a hotbed of intrigue or danger. You're changing the subject. Should I drive in?"

"No. I'm fine." Or she would be, if her nerves ever quit pinging.

"So you say." A beat passed. "What was in the package other than a ticking clock?"

"I don't know that there *was* anything else in there. I'll ask the detective later. He said he'd stop by after they finish canvassing the neighborhood."

"I bet there was a message inside. You'll let me know about any new developments, right?"

"I'll text you with important updates."

"Your definition of important and mine don't mesh. If I got one letter like any of the vile missives directed at you, I'd be rethinking my profession."

"Then it's lucky you picked a job where your clients can't complain."

"Ha-ha. Are you going to talk to Cate?"

"I asked the detective to get word to her that I'm fine."

Another sigh. "Look, why don't I come in tonight? We could go shopping tomorrow, have lunch, make a Ted Drewes run. It's been ages since I've had a marshmallow concrete, and I'm in the mood for frozen custard."

Pressure built in Eve's throat.

Grace's plate was already full. Too full. No surprise, given the short supply of forensic pathologists with her credentials, especially in rural areas. Carving out a weekend to babysit her sister would eat into what minuscule free time she had.

No way could she agree to that sacrifice—much as she was tempted to accept. While a whole day with her sister would be a treat . . . and a welcome diversion from this afternoon's nastiness . . . it wouldn't be fair to Grace.

"I appreciate the offer—but my goal this weekend is to paint the living room. Now, if you'd like to help with that . . ." The corners of Eve's lips twitched. Considering how much Grace hated do-it-yourself home projects—with painting at the top of the list—it would be fun to see how fast she backtracked.

"Uh . . . I guess I could do that if you really need another pair of hands, but I do have a ton of paperwork to catch up on."

"No worries. I'll put on up-tempo music and groove to the beat while I paint. It'll be a blast."

"If you say so."

The doorbell chimed, and Eve jerked, fumbling the almost-empty soda can. "I have to run. I think my detective's back."

"I'll watch for a text update. In the meantime, be careful."

"That's my plan. Let's organize a sisters weekend as soon as Cate's done with her undercover assignment." She finished off the soda and pitched the can in her recycle bin.

"I like that idea. Talk to you soon."

Eve picked up her pace as the doorbell chimed again. Assuming that was Brent Lange, he must be anxious to talk with her.

Perhaps he and his colleague had found a lead that would help them identify the perpetrator.

That would be encouraging. If she knew they were on the trail of the person who'd risked a felony charge by leaving a fake bomb, it was possible she'd even sleep tonight.

Yet as she caught sight of the dark-haired detective through the sidelight on the door, a sixth sense told her that wasn't the news he was planning to deliver. That whatever Brent Lange was about to tell her would be far from comforting.

Her step faltered . . . but delaying the inevitable wasn't going to change it. She had to face whatever was ahead.

Wiping her palms down her leggings, she straightened her shoulders, gripped the knob, and pulled the door open—praying that whatever Brent had to say wouldn't unleash yet another surge of sleep-banishing terror.

3

BASED ON HER BODY LANGUAGE, Eve was prepared for bad news.

That made this a bit easier—but not by much.

"We're finished." Brent motioned toward the hall behind
her. "May I come in? I'd like to bring you up to speed before
I take off."

"Sure." She moved back, pulling the door wide. "The living
room's on your right."

He stepped past her but halted in the arched doorway of
a construction zone as he took in the scene.

Big swaths of mudding swirled over the walls, indicating
serious drywall patching had been done. The floors were covered with tarps, and a ladder was propped against a built-in
bookcase. Most of the furniture had been shoved into the
middle of the room, leaving the couch and side chairs inac-
cessible.

"Oh. Sorry." She stopped beside him. "I forgot there's no
place to sit in here. Let's try the kitchen."

She headed toward the back of the house.

He followed, skirting around a spattered paint pan that
contained two used rollers and brushes of varying sizes.

"Looks like you're doing big-time remodeling."

"A fair amount. I bought the house at a bargain price—but that was because the older couple who called it home for fifty years hadn't updated anything. However, it has solid bones and great potential. The kitchen and my bedroom are finished, and the living room is up next. That's my weekend project for the foreseeable future."

He followed her through another doorway, stopping on the threshold to survey the bright, airy, contemporary space.

"Not what you expect in a mid-century Cape Cod, is it?" She leaned back against the granite-topped island, crossed her arms, and grinned.

That was putting it mildly.

"No."

He gave the room a slow sweep. Evening sun spilled through a skylight in the vaulted ceiling above the dining nook, spotlighting a round bar-height table and four matching stools with backs. Stainless steel appliances and a light-colored oak floor contributed to the open feeling. Beyond the dining nook, a comfortable seating area featured a gray-and-white patterned L-shaped sofa in front of a fireplace with a raised hearth.

"There used to be two walls back here." Eve swept a hand around the cheery space. "The kitchen was a cubbyhole, with a door that led to a tiny breakfast room, which in turn led to a small den. Ripping out walls was my top priority. And would you believe there was indoor/outdoor carpeting on top of this hardwood floor? The glue was a mess to get off."

"Did you do all this yourself?" He could handle basic home handyman chores, but tearing down walls? Refinishing floors? Out of his league.

"The majority of it. I had a construction crew come in to take out the weight-bearing wall and put in a new support beam, and I left the granite and skylight installation to the experts. Otherwise, this is my handiwork."

"You finished all this in six weeks?"

"No. I closed on the house a month before I terminated the lease on my apartment." She arched an eyebrow at him. "How did you know when I moved in?"

"A background check is SOP for the victim of a bomb threat."

"Why?"

"Sometimes we spot a piece of information that helps us put the pieces together."

"Did you in my case?"

"Nothing beyond the obvious. Given your profession, a disgruntled listener would be the logical suspect—especially after the note we found in the package."

Color leeched from her face, and she felt for the stool tucked under the island behind her. Sank onto it. "So there *was* a message. My sister thought there might be."

He pulled out his cell and scrolled through his photos. "It's already in the lab, along with the package. But I snapped a picture to show you." He walked over and handed her the phone.

"'Be silent . . . or be silenced.' Short and to the point." A slight quaver ran through her voice as she passed the phone back. "What happens next?"

"We'll go over the package and its contents with a fine-tooth comb. My colleague and I also walked your entire yard and the perimeter of your house. We didn't see anything suspicious—nor did the CSU tech. Our assumption is that the person who delivered the fake bomb came and went fast and was careful not to leave any evidence behind—other than the package."

"Do you think your lab will find anything on that?"

"I'm not counting on it. TV crime shows get a ton of law enforcement details wrong, but they *have* helped bad guys learn how to avoid detection."

"Then this person could walk."

"That's a possibility—but we'll work this until there's nothing left to work."

She scrubbed at her temple, and the stretchy band on her hair finally lost its grip.

He snatched the elastic circle as it fell and dropped it on the island.

"Impressive reflexes." She flashed him a smile and tucked her side-parted, shoulder-length hair behind her ear. "So . . . what about the threat inside the package? Do you think this person will follow through?"

She was trying to present a calm front, but the rapid pulse beating in the hollow of her throat sabotaged the effort.

Much as he hated to scare her, sugarcoating the truth could put her at further risk. Forewarned really was forearmed.

"Do you mind if I sit?" He indicated the stool next to hers.

A flush washed over her cheeks. "Please—and I apologize for my bad manners. Would you like a glass of water or a soft drink?"

"No thanks—and no apology necessary. You have more important things to think about." He settled on the stool and angled toward her.

"And worry about?" She picked up the elastic band and scrutinized him.

"Maybe. We should assume that anyone who would risk a prison sentence to put that package on your porch isn't playing games. The message inside would suggest the culprit is a disgruntled listener." He linked his fingers on the cool granite. "How much of the negative feedback you get is general—like this—versus focused on your position on a particular topic?"

"Doug and Meg at the station would be the ones to ask about that, but my sense is that most listeners who call and write want to talk about a specific issue. As I told you earlier, we hear from a few regulars, but they're in the minority."

"Do you know who they are?"

"Only first names."

"We may want to get a court order for a phone trap on the calls coming in to your program."

"Doug will be happy to cooperate—but I think that's a dead end. My regulars are mouthy, but they seem like ordinary people who are taking advantage of the opportunity to vent."

Brent rested an elbow on the island. "Yet the message suggests it's from a listener."

"Suggests." She gave him a keen look. "You've used that word twice. Are you thinking that could be a red herring?"

The fear she was struggling to control hadn't short-circuited her brain.

"It's possible. Do you have any enemies in your private life?"

"No. I stay off the grid and do projects like this." She waved a hand around the kitchen. "I also exercise, and I volunteer with a couple of organizations. I'm not at odds with anyone in my private circle."

"No serious ex-boyfriend who may not be happy about a breakup?"

She played with the stretchy band, watching him. "I thought you did a background check."

"I didn't go that deep."

"I'll save you the trouble. I have one serious ex. We went out for eighteen months but parted amicably two years ago—a breakup he initiated. He was a lawyer with his eye on a political career and was concerned the controversy I attract could derail those ambitions. So no issue there."

Her ex had dumped her because he couldn't take the heat generated by her profession? Had put his goal of an elected office above a personal relationship?

What a loser.

And definitely not worthy of the woman sitting across from him.

He and Eve Reilly may have met less than three hours ago,

but it didn't take long to recognize character. She was the real deal—strong, intelligent, principled, courageous, caring . . . not to mention beautiful.

Too bad he wasn't in the market for a relationship.

But even if he was, dating someone who was part of an investigation was a no-no.

He hooked one foot on the rung of the stool. "So we can write him off." In more ways than one.

"I'd say that's a safe bet. I haven't seen or spoken to him since the day we broke up. I did hear through the grapevine that he's dating someone else. So I doubt I'm on his radar anymore."

"You're certain you have no other personal enemies?"

"Yes. This has to be related to my job." She twined her fingers together in her lap. "You said a few minutes ago that the person who did this isn't playing games. Does that mean you think this will escalate if I don't shut up, like the message told me to do?"

"It could. I'd treat this as an active threat."

"Meaning?"

"Use caution and common sense. Pay attention to your surroundings while you're out and about. Stay away from dark alleys. Don't wander around by yourself at night. Do you by chance have a concealed carry permit?"

She swallowed. "No. While I fully support the constitutional right to bear arms, guns make me nervous. Even if I had one, I don't know that I could ever pull the trigger."

"You might be surprised what you could do in the face of an imminent threat."

She tipped her head, scrutinizing him. "Is that experience talking?"

Yeah, it was.

But he wasn't discussing that subject today.

"Let's just say I've been in a few dicey situations during my law enforcement career."

"That's the same kind of vague answer Cate gives me whenever I ask questions about her experiences on the street. But no worries. I respect people's privacy. We all have subjects that are off limits. Any other advice?"

"Would your station spring for personal protection while we try to sort this out?"

Her eyes widened. "You mean like . . . a bodyguard?"

"Yes."

"Isn't that overkill?"

"I don't know—and I don't like unknowns. It's always better to be safe than sorry." .

"Well, a bodyguard's not going to happen. The station doesn't have a budget for anything like that. I have a decent audience, and ad revenues have been rising as my reach expands with more and more syndication deals, but protection would have to be on my dime. And that would be a big price to pay for a little peace of mind."

He couldn't argue with that—and her answer didn't surprise him. Few people had the financial resources to fund personal security.

Truth be told, with most victims of a hoax like this, he wouldn't have broached the subject. It was possible this was a one-off. Someone had decided to take a big chance to make a point—and was hoping the impact was sufficient to shut Eve down. If the attempt failed, they might chalk it up to a nice try and be glad they got away with it once.

Yet he couldn't shake the feeling there was more to this. That someone had Eve in their sights—and wasn't about to be deterred by one failure.

But given her pallor, the notion of a bodyguard had only added to her stress—and beyond a gut feeling, he had nothing to justify pushing the idea.

Backpedal, Lange. Tone down the warning and reassure her. She won't sleep a wink tonight if you leave her like this.

Standing, he kept his expression neutral. "In that case, go with the watch-your-back plan. In the meantime, I'll put pressure on the lab to get to the package ASAP. I'll also call Doug Whitney about reviewing the recent negative communication you've received and get the paperwork started for a phone trap on the calls coming in to your program's 800 number."

She slid off her stool too and twisted her wrist to see her watch. "Long day for you. You missed dinner."

"I never expected regular hours in this job. I'll hit a drive-through on the way home."

Her gaze flicked to his left hand.

The lady was doing a ring check.

"Um . . . I don't have a bunch of food in the house, but I'd be happy to make an omelet or throw together a quick stir-fry if you'd like to forego the fast food. I feel like it's the least I can do after ruining your Friday night."

Dinner with Eve Reilly.

Tempting.

Very tempting.

But mixing business and pleasure wasn't smart.

And an evening with Eve would be all pleasure.

"Thank you for the offer, but I should be going."

"Of course." She gave him a smile that was a tinge too bright. "I'm sure you have places to go and people to see."

In other words, she thought he had a date.

A misconception he didn't intend to let stand, even if he wasn't looking for a new relationship.

He'd figure out why later.

"Not tonight—but I have a full day tomorrow, and there are a few things I have to take care of before then. As for my evening—you didn't ruin it. If I hadn't been working, I would have gone for a run . . . and given how hot it is, you may have saved me from a case of heatstroke."

44

"I'm glad something positive came out of this day." Unless he was mistaken, a hint of relief softened her features at the news his evening plans didn't include a hot date.

His spirits took an uptick—for reasons he refused to analyze.

He followed her to the foyer, waiting as she flipped the lock and twisted the handle. "I noticed your security system keypad by the back door. I assume you use it."

"Yes. Having a sister in law enforcement means I get frequent lectures on home safety. I'd have one anyway, given what I do for a living."

"Smart." He continued past her to the small front porch. "I'll keep you informed about our progress." He motioned behind her, toward the paint cans. "Good luck with your weekend project."

"Thanks. As soon as I eat, I'm going to dive in."

"Don't work too hard."

Her mouth bowed. "I was born with a hard-work mindset. What can I say? Thanks again for everything."

"My pleasure."

He followed the paved path to the sidewalk in the quiet neighborhood, where the residents were once again going about their normal routines.

People were walking dogs.

Children were riding bikes.

The hum of lawnmowers, a distant train whistle, and the jingle of an ice cream truck mingled in the evening air.

For Eve's neighbors, life had returned to normal.

But hers wouldn't be the same again for quite a while.

He circled his car to the driver's side, glancing back at her house.

A light was on in the living room, peeking around the edges of the closed shades, and a shadow moved past the window as he slid behind the wheel.

Eve might be up late painting tonight, but a propensity for hard work would be only one of the reasons.

She'd also be thinking about what happened today—and wondering if there was more to come.

As he pulled away from the curb, he could relate.

Because that's exactly what he'd be doing too . . . well into the night.

———

"Hey, Buzz . . . weren't you working in that neighborhood today?"

Buzz Lander shifted his attention from the TV above the bar to Suds, who was guzzling beer like there was no tomorrow.

"We both were." On his other side, Crip swigged his own beer and continued to watch the coverage of the bomb scare on the cul-de-sac a few blocks from their painting job. "You shoulda heard all the sirens." He grabbed another handful of popcorn and shoved it in his mouth.

Buzz hid his disgust behind the rim of his mug.

Both of these guys were morons who didn't have a clue about what really mattered. All they cared about was making enough money to keep the fridge full of beer and brats. Neither of them ever gave a thought to the future.

But the three of them had a history . . . and the job they'd gotten him with the painting company after he came back from California was an easy gig that gave him time to do other things.

More important things.

And it didn't hurt to hang out with these two on Friday nights once in a while. It was what most guys their age did. Even if he had to put up with the asinine high school nicknames they refused to leave in the past.

"Who'd have guessed Eve Reilly would end up looking like that." Suds swigged his beer and shook his head. "All I remember from high school is her frizzy hair."

"Nah—you're thinking of her sister Grace." Crip kept chowing down on the popcorn. "She was a year behind us. Eve was a year ahead of us. Isn't that right, Buzz?"

"Yeah. I think."

To tell the truth, he didn't remember either sister all that well from high school. Best as he could recall, they were both A students who took all the advanced courses. They'd never shared a classroom with him—or any of his group. He'd seen them in the cafeteria or study hall once a week, max.

But he knew all about Eve now.

"So what do you think about that?" Crip waved salt-encrusted fingers toward the screen, where a photo of her was displayed in the bottom corner while the reporter talked to a cop in the center. "Why would someone pull a stunt like that over a stupid radio show?"

Because it wasn't stupid.

It was dangerous.

"Yeah. I mean, if they catch that guy, he could go to prison." Suds waved at the bartender and held up his empty mug. "He took a big chance."

"Maybe he thought it was worth it." Buzz sipped his beer, nursing the drink. No way did he want to risk getting a DUI. That could ruin a person's life.

"I don't see how pulling a prank like that would be worth it. What did it accomplish?" Crip scraped the last of the popcorn from the bowl.

"He may have left a message." Buzz watched the screen as the camera zoomed in on Eve, sitting on a bench behind the yellow tape, talking to a tall guy in a jacket.

"What kind of message?" Crip stared at him.

"I don't know. Could be someone doesn't agree with her politics."

Suds snorted. "I don't agree with a lot of people's politics. That doesn't mean I go around putting bombs on their porch."

"Fake bombs," Crip said.

"Whatever." Suds waved a hand. "It's still dumb. People are entitled to their opinions. This is a free country with free speech. If someone doesn't like what she says, they can get their own radio show."

Crip chortled. "I can just see you on the radio. You don't know current events from the Current River."

"Hey—people could be interested in the river. I know fishing inside out. And that wouldn't get me bombs on my doorstep, either. I'm sick of politics anyway." He scanned the screen again. "Why a chick with her assets wants to waste time on all those heavy topics is beyond me. She ought to do a show on a froufrou subject, like cooking or makeup or interior decorating. Don't you think so, Buzz?"

"Yeah."

Double yeah.

And it was possible she'd switch gears, after this scare.

"How come you're so quiet tonight?" Crip nudged him.

"Long day."

"I hear you. Any big weekend plans? Hot dates?"

"Nope."

Crip sighed. "Me either. But I bet Eve's got guys falling over themselves to take her out." He motioned toward the screen with his mug. "What a looker. She sure didn't deserve what happened today."

Buzz bit back the retort that sprang to the tip of his tongue. Disagreeing with his buddies would only raise questions.

But the truth was, she deserved everything she'd gotten—and more.

He took another sip of beer while Crip and Suds continued the conversation.

And maybe she'd get it.

Maybe there'd be an Act II to today's performance.

It was certainly worth thinking about.

How ironic that she'd been the one sent to cover the Eve Reilly drama for tomorrow's paper.

Carolyn Matthews stepped out of her shoes and picked up the TV remote. Late as she'd worked on her article, there wasn't much chance she'd catch any of the TV coverage—but with a breaking story like this, there could be an update at the end of the late-night news.

She tuned out the sports and wandered into the kitchen. A glass of wine would be an excellent end to the evening. Her story was finished and turned in—and Eve Reilly had to be running scared.

Carolyn smiled and pulled a bottle of chardonnay out of the refrigerator. Uncorked it and poured a generous glass. Took a sip.

Perfect.

The announcer's voice drifted into the kitchen from the living room, and she tuned in as he returned to the lead story.

"At this hour, the police say they don't yet have any suspects in custody for the fake bomb that was planted on radio personality Eve Reilly's porch late this afternoon. They're continuing to work the case, and they've asked anyone who may have information about the perpetrator to call the tip line." He gave the number as it flashed on the screen.

So there was nothing new. No leads.

Nor would there be, if fate was kind.

Carolyn took another slow sip of wine, letting the taste linger on her tongue as she shut off the TV.

Whether the incident would spook Eve enough to make her rethink the risk of hosting a controversial radio show remained to be seen.

But she had to be scared. You'd be stupid not to be.

And Eve Reilly wasn't stupid.

Carolyn's lips curved up.

Whatever the outcome of today's little caper, she and Doug would have much to talk about at their lunch on Monday.

Al FRI., AUG. 24, 10:50 P.M.

Have u seen the news?

Dan FRI., AUG. 24, 10:56 P.M.

Yes. I was going 2 contact u. The window is open.

Al FRI., AUG. 24, 10:56 P.M.

Agreed.

Dan FRI., AUG. 24, 10:57 P.M.

This will take careful coordination. Are u in?

Al FRI., AUG. 24, 10:57 P.M.

Yes.

Dan FRI., AUG. 24, 10:58 P.M.

I'll be back n touch with further direction. Stand by.

4

THAT'S A WRAP, EVE. Great show."

As Ryan's voice came over her headset, Eve gave the technician behind the large window that separated the studio from the sound booth a thumbs-up. "Thanks. I'll be out of here in thirty seconds."

"No hurry. Joe went to get a cup of coffee, and the eight o'clock news break is just starting to roll."

"I'm ready to call it a morning anyway." She removed the headset, slipped her notes and background material into a tote bag, and stretched her back before exiting the studio.

Doug was waiting for her in the hall. "Busy morning. Ryan said the phones were ringing off the hook."

"Did you catch the whole program?"

"Yeah. I think it was smart to tackle the bomb threat up front and open the show to discussion."

"No sense ignoring the elephant in the room. What did you think of the comments?"

"Your supporters were out in force—a bunch of them pretty worked up."

"I know. What surprised me more were the calls from a few of my regular critics offering *their* support. I know the police think one of them could have left the bomb, but I'm sticking with my conviction that they're more words than action."

"Speaking of the police, I spoke with your detective twice over the weekend. They already have a court order for a phone trap on your call line, and Ryan tagged the regular callers for him this morning. He also wants to come by as soon as Meg can pull together a file of negative correspondence."

As if on cue, the door at the end of the corridor opened and the station's newest administrative assistant hurried down the hall.

Eve lifted a hand in greeting as she approached. "Were your ears burning?"

"You were talking about me?" She joined them.

"All positive comments."

"I have to deal with several urgent emails." Doug took a swig of coffee. "Meg, let's talk once you're settled in for the day."

"Sure. I'll be there in five."

As the program director continued down the hall toward his office, Meg touched her arm. "Are you okay?"

"Fine."

"Any news from the police on possible suspects?"

"No. I haven't talked to the detective since Friday night. I'm assuming there's nothing to report. But he's planning to come in and review the negative correspondence I've gotten recently. Doug's going to ask you to pull the latest nasty-grams."

"I'll give it top priority. You heading out now?"

"Yes." She waved at Joe as he passed on his way to the studio for his two-hour show to finish out the drive-time programming. "I have a blog post to write and a talk to prepare for an upcoming event. I also want to get in a spinning class today."

Meg sighed. "I admire your dedication to exercise. I wish

I could fit in workouts too. I think I put on three pounds at Bob Evans on Saturday."

"I thought you were dieting."

"I'm trying." Meg fiddled with the strap of her shoulder purse and shifted her weight. "But Steve was in the mood for a splurge, and he doesn't like to indulge alone."

No, he wouldn't.

She'd only met Meg's husband on a couple of occasions—including the station's annual barbecue in July—but he didn't strike her as the flexible type. More like the kind of guy who would put himself first.

In other words, the polar opposite of the detective who'd spent most of Friday evening in her neighborhood, making her feel like her welfare mattered to him. Could just be part of Brent Lange's professional persona—but it felt like more than that. Some people were caring by nature.

From her few brief encounters with Meg's husband, he didn't seem to be one of them.

"Maybe you can mitigate the splurge this week with diet lunches."

Meg hefted the small insulated carrier in her hand. "Salads are on the menu every day."

"That will help—and if you ever want to dip your toes into spinning, I'd be glad to schedule an evening session and introduce you to it. The workout is amazing."

"I'd like that . . . but I try to keep my evenings free for Steve. Other than Wednesdays, when he bowls and I go to a Bible study class."

"Would a Saturday morning work?"

Meg chewed on her lip. "We like to stick close together on the weekends." She summoned up a smile that didn't quite reach her eyes. "We're still kind of newlyweds."

"Doesn't he have any other outside activities besides bowling?"

"No. He's active on his job, so he's happy to chill out in the evenings with TV."

And Meg couldn't go to the gym with her while her husband watched TV because . . . ?

But Eve let it pass.

Sowing seeds of discontent in a young marriage wasn't wise—even if she *was* picking up an undercurrent of negative vibes.

"Well, the offer stands if you ever change your mind. I'll see you on Wednesday."

"I'll be here. And Eve . . ." She touched her arm again. "I know I've said this already, but thank you again for whatever influence you exerted to help me get this job. It's been a godsend."

"It was my pleasure. I remember how conscientious you were in high school, and I knew you'd be a perfect fit here. I'm glad it worked out."

"Me too." She motioned down the hall. "I should get with Doug to talk about pulling your correspondence. I'll think about that spinning class."

"Anytime." Eve hoisted her tote bag and watched the other woman walk away.

Strange that the two of them had reconnected at this stage of their life. While they'd never been close in high school, it had been hard not to feel a bit sorry for the slightly overweight, shy teen with the nerdy glasses and lank hair. Pulling her into an occasional lunch back then had been a no-brainer.

And recommending her to Doug hadn't required a second thought.

Meg Lassiter—Jackson now—was one of those gentle souls who'd always seemed in need of TLC.

And unfortunately, despite the attention Meg claimed her husband lavished on her, Eve would be willing to bet she wasn't getting much tender loving care from the man she'd married.

———

She was waiting for him, as usual, at the bar.

Spirits lifting, Doug stopped inside the door of the popular downtown restaurant and adjusted the knot in the tie he always wore on Mondays.

The day he met Carolyn for lunch.

A niggle of guilt nipped at his conscience, and he frowned. That was ridiculous. There was no reason to feel guilty. This was a professional lunch between a mentor and a mentee. Nothing more. Yes, he'd been flattered after she'd sought out his advice eight months ago after they met at a journalism dinner event, but there was nothing personal about their get-togethers. They always talked about work.

He might like the warmth in her eyes . . . and her habit of resting her fingers on his hand when she made a point . . . and how her gaze never strayed while they talked, as if he was the most important person in the world—but he was a happily married man, and she was twenty years his junior.

Yeah, but she makes you feel young and hot again—and you like it. Too much.

Okay.

That was true.

But what guy wouldn't be flattered by a pretty face who wanted to talk to him about more than bills and leaky roofs and college woes and in-law problems?

He blew out a breath and smoothed down his tie. Those were the only kinds of topics he and Alison ever discussed anymore. He couldn't even recall the last time he'd felt the tiniest zing of romance between the two of them.

But every Monday at eleven-thirty, Carolyn reminded him of what he was missing.

And if their innocent lunches gave him a lift—what was the harm in that?

She caught sight of him and raised a hand in greeting, her welcoming smile drawing him forward.

He wove through the bar toward her, tamping down another wave of guilt. His lunches with Carolyn were totally aboveboard and 100 percent business.

Except you enjoy them too much . . . and you're flirting with danger . . . and you're being unfair to Alison.

Fine.

That was all true.

And while nothing untoward had happened yet, if this kept up . . . if Carolyn ever gave him the slightest indication she was interested in taking their relationship to a different level . . . the urge to cave would be strong.

He should put an end to these meetings, remove the temptation.

And he would.

Soon.

But not today.

"I was beginning to think you'd stood me up." Carolyn slid off the stool as he joined her.

"Sorry. It was crazy at the station this morning."

"I'll bet, after that fake bomb stunt."

"I saw your article about it in Saturday's paper. First-class reporting."

"Thanks. I'm continuing to follow the story, but my sources at the PD say there's nothing new."

"That's what Eve told me too." He motioned toward the dining room. "Shall we claim our table?"

"By all means. I'm starving."

She preceded him to their usual spot, plucked up her napkin, and draped it over her lap. "How's Eve holding up?"

"The woman is a rock. In her shoes, I'd be seriously spooked. Are you having the usual?"

She gave a low, throaty laugh that juiced his libido. "You know me too well."

"Your lunch preferences, in any case." He swallowed, gave the order to the waiter, and handed the man the menus.

"I assume the police think the bomb person is a disgruntled listener."

"They're not saying much, but that would be my guess. The detective's going to come by to review all the negative social media communication Eve gets. They also put a trap on our incoming phone line for the show."

"And she's not worried?"

"If she is, she's doing a masterful job covering it."

"You have to admire her guts—even if she could be taking a big chance. There's a surplus of nuts out there these days. I'm not sure it's worth putting your life at risk for a show."

"What would you do in her place?"

She gave him a rueful look. "I wish I had that problem."

"Your day will come." Carolyn hadn't been coy about the fact that her long-term plans included developing an on-air radio personality. It was why she'd sought him out. But as he'd told her—and she understood—those kinds of opportunities were few and far between. The number of slots in a twenty-four-hour schedule was limited.

"I'm beginning to wonder about that."

"My advice hasn't changed. Keep plugging away with your podcast, build your audience—and when an opening comes along, you'll be ready. That's how Eve broke through."

"I know. I've studied her success. It's inspiring. But back to this bomb situation. Is she taking any special precautions?"

"Not that I know of, although I expect she's watching her back."

"Are you worried about her?" Carolyn picked up a bread-stick and twirled it in her fingers. "I mean, what if something happens to her? Are you going to feel any sense of responsibility? It would be terrible to have to live with that kind of guilt."

Yeah, he knew all about guilt. He was feeling a ton of it just sitting here enjoying the company of an articulate, vivacious, attractive woman who wasn't his wife.

But guilt over Eve?

That wasn't a concern he'd considered.

"To be honest, I haven't given that much thought. I'm hoping the police find the perpetrator and put this to bed."

"I hear you." She pulled a folder out of the small portfolio she always brought to their lunches. "I wanted to show you the topics I'm thinking about introducing on my podcast, get your take. I think they may attract a bigger audience."

"Sure. Let's take a look."

During the remainder of their lunch, he focused on their programming discussion—and tried to ignore the faint, alluring scent that clung to Carolyn's hair and drifted his direction whenever she turned her head.

By the time their separate checks came—another attempt to ensure these lunches remained aboveboard—he was running late for his early afternoon meeting.

But breaking away was hard. Carolyn was in no hurry to leave either . . . and a whole week stretched ahead of him until he saw her again.

Yet another sign he was teetering on the edge of danger with this woman.

And risking a twenty-two-year marriage had never been in his plans.

He loved Alison.

He did.

So he wasn't about to make a stupid mistake he'd regret to his dying day thanks to a midlife crisis.

Taking Carolyn's arm, he guided her through the lunch crowd, toward the door.

"If you ever have an open slot at the station, you know I'm waiting in the wings." Carolyn paused at the exit to toss out her usual parting comment—no less than he'd expect from an ambitious twenty-eight-year-old.

"You're on my list."

"Near the top, I hope." She rested her fingers on his arm and smiled.

"Very."

"Good to know." She removed her hand. "I'll be following the bomb scare story until it's resolved. If you get any inside information, I hope you'll think of your favorite reporter."

"Naturally."

Grinning, she wiggled her fingers and sauntered down the street toward her car.

Once she disappeared in the crowd, he turned the other direction and picked up his pace back to the station.

A two-hour meeting with the sales folks about ad revenues wasn't going to be the highlight of his day—but if that detective stopped by to go over the material Meg was compiling, he'd have an excuse to duck out.

His cell began to vibrate, and he pulled it out.

Alison.

His conscience pricked again.

The impulse to ignore the call was strong—but he forced himself to answer. "Hi, hon."

"Hi." She sounded frazzled . . . as usual these days. "Am I interrupting anything?"

"I'm getting ready to go into a meeting, but I have a minute."

"I won't keep you. Your mom called. She seems lonely. If you have a spare half hour, you may want to swing by after work tonight. I think she could use a lift."

Couldn't they all.

But stopping at the assisted living facility where his parents had lived for the past three months wouldn't give *his* spirits a boost. The place was downright depressing.

"I'll see what I can do."

"Bree called too. She's got more roommate issues."

"That's what comes from having a room to herself at home all these years. She's been on campus what? Ten days?" He stopped at the corner to wait for the light to change. "She needs to give this other girl a chance, learn to accommodate."

"I told her that. You may want to call her and reinforce my message."

"I'll touch base with her later this afternoon. Anything else?" A hint of impatience crept into his tone, but he didn't attempt to mask it. After the past, pleasant hour, he wasn't yet ready to dive back into the reality of his life.

"No. I'll see you tonight."

The light changed, and the crowd surged across the street. "I'll let you know my ETA." He shoved the phone back in his pocket.

Calls like this were why he enjoyed his one-hour escape each week with Carolyn.

And why it was so difficult to give up that pleasant reprieve from real life . . . despite the danger.

"Knock knock. Anyone home?"

At the question, Eve jerked around in the chair she'd claimed on her small deck and grabbed her teetering laptop.

Olivia sent her an apologetic look and continued across the lawn, a covered plate in her hands. "Sorry. I didn't mean to startle you. I should have called out sooner, given all the excitement we had on Friday."

Eve stood and met the woman at the edge of the deck, reaching down to take the plate. "Don't worry about it. I was deep in thought, trying to come up with ideas for the speech I'm giving on Saturday. It's been kind of hard to concentrate. Come on up."

The older woman joined her on the deck and took the chair she indicated. "I can certainly understand why you'd be distracted. A bomb scare, of all things! Here in our quiet little neighborhood." She shook her head. "What's the world coming to?"

"A question I think about every day."

"I know—and it's not a pleasant topic. I hoped my brownies would sweeten your afternoon."

"Guaranteed. Will you share? I could pour you a cup of coffee."

"No, those are all yours. I kept a few for myself at the house, though—not that I need the calories." She patted her trim waist.

"I don't think you have to worry." Eve pulled one of the rich squares from beneath the plastic wrap. "And I for one could use a helping of comfort food today. I'll work off the calories later at my spinning class."

"Having an outlet for stress is smart."

"More now than ever." She took a bite of the brownie, letting the chocolate dissolve on her tongue.

"I listened in on your show this morning. I thought you handled the whole matter with aplomb."

Eve's throat tightened.

While Olivia was a new friend in her life, the older woman had gone out of her way to welcome her to the neighborhood. And since she'd confessed early on that she didn't have a political bone in her body and hated controversy, her neighbor's effort to listen to the program was touching.

"I appreciate the encouragement—and also that you tuned in. I know my program isn't your thing."

"I worry about you, my dear." She patted her hand. "Has

there been any news from the police? I hate to think the crazy person who left that fake bomb is still on the loose."

"I haven't heard anything, which leads me to believe there haven't been any breaks in the case."

"That's unfortunate. Are the police concerned that this person could come back?"

"I don't think they've ruled out that possibility." Especially given Brent's suggestion about personal security.

But Olivia didn't have to know that. It would only make her worry, and it wasn't as if there was much chance her older neighbor would be in the line of fire if the person did decide to pay a repeat visit.

"That's troublesome. Do you think you ought to beef up your security here at the house?"

Eve pulled a tissue out of her pocket and wiped the chocolate residue from her fingers. "I've got a first-class system. Once I arm it, no one can get in without me—and the police— being informed."

"But that wouldn't prevent someone from leaving another bomb on the property."

There was that.

"If this person comes back, I doubt they'll try the same technique twice."

At least she hoped not.

"You're probably right. But I do hope you'll be careful."

"That's my plan."

"Well . . . you have work to do and I have a soap to watch." She winked and rose. "If I can ever be of help, though, don't hesitate to call. I may not move as fast as I used to, but I can dial 911 as quick as anyone."

"I'll keep that in mind—and thank you."

"No thanks necessary. This is what neighbors do. Enjoy the rest of those brownies—and keep your phone close at hand when you're outside . . . just in case."

With that encouraging thought, her neighbor lifted a hand in farewell and recrossed the lawn.

Eve glanced around her backyard, a tiny tingle of trepidation prickling through her.

She didn't need Olivia's warning to remind her to be on red alert. Ever since she'd found the fake bomb, she'd been looking over her shoulder and jumping at every tiny noise—not how she'd ever intended to live her life.

So while reasonable precautions were prudent, she'd carry on as usual otherwise . . . although that would be much easier to do if the police identified the person who'd left the fake bomb.

She picked up her cell. Weighed it in her hand.

Brent Lange had said to call him anytime. All she had to do was scroll through her address book, press his number . . . and ask for an update.

However . . . if he had anything to report, he'd have called her—as he'd promised. The detective struck her as the kind of guy who kept his word.

She set the phone on the table and sank back in her chair.

Bothering him at work simply to hear his resonant, reassuring voice was selfish. For all she knew, the man could be at a crime scene.

So she'd wait for *him* to call *her*.

And until then, she'd continue to do what she'd been doing—and what Olivia had advised.

Be super careful.

Because even though her life had been quiet since Friday night, she couldn't shake the feeling that there was another threat hovering in the wings.

"Until next time, this is Carolyn Matthews signing off."

Carolyn ended the podcast with one keystroke, sat back in her chair, and took a sip of water.

That had been an excellent program.

Excellent enough to deserve a slot on real radio.

Yet no matter how hard she'd pushed Doug, he'd given her no specific promises.

She screwed the lid back on her water with more force than necessary.

After eight months stroking his ego and playing the charm card, she should have gotten concrete results by now.

Shoving her chair back from the computer, she rose and began to pace.

Too bad Eve hadn't buckled after the bomb scare. That would have made life much simpler. But apparently the woman wasn't intimidated by physical threats.

Still . . . there were other ways to make people squirm.

Carolyn wandered into the kitchen. May as well finish off the bottle of wine in the fridge. There wasn't more than a glass or two left.

She pulled it out, removed the cork, and poured a generous serving, swirling the golden liquid as she mulled over how best to proceed.

There was one card she hadn't yet played in her break-into-radio campaign. One she'd been holding in reserve in case the opportunity presented itself . . . or nothing else worked.

This could be the moment to put it on the table.

She took a slow sip of wine and walked over to the picture window in her condo, giving the city lights below her a slow sweep. Not a bad view—but a larger . . . higher . . . unit would offer a more impressive panorama.

That wasn't going to happen on her reporter's salary—although it would be within the realm of possibility if she ever got the chance to host her own radio program.

Propping a shoulder against the edge of the window, she watched the traffic below. Thanks to the new office building that was under construction, all vehicles were being diverted north, toward less-savory side streets in the city. An unappealing but necessary detour if the drivers wanted to reach their destination.

Maybe that's how she should view the card she held. She didn't have to like using it . . . but if it got her where she wanted to be?

Worth considering.

Carolyn returned to her desk and pulled out the file she'd been holding in reserve for months. Set it beside her computer.

She didn't have to decide tonight.

But she couldn't wait too long or the window would close.

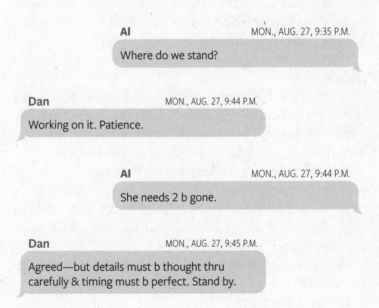

Al   MON., AUG. 27, 9:35 P.M.

Where do we stand?

Dan   MON., AUG. 27, 9:44 P.M.

Working on it. Patience.

Al   MON., AUG. 27, 9:44 P.M.

She needs 2 b gone.

Dan   MON., AUG. 27, 9:45 P.M.

Agreed—but details must b thought thru carefully & timing must b perfect. Stand by.

5

"THANKS FOR CALLING THE SHOW" —Eve double-checked the name on the phone monitor—"Denise. What's on your mind today?" She glanced at the clock. Seven minutes to go on her Wednesday program. She should be able to take one more call unless this one ran long.

"I wanted to weigh in on that big protest at the abortion clinic yesterday."

"Sure." The massive turnout of picketers, a cooperative effort by a number of churches, had elicited more than a few comments on today's program—but it was impossible to tell from this woman's tone where she stood on the issue.

The caller didn't leave her guessing for long.

"I get that people have a right to protest peacefully, but I think it's terrible to subject women already under stress to more grief. Abortion is a personal decision, and it's nobody's business but the woman's."

Out of the corner of her eye, Eve caught a movement in the sound booth.

She looked over.

Brent Lange was standing behind Ryan.

Her heart missed a beat as he lifted a hand in greeting.

"Hello? Are you still there?"

At the caller's query, she forced herself to refocus. This topic was important and required no less than her full concentration despite the very distracting man standing ten feet away who was watching her every move.

She swiveled her chair to eliminate the appealing view in the sound booth. "Yes. I'm here. And I have to disagree with you. The woman isn't the only one affected by her decision. So is the unborn child."

"It's not a child until it's born."

"So you agree with late-term abortions?"

"Umm . . . up to a point."

"What point?"

"Well . . . after the baby could live on its own outside the womb, it would be wrong to abort it."

"No baby can live on its own outside the womb. Even full-term babies have to be fed and changed and clothed and sheltered from the elements."

"That's not what I mean. They should be able to survive with basic care."

"So you're saying a premature baby who requires medical intervention isn't really a baby, and we're under no obligation to help him or her live."

"No. I'm not talking about that either." Frustration etched the woman's words. "I mean earlier than that, when it's just a mass of cells—that's not a baby."

Since the caller wasn't able to defend her original position, she was shifting gears.

Typical.

"Again, I have to disagree. Did you know a baby's heart begins beating one month after conception—before most women realize they're pregnant? At six weeks, brain waves can be detected. By week ten, the baby has fingers and toes, and all essential organs have formed. So when is this child not a baby?"

"Look . . . you're making this more complicated than it has to be. A woman has a right to decide whether to have an abortion. I mean, it's her body."

"That's not quite true, either. While the baby is *inside* her body, it has distinctive DNA. He or she is a unique individual from the moment of conception."

"But it couldn't live without the mother—and she ought to have the right to decide what to do with it."

"You mean whether to carry her baby to term—or kill it?"

"Kill is a harsh word."

"So is abortion." Eve rested her elbows on the table in front of her and linked her fingers. "You know, in discussions on this topic I always hear about the rights of women—but who watches out for the rights of the unborn? Why do we treat babies in the womb differently than babies who've been born? Have we as a society decided that the most vulnerable among us aren't worth protecting? And who's next on the hit list? The elderly? The disabled? Anyone who's not productive as defined by the self-proclaimed enlightened members of our so-called civilized society? Let's talk about this a little more."

As Eve launched into one of the subjects that was near and dear to her heart, an awareness of Brent's proximity simmered in the back of her mind.

But when it came to the causes she believed in, not even a tall, dark, and handsome detective waiting in the sound booth could distract her from her message.

No wonder Eve Reilly raised hackles.

As Brent listened to her conversation with the caller and watched the gestures, body language, and facial expressions the radio audience wasn't privy to, one thing became crystal clear.

This woman was passionate about what she believed—and

she wasn't afraid to tackle hard topics. Nor was she afraid to take a stand that was unpopular in many circles.

A stand that, in this case, she was defending with absolute conviction and rational, hard-to-refute arguments.

Her response might be impassioned, but it was also reasoned and fact-based.

In the end, she demolished the hapless caller—but she did it respectfully and civilly, without ever resorting to belittling or dismissive language.

Quite a way to end the morning show.

Except . . . she turned toward the sound booth and held up her index finger.

"She's taking one more call." Ryan adjusted his headphones as he spoke over his shoulder.

Eve pressed a button on the console in front of her. "Good morning. I don't see any ID on my monitor. With whom am I speaking?"

"My name's Andrew."

"Welcome, Andrew. We've got time for one more quick question or comment. What's on your mind today?"

"I have a question." The man's voice had an odd, sort of disembodied quality to it.

Brent's antennas went up.

"Shoot."

"You seem pretty conservative in your opinions and values."

"Guilty as charged—and no apologies. What's your question?"

"Given the moral high ground you advocate, I wondered how you justified dating a married man eight years ago, while you were a high school teacher. Don't you think that's inconsistent with the image you present to your listeners?"

Given Eve's slow blink and her sudden intake of breath, the caller's left-field comment had totally blindsided her.

It had blindsided him too.

As far as he could tell from his interactions with the woman sitting in the studio—along with the information gleaned from his background check—she was as genuine as they came and rock solid in her values.

Yet for the second time in six days, she'd had a bomb dropped in her lap.

There wasn't much chance the timing was coincidental, either.

On the other side of the window, Eve's demeanor morphed from shocked to analytical, and he could almost hear the gears whirring in her brain.

She leaned forward, the white knuckles of her clenched fingers her sole outward sign of stress as she spoke in a calm, rational tone.

"Andrew, I wish I had time left in my program to dig into the subject you broached, but we're down to a minute and a half. I'll have to address this on Friday—but let me assure all of you listening that the situation was not what it appeared to be, despite the way Andrew framed it."

Her wind-down music began to play in the background, and Eve signaled Ryan to cut the volume.

The music faded out as she continued. "I'll also be blogging about this topic later this afternoon if any of you would like to hear an explanation sooner. But let me be crystal clear. I would never condone dating a married man. It goes against every principle I believe in about the sanctity of marriage. This will be my lead-off topic on Friday. In the meantime, visit my blog later today for more details." She signaled Ryan, and the music volume rose. "Until Friday, this is Eve Reilly, fighting the good fight."

While Ryan flipped switches on the board in front of him, Brent focused on Eve.

If she remembered he was there, she gave no indication of it.

For a full thirty seconds, she remained where she was. Motionless.

At last she took off her headset and began to gather up the papers on the table in front of her.

"Boy . . . that came out of nowhere." Ryan was watching her too. "Eve can't catch a break lately."

"Did you see any ID on that last call?"

"No. My screen was blank, like Eve's."

Translation? The caller hadn't wanted to be identified.

Eve headed for the door, and he did the same. They both emerged into the hall at the same time.

Doug Whitney was waiting for Eve.

"What the heck just happened in there?" The man looked frazzled.

"I wish I knew." She angled away from the program director. "Good morning."

"Morning." Brent stopped beside her.

Doug finally noticed him. "Oh. I didn't know you were coming by again today."

"I have to be downtown later this morning for a meeting, so I thought I'd swing by with a few questions for Ms. Reilly that came up from the review I did yesterday of her hate mail. It appears I arrived as phase two of the attack was kicking off."

Doug stared at him. "You think this is related to the fake bomb?"

"The timing seems too close to be coincidental. Since the person couldn't physically intimidate Ms. Reilly into silence, they may be resorting to other tactics."

"And this one could be even more damaging." Doug ran his fingers through his hair and transferred his attention back to Eve. "Undermining your audience base could have dire consequences for ad revenue."

"I'm aware of that—but I think we can contain this once I explain the situation to listeners."

"Tell me that guy's allegation was a total fabrication."

She took a deep breath. Let it out. "It's not true in terms of how the caller positioned it." She turned to him. "You should sit in while I brief Doug if you think this is relevant to the bomb incident."

"Let's use the conference room." The man started down the hall.

Eve fell in behind him, but when Brent touched her arm she swung back. "Could you use a coffee refill?"

She studied the empty mug in her hand. "Yeah. There's a pot in the break room."

He took the mug from her icy fingers. "I found it while I was here yesterday. Cream or sugar?"

"Both. Heavy on the sugar. The conference room is around the corner up there." She motioned ahead of her, where Doug had already disappeared.

"I'll be there in three minutes."

She nodded and continued down the hall, back straight, step confident, head high.

But those chilled fingers had given her away.

They also suggested the listener's claim had some basis in fact. He may have twisted it to suit his purposes, but there was a nugget of truth in there somewhere.

And that was bad.

While Eve didn't appear to be a quitter . . . and she might be willing to stand up to a bomb threat . . . this latest attack was much more insidious. Undermining the moral character of a public figure who espoused traditional, conservative values could bring about a bloodless coup.

Doug's first concern, about her audience and ad revenues—the lifeblood of a radio station—had been telling.

If Eve's credibility with her listeners was compromised and they deserted her, she wouldn't have to quit. The show would be cancelled.

Plus, once you planted doubts in people's minds, they had a tendency to believe the old where-there's-smoke-there's-fire adage, regardless of the truth.

Eve was articulate and had natural eloquence—but even an expert communicator would have difficulty combating this kind of foe.

Still . . . if anyone could do it, his money was on Eve Reilly.

Someone was really out to get her.

As Eve sank into a chair in the conference room while Doug handled a quick phone call in his office—no doubt related to the bombshell that had been dropped in the waning moments of her program—she forced her lungs to keep inflating and deflating.

Never in a million years had she expected that unfortunate chapter in her life to see the light of day again. It was ancient history—and none of the parties involved would benefit by rehashing it.

So how had this caller found out about it? And was he the person who'd dropped the fake bomb at her house, as Brent had suggested? Was this a continuation of his campaign to silence her?

None of those questions were her immediate concern, however.

First, she had to tell her story to Doug and Brent—and hope they believed what she had to say.

Then she'd put all her efforts into damage control with her audience.

Brent entered the room first, set her mug on the table, and took the seat beside her. "You okay?" Warmth radiated from his dark brown eyes.

She wrapped her cold fingers around the ceramic, fighting a sudden disconcerting urge to lean into this man and draw strength from his steady presence.

But she wasn't a leaner. Never had been, never would be. She could hold it together until she was alone.

After that, all bets were off.

"Eve?"

At his gentle prompt, she took a sip of the coffee and carefully set the mug on the table in front of her. "I'll be fine. I just never expected to have to deal with this. Do you honestly think that call is related to the fake bomb?"

Doug came in on the tail end of her question and slid into the chair across from them. "I'd like to hear the answer to that question too."

"I think it's possible. The quality of the voice on the call caught my attention. I suspect the person was using voice-altering software. We can check your 800 carrier's log for the number, but I wouldn't be surprised if it came from a burner phone that's already been disabled and pitched."

"Does that mean we can't even find out where it came from?" Eve picked up her coffee again, more to keep her hands busy than because she needed a caffeine boost.

"Not without a specific court order for that number—and since there was no overt threat, that would be difficult to obtain. But my gut tells me it's related to the bomb incident."

"If you're right, that would indicate this guy means business—and may not be willing to quit until Eve does. Not the best news I've had today." Doug rested an elbow on the table and massaged his temple. "So what's the scoop on this caller's story, Eve?"

She gripped her mug. Everything would be fine.

It had to be.

Just tell the truth and put the rest in God's hands, Eve.

With that admonition echoing in her mind, she dived into the story. "Eight years ago, when I was twenty-four and launching my teaching career at a private high school, I met a man who was ten years older than me at a teacher workshop.

He was one of the presenters. I ended up sitting at his table for lunch, and we hit it off. He called a few days later, invited me to dinner, and I accepted. For the record, he wasn't wearing a ring."

"But he was married?" Doug leaned forward.

"Yes—but I didn't know that."

"Didn't you ask?"

"No. In those days, I thought the best of people. It never occurred to me anyone would openly cheat on a spouse—and I would never have pegged this guy as a cheater."

"Why not?" Brent joined in the questioning.

"He came across as honest, clean-cut, well-educated, and straightforward. He had a responsible job in education and appeared to be committed to the welfare of students. The man radiated integrity. And it wasn't as if he took me to sleazy bars or met me in dark, out-of-the-way places."

"How did you find out the truth?" Brent was watching her with an intent, penetrating look she suspected had made more than a few criminals fold under questioning.

Yet empathy radiated from his pores—as if he was searching for the facts, but nevertheless believed in her.

She telegraphed a silent thank-you.

"From his wife, who stormed into a restaurant where we'd met for dinner and proceeded to shriek to everyone in the place that her husband was having an affair."

Doug cringed. "Ouch."

"Ouch is a vast understatement. I was mortified and hurt and angry and shocked and . . . you name the emotion, I was feeling it."

"What did your friend do?" Brent leaned closer, almost as if he wanted to take her hand.

Now wouldn't that be nice?

She linked her fingers in her lap, fighting the temptation to initiate that inappropriate contact.

"He turned beet red, apologized, and beat a hasty retreat with his wife."

"Did you ever hear from him again?" Brent folded his arms and leaned back, his jaw hard.

"Once. He sent a letter. Unsigned, no return address. He said his wife had been emotionally strung out for years, was on a variety of medications, and that life at home was a living hell. He'd thought about divorcing her but felt that was wrong."

"Yet dating another woman—and misleading her—wasn't?" Brent narrowed his eyes.

She shrugged. "I can't speak to his reasoning. All he said was that he was lonely, and the connection he'd felt with me had been too strong to ignore. He claimed he would have told me the truth down the road—but he also admitted he enjoyed our dinners and the respite they gave him from his problems at home. He said he'd never done anything like that before, and never would again. At the end, he apologized, wished me well—and that was that."

"No one knew about this liaison?" Doug frowned.

"Liaison isn't the appropriate word. Friendship would be more accurate. We met for dinner five times. There were never any romantic overtures."

"Didn't you think that was odd after five dates?" This from Brent.

"No." She met his gaze straight on. "I told him up front how I felt about casual intimacy. That I wanted to get to know any man I dated on other levels—intellectual, social, spiritual, emotional—first. He accepted that."

"And you never heard from him again?"

"No."

"Did anyone else know about this?" Doug repeated his question.

"I told my sisters and my most recent boyfriend. I guarantee my sisters have kept it to themselves, and my ex-boyfriend would have no reason to spread the story around. As for the man who started all this—I doubt he'd share the embarrassing tale."

"What about his wife?"

"I'm not confident she was as discreet, based on a look I got once from a woman I met at an educational event, who I later found out knew her. But it's been a dead subject for years, and my only fault in the situation was trusting this man too much."

Doug tapped a finger on the table. "What are you planning to say in your blog post today?"

"Exactly what I told both of you—along with a warning to all my listeners who are dating to be careful, because it's easy to find yourself in a compromising situation if you're too trusting."

"Let's hope they buy your version."

"It's not my version. It's the truth." Eve lifted her chin—but the show of bravado was nothing more than that. Pure show. If her own boss was having doubts about her moral character, that didn't bode well for the reaction of strangers.

"I didn't mean it like that. I'm in your corner, Eve." Doug touched her shoulder and rose. "I'll deal with any fallout from advertisers and try to keep knee-jerk reactions at bay while we monitor audience feedback." He shifted his attention to Brent. "Did you want to talk with me while you're here?"

"No. I just have to ask Ms. Reilly a few questions."

"In that case, I'll head back to my office. The conference room is free until ten, so no hurry to vacate." He reached over to shake Brent's hand. "Thanks for your work on this case. Anything more we can do to help, give us a shout."

"I'll do that." Brent rose and gripped his fingers.

He remained standing, and after Doug exited he picked up

his disposable cup. "I'm going to get a refill. Would you like a warm-up?" He indicated her half-empty mug.

"I'm fine."

"Give me two minutes."

As he disappeared out the door, half-closing it behind him, Eve let out a shaky breath.

Her reassurance to Brent seconds ago had been a lie. She wasn't fine. Not even close.

First a fake bomb on her doorstep, now a bomb of a different kind. Both calculated to intimidate and ruin her career.

And maybe they would.

Maybe forces beyond her control would ultimately torpedo her radio program and silence her.

But she wasn't going down without a fight.

Eve Reilly had never been a quitter. As far back as high school, the yearbook had named her Most Likely to Beat the Odds.

That hadn't changed.

Assuming she could convince her audience that today's caller had a hidden agenda, she'd weather this latest attack and go on to fight another day.

Unless her nemesis had more firepower in his arsenal, ready to deploy if this latest tactic didn't work.

Not the most optimistic thought—but she had a sinking feeling it was a very real possibility.

Meaning that for the foreseeable future, she'd be looking over her shoulder, trying to anticipate his next move . . . and watching for danger in every shadow.

6

BRENT REFILLED HIS CUP, set the pot back on the warmer, and took a sip of the strong brew as he retraced his steps to the conference room.

It was lucky he'd decided to stop by the studio and see Eve in person rather than provide a case update by phone. Otherwise he wouldn't have been on hand to witness the latest bomb being dropped.

The providential timing also helped mitigate his guilt over what, until the final minute of her show, had been an unnecessary trip. He didn't require a face-to-face with Eve to bring her up to speed. A phone call would have sufficed, given how little news he had to offer.

But the simple truth was he'd *wanted* a face-to-face. Hard as he'd tried to keep the red-haired radio personality from infiltrating his thoughts over the past five days, she'd popped into his mind too often to count.

Which explained why he'd shown up at the station at seven-forty-five even though his meeting a few blocks away wasn't until eleven.

Not his smartest decision if he wanted to avoid the complications relationships entailed—but now he had a professional excuse to spend a few minutes in her company.

He paused outside the conference room, resettled his jacket on his shoulders with a shrug, and entered, shutting the door behind him.

"Sure you don't want a warm-up?" He motioned toward her half-empty mug.

"No, thanks."

He took the chair beside her. "I wanted to brief you on where we are with the case."

"Does that mean there've been new developments?"

"Nothing specific." He set his cup to the side and angled toward her, resting one elbow on the table. "The lab didn't come up with any leads from the bomb package or the note. We ran basic background on the Monday callers Ryan identified as regulars once we isolated their cell number, but no red flags popped up."

"I didn't think they would. What about the social media comments and letters Meg pulled?"

"I spent several hours going through those yesterday, looking for patterns, flagging the ones that came across as threatening."

"You must have ended up with quite a stack."

"I did. However . . . I couldn't detect any pattern in the threats—and most weren't specific. A few of them wished you ill but didn't indicate they personally intended to cause any harm."

"Where does that leave us?" Faint furrows creased her brow.

No place good.

But he wasn't ready to admit defeat.

"Until this morning, I'd have said we were in a waiting mode to see if the person who left the package took any further action now that you've made it clear you weren't intimidated by the fake bomb. Today's call answered that question."

"In other words, this game isn't over."

"It doesn't appear to be."

"And we're no closer to an answer than we were on Friday." The corners of her mouth drooped.

"We don't have an ID, no—but the language today's caller used suggests we're dealing with someone well-educated. 'The moral high ground you advocate' and 'inconsistent with the image you present' isn't the typical speech pattern of the average person on the street."

The twin grooves on her forehead deepened. "That's almost scarier. Someone who's smart and savvy is a more formidable foe."

He couldn't argue with that.

"That's why you should keep watching your back."

"You think he'll try again if this doesn't work?"

"Let's just say I wouldn't be surprised if there's another attempt to silence you."

She swallowed, watching him. "Yet he hasn't done anything to physically harm me."

Her comment was straightforward—but the underlying question was clear.

"Yet."

She sucked in a breath. "So you think that may be coming."

"I don't know. It depends on the strength of his feelings and how committed he is to whatever purpose is motivating him. Whether he would resort to actual physical violence is a huge question mark."

"In that case, until this is resolved, I guess I should keep my pepper gel close at hand." She offered him a shaky smile and picked up her coffee.

"You could also reconsider personal protection—or take a hiatus from your show."

Her nostrils flared, and she lifted her chin. "I'm not spending a fortune on a bodyguard—and I'm not going to slink away and let this guy win. This is America. People have a right to express their opinions. What kind of message would it send if I let this guy bully me into silence?" She set her cup on the table with more force than necessary. "This is as bad as the Antifa zealots who show up at rallies and protests hiding behind black hoods and masks and beat up people whose opinions they don't like. That's not how this country works."

Man, she was a sight to behold when she got worked up, with her green eyes flashing and energy sparking off her like a transformer gone haywire.

"You don't have to convince me, Eve. I'm on your side. And I admire your convictions. But you also have to take care of yourself."

"I'll be careful."

That might not be enough.

Yet what else could he suggest? The PD didn't have the resources to offer protection to citizens, and he couldn't dispute the expense of private security.

Much as he disliked the thought of this woman being exposed to the risks that holding her ground entailed, he had to admire her willingness to stare this threat in the eye without backing down.

"The advice I gave you on Friday stands."

"Duly noted."

There was nothing else to say. This meeting was over.

But he didn't want to leave.

He leaned back in his chair and folded his arms. "How did the painting go over the weekend?"

Eve seemed as surprised as he was by the off-topic question that spilled out of his mouth, but she recovered quickly—as if she too was happy to have an excuse to continue the conversation.

"Very well. Other than spinning class and church, I never ventured out the door. My neighbor, Olivia, came over for a few minutes with homemade pumpkin bread—and a question about her cellphone. She's a sweetheart, but she's lost in our wired world. Anyway, I focused on making progress in the house. I'm happy to report that the hall and living room ceiling and walls are finished. Next up is the hardwood floor."

"How did you learn to do all that?"

"YouTube." She grinned.

"Seriously?"

"Yep. It's amazing what you can pick up from those DIY videos." She tipped her head. "I get the feeling you're not the home handyman type."

"I never had an incentive to be. I lived in an apartment until I bought an updated condo four years ago."

"Your dad wasn't into home maintenance projects either?"

Uh-oh.

This wasn't the direction he'd expected their conversation to go.

He shifted in his seat and picked up his coffee, keeping his tone casual. "I was raised by my grandparents. My grandfather was an accountant who didn't like hands-on projects."

Like home repairs—or raising his daughter's illegitimate son.

Several beats ticked by as Eve scrutinized him, and he had the uncomfortable feeling she'd picked up the lingering residue of resentment from his childhood days that he'd never quite been able to vanquish.

"Do you have any siblings?"

"No."

"Mmm. An only child raised by an older couple. That could have a few downsides."

More than a few.

And she was giving him an opening to talk about them.

But he hadn't shared his history with anyone other than his best friend. Even with Adam, it had taken months to establish a sufficient trust level to risk confidences.

So how weird was it that he was tempted to spill his guts to a woman he'd met a mere five days ago?

He should get out of here before he caved and did something he could regret.

"It had pluses and minuses." He pushed back his chair and rose. "I have to get to that meeting I mentioned."

"Okay." She stood more slowly and took a sip of her sweetened brew. Grimaced. "Yuck. Cold coffee ranks right up there with soggy Reuben sandwiches on my most-unappetizing list." She grinned at him.

Hard as the lady dug in her heels on matters of principle, she knew how to read the signals—and when to back off—in interpersonal relationships.

Another check in her positive column—not that he was keeping score.

"My list would include instant mashed potatoes."

She gave him a look of mock horror. "Perish the thought! In the Reilly family, the potato is sacrosanct."

One corner of his mouth twitched. "That's a mite stereotypical."

"But true. Thanks to my mom's heritage, though, we're not entirely one-dimensional in our culinary tastes. After she died, Dad made an effort to expose us to Greek food and culture while we were growing up. In fact, I make a mean moussaka. And my sister Grace whips up world-class baklava."

"What's Cate's specialty?"

"Eating."

A chuckle erupted from his chest. "I have a feeling she and I would hit it off." He motioned toward the door. "Are you hanging around here for a while or taking off?"

"Taking off."

"Why don't I walk you out?" He couldn't offer round-the-clock protection, but he could see her to her car.

"You don't have to bother."

"It's no bother." Without giving her a chance to respond, he crossed to the door, opened it, and waited.

She propped a hand on her hip and squinted at him. "Why do I get the feeling you're not giving me a choice?"

Because he wasn't.

But Eve wouldn't tolerate high-handedness. That much was already clear to him. Better to reposition his "offer" and let her make the smart, rational choice—which she would, given everything he knew about her.

"If you prefer to walk out alone, I'm not going to stop you—but I don't know why you'd turn down an armed escort." He pushed his jacket aside to reveal his Sig Sauer.

Her gaze dropped to his weapon. Returned to his face. "Excellent point. I'm ready whenever you are." She picked up the tote bag from beside her chair and eased past him.

The ride down in the elevator they shared with several other people was silent, but as they walked to her car she spoke again. "They do have decent security in the garage, you know."

Given the downtown location and the crime rate in the city, that wouldn't surprise him.

But decent wasn't adequate if someone was determined to get in.

And he suspected she knew that.

His assumption was validated moments later when a car backfired and she jerked, losing her grip on her tote.

After giving the garage a fast sweep, he bent to retrieve the bag.

She did the same.

Their heads bumped.

"Ow!" She pulled back, rubbing her temple.

"Sorry about that." He handed her the tote and did another swift scan.

Nothing was amiss.

"I must be a little jumpy." She clenched her fingers around the handle of the bag.

"That's not a negative in light of everything that's happened. It means you're on alert and ready to react if the situation warrants it."

"Or overreact." She pointed to his forehead. "You may end up with a bruise once that red spot fades."

"I've dealt with worse injuries." He took her arm and guided her forward, picking up his pace. "Let's get out of the traffic."

She stayed close while they completed the short walk to her car—and he tried without much success to ignore the faint, spicy hint wafting from her hair.

"Thanks for the escort." She fished her keys out of her bag and hit the button on her autolock fob.

"Happy to do it. I'll be in touch if we uncover anything worthwhile—and let me know if there are new developments on your end. You have my direct number, right?"

"Yes."

"Don't hesitate to use it, night or day. I don't punch a clock."

"Thanks." She tossed her bag onto the passenger seat and slid behind the wheel.

Say goodbye, Lange.

He retreated a step. "Lock your doors and drive safe."

"Always." She smiled. "I have a perfect record—as you must know from your background check."

"Keep it that way." He hiked up one side of his mouth, turned, and headed for his Taurus.

Behind him, her engine came to life.

The temptation to watch her drive away was formidable—but he fought the urge. It was important to maintain a professional distance.

And not just because she was the victim of a crime he was investigating.

Getting close to any woman wasn't in his plans.

An extreme position, admittedly, given that most of his colleagues were married.

Yet after what he'd put Karen through, subjecting a spouse to the constant worry of whether or not this would be the day he was killed in the line of duty didn't seem fair.

While the odds were in his favor . . . and the majority of law enforcement professionals played them . . . he'd come close enough to being a statistic to know there were no guarantees about tomorrow with this job.

Maybe one of these days, if the loneliness pressing in on him these past few months became too oppressive, he'd trade his badge for a ring.

But he'd never really given that option any serious thought.

Or he hadn't, until a gorgeous redhead with a passion for commendable principles entered his orbit five days ago.

———

"Hi, Doug. Sorry to bother you in the middle of the workday, but I heard about the last-minute caller on Eve Reilly's show this morning. If you have a minute, could you give me a ring and fill me in? This may deserve a follow-up to my Saturday story. I'd have texted, but I can talk faster than I can type. Thanks."

Doug erased Carolyn's message and leaned back in his desk chair, phone in hand.

Of course he'd return her call. She was in reporter mode, giving him a legitimate excuse to talk with her. But there wasn't much he could offer. The police had no idea who'd placed that call in the waning moments of Eve's show. A follow-up story wouldn't warrant more than a few lines of copy.

Still, talking to her would be the bright spot in his day.

Another warning sign he was getting in too deep.

And another reminder of the parallels between his situation and the one Eve had found herself in eight years ago.

Expelling a breath, he reached around and rubbed the back of his neck.

Much of what she'd said earlier this morning had hit too close to home.

No, he didn't have a wife with emotional problems. And no, he wasn't misleading anyone about his marital status.

Yet now that he and Alison were drifting apart and his days were filled with nothing but a myriad of family and work issues, he could relate to a guy who'd succumbed to loneliness and flirted with a clandestine romance.

That's why a quiet interlude each week with a pleasant companion who brought no baggage to the table was appealing—and hard to resist.

But it was also dangerous.

Look what had happened to Eve—and she was totally blameless.

He was too.

So far.

And returning Carolyn's phone call wasn't going to change that.

Before he could second-guess himself, he tapped in her number.

She answered on the first ring. "Hi, Doug. Thanks for getting back to me."

As usual, her throaty voice jacked up his pulse. "No problem. I'd have called sooner, but it's been crazy here all morning."

"I bet. I heard about the call from a colleague and went online to listen. What's the story?"

"There is no story, according to Eve." He gave her a quick recap. "She'll be posting all that on her blog this afternoon, so I'm not telling you anything the world won't soon know."

"Do the police think this is the same person who planted the fake bomb at her house?"

"The detective is convinced the timing is more than coincidental."

"How's Eve holding up?"

"She's not a quitter. If we can contain this and hang on to her audience, she should be fine—but if listeners begin to desert her or ad revenues dip . . . well, radio is a numbers game."

"Someone thought this through."

"Yeah."

"I may do a brief follow-up article, but I'll wait to see what Eve writes on her blog. I know she's not talking to the press, but do you want to make any comments on the record?"

"No. I'm hoping the less said, the better."

"I hear you. So what happens if the show tanks?"

He frowned at the question. They weren't just talking about a show here, but Eve's career. "I don't think any of us have thought that far ahead yet."

"I can understand that. This came out of the blue. But from what I know about radio and ad revenues, if the money dries up, a show can get yanked fast. I figured you were already thinking about what to do with that potentially empty slot."

Like maybe give her the chance she'd been itching for to break in?

An image of a shark circling a wounded swimmer flashed through his mind.

It wasn't a pretty picture.

Doug swallowed past the unpleasant taste in his mouth, a tiny bit of Carolyn's allure fading. While she'd made no secret of her ambition, he'd never pegged her as ruthless. As someone who would heartlessly cash in on another person's misfortune.

"Doug?"

"Yeah. Yeah, I'm here." He stood. "Look, I, uh, have to run. Like I said, it's kind of chaotic here."

"I can imagine." A few seconds ticked by, and her tone warmed as she continued. "I hope I wasn't out of line asking about the future. I'd hate for you to be caught unprepared if this situation goes south. You've built a fabulous career and contributed a huge amount to the station."

"My career isn't the one on the line here."

"I'm glad to hear that. I'll let you get back to work—but I also wanted to tell you I used those ideas we discussed Monday on my podcast. If you get a chance, I'd love for you to listen and give me some feedback over lunch next week."

"I'll do my best to tune in. Talk to you soon."

He pressed the end button, dropped the handset back into the cradle, and walked over to the window that overlooked the city six floors below.

That had been a strange conversation.

And it hadn't left him feeling warm and fuzzy.

Carolyn's interest in a radio slot was no secret. She'd been up front about that from day one.

But he'd never made any promises, done anything to lead her to believe she was next in line if an opening did come up. Sure, he'd consider her for a trial run if an appropriate slot ever became available—although that had always been a long shot, as he'd been careful to communicate.

Or it had been until Eve became a target.

Doug froze as a police car tore past the building, lights flashing, in pursuit of someone who'd stepped outside the law to achieve an end that was important to them.

Like hosting a radio program?

No.

He shook his head.

That line of thought was nuts.

Carolyn was a smart woman and an ace reporter. She was

prepping herself for a higher-profile career, but she was playing by the rules.

And perhaps she was also playing him.

Not an angle he'd ever acknowledged, but possible.

Yet taking advantage of a man in the throes of a midlife
crisis, while of questionable morality, wasn't illegal. Nor did
it have any connection to Eve's problems.

Carolyn didn't have any connection to Eve's problems, other
than covering them for the paper.

She wouldn't jeopardize her career—her entire future—by
doing anything risky or on the shady side of the law, even if
she did have the investigative skills to dig deep into someone's
background and ferret out dirt. She was too smart to use that
kind of information for nefarious purposes.

And she was certainly too smart to plant a fake bomb.

Yet as his phone began to ring again and the advertising
manager's name appeared on his screen, he couldn't kill the
tiny seed of doubt that had suddenly sprouted to life in his
mind.

She may have pushed too hard.

Carolyn tapped a polished nail against her desk and slipped
her cell into her purse as Doug ended their call.

He was pulling back.

And at this stage, with a slot in the drive-time programming
on the cusp of opening, that was disastrous.

Now, of all times, she needed him in her corner.

She checked her watch, rose, and slung her purse over her
shoulder. Unless she hurried, she'd be late for the interview
she'd scheduled to flesh out tomorrow's story on the latest
scandal to rock City Hall. But letting Doug's call roll—or
rushing their conversation—hadn't been options. Being tardy
was a small price to pay for the potential payoff.

Except *Doug* had rushed to end the call.

Putting her phone to her ear to discourage conversation with any of her colleagues, she strode down the hall of the newspaper offices, mind firing on all cylinders. She had another card she could play to win his support—but it wasn't one she wanted to use.

She wrinkled her nose.

Nice as Doug was, sleeping with someone her father's age held zero appeal.

If it helped advance her career goals, though?

Tolerable.

And it would be a cinch to set up. All she had to do was crook her finger and he'd fall into her arms.

Given how well that tactic had worked when she'd been angling for a promotion to an investigative slot, there was no reason to think it wouldn't again. The man was ripe for plucking.

But she didn't want to pluck him unless there was no other option.

So the best plan was to curb her ambitions—verbally at least . . . continue to play the charm card with Doug . . . and see what kind of fallout there was from the call Eve had received today.

Given her conservative audience, there could easily be a mass exodus of both audience and sponsors.

That was the ideal outcome. It would open the window she'd been angling for with no further effort on her part.

And as long as she kept Doug in her corner—her top priority for the immediate future—the opportunity she'd been waiting for could be much closer than she'd ever dared hope.

E VE GAPED AT THE TALLY on her blog post.
      Four-thousand-plus comments since her response to
this morning's caller had gone live six hours ago?

She leaned closer to her laptop to confirm the number.

Her eyes hadn't deceived her. The precise figure was 4,652.
Wow.

She sank into the desk chair in her home office and scrolled
through a few of the entries.

They appeared to be trending favorable by a large margin.
Excellent.

Her cell began to ring, and she skimmed the screen before
putting it to her ear. "Hi, Doug. What's up?"

"Have you seen the response to your blog post?"

"I'm looking at the number as we speak. It's phenomenal.
I don't get that many comments in a month, let alone six
hours."

"Obviously your caller hit a hot button with listeners."

"No kidding." She twisted her wrist to see her watch. "Are
you still at the office? It's after seven."

"I know. I asked Meg to stay late too and spot-check the
comments, give us a read on positives versus negatives. But

if the random sampling I did is any indication, your listeners appear to be supportive."

"That's my take from the few I've scanned. You do realize Meg will be there until midnight culling through them for any negative remarks that may interest law enforcement—unless you rein her in. She's super conscientious."

"I know. I already talked to her about a cutoff. I also assigned a couple of other people to help with the task. We can pick it up again tomorrow. Have you heard anything more from the detective?"

"No." Unfortunately.

"I don't think they have much to work with on this." He sighed. "You doing okay?"

"Hanging in. I did back-to-back spinning classes, and now I'm going to start stripping the hardwood floor in my living room. Physical activity is a great stress reducer."

"Refinishing floors definitely qualifies. I'll let you get to it."

"Would you ask Meg to give me a call if she comes across any comments that raise a red—"

Ding dong.

She fumbled the cell and pivoted toward the hall.

"Eve?"

"Sorry." She tightened her grip on the phone. "Someone's at my door."

"Don't open it until you're certain it's safe." Concern sharpened Doug's voice.

"Trust me, that's the plan."

"You want me to stay on the line until you see who it is?"

She quashed her first inclination to decline. Brent's advice to watch her back and take extra precautions was sensible. Accepting Doug's offer would be smart.

"Sure. Give me a sec." She exited the office and hurried down the hall, staying in the shadows as she approached the front door and sidled up to one of the sidelights to peek out.

Eve blinked.

Why on earth was Grace in town in the middle of the week?

"Eve? Is there a problem?"

Doug's urgency refocused her. "No. It's my sister. Thanks for staying on the line."

"Glad to do it. I'll be in touch tomorrow with a firmer handle on the tone of social media response."

The bell chimed again.

"Thanks. Talk to you then." She ended the call and opened the door. "What are you doing here?"

"Hello to you too." Grace breezed past, the large white bag in her hand leaving a tantalizing aroma in its wake. "Shut the door."

Eve complied. "Why are you here?"

Grace stopped on the threshold of the living room to survey the walls. "Nice job. Love that shade of gray." She continued toward the kitchen. "I brought dinner. Tell me you haven't eaten yet."

"I haven't eaten yet." Eve followed on her heels. "Grace."

Her younger sister deposited the food on the island and began to unpack the bag. "What?"

"For the third time—what are you doing here?"

"Aren't you happy to see me?"

"That's not what I mean, and you know it. You never drive to St. Louis in the middle of the week. What's going on?"

Rolling her eyes, the youngest Reilly tucked her wavy, ginger-colored hair behind her ear and stuck her hands on her hips.

Classic Grace.

At five-four, she was the shortest of the sisters—but her poise and authoritative bearing more than compensated for her lack of height.

"I listened to your program this morning."

Oh.

She hadn't considered that or she'd have called Grace hours ago.

Eve folded her arms. Putting her sister on the defensive could buy her a few seconds to regroup. "That's out of pattern for you, isn't it?"

"I make no apologies for not being a morning person. I gladly concede that title to you and Cate. But as it happens, I had an early call about a suspicious death, which meant I was on the road at seven. I tuned in, assuming your program would wake me up. Boy, did it." She scowled. "So when were you going to tell me about this latest attack?"

"After I finished processing it—and attack may be too harsh a word."

"No, it's not. Somebody is gunning for you."

Eve flinched. "Also a harsh word."

"But true. First a bomb, now a personal strike. Have you told Dad?"

"Heavens, no. Why would I bother him about this? He's thousands of miles away. It's not as if he could do anything except worry."

"I suppose that's true—but you *have* alerted the police, right?"

"As a matter of fact, the detective handling the case happened to be on hand when the call came in."

Grace's eyebrows peaked. "He came to the station before eight in the morning?"

"Yeah. He dropped by to bring me up to speed on the case."

"At that hour?" Her sister squinted as she repeated her comment.

"I get off work at eight. He didn't want to miss me."

"He must have had big news if he made the effort to talk with you in person."

"Not really. He was in the area for a meeting and decided to swing by."

"Yeah?" Grace scrutinized her. "Most cops I know don't revisit crime victims unless there's a substantive motivation." She tipped her head. "How old is this guy?"

Eve frowned at the non sequitur. "I don't know. Thirty-something?"

"Good looking?"

Ah. So that's where her sister's line of questioning was going.

Play this cool, Eve, or Grace will pounce like a cat toying with a trapped mouse.

She tried for a casual inflection. "I suppose—but his appearance hasn't been my main concern these past few days."

A speculative gleam sprang to life in Grace's hazel irises. "Is he married?"

Warmth rose on Eve's cheeks.

Shoot.

The bane of redheads strikes again.

She moved to the cabinet and retrieved two glasses, angling away from her sister's discerning eyes. "We didn't discuss that."

"But you did a ring check."

Yeah, she had—and denying it would only send Grace further down the path she was already traveling.

"Isn't that standard procedure?"

"And . . . ?"

"He wasn't wearing a ring—but that doesn't mean he's single."

Except he was.

Eve knew that as surely as she knew the sparks arcing between her and the handsome detective hadn't been one-sided.

"The situation has possibilities, though." The corners of Grace's lips rose a hair, and she went back to unpacking the food. "I brought chicken broccoli, sweet and sour pork, and spring rolls. I hope you're hungry."

"I am—and that menu is a vast improvement over the omelet I was going to make." Thank goodness her sister had moved on to a safer topic.

"You don't eat right."

"Yes I do. I'm very health conscious."

"Only in terms of spinning and biking. But you *are* very adept at sidestepping topics you don't want to discuss—especially in the personal realm. By the way, I thought the rebuttal you posted on your blog was perfect."

"You've read it?"

"Of course I've read it." Grace pulled two plates from the cabinet and turned to her. No trace of levity remained in her demeanor—or her tone. "This whole thing stinks, Eve. I'm so sorry for what you're going through. And I'm worried about you. To answer your earlier question, that's why I'm here."

Pressure built in Eve's throat, and her vision misted. She and her sisters might lead very different, busy lives, but when push came to shove, they were the Three Musketeers.

Without a word, she crossed to Grace and gave her a hug.

Her younger sibling held on tight.

"Thank you for tackling the long drive here—on the tail end of rush-hour traffic, no less—after your early start today."

"What are sisters for if they can't give each other moral support?" Grace pulled back, swiping a finger under her lashes. "You know, if we don't eat this food soon, we're going to have to nuke it."

"Then let's dive in."

Eve finished getting their drinks, helped herself to generous portions from the containers Grace had set on the island, and carried her plate to the table. Grace joined her a moment later, also with a heaping plate.

How someone so tiny could chow down like a sumo wrestler without gaining an ounce was beyond her.

"I wish I could eat like that." She sent Grace's plate an envious glance.

"Your sedentary job doesn't help . . . but you could always exercise more."

"I hate exercise—spinning and biking being the exceptions. And I do as much of those as I can fit into my schedule. You just have Mom's fast metabolism." Eve folded her hands. "You want to say the blessing?"

"It's your house. I'll let you do the honors."

Eve dipped her chin, offered a quick prayer, and began eating.

"Mmm. I haven't had Chinese for a while. This is delicious." Grace spoke around a mouthful of food.

"I agree. The one thing that could improve this meal would be your baklava for dessert."

"Sorry. That's always a weekend project. It requires a large block of uninterrupted time. I promise I'll make a batch for Christmas, as usual."

"That would be—" Eve cocked her head at a faint scratching noise in the vicinity of her back door.

"What's wrong?" Grace stopped eating.

Pulse leaping, she dropped her volume. "Someone's fooling around with the lock on my back door."

Grace slid off her chair, grabbed her oversized purse, and pulled out the compact Beretta she always carried. "Don't you have a motion sensor on the light by that door?" The question was so soft Eve had to strain to hear it.

"Yes."

But it wasn't working. Outside the drawn shades, her deck and yard were dark.

"Get behind me and call 911." Grace aimed her pistol at the door, arms stretched in front of her.

The knob rattled slightly, and Eve snatched her cell off the table.

She punched in the first number with a shaky finger as the door swung open. Froze as a black-clad figure stepped into view.

"Cate?" Her sister's name came out in a squeak.

"What are you doing here?" Grace's stance relaxed a hair. "I thought you were undercover."

"I am." Cate closed the door behind her and motioned toward the Beretta. "You can put your weapon away now."

Grace lowered the gun. "Why didn't you call to let us know you were coming? I could have shot you."

"I wasn't certain I'd be able to pull this off until the last minute."

"You could have knocked, you know." Grace stashed her pistol.

"I didn't want to call any attention to my arrival. And I didn't know you were here with your trusty Beretta. I didn't see your car out front."

"I had to park three houses down. The people across the street have birthday balloons on their mailbox. I assume there's a party in progress."

Eve pressed a hand to her chest. "I think you took a year off my life."

Cate crossed the room, detouring around Grace to stop in front of her. "I'm not the one who seems intent on doing that. How are you holding up?"

"I'm fine. Or I was, until you almost gave me apoplexy."

After a swift, skeptical once-over, Cate pulled her into a tight hug. "Look who's talking about apoplexy. You're keeping me awake nights, you know."

Eve hugged her back. "You need to stop worrying. I can take care of myself. *You're* the one putting your life on the line every day. And aren't you taking a chance by coming here?" She eased away to study her sister. "Couldn't this blow your cover?"

"I worked it out with my handler. I'm good for thirty minutes. Fill me in on everything that's happened." She flipped the tail of her long, dark auburn ponytail over her shoulder.

"You want to eat while we talk?" Grace motioned toward the island. "I brought more than the two of us can finish."

Cate sniffed and surveyed the food. "Do I detect sweet and sour pork?"

"Yes." Grace retook her seat.

"I'm in."

While Cate helped herself, Eve got her a Diet Sprite and set it on the table.

"Thanks for keeping my favorite on hand." Cate slid onto a chair and lifted the can in salute.

"You're welcome."

"Be thankful I don't have exotic, expensive tastes like our sister does." She tapped the bottle of Tazo mango iced tea sitting in front of Grace.

"Can I help it if my palate is more discerning than yours?" Grace sniffed.

Cate scooped up a forkful of rice and shook her head. "What can you do? The baby of the family is always spoiled."

Grace stuck her tongue out at Cate.

"I rest my case." Cate grinned at her.

"Hmph." Grace sent a pointed look toward their eldest sibling. "At least I'm not a control freak, like certain people I could name."

"Truce, you two." Eve stifled a smile. The good-natured bickering between her older and younger sister was always a hoot.

"I'll second that." Cate continued to eat. "Now tell me everything."

Her sister listened while Eve recounted the events of the past five days, ending with the response to her blog post earlier in the day.

"And here's another news flash. The detective handling the case has gone above and beyond to keep Eve up to speed." Grace smirked at her. "He even dropped by the station early this morning." She gave Cate an elbow nudge and waggled her eyebrows.

"It was a professional visit, and he didn't stay long." Eve sent Grace a silent back-off glare.

Her sister ignored it and took a swig of iced tea.

If Grace kept this up, she might have to supply her own high-end beverage on future visits.

"The fact that he came by is . . . interesting." Cate appraised her.

Eve tried not to squirm. "I'm glad he did, given the call I got at the end of the program."

"But that wasn't the motive for his visit." Cate swirled the soda in her can. "I wonder what prompted it?"

Instead of replying, Eve slid a forkful of food into her mouth.

"I can guess." Grace finished her dinner and broke open her fortune cookie.

"I can too." Cate tapped the edge of her plate with her fork.

Drat.

Her sisters were way too intuitive.

When she remained silent, the corners of Cate's mouth twitched. "Your reticence is telling. But I'd be happy to give you a bit of intel on Brent Lange. Assuming you're curious about him, that is."

Her control-freak sister was going to make her admit she wanted to know more about the man.

Fine.

She was hosed anyway. Grace and Cate had already figured out she was attracted to him.

Not that she intended to admit that.

"I wouldn't mind some background." She tried for a conversational tone. "He ran plenty on me, and turnabout seems fair play."

"Nice try." Cate set her fork down, her expression smug. "To cut to the chase, I haven't run into him much. He's been in patrol most of his career. But I asked my handler to do a little digging after he told me Brent was on your case. The report is all positive. He's well-respected in the ranks, a total pro, honest, brave, and has absolute integrity. And since I know you're dying to ask but won't—he's never been married and, as far as I can tell, doesn't have a steady girlfriend."

Hallelujah!

But Eve did her best to mask that reaction. Just because the man was available and his behavior suggested he could have more than a professional interest in her didn't mean she—or her sisters—were reading him correctly.

She was not going to get carried away with adolescent romantic fantasies about a man she hadn't known a week ago.

"He sounds like a keeper." Grace bit into her fortune cookie.

"That's the word on the street." Cate checked her watch, polished off the remains of her dinner, and broke open her own cookie. "I have to run."

"Are you certain it's safe for you to be here?" Eve moved her plate aside. "I mean, I'm touched you went to all this effort to come by, but I thought you said you were incommunicado until this assignment was over?"

"I am—but I wanted to see you. You know me . . . the control freak." She aimed a wink at both of her sisters.

"Let me go on record as being fine with your control-freak tendencies . . . even if you *were* a tiny bit bossy—and overprotective—after Mom died." Eve gave her a thumbs-up.

"A tiny bit? Ha!" Grace snorted. "I'll never forget how you intimidated my dates with your gestapo-like third degree—and you're a mere four years older than I am!"

"Someone had to vet those guys, and Dad thinks the best of everyone. Didn't I steer you away from that smooth-talking senior whose sole intention was to add a notch to his belt?"

"There was that." Grace lifted her iced tea in acknowledgment. "You do have excellent instincts about men."

A brief shadow passed over Cate's face, gone so quickly Eve would have missed it if she hadn't been watching her sister.

What was that all about?

As far as she knew, Cate was focused on her career and hadn't had a serious dating relationship in years.

Her sister stood and changed the subject. "My time's up."

"How long is this assignment going to last?" Eve slid off her chair too.

"Until it's done."

"Gee. That's helpful."

"The job is open-ended. I knew that when I signed on."

"Are you liking it?" Grace joined the conversation.

Cate shrugged. "I'm not certain it's my thing—but I'm glad I'm giving it a shot. I've always wondered about the allure of undercover work. What does your cookie say?" She motioned to the crispy piece of twisted dough beside Eve's plate.

She picked it up and broke it open. Once again, her cheeks warmed.

"Well?" Grace leaned forward.

"These are silly." Eve wadded up the slip of paper.

Cate gave each of them a hug and continued to the back door. "Retighten your porch bulb after I leave. We had someone loosen it earlier so I could come and go in the dark. Now spill your fortune." She paused by the door.

Double drat.

Her sisters would have a field day with this—but she was stuck.

"It said, 'The one you love is closer than you think.'"

"That's a big improvement over the 'stay the course' I got." Grace waved her slip of paper in the air. "And timely too—don't you think, Cate?"

"Yep. See you two soon, I hope."

"Be careful." Eve joined her at the door.

"My number one rule. Give me three minutes, then tighten the bulb. Love you guys."

Without waiting for a response, she slipped into the darkness.

Eve stayed by the door while Grace cleared the table. At the three-minute mark, she twisted the bulb until it was tight and locked the door.

"Cate looks tired." Grace carried their plates to the sink.

"I imagine undercover work brings a whole new level of stress to the job." Eve gathered up the empty food containers. "I hope coming here didn't put her in any danger."

"I got the impression she had it covered. So . . . what were your plans for the evening before Cate and I descended?"

"Stripping floors."

"Oh."

At Grace's obvious dismay, Eve grinned. "Don't worry. I'm not going to ask you to help me. How long were you planning to stay?"

"About another hour."

"Why don't we make a Ted Drewes run?"

Her sister brightened. "Now you're talking. I can already taste that marshmallow concrete."

"Give me five minutes to change out of my spinning clothes."

"No worries. I can respond to messages while I wait."

Eve headed for the hall, heart lighter, as Grace slid onto a stool, fingers already working the keyboard on her cell. She wouldn't get much done on her floors tonight, but an outing for frozen custard with her sister was exactly what she needed to lift her spirits.

Yet the fact that both Grace and Cate had felt compelled to stop by was unsettling. Despite Cate's tendency to shift into protective mode, both she and Grace were levelheaded and not inclined to overreact.

Conclusion? Their impromptu visit suggested that worry—and caution—were warranted.

However . . . it was possible that once she weathered this latest attack, her tormentor would give up.

Either that, or resort to more extreme measures. Ones that could actually produce physical harm.

She shuddered as she pulled a pair of shorts and a T-shirt from her dresser.

Maybe she ought to think about forking out the money for personal security after all. The cost might not be as outrageous as she expected.

But letting this guy put a dent in her budget, allowing him to impact her life in a material way, would give him a victory of sorts.

That didn't sit well.

On the other hand—it wouldn't hurt to call and get prices tomorrow in case she caved.

And since Brent could probably recommend a firm, that gave her a legitimate excuse to call him.

Her spirits took another uptick.

She finished dressing and slipped on a pair of flat sandals, a smile playing at her lips.

Much as she'd enjoy this outing with Grace, wouldn't it be fun to visit St. Louis's iconic custard stand with Brent?

But she had to get through this crisis first. There'd be time to think about the future afterward.

Assuming there was a future.

Expelling a breath, she picked up her purse. That dark thought needed to be banished ASAP.

Yet hard as she tried to shake it off, an unsettling sense of jeopardy hovered at the edges of her consciousness, clinging as persistently as the oppressive humidity of a St. Louis summer day.

8

"WATER BREAK." Adam Moore stopped, pulled the bottle off his waist pack, and took a long gulp.

Brent followed his best friend's example. Running in this heat without adequate hydration was dangerous, even if they *had* waited until after the sun set to log a few midweek miles.

They drained their bottles in silence.

"You've been quiet tonight." Adam slid his empty bottle back into place.

"Long day."

"Transitioning to a new job is always rough. They give you any interesting cases yet?"

"Yeah. Did you hear about that fake bomb someone left at a local radio show host's house?"

Adam stared at him. "You're working the Eve Reilly case?"

"I was the closest detective when the call came in last Friday. I take it you've been following the media coverage?"

"Hard not to. The press has been all over the story." He propped his hands on his hips. "That's a high-profile assignment for a rookie."

Brent coaxed out a few more drops of liquid and stowed his bottle. "After ten years as a cop, I'm not exactly new to law enforcement."

"You're new to the detective ranks." Adam swiped off a bead of sweat tracking down his temple. "So tell me about Eve Reilly. Is she as dynamic in person as she is on the radio?"

That was *not* a topic he wanted to discuss.

"Yes. Let's run." He took off, leaving Adam no choice but to follow. If he picked up the pace, maybe his once-a-week running partner would focus on pounding the pavement and forget about conversation.

His buddy caught up to him in a few strides. "Why don't you want to talk about her?"

So much for any hope of avoiding that subject.

Time for evasive maneuvers.

"I'm happy to talk about her—but I've only seen her twice. Why are you interested in her?"

"I like her show."

"I didn't know you were into talk radio."

"I'm not—but Rebecca got me hooked on Eve's program." He dodged another jogger who was running the opposite direction. "I tune in while I'm driving to work, unless I'm practicing an opening statement or closing argument—a frequent activity if I'm alone in my car."

"You ever get any strange looks from fellow commuters while you do that?"

"Not often. These days, most people assume I'm on a hands-free call. But at a stoplight a couple of years ago, I noticed the passenger in the adjacent car watching me with a weird expression. She had her window open, so I cranked mine down too and called over to her that I was a prosecuting attorney practicing for court."

"What happened?" With Adam, there was always a punch line.

"She rolled up her window, nudged the guy behind the wheel, and they left me in the dust the minute the light changed. Of course, given that I was on my way to that mystery-dinner costume party we were both invited to, my Lord Voldemort outfit probably didn't give me much credibility."

Brent laughed out loud—and after the frustration of five fruitless days spent trying to untangle Eve's situation, the brief moment of levity was refreshing.

"I remember that party—but not my costume."

"It wasn't memorable, like mine. I still can't believe Rebecca gave me a second glance while I was dressed in that getup."

"She did more than that. She married you."

"Yeah."

The deepening dusk shadowed Adam's face, but Brent could hear the smile in his voice.

Must be sweet to have a beautiful, intelligent, articulate, caring, witty wife to go home to.

An image of Eve materialized in his mind.

As if Adam had sensed the direction of his thoughts, his friend returned to his original line of questioning. "So what's your famous client like?"

Beautiful, intelligent, articulate, caring, witty.

But he wasn't going to say any of that.

"She's not a client. She's a crime victim."

Adam waved a hand. "Don't throw technicalities at me. Just answer the question."

He chose his words with care. "She's putting up a brave front—but she's scared."

"Who wouldn't be in her shoes? You have any leads?"

Brent looked over at him. "Are you asking that as an assistant prosecuting attorney or a friend?"

"I don't have my lawyer hat on tonight."

"In that case, leads are few and far between—but there *was* a new development this morning."

Brent filled him in on the call—but Adam zeroed in on a different part of the story. "Why were you at the station?"

"I already told you. While I was downtown for a meeting, I stopped in to give her an update."

"If you haven't had many leads, how much of an update could there be?"

Leave it to a trial attorney to pull out the most pertinent—and incriminating—fact.

"Like I told you, she's scared. I figured showing up in person would reassure her I'm giving her case a high priority."

Silence except for the slap of their shoes against the pavement and the faint wail of a siren in the distance.

Brent braced for Adam's follow-up.

Nothing came.

Finally he risked a sidelong glance at him.

Adam was grinning.

As if sensing his scrutiny, his friend met his gaze, making no attempt to hide his amusement.

"What's so funny?" As the question spilled out, Brent stifled a groan. If he wanted to change the subject, giving Adam a chance to expound wasn't his smartest tactical move.

"Your last comment." Adam transferred his attention back to the path.

"I don't see the humor in reassuring a crime victim I'm keeping her case top of mind."

"Keeping her *case* top of mind—or keeping *her* top of mind?"

As usual, his friend had cut straight to the chase.

Instead of responding, he broke into a sprint, giving the well-lit area a sweep. This was a safe part of town—and the park was full of people who'd waited until the temperature cooled at dusk to clock their daily miles—but once a cop, always a cop.

"Hey . . . was that sudden burst of speed a new training technique—or an avoidance tactic?" Adam drew up beside him again.

He could pretend he was too winded to talk, but his buddy

would see through that in a heartbeat. Between his running and regular gym workouts, he was in excellent shape.

"No comment."

"Must mean you have a personal interest in the lady."

"Jumping to conclusions is dangerous, counselor."

"It's not a jump if the evidence points that direction."

"You know I'm not in the market for a relationship."

"I thought that might change after I got married."

"Nope." Even if life *had* been lonelier since his friend's wedding six months ago. Adam was diligent about staying in touch, but it wasn't like the old days when they could call each other up at four o'clock and book an impromptu dinner together.

"I think you're nuts."

Brent forced a lightness he didn't feel into his tone. "Don't hold back. Tell me how you really feel."

"You know how I feel. I've been up front about it ever since you declared a moratorium on dating."

"I date."

"Only if you're pressured into it for a couples-oriented social event. And never the same woman twice."

"So? I don't want to lead anyone on."

"Where does that leave you with Eve Reilly?"

Good question.

Once this case wrapped up, he'd be free to ask her out— but unless his instincts were failing, a date with her would simply whet his appetite for more.

And that could undermine his resolve to walk a wide circle around commitments.

They rounded the last curve in the path and entered the home stretch.

"Assuming I was interested—and I'm not admitting I am—I don't have to make that call yet."

"You want my advice?"

"If I say no, will you back off?"

"What do you think?" An elbow connected with his rib cage, and his friend chuckled.

He gave a protracted sigh. "Fine. Say your piece."

"I'll give it to you in a nutshell. The situation with Karen was unfortunate. I know she was traumatized, and I know you were freaked out by her reaction. I get that. But not every female is incapable of dealing with risk. In my experience, women in general are incredibly strong."

Again, an image of Eve materialized in his mind. She fell into the strong category—and she had spunk and smarts to match.

But it didn't matter how strong she was. Putting the kind of life-and-death stress his job entailed on someone he loved would test their fortitude—and it would be selfish.

Period.

Even if most of his colleagues agreed with Adam's viewpoint—and lived their lives accordingly.

But they hadn't been through what he'd experienced. And he never wanted to go down that road again, or cause anyone that kind of emotional distress.

"Are you thinking about what I said, or did you tune me out?" Adam pulled slightly ahead.

"I didn't tune you out."

"But you're not reconsidering your position."

He didn't respond.

"I'll assume my take is correct." Adam blew out a breath. "But I'm betting the right woman could change your mind, if you gave her a chance."

Brent finished the last hundred yards in silence, and Adam let the subject drop as they cooled down and parted for the night.

Yet as he drove home alone in the dark . . . as he pictured the bare-bones condo in desperate need of a few decorating touches that would give it warmth and personality . . . his friend's last comment replayed in his mind.

New as Eve was in his life, his intuition told him she might be the woman who could change his mind about a serious relationship.

If he could ever put the specter of Karen's legacy to rest.

Meg's radio station gig wasn't working for him.

Steve shoved aside the drapes in the living room and scanned the street in front of the house again.

No sign of her, and it was after nine.

She should have been here to greet him when he got home from his Wednesday bowling-and-pizza night. He expected that—and she knew it. If a man couldn't count on his wife to put him first and keep his home running smoothly, what *could* he count on?

His dad hadn't been right about much, but he'd nailed the role of wives. Their primary job was to keep their husbands happy.

A job his mother had failed at—big-time—thanks to that corporate position she'd taken. Once she had her own money, she hadn't wanted—or needed—her husband or son anymore.

He fisted his hand and kicked the baseboard.

After his experience with dear old Mom, it was no wonder he'd vowed to someday find a woman who could be controlled—and who would never be a flight risk.

Meg had fit the bill.

Or she had, until he'd relented after the miscarriage and let her apply for that stupid job at the radio station he'd never expected her to get.

How could he have known Eve Reilly would intervene, convincing management to give his wife the position over better-qualified candidates—and putting ideas in her head about exercise classes and dieting and becoming more active in her church?

He gritted his teeth and muttered a few choice words he'd picked up years ago from his dad. Thanks to Miss Radio Personality, his wife was starting down the same path as his mother.

And he couldn't let that happen.

He yanked out his cell.

She either had to quit—not a choice she appeared inclined to make—or the job had to go away. Especially after tonight. Working late wasn't acceptable . . . even if he'd only arrived home ten minutes ago himself.

Finger poised to jab in her speed dial number, he paused as headlights appeared at the end of the street.

Fifteen seconds later, a car swung into the narrow access lane beside their house.

Finally.

Shoving the cell back in his pocket, he stomped into the kitchen, positioned himself a few feet from the back door, and crossed his arms. It wouldn't take her long to appear. Since the single-car attached garage was his, she always parked in the alley behind the house.

Two minutes later, the door opened.

She halted as soon as she saw him. Offered a tentative smile.

He didn't return it.

"Hi, hon. Sorry I'm late." She closed the door but waited inside—as if she was uncertain of her welcome.

"It's after nine."

"I know. I texted you about what happened at work. Didn't you get my message?"

"I got it—and I didn't like it. Your salary doesn't justify working long hours."

"Doug said they'd add overtime pay to my check, given the unusual circumstances." She eased into the room and deposited her purse on the counter. "How was bowling?"

"I don't want to talk about bowling." He moved toward her.

A flicker of fear flared in her eyes . . . as if she was worried he might hit her.

Good.

He wanted her submissive and compliant. That's how a wife—a woman—should be.

But physical violence wasn't necessary. There were much more effective ways to exert control, as he'd learned from his dad.

However . . . they only worked if you kept a woman isolated and dependent.

That's why Meg's job had to go—sooner rather than later.

He stopped in front of her, lifted a hand as she watched him with trepidation . . . and stroked his fingers down her cheek. "I'm worried about you, babe. The situation at that station is dangerous."

"N-not for me."

After a few beats, he motioned to the kitchen table. "Let's sit."

She hesitated—but when he pulled out a chair and waited, she slid onto it.

"Today was unusual, Steve." She leaned toward him as soon as he was seated, posture taut, twin furrows creasing her brow. "Like I told you in the text, after that call came in, the station was in a frenzy. They wanted me to monitor the reaction on social media. I could have stayed until midnight, but Doug insisted I come home."

"Does that mean you'll have to work late tomorrow night too?"

She shifted in her seat. "I don't know. Until we get past this craziness, everyone's schedule is thrown out of whack—but it can't go on forever. Whoever is causing Eve all this grief will eventually give up."

"Or *she* will."

"No." The definitive shake of Meg's head left no room for argument. "She's not a quitter."

"Maybe she won't have a choice. After today, her audience could desert her."

"In light of all the support she's receiving on social media, I don't think that will happen."

Neither did he, after reading a fair sampling of the comments on her blog. Near as he could tell, they were running 90 percent in her favor.

"Then you should think about resigning."

"Steve." She reached for his hand, her demeanor beseeching. "I enjoy the job, and I'd like to stick with it awhile. The long hours won't last. But I know you're concerned. So why don't we compromise? After we get past the current crisis, I could ask Doug if he'd let me work through lunch. That would get me out of there an hour earlier, and I could have supper underway before you get home."

"Until the next crisis hits."

"I'm not expecting anything else like this to come up in the foreseeable future."

"But it could." He pulled his hand free of her cold fingers. "I think you have to decide which is more important—your job or our marriage. Didn't we agree you'd be a stay-at-home wife?"

"Yes." She linked her fingers into a tight knot on the table. "I just didn't realize how lonely I'd be here all day by myself. My old job wasn't great, but I liked the social interaction. It would be different if I had a child to care for, but with all the complications from the miscarriage, that may never happen." A sheen appeared in her eyes.

"I talked to the doctor. He didn't rule out the possibility of you getting pregnant."

"No—but the odds aren't in our favor. And I always wanted to be a m-mother."

"That could still happen."

"Until it does, though, the job fills up my empty days."

Meaning if they never had children, she'd push to keep working.

Not acceptable.

"We could always consider adopting." That wasn't a serious option, but it could be a bargaining chip to help him achieve his goal if Eve's show continued.

Her jaw dropped. "I thought you'd nixed that."

"I may reconsider if it's that important to you—and if we don't have any success having our own children."

She bit her lip and studied him. "An adopted child *would* be our own child."

"Of course." He waved aside her comment. Having a rug rat by any method was unappealing. Kids were disruptive. But if they kept Meg in the house? Worth the sacrifice. She'd be the one taking care of them anyway. "Here's the thing, though. From what I've heard, adopting is almost a full-time job."

She chewed on her lip again. "I'll tell you what. Why don't we give ourselves six months to get pregnant? If that doesn't happen, we'll start the adoption process—and if it's too time consuming, I'll quit my job to handle all the paperwork and other details."

Six months.

Too long.

He wanted her home now.

And he wasn't changing his time frame.

But until the radio show she'd been hired to assist with was history, why not play along with her plan? It would buy him breathing room to figure out how to accelerate the process.

"I can live with that." He took her hand, stood, and pulled her to her feet. "In the meantime, why don't we work on beating the odds your doctor gave us? I've been missing you all day."

Her shoulders drooped a tiny bit, but she masked her dismay well. "Sure. Give me ten minutes to freshen up?"

"No problem."

He bent and kissed her.

Meg responded—as always—despite the shadows beneath her lower lashes and the faint lines of weariness at the corners of her mouth that testified to her long day. Food and sleep had to be high on her priority list.

But it was important for her to remember he came first.

He drew back and played with a lock of her hair. "Go ahead and get ready. Wear that skimpy black outfit I got you."

The one she didn't like.

The one she'd kiddingly said made her feel like a hooker.

Except deep down she hadn't been kidding. The revealing scrap of lingerie wasn't anywhere close to her style.

He liked it, though—and he especially liked how he felt making her wear it.

"Okay." She backed off, rubbed her palms on her slacks, and disappeared down the hall.

Steve strolled over to the fridge and took out a beer. He'd had his fill already tonight, but Meg hated the smell of beer—and the taste of it when he kissed her.

This would remind her who ran the show.

He popped the tab and took a long pull, thinking about what he would do to her in a few minutes.

His mouth curled.

Definitely some stuff she didn't like—but enough she did enjoy to keep her satisfied. Balancing the two was always fun.

He took another sip and wandered over to the back window, which overlooked the minuscule patch of grass that could use cutting.

Meg would have to get on that this weekend. Relegating lawn chores to her had been one of his stipulations if they exchanged his apartment for a house. After a full day of physical labor, sweating behind a lawnmower held no appeal.

Propping a shoulder against the wall, he watched a feral cat slink through the darkness, scavenging in the trash bins for a few tasty morsels.

Meg wasn't the prettiest or smartest or most adventurous woman he'd ever met, but she'd been easy to win, thanks to her weight issues and the loser parents who'd pulverized her self-esteem. It had been pathetic how fast she'd succumbed to a few compliments and kisses.

And she didn't want to lose him. Didn't want to lose the way he made her feel when he was in one of his generous moods. A little sweet talk, a few gentle touches, a thoughtful gesture here and there—she was putty in his hands.

Grinning, he finished off the beer, tossed the can, and headed down the hall five minutes early.

She'd hate that. Being caught in the middle of a shower always embarrassed her.

But he'd tell her he couldn't wait any longer to be with her.

The truth, though?

It was all about control.

Buzz double-checked the clothing laid out on his bed, ticking off the items one by one as the evening news played on the screen behind him.

Everything was there, ready for his trial run this weekend.

He fingered the black T-shirt, then picked up the brass knuckles and slipped them on. An old-fashioned weapon, but effective—and quiet.

As was the Ka-Bar knife.

It was amazing how available this kind of gear was on the open market.

And he knew how to use it all.

He set the knuckles back on the bed and took a deep breath. Blew it out.

There was no reason to be nervous. He'd already done most of this in his previous life on the West Coast.

But the task dangling before him was much higher profile— and this weekend's mission would confirm he was up to the job.

If all went well, he'd move on to—

"And now, we have an update on last week's story about the fake bomb that was left at radio personality Eve Reilly's house six days ago."

Buzz swung toward the screen, tuning in as the anchorman recapped today's events, beginning with the call to the station during Eve's program.

"At this hour, the police have no suspects, but they continue to work the case. While no one in law enforcement has confirmed there's a link between the bomb threat and call, they did acknowledge they're exploring that possibility. We'll keep you updated as new developments arise."

Buzz picked up the remote and pressed the off button.

No mention that Eve had any plans to take a hiatus from her show.

Too bad.

Her ideas were dangerous—and the fact that she had a huge platform to present them to gullible people who could be easily swayed by articulate, if erroneous, arguments made her dangerous.

She had to be shut down.

And given all that had happened, she would be.

Especially if the siege she was under continued.

Because everyone had their breaking point.

9

THE TALK HAD GONE WELL —even if far too many of the questions from the audience had been related to the furor in her life during the past week rather than the topic of tonight's program.

Hopefully morbid curiosity about her personal tribulations wasn't responsible for the large turnout. That would be an ego buster, and after all—

"Wonderful job, Eve."

She swiveled as a female voice spoke behind her. The school principal was approaching, several members of the audience in her wake.

"Thank you."

"We so appreciate you giving up your Saturday night to join us."

"It was my pleasure. And it's a special treat to speak to parents and teachers of young teens. That's the perfect age to lay a solid grounding in the principles that define America."

"I couldn't agree more. As you pointed out in your speech, few young people understand how our government works—or why it was structured as a constitutional republic. We have to do a better job teaching civics in our schools."

"Hear, hear." An older gentleman spoke up behind the woman.

The principal smiled. "A number of people had questions they didn't get a chance to ask during the Q&A. Can you spare a few minutes to chat with them?"

Eve stifled a sigh. It was almost nine o'clock . . . she'd been up since six . . . yesterday's fast and furious show had exhausted her . . . and stripping floors all day had taken a physical toll.

But she owed every gig her best effort. It was always possible a simple conversation could be the catalyst that encouraged someone to take a deeper interest in defending the country's founding principles.

"Of course."

Thirty minutes and more than a few questions later, as she finished the impromptu Q&A and collected her purse and notes, the principal rejoined her.

"Sorry to keep you this late. If it's any consolation, you should be flattered by all the questions. Only on rare occasions does anyone hang around after our evening PTA programs."

"Then I'll definitely take this as a compliment." She scanned the empty middle-school theater. "Looks like we've closed down the place."

"We have. I'll be around for a few more minutes, turning off lights, locking doors, and ducking into my office to pick up a stack of reports I have to read tomorrow. You're welcome to hang around if you'd like to walk out to the parking lot together."

Wait another ten or fifteen minutes when she was dead on her feet?

No way.

This was a safe area of town, the parking lot had plenty of lights, and her car wasn't far from the entrance.

Besides, while she didn't have a Beretta stashed in her purse, as Grace did, she had her trusty pepper gel.

"Thanks, but I'm ready to call it a night. May I leave through the lobby?"

"Yes. The door will lock behind you." The woman extended her hand. "Thank you again—and let me add my voice to the personal support expressed tonight by many of our members."

"I appreciate that." She returned the principal's firm squeeze. "Enjoy your weekend."

"You too."

Eve trekked toward the lobby, digging through her purse for the small canister of gel. As she pushed through the door, she pulled it out and paused to peruse the area.

Two cars remained in the parking lot. No one was in sight, and the expanse of asphalt was well lit. This was also a low-crime, upper-middle-class section of town populated by professionals.

If she wasn't spooked by the incidents of the past week, she wouldn't even have bothered to dig through her bag for the gel.

Not that she'd ever share that with Cate. After her detective sister's reminders to always expect the worst—and be prepared to deal with it—she'd be appalled by that admission.

But living in fear was the pits.

Given present circumstances, however, an extra dose of caution was prudent.

Tightening her grip on the container, she crossed the lot toward her Camry, one finger on her autolock button, the other poised on the flip top of the gel.

Ten feet from her car, she unlocked her door. In a handful of seconds she'd be safely inside her vehicle.

Picking up her pace, she gave the lot another sweep.

All clear.

At the door of her car, she glanced into the backseat—

another rule Cate had pounded into her sisters' heads. One she always followed.

No one was hiding inside, waiting to pounce.

Without lingering, she slid behind the wheel . . . locked the doors . . . and exhaled.

She was safe.

All that worry, all those precautions, had been for nothing.

No complaints, though. It was smarter to overprepare for trouble than be caught—

Eve froze.

Stopped breathing.

The folded sheet of paper on her dashboard hadn't been there when she'd left her car almost three hours ago.

Slowly she reached for it. Lifted the top edge of the thin sheet. Read the typed words.

> Final warning. Shut up or die.
> A nife can stab more than tires.

Sweet mercy. Would this never end?

Heart pounding, she read the note again.

Frowned.

What was that about her tires? They were fine—at least the ones on the driver's side that were visible from the auditorium.

But the car did seem to be listing slightly.

Were the other two flat?

Should she get out to check?

No. Not with this note in her hands. Whoever had gotten into her car and perhaps slashed her tires could be hiding nearby. They might not know how to *spell* knife, but they could very well know how to use one.

A call to 911 would be appropriate, but a police officer she didn't know would show up . . . and talking to a stranger— however nice he or she was—held zero appeal.

She wanted a familiar face here. Someone whose very presence was reassuring and inspired confidence.

And she knew just the face she wanted to see.

———————

The patrol officer had stayed in his car, as requested—close to Eve's Camry, to assure her help was at hand if needed—but he hadn't approached her.

Good man.

Brent parked beside the cruiser, and the officer slid out of the vehicle.

Myers.

Perfect.

After two decades on the job, the man had street smarts and excellent people skills. Taking the initial report was his responsibility, but he'd cooperate to mitigate the stress of this latest incident as much as possible for Eve.

"Lange." The man held out his hand as he approached.

"Glad you were the responding officer." Brent returned his firm shake.

"You got a hot one right out of the gate with this case."

"No kidding. You want to tag team tonight's incident?"

"Sure. You can take the lead if you want. You know the drill—and what I need for the report."

"Thanks."

"No problem. Shall we?" He indicated Eve's car.

Brent continued toward the Camry as Eve slid out from behind the wheel. She had on more makeup than usual, but it couldn't disguise her slight pallor or the taut line of her mouth.

"Thanks for coming." She addressed the comment to him, giving his jeans and T-shirt a quick perusal before shifting her gaze to include Myers.

Brent indicated the uniformed man. "This is Officer Myers."

He turned back to her. "Have you gotten out of the car since you called me?"

"No."

"Have you seen anyone?"

"Only the principal. Officer Myers spoke to her as she was leaving."

"Give us a minute to walk around the car."

He and Myers circled to the other side.

Considering the slight tilt of the vehicle, he wasn't surprised to discover two flat tires.

While Myers dropped to the balls of his feet and inspected the back tire, he did likewise in the front.

The man joined him less than thirty seconds later. "Half a dozen punctures in the sidewall."

"Same here." He rose.

"Nasty prank."

Too bad that wasn't all it was.

"There's a note too." He rejoined Eve, who was leaning against the car, arms tightly crossed. "They're flat."

"I assumed they would be."

"Would you like to sit while we talk?" He motioned toward the driver's seat.

"I'd rather stand."

He gave the area another slow scrutiny. Everything appeared to be calm—and it was unlikely the perpetrator was lingering, now that law enforcement was on the scene. Today's mission had been accomplished. Why hang around and risk being spotted?

"That's fine. Walk us through what happened this evening."

Myers took notes as Eve told her story. Brent asked the necessary follow-up questions, but her account was thorough—and she provided her contact information to the officer without being prompted.

"You know the routine." Myers flashed her a quick smile.

"I've had recent experience—sad to say." Her lips rose a hair, then flattened again. "Any idea how someone got into my locked car without doing any damage—other than to my tires?"

"All it takes is a wedge for the top of the door and a long rod." Myers continued to jot in his notebook. "Power locks give a false sense of security. And jamming devices that prevent the car from locking even though you hear the familiar click are all over the open market. Car alarms can help—but those aren't infallible either."

"That's not the most comforting news I've heard today." She motioned to the sheet of paper on the passenger seat. "There's the note. Obviously I already touched it."

"No worries." Brent pulled a pair of latex gloves out of the back pocket of his jeans. "We have your elimination prints on file from the fake bomb incident. But I doubt we'll find anyone else's on this. As I've mentioned, these"—he held up the gloves—"are a criminal staple these days—just like they are for law enforcement. Give me a minute to grab an evidence envelope from my car."

Myers continued to scribble in his notebook while Brent retrieved the envelope, placed a call to the Crime Scene Unit, and tugged on his gloves.

Eve moved aside as he reached across the driver's seat and picked up the single sheet of paper. Read it. Showed it to Myers before sliding it into the bag. "You have any other questions?"

"No." The man stowed his notebook.

"CSU will be here soon. Can you wait around until they show up?"

"Sure." Myers angled toward Eve. "Don't hesitate to call us if there are any new developments, ma'am—but you're in capable hands with Detective Lange. My report from tonight will be available by tomorrow if you want a copy for insurance purposes."

"Thank you—and thanks for responding so fast."

He nodded in acknowledgment and returned to his cruiser.

Brent filled out the envelope, ending with the chain of custody section, then refocused on Eve. "Do you want the car towed, or would you prefer to have someone replace the tires here?"

"What do you recommend on a Saturday night at this hour?"

"I'd have it done here—but that would have to wait until tomorrow. I can ask Patrol to have an officer swing by overnight and keep an eye on your vehicle if you want to consider that option. I'll also give you the names of a few reputable outfits that can take care of this—and I'd be happy to run you home."

She rubbed at the twin grooves above her nose. "I've disrupted your evening too much already. I should let you get back to whatever you were doing."

"The book I was reading can wait." He might not admit to his colleagues that he spent his Saturday nights on such a low-key pursuit—but Eve would appreciate his choice of leisure activity.

And maybe even be glad he wasn't out barhopping . . . or on a hot date.

"You were reading?" She stared at him.

He hitched up one side of his mouth. "Yeah. I learned how in first grade."

Soft color stole across her cheeks. "Whoops. That didn't come out right. I didn't mean to insult you. But in my defense, I haven't met many men who spend their Saturday nights reading."

"Their loss—and no offense taken."

"Thanks. What are you reading?"

"I'm alternating between a novel and a nonfiction book."

When he mentioned the titles—one about the relationship

between John Adams and Thomas Jefferson, the other a best-selling thriller—she arched an eyebrow. "Quite a contrast."

"My reading taste is eclectic."

"I can see that. I enjoyed the Jefferson/Adams book."

"That doesn't surprise me, now that I'm becoming acquainted with your interest in the workings of our government. Do you also read fiction?"

"Yes. At the moment I'm immersed in a heartwarming series set in a charming seaside community in Oregon. With all the turmoil in my life, it's soothing to visit a place where everyone cares about everyone else." She let a beat pass. "If you're certain you don't mind giving me a ride, I'll go with the change-the-tires-here option and take you up on your offer."

His spirits lifted. For once his Saturday evening wouldn't end in a solitary pursuit.

"The offer stands."

"Should I lock my car? As if that will keep it—or me—safe."

"No. The CSU tech will do that after he or she is finished. And locking your car *is* a deterrent in most cases—but for the immediate future, check your door afterward to be sure it's not still open, in case someone happens to be using a jamming device."

"For those to work, that someone would have to be nearby, watching for you to get out and lock your car—right?"

"Yes."

"So if whoever left the note used one, he's been tracking my schedule and knew about my speaking engagement."

"That would be a reasonable assumption. You ready to go?"

"I have one more question first." She swallowed. "The note said this was a final warning. That next time I'm not going to walk away. Do you think this is another scare tactic—or a serious threat this person intends to follow through on?"

He knew what she wanted to hear—but he couldn't give

her that assurance. Not when his gut was signaling a red alert. Telling him the situation was ratcheting up.

And he trusted his gut. Only on rare occasion had it let him down—or led him astray.

"I think increased caution is in order." He tried for a measured tone, despite the apprehension prickling in his nerve endings. He wanted her attentive, but not panicked. People who freaked out lost their ability to think clearly—and made mistakes.

Sometimes fatal ones.

"As in I should bite the bullet and shell out the money for personal security?"

"If you can swing it, that wouldn't be a bad investment at this point. Your home security system is first class, so you'd only need a bodyguard part-time, while you're out and about. And I hope not for long."

She expelled a breath. "Okay. I'll give it serious thought. Can you recommend anyone?"

"Not officially."

"How about unofficially?"

"A former County detective opened a PI/security firm a number of years ago called Phoenix Inc. It's top-notch. All of the PIs have law enforcement backgrounds—police detectives, Secret Service agent, undercover ATF operative. If I ever wanted protection, that's where I'd go."

"Sold. I'll give them a call and get pricing information."

"Be ready for sticker shock. That kind of expertise doesn't come cheap."

"Thanks for the warning."

"Shall we?" He motioned toward his car.

"Yes. I'm ready to go home."

But he wasn't.

And as they walked to his vehicle . . . as he held the door for her and she slipped inside . . . a powerful temptation to extend the evening swept over him—despite the warning flashing in his brain.

The smart choice was clear. If he didn't want to get involved with this woman, he should walk her to her door—and walk away.

Fast.

Except he didn't feel smart tonight.

He felt lonely.

And loneliness was a potent motivator.

Maybe by the time he pulled into her cul-de-sac he'd find the strength to make a quick exit.

But he wasn't betting on it.

10

EVE DIDN'T WANT BRENT to walk her to the door— and walk away. Yes, she had a top-notch security system . . . but after tonight's scare it would be nice to have company for an hour or two.

One man in particular.

Could she entice him to stay?

As they traversed the dark streets, the silence broken only by the hum of tires against pavement, Eve peeked at the man behind the wheel.

His jaw was hard, his brow furrowed—and his frequent glances in the rearview mirror suggested he was on high alert.

The man oozed confidence and competence.

No wonder she always felt safe in his presence.

And feeling safe was a top priority tonight.

But that's not the main reason you want him to stay, Eve.

She exhaled. Okay, fine. She could admit the truth. Yes, she liked Brent Lange.

A lot.

But who wouldn't? What was not to like? The man was smart, conscientious, reeked of integrity, had a solid reputation among his peers—and was one hunk of handsome, appealing masculinity.

The latter attribute was on full display tonight, thanks to a snug T-shirt that showed off his broad chest and impressive biceps, plus a pair of broken-in jeans that hugged his lean hips and muscular legs.

No wonder her already elevated adrenaline had gone off the charts when he'd stepped out of his Taurus in the parking lot.

She shifted in the seat and tugged at the neckline of her suddenly too-tight mock turtleneck.

Cate's intel suggested Brent didn't have any steady female companionship—and the fact he'd been reading on a typical date night appeared to support that conclusion.

That didn't mean he'd be interested in getting to know her, however. Hadn't he turned down her last offer to stay awhile on the night she'd found the fake bomb?

But what did she have to lose by trying again?

"Home sweet home." He pulled into her cul-de-sac and guided the car toward her house.

It was now or never.

Taking a deep breath, she strove for a nonchalant tone. "I know it's getting late—and you have your book waiting for you—but can I offer you a drink? And maybe dessert? I don't make killer baklava like Grace does, but my carrot cake is a family favorite."

Thank goodness her restlessness had compelled her to whip one up today in between stages of working on the floor, or all she would have been able to offer was yogurt.

A dessert unlikely to persuade anyone to hang around.

The seconds dragged by as he swung into her driveway and set the brake.

Message received.

Inviting him in had been a bad idea.

She needed to lighten up the atmosphere and try to salvage this awkward situation.

"On the other hand, if you do stay I may put you to work

helping me refinish floors." She forced up the corners of her mouth. "For someone who's not into DIY, that wouldn't be the best—"

"I love carrot cake."

The rest of her sentence died in her throat.

He angled toward her, but his shadowed face was impossible to read. "I won't be able to stay long, though. I'm ushering at the early service tomorrow morning. But I can't pass up carrot cake."

The encouraging news that Brent was a churchgoer registered at a peripheral level—but it was the end of the sentence that captured her attention.

He was staying!

She tried to contain her elation. "Great. And I totally understand about the early service. I'm used to getting up before dawn for my show, so I always go then too."

May as well let him know church was part of her regular schedule too. Shared beliefs and interests were the building blocks of relationships, after all.

In case that was where they were headed.

"Good to know we're on the same page."

The dimness in the car masked his features, but she had the distinct feeling he was talking about more than their Sunday church habits.

"Uh-huh."

Real articulate, Eve.

At least he couldn't see her eye roll in the darkness.

"I'll get your door." He circled around the hood, then followed her to the front porch and waited while she fitted the key into the lock.

Or tried to.

It took three fumbling attempts to insert the thing.

Sheesh.

You'd think she'd never invited a man into her home.

Once the door swung open, he joined her in the foyer, her security system beeping in the background.

"Follow me to the kitchen and I'll shut that off. As you can see"—she waved a hand toward the empty living room—"this remains a work in progress. But I should finish the floors in a week or so."

She continued to the back of the house, deactivated the alarm, and dropped her purse and notes on the counter. "I have coffee, tea, Diet Sprite, and mango iced tea."

"Mango iced tea?" The corners of his eyes crinkled in amusement. "That's not an option I often get."

"It's Grace's favorite. I always keep a few bottles on hand. Want to try it?"

"No thanks. That's too exotic for my tastes. Coffee is fine."

"Full strength or decaf?"

"The higher the octane, the better. What do you prefer?"

"This late at night I drink herbal tea."

"In that case, don't bother with the coffee. I'll have a soda."

"It's no bother. I've got a one-cup brewer. But won't full-strength java keep you awake all night?" She pulled out the bag of coffee and measured a generous portion into the filter.

"Unless I guzzle a pot of caffeine, it doesn't affect my shut-eye. One cup won't make a dent."

"I wish the same was true for me. Have a seat." She indicated the stools at the island and filled two mugs with water. "I'll have this ready fast."

But he didn't sit.

Instead, he strolled around the island—closer to her. "Can I help?"

"Um . . ." The subtle, distinctive scent of his aftershave tickled her nose—and turned her brain to mush. "All I have to do is c-cut the cake."

He grinned, either unaware of her discomfiture . . . or

enjoying it. "Can I lick the icing off the knife? That will take me back to my childhood."

As the image of him engaged in that activity flashed through her mind, her heart lurched.

"Uh . . . s-sure." She cleared her throat and backed away, toward the fridge.

Thank heaven he didn't follow.

Once there, she set their mugs on the counter, opened the door, and stuck her face in as far as she could. If she was lucky, the chilly air would chase the warmth from her cheeks.

The cake was front and center among the meager items on her shelves—but he couldn't see that from where he was standing—so she lingered on the pretense of moving the contents around to reach their dessert.

Too bad she couldn't further stretch out the retrieval, but if she dawdled too long he'd get suspicious.

Pasting on a smile that was a tad too cheery, she withdrew the cake and held it out for him to inspect. "Ta-da."

The confection in her hands distracted him long enough for her to get her act back together.

Sort of.

"Wow." He ogled the swirls of cream cheese icing. "That looks fabulous."

"It's my specialty—after moussaka." She deposited it on the counter and cut a generous slice for him and a smaller one for her. "Why don't you take these over to the table while I get the beverages going?"

"Don't I get a crack at the knife?"

Her heart missed a beat. "Uh . . . sure." She held it out.

"This will be a treat." He took it from her, his lean fingers brushing her hand.

The treat was all hers as she watched him lick the blade clean.

"Thank you." He handed her the knife back, his gaze locking with hers. Warming. Igniting.

Oh man.

This was bad.

Very bad.

She never got hot and bothered over a man she barely knew.

Change the subject, Eve.

Right.

"There are, uh, forks in the drawer beside the sink, and napkins in the cabinet above."

"Got it." He picked up the plates and retrieved the items she mentioned while she put her water in the microwave and poured his into the coffeemaker. "I'm going to enjoy every bite of this. Homemade cake isn't on my menu very often these days."

"Not a baker, huh?"

"Not a chef, period. I don't have the time—or the inclination—for the culinary arts. I'm more in Cate's camp—eating is my specialty."

"I don't dally in the kitchen, either. If I have any openings in my schedule, I'd rather bike or spin. But I know all the basics."

He inspected the cake. "This is way beyond the basics."

"I do excel at a few items."

She swiveled away and fiddled with the coffeemaker. While she'd shared pieces of her history with him over the past eight days, he'd told her nothing about his background other than a brief reference to his grandparents. Yet he *had* mentioned his childhood a few minutes ago. Would he be willing to offer her a few tidbits about his growing-up years tonight?

Why not test the waters?

"So did licking the knife bring back happy memories from your childhood?" She kept her tone casual and conversational.

Behind her, the thump of ceramic against wood told her he'd deposited their plates on the table.

Several silent seconds ticked by.

Shoot.

Introducing a potentially sensitive subject had been a bad call.

Fix this, Eve, or he's going to leave as soon as he scarfs down his cake. Like he did last time, after the subject of his grandparents came up.

"Um . . . do you want cream or sugar?"

Of course he didn't. Brent was the kind of guy who took his coffee black and strong, with no hint of sweetness.

But the innocuous question would break the uncomfortable silence.

"No thanks."

The microwave pinged, and she took out her mug. Added a bag of her favorite, soothing peppermint tea.

Yet as she retrieved his mug from the coffeemaker, the almost palpable tension emanating from her guest might be too much for even her favorite comfort beverage to overcome.

———————

He shouldn't have caved and accepted Eve's invitation.

This cozy kitchen that invited the sharing of confidences was undermining his resolve to keep his distance.

Though truth be told, it had been crumbling from the moment he'd met her.

Brent regarded the cake he no longer wanted and curled his fingers in his lap.

Walking through her door had been his first mistake—but why had he set himself up for further danger by tossing out that remark about licking the knife . . . and childhood memories? If he hadn't made that stupid comment, she wouldn't have asked the follow-up question he'd ignored.

Thankfully she hadn't repeated it. No doubt she'd realized it was an off-limits topic.

Or it had been all these years.

So what was with the sudden urge to talk to a virtual stranger about painful episodes from his past he'd never shared with anyone but Adam?

It didn't make sense.

Yet it felt right.

He rested his elbow on the table and pressed his knuckles against his mouth.

Should he take a chance with this woman, share some of the wounds in his soul—or play it safe and shut down, as usual?

Eve turned, both mugs in hand, and walked toward him. Her wary expression indicated she'd picked up the negative vibes bouncing around the room.

Given her intelligence and intuitive abilities, that wasn't surprising.

She joined him at the table and gestured toward his cake. "Go ahead and dig in."

He picked up his fork, his pulse racing as fast as it had during the tense standoffs that were the lot of a street cop, when one wrong move could change the landscape of a life forever.

Just as tonight could, if he gave into the urge to open his heart.

"Is everything okay?" Eve's tentative question refocused him.

"Yeah." He poked at his cake. "Sort of."

She wrapped her fingers around her mug. "I'm sorry if I ventured into restricted territory—or said anything to upset you."

"It's not what you said that upset me." Why deny his angst? It was obvious Eve had tuned in to his emotional state. "It was the memories your question stirred back to life."

She studied him, as if waging an internal debate—then released her mug and rested her fingers lightly on top of his. "I'm not a bad listener, if you need a sympathetic ear. On the other hand, I won't take offense if you want to talk about the weather, eat your cake, and go home to your book. We all have too much pressure in our lives as it is. I don't want to add to yours."

Her gentle touch, the empathy and kindness in her deep green eyes, and the no-penalty escape she'd offered cinched his decision.

If he couldn't take a chance with this caring woman, he was doomed to live in an emotional vacuum forever.

He examined the slender fingers covering his. Filled his lungs. "I appreciate that—but I'd like to stay awhile . . . and answer your earlier question." He exhaled, psyching himself up for a point-of-no-return leap. "No, licking the knife didn't bring back happy memories from my childhood. That treat wasn't part of my normal routine."

To her credit, she didn't pounce on him with a follow-up question. She simply withdrew her hand and waited, giving him the space and time to decide what—and how much—to share.

He set his fork back down and linked his fingers on the table. "I told you once I was raised by my grandparents."

"I remember."

"It wasn't an ideal situation. I wasn't a welcome addition to their household."

"Then how did you end up with them?"

He stared into the dark depths of his coffee and dredged up the story that had shaped his life. "My mother died in childbirth at nineteen without ever revealing the name of my father. Since she was an only child, and our few distant relatives were scattered around the country, I'd have gone into the foster system if my grandparents hadn't taken me. So after consulting with their pastor, they did their Christian duty. And that's what I always felt like. A duty."

The room went quiet, the admission hanging in the air between them.

He lifted his head, and at the compassion radiating from her, he nearly lost it. No one had ever looked at him with such gentleness and empathy. It was almost as if Eve could feel the pain that had plagued him for decades—which was crazy.

Yet it felt real.

"I'm sorry, Brent." The ache in her whisper tightened his throat. "I can't imagine growing up in that kind of environment."

He gave a stiff shrug, hanging on to his composure by a hair. "I survived."

"Are your grandparents still living?"

"No. My grandmother died eight years ago, my grandfather eleven months later. After they retired to Florida when I was twenty, I didn't see much of them." He picked up the fork, ran the tines through the icing, and let the sweetness dissolve on his tongue.

But it couldn't mask the lingering bitterness he'd tried for years to vanquish.

Eve leaned forward, concern etching her features. "They didn't neglect you—or mistreat you—did they?"

"Not in the way you mean. I always had enough to eat, clean clothes, and a warm place to sleep. As long as I followed the house rules, life was placid. But they were aloof people, and it was a lonely childhood. That's why I developed such a love for reading. Books let me escape to happier places."

Eve's eyes began to shimmer. "Given your home life, I can't believe you turned out as normal as you did."

If only.

"That depends on how you define normal. I have a career I enjoy. I have a faith that sustains me, thanks to a youth leader at our church who took me under his wing when I was nine. I show up for work, pay my bills, take a vacation once in a while, volunteer with Big Brothers. But not every part of my life is normal."

"Such as?" Eve's question was mild, undemanding—and if he didn't want to answer it, she wasn't going to push.

He took a sip of his coffee . . . debating.

This was the part of the conversation he'd most dreaded—and he still wasn't certain he could crack the door wide enough to let her in.

The strains of "I Won't Back Down" filled the kitchen, and despite the tension rippling through him, a grin twitched at his lips. That had to be the ringtone on Eve's cell. It fit her to a T.

She glanced at the counter, an annoyed frown marring her forehead.

"Tom Petty is calling." He picked up his mug. "Go ahead and answer."

And give me a couple of minutes to hash out my dilemma.

Although he didn't speak those words, she seemed to hear them—because after a brief hesitation, she slid off her chair.

"Hold your thought. I'll be back in a sec." She crossed the room to retrieve her cell.

Leaving him to figure out how far he wanted to take this tonight—and whether he had the courage to go the distance.

11

O F ALL THE INOPPORTUNE TIMES for the phone to ring!

Eve snatched the cell off the counter and scowled at the screen.

Grace.

It figured. Her sister's timing had never been the best.

She pushed the talk button, held up an index finger to Brent, and hurried into the hall.

This was *not* going to take more than one minute!

However . . . her guest was probably glad for the reprieve. It would give him a chance to decide how he wanted to proceed—or if he even wanted to continue their conversation.

Much as she hoped he would, pushing would be a mistake. He'd already shared far more tonight than she'd expected— which was why she'd beaten back the temptation to let the call roll. In his shoes, she would have appreciated a chance to weigh the pros and cons before wading into murky waters.

"Hello? Eve? Are you there?"

Oops.

She'd forgotten to greet her sister.

"Yeah, I'm here. What's up?"

"Does something have to be up for me to call you?"

143

"Uh . . . no." She ducked into her bedroom and closed the door. "I just thought you might have news."

"I'm not the one in the headlines these days. What's the latest with *you*?"

She hesitated. Telling Grace about tonight's incident was a given, but if she dallied to explain the details—and answer all the questions her sister would throw at her—Brent could get tired of waiting and leave as soon as she returned.

"I do have an update—but can I call you back later?"

A few seconds ticked by.

"Why are you out of breath?"

Was she?

"Um, I'm kind of busy at the moment."

More silence.

"Do you have company?"

Grace's ability to link seemingly disparate pieces of information and come to accurate conclusions was amazing.

It was also irritating in certain circumstances—like this one.

"I gave a talk tonight, remember?" If she dodged the query, maybe her sister would drop the subject. "I only got home twenty minutes ago."

"That doesn't answer my question."

No, it didn't.

And Grace was as tenacious as ever.

"I'll explain later."

Three beats ticked by.

"Is your detective there?"

Eve blinked. How in the world had her sister come to *that* conclusion?

No matter. She was stuck. Short of an outright lie, there was nothing to do except admit the truth.

"Yes . . . on official business." Sort of.

"Has there been another attack?" Grace's tone sharpened.

"Yes—but nothing physical. It was indirect, like the other two. I'll explain everything when I call you back."

"Is the detective still questioning you?"

More like baring his soul—unless this ill-timed call had jinxed everything.

"We're finishing up."

"So you'll call me back soon?"

"As soon as I can." She cracked the bedroom door and cocked her ear. A quiet clunk suggested Brent had set his mug down—meaning he'd remained at the table.

"Fine. I'll let you go. But one piece of advice. Unless you want him to disappear forever after this case is over, try to give him *some* indication you're interested."

Already done. Inviting the man in for coffee and cake was about as clear as she could make her interest at this point.

But her sister didn't have to know that.

"I'll keep that in mind."

"Don't just keep it in mind. Spit the words out."

"I don't think spitting will endear me to him."

"Very funny. I'll be waiting for your call—and a full report."

The line went dead.

And none too soon.

Phone in hand, Eve hurried back to the kitchen. "Sorry about that. It was my sister."

"Grace?"

"Mmm-hmm." She retook her seat. Brent had eaten several bites of his cake while she was gone, and his mug was half empty. "If you want a refill, let me know."

"I'm fine for now." He took another sip, and one side of his mouth flexed up. "I like your ringtone. It suits you."

"Cate says it's indicative of my stubborn streak."

"I meant it as a compliment."

"Thanks. I'm impressed you recognized it."

"I'm a fan of oldies but goodies." He forked a piece of cake. "Here's the name of a reputable tire service, as promised." He slid a face-down business card toward her, the information jotted on the back.

The conversation had degenerated to ringtones, music, and flat tires.

Drat.

He wasn't going to pick up the discussion where they'd left off.

But the choice about whether to continue was his, and she had to respect his privacy—despite the dozen questions in her mind clamoring for air time.

"I appreciate the recommendation." She moved the card aside, away from the sticky icing.

"You haven't touched your cake." He motioned toward her dessert.

She summoned up a brief smile. "You did manage to get ahead of me."

"Why don't you tackle it while I finish what I was telling you when the phone interrupted us?"

His tone was calm. Conversational. Impersonal almost. As if what he was about to say didn't matter in the least.

But it did.

Not only to him, but to them.

Trust was everything in a relationship, and his willingness to continue after having a chance for second thoughts spoke volumes.

Spirits rebounding, she picked up her fork, broke off a bite of the cake—and waited.

He took another sip of coffee, set the mug down, and looked at her. "My grandmother always baked a cake for my birthday. Once a year I got to lick the knife."

Once a year.

Somehow she knew that simple fact was significant.

Twin crevices dented his brow. "I don't know why I made that comment tonight about licking the knife. Instead of bringing back happy memories, it reminds me how sterile and empty my life was the other 364 days of the year—including

Christmas. After church, I opened a few practical presents like socks and shirts. Later, my grandmother fixed dinner, my grandfather disappeared into his study, we ate, and I read in my room until bedtime."

Eve tried to imagine that sort of subdued holiday, where everyone in the family passed most of the day in solitary pursuits.

Failed.

The Reilly Christmas always meant mounds of presents, laughter, board games by the fireplace, joyful holiday carols playing in the background, and a sense that God was in his heaven and all was right with the world.

"I'm sorry, Brent." She gentled her voice. "A child's Christmas should be filled with the makings of happy memories."

He shrugged. "I got used to it—and got past it."

No, he hadn't, or it wouldn't be haunting him two decades later.

But she left that unsaid.

"Did you have any friends while you were growing up?"

"Yes." The shadows on his face brightened a shade. "Adam Moore was my best bud in grade school. Still is. His family always welcomed me whenever my grandparents let me visit. I was there often enough to recognize what I was missing in my own home and to get exposure to a normal family situation."

"Thank God you had that."

"I did—and do—every day."

"When did you leave your grandparents' house?" Calling it home would be too much of a stretch.

"College. I went to an out-of-state school and never lived in their house again."

Their house—not our house.

Her heart ached for the little boy who'd never felt welcome in his own home—and for the grown-up man who bore the scars.

"Did you stay in touch?"

"I called every few weeks, and I dropped by once in a while. My last visit was ten years ago. I'd been on a retreat, and afterward I got the urge to give my grandparents a gift. I knew they'd always wanted to take a cruise, and since I had the County job by then—and a regular salary—I decided to surprise them. A last-ditch effort to connect, I guess. I also wrote them a letter that was a bit on the sappy side."

In other words, he'd taken a risk and bared his soul.

She leaned forward. "What happened?"

"They thanked me for the cruise."

"What about the letter?"

"They said they'd read it after I left."

"Did they?"

"I don't know." A muscle clenched in his jaw. "They never mentioned it again."

Merciful heaven. How could they have treated their own flesh and blood with such coldness?

"I'm so sorry, Brent." Somehow she managed to choke out the words.

"Hey." He touched her hand. "It's okay."

No, it wasn't.

But she couldn't change the past. All she could try to do was ensure he had a better future.

As she struggled to get a grip on her emotions, he spoke again.

"Eve—I didn't introduce this subject to dwell on the past or to elicit sympathy. I brought it up to help you understand how my childhood shaped me . . . and why I'm deficient in certain areas of my life."

"None that I can see."

"You would in time." He linked his fingers on the table. "Let me cut to the chase. As you've probably deduced, my grandparents weren't the most demonstrative or warm people. I witnessed few exchanges of affection between them, and they were no different with me."

"What about when you were a young child? Didn't they kiss you good night or . . . or comfort you if you were sad or hurting?" Surely they had a *few* loving qualities.

"No. They were stoic personalities. There wasn't much laughter in the house, nor were tears allowed. Everyone was expected to suck it up and carry on. As a result, I learned to be self-sufficient and to keep my emotions on a tight leash. That's been an asset in my work—but less so in my personal life. In fact . . . it's been a significant problem."

All of a sudden, the gentle rain that had begun falling as they'd arrived at her house intensified. The drops hammered against the skylight, adding to the drumbeat of tension in the room as she tried to process all he'd told her.

The man sharing her kitchen table had given her a bunch of facts—most of them heartbreaking. Yet there had been one revealing omission.

He hadn't talked about how his bleak childhood had made him feel.

Or how he felt now.

And why would he, after being raised by two such cold people? After spending his youth in a joyless environment where emotion was discouraged? After his one outreach as an adult had been rebuffed with callous indifference?

After all, if you didn't get close to anyone, you couldn't get hurt.

But people who never allowed themselves to feel emotions— or make connections—could have difficulty forming social attachments.

Was that why he'd never married? Was that what he'd been trying to tell her with that last comment? That he wasn't the best husband material?

Or was she reading too much into his remark?

No way to be certain unless she asked for clarity . . . with as much diplomacy as she could muster.

She pressed a finger on a stray crumb and deposited it on her plate, speaking slowly as she formulated her response. "I'm trying to read between the lines here, and I may be off base—but I'm interpreting what you said to mean you haven't always been as successful in relationships as you've been in your career. And that this may be why you've never married."

The corners of his mouth rose, but there was no humor in his eyes. "Are you certain you didn't double major in psychology?"

"Psych 101 was as far as I went. Western history and political science were my focus."

He arched an eyebrow. "How did you end up in education?"

"History and poli sci majors don't get a ton of job offers. The teaching gig in a private high school fell into my lap, and I grabbed it. Doing the blog on the side allowed me to use my degrees—but I'd still be teaching if that hadn't taken off and led to the radio program. I enjoyed working with young people."

"Well, you would have done well in psych. You nailed the problem. I tend to keep my emotions close to my vest, and that isn't conducive to starting—or maintaining—a relationship."

Careful, Eve.

"Is that conclusion based on assumption—or experience?"

"Experience."

Meaning he had at least one failed relationship in his past—perhaps more.

And they must have come to ugly ends if they'd scared him off of trying again—and impelled him to warn her he was damaged goods.

Except he wasn't.

If his emotions were buried too deep to retrieve . . . if his ability to connect with another person was too broken to salvage . . . if he truly believed he was destined to live his life alone . . . he wouldn't be in her kitchen tonight, sharing such painful secrets from his past.

Nor would he be here if he didn't care for her a great deal. Maybe more than he'd ever cared for any other woman.

But would he be receptive to her conclusions—or think she was glossing over wounds he was convinced had left permanent damage?

Only one way to find out.

Once again, she reached out and covered his linked fingers with hers. "I can't speak to your past serious relationships—"

"Relationship. Singular. These days I never let my interactions with women get past the superficial conversation stage. Karen was the one exception."

That piece of news—plus the flicker of pain that flared in his dark brown irises—put a different spin on the situation . . . and revealed more than he'd perhaps intended to share.

The deep-seated fear behind Brent's unwillingness to connect had been turbocharged by his one serious relationship that had gone south.

"Do you want to tell me what happened with her?"

The rain continued to pound overhead as she held her breath and waited for his response.

At last he swallowed. "That's a story for another day. It's getting late, and I should be going."

Eve released the air in her lungs, doing her best to mask her disappointment.

He was done sharing for tonight.

Yet she should be thankful he'd opened up as much as he had and given her new insights.

The story about Karen could be a key piece of what made this man tick, but it would have to wait for a future tête-à-tête—unless he was so spooked by all he'd revealed tonight that he cut her off cold.

She had to reassure him the risk he'd taken was worthwhile . . . and appreciated.

"Okay." She called up the ghost of a smile. "I'm grateful

you told me as much as you did. I know it can be tough to open up like that."

"Honestly?" His gaze locked with hers. "It wasn't as hard as I expected—and that's a tribute to you. You have excellent listening skills."

"Is that why you told me? Because I was a receptive sounding board?"

She already knew the answer to that question, but it was important for him to acknowledge it to her—and to himself. If he wanted to override his instinct to back off when the subject matter got too personal, he had to learn to talk to people he could trust.

Like her.

And he did want to conquer his problem. Otherwise he wouldn't have risked what he had tonight with her.

As she waited him out, he shifted in his chair. Swiped his thumb over a stray piece of icing on his plate. Picked up his mug of cooling coffee.

The dark liquid sloshed against the edges.

Telling.

This strong, capable, accomplished man who'd gone head-to-head with very bad people on the streets was big-time scared.

Her heart melted.

He squared his shoulders, as if preparing to face an enemy. "No. I told you about my past because I feel a connection between us—and I'd like to get to know you better . . . even if that's not smart." Grooves of tension bracketed his mouth. "I shouldn't have caved and come in tonight."

Uh-oh.

That wasn't encouraging.

Was he regretting how much he'd shared?

Jump in here, Eve, or this could go downhill fast.

"Um . . . you do know that I'll keep everything you told me confidential."

"Yes."

"Then why isn't it smart for us to see where a friendship could lead?"

"For a couple of reasons—including the issue we talked about tonight. I've listened to you on the radio, Eve. You put it all out there for the world to see, facts and opinions and feelings. You're an open book in the best sense of the term. You don't hold back, and what you see is what you get. You deserve someone who can reciprocate."

"After the past hour, I'm pretty sure I'm looking at someone who can. With me, anyway—and in a relationship, that's all that counts."

"One evening doesn't change the habits of a lifetime."

"It's a first step. And for the record, I also feel the connection between us. I hoped it was mutual. Now that I know it is, I can see promising possibilities ahead."

"I'd like to say the same." His tone was sad. Defeated. "But there's another barrier."

The strains of "I Won't Back Down" riffed through the kitchen again.

Eve glared at her cell. "I'm letting that roll."

"If you want to get it, that's fine. I have to go." He stood abruptly, as if the urge to flee was too strong to resist. "The cake was great."

She checked his plate.

Empty.

When had he finished his dessert?

"Let me get you another piece to take home."

He edged toward the doorway to the hall. "You don't have to do that."

She ignored him.

Brain whirring at warp speed, she retrieved the cake from the refrigerator. As she cut another generous slice and encased it in plastic wrap, his barrier comment kept looping through her mind.

What was the other obstacle between Brent and a relationship?

If she could detain him a few minutes, there was a chance he'd tell her—and she needed to know. Otherwise she wouldn't be able to address it.

She slid the cake back into the fridge and turned.

He was already waiting in the doorway between the kitchen and hall, keys in hand.

Her spirits tanked. There would be no more conversation tonight.

Stifling her frustration, she crossed to him and passed over the cake. "Would you like to borrow an umbrella?"

"No thanks. I can run to the car." He walked toward the foyer, leaving her no choice but to follow. "I'll let you know as soon as the lab weighs in on tonight's note and any findings from the CSU."

"I'm not holding out much hope for helpful news."

He stopped at the front door and angled toward her. "You'll give Phoenix a call?"

"Top of my list tomorrow—after I arrange to get new tires put on my car."

"Do you have to be anywhere in the morning?"

She could lie to take advantage of the implied offer of a lift—and a chance to see him again—but working on the floors was the primary item on her schedule for tomorrow.

"No. Under the circumstances, I think God will overlook my absence at church."

He hefted the cake. "I'll enjoy this. Thanks again."

"I have more if you run out—and I'm always available if you want to talk."

He didn't bite. "I appreciate that." Turning away, he reached for the knob.

In five seconds, he'd be gone.

A bold idea sprouted in Eve's mind, and she stopped breathing. Brazen wasn't her style—but letting him leave without impressing on him how much he'd come to mean to her in their short acquaintance felt like a mistake.

"Brent."

He paused. Slowly pivoted back toward her.

Without giving herself a chance to get cold feet, she closed the distance between them . . . rose on tiptoe . . . and brushed her lips over his.

He froze as she lowered herself to her heels.

"They say actions . . . speak louder than words." Her sentence came out choppy, as if she was winded. "That action is to let you know how much I care about you—and that I'm willing to work with you on whatever other obstacle you think stands between you and romance. The sparks we're generating deserve to be explored."

His nostrils flared, and his chest rose and fell as fast as if he'd run a hundred-meter dash. "You don't play fair."

"I'll always play fair with you. But I'm not afraid to go after what I want—or let you see how I feel."

"A classic example of the difference between us."

"You opened up tonight. If you can do it once, you can do it again—until it becomes a new habit."

"That could take a long time."

"I'm on no deadline."

A gust of wind sent a spray of cool mist through the door.

"I'll call you." He moved to the porch. "In the meantime, watch your back."

"That's my plan."

No commitment other than a phone call—but she'd take it.

He hesitated . . . then spun away and jogged down the walk through the rain.

Eve watched from the door until nothing but the dim glow of his receding taillights remained. As far as she could tell, he never looked back.

With a sigh, she locked the door and wandered back to the kitchen, where the faint scent of his aftershave lingered. Closing her eyes, she inhaled it—and tried to gear herself up for the call to Grace. Her sister was going to ask pointed questions about her guest, that was a given.

Sad to say, she wouldn't have the answers to many of them. Especially the key one.

Because while she could assure Grace she'd made her interest crystal clear to Brent, she had no idea if he would follow up—or give up.

And between that uncertainty and this evening's new threat from her tormentor, it was going to be a long night.

At least she'd make serious headway on her floors.

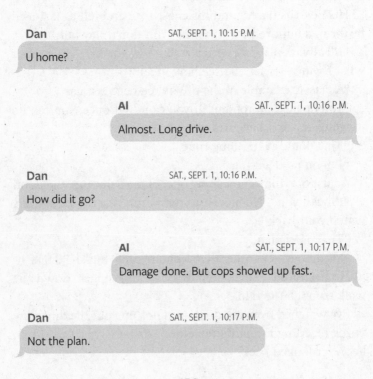

Dan   SAT., SEPT. 1, 10:15 P.M.

U home?

Al   SAT., SEPT. 1, 10:16 P.M.

Almost. Long drive.

Dan   SAT., SEPT. 1, 10:16 P.M.

How did it go?

Al   SAT., SEPT. 1, 10:17 P.M.

Damage done. But cops showed up fast.

Dan   SAT., SEPT. 1, 10:17 P.M.

Not the plan.

Al SAT., SEPT. 1, 10:18 P.M.

I know. But ready 4 next step.

Dan SAT., SEPT. 1, 10:20 P.M.

Need to think about that.

Al SAT., SEPT. 1, 10:20 P.M.

I can handle.

Dan SAT., SEPT. 1, 10:22 P.M.

Window is closing. Can be no mistakes.

Al SAT., SEPT. 1, 10:22 P.M.

Won't b. U have plan?

Dan SAT., SEPT. 1, 10:23 P.M.

Yes. Finalizing details. Will text 2morrow.

Al SAT., SEPT. 1, 10:23 P.M.

What is timetable?

Al SAT., SEPT. 1, 10:26 P.M.

U there? Timetable?

Dan SAT., SEPT. 1, 10:27 P.M.

Soon. In two weeks, ER will be gone.

12

DOUG HAD SHOWN UP —and the corners of his lips rose when he caught sight of her waiting in the restaurant's bar—but his face didn't brighten like it always did. He was also late.

Neither boded well for their weekly lunch.

Giving him her warmest smile, Carolyn slid off the stool and wove through the crowd in the foyer toward him. "I thought you'd stood me up." She used the coy, teasing tone men seemed to like. "I was afraid I'd have to eat alone."

"Sorry. I was stuck in a meeting." The apology was perfunctory, and he did no more than glance at her before motioning toward the dining room. "Ready for lunch?"

"Sure."

She took the lead, weaving through the other diners toward their usual table, and slid onto her chair. As she picked up her napkin, Doug signaled for the waiter.

He wasn't wasting any time on small talk, trying to stretch out their lunch as long as possible.

Another bad omen.

"I can't linger today." He straightened his silverware. "It's crazy at the station."

"I can imagine." But the undercurrent of tension in the air suggested there was more to his haste than work issues.

The waiter appeared, and after they gave him their orders she focused on Doug. "You seem more stressed today than last week. Fallout from the last-minute bombshell that caller dropped on Eve's show Wednesday?"

"No. She handled the response masterfully on her blog and on Friday's program."

Yes, she had.

It was hard not to admire the woman, even if you wanted her programming slot.

"She's a pro."

"Yeah." Doug brushed at a speck on the tablecloth. "And the sponsors are sticking. So we're holding our own at present."

"That's positive news." For Eve—and the station—anyway. "Any recent developments on the case?"

"Yes—but we're keeping the latest under wraps. Eve doesn't want it broadcast to the public."

She called up her flirty smile. "I'm not the public."

"No. You're press." He picked up his water and took a sip, avoiding eye contact.

O-kay.

Her phone call to him after Eve's Wednesday program must have done more damage than she'd estimated.

This required finessing.

She touched his forearm and put on her worried face. "Doug . . . you know I'd never divulge a confidence. I'm not here as a newspaper reporter. We have a . . . friendlier . . . relationship than that."

His gaze dropped to her fingers. Lingered. Then he swallowed and eased his hand away. "I thought we did too."

Thought.

Past tense.

Fighting back a wave of panic, she retracted her fingers and smoothed out the napkin on her lap. Something was very wrong.

And avoiding the issue wasn't going to fix it.

Since charm alone no longer appeared to be working, she might have to turn up the heat and resort to the plucking option—as soon as she convinced him she'd been on overload after a tough morning at work on Wednesday, and apologized for coming on too strong about her radio ambitions. Doug, of all people, would understand the difficulty of coping with stress.

She leaned toward him, making no attempt to hide her concern. "You're not yourself today. What's going on?"

Wadding up the napkin in his lap, he finally gave her his full attention. "I need to ask you a question."

A tingle of unease slithered down her spine. "This sounds serious."

"It is."

"All right. I'll do my best to answer."

He scanned the room, leaned closer to her, and lowered his voice. "Do you know anything about that call Eve got on her program last Wednesday?"

For a few seconds, the tinkle of cutlery against china, the clink of ice in glasses, and the background hum of conversation and laughter faded as she digested his question—and the implications.

Doug suspected she'd played a role in Wednesday's incident. That her ambition had driven her to take desperate measures to unseat Eve and create a slot for herself.

Perhaps he even thought she'd been involved in the fake bomb and the latest incident he'd referenced.

Wow.

The man was much more astute—and far less blinded by attraction—than she'd deduced.

They were on dangerous ground here, and she had to think the situation through.

"Why would you ask me that?" She stared at him, her shock real rather than manufactured, buying herself a few moments to regroup.

His attention remained riveted on her. No eye shifting now. "Because I know you want a chance on radio . . . and you've always followed Eve's career . . . and you were clear in your call on Wednesday that you'd be interested in her slot if the situation the caller created blew up."

She swallowed past the expletive that popped onto her tongue.

All these months she'd been convinced she had Doug snowed.

But apparently hormones hadn't disengaged the left side of his brain.

"I was super stressed Wednesday, and I overstepped. I'm sorry for that. However, I make no apologies for being ambitious."

He saw through her hedge. "I don't expect you to. Eve was also ambitious. But she got her chance through hard work rather than resorting to subterfuge."

Despite the sudden churning in her stomach, Carolyn managed to keep her brain firing.

There was only one way to play this unexpected turn of events.

She snatched up her purse, pulled out a twenty, tossed it on the table, and stood. "I expect it's too late to cancel my order. Take my lunch back to your office for someone to enjoy. I've lost my appetite."

Lifting her chin, she walked away.

Before she got three steps, he spoke. "Carolyn. Wait."

She paused. Exhaled.

Her bluff had paid off.

After letting him sweat for a few beats, she angled back, shoulders taut. Like anyone's would be if they'd been accused of orchestrating the kind of coup her mentor had suggested.

Doug had risen, and he circled around the table to join her, keeping his voice low. "I'm sorry if I offended you."

The words were appropriate—but he looked more uncertain than sorry.

"I can't believe, after all the months we've known each other, that you'd think I could do such a terrible thing."

"Ambition can be powerful—and temptation can be hard to resist."

At such close proximity, the creases in his face were more pronounced than usual. Definitely a man past his prime.

The appeal of the plucking option continued to wane.

But in light of that remark about temptation . . . and judging by the hunger in the depths of his eyes . . . she might still have a certain amount of power over him if they could get past this glitch.

And she'd use it if necessary, distasteful though it would be.

She softened her stance—and tone. "What kind of temptation?"

His features tightened, almost as if he was in pain. "To have something that isn't in your best interest."

Doug wasn't talking about the radio show she coveted.

He was talking about coveting her.

That was reassuring—but for now, she'd play the innocent. "Why wouldn't the chance of a radio job be in my best interest?"

"I'm not saying it isn't—but rushing an opportunity could be a mistake. There are repercussions for every decision."

Like cheating on your wife?

But that was his problem. Her sole concern was her career. "Not all repercussions are bad. And I've always believed you should seize opportunities, because they may not come again." She smoothed out a crease in the lapel of his sport jacket. "That doesn't mean I believe you should resort to anything underhanded to foster them, however."

He studied her, conflict scoring his features. "I'd like to think you're being honest with me."

"As you should. Always think the best of people—especially friends who've given you no cause to distrust them."

Her response didn't placate him. "Carolyn—I want to give you the benefit of the doubt. But your call Wednesday . . . it bothered me." He massaged the puckers on his forehead. "Can you assure me you've had nothing to do with all the troubles plaguing Eve?"

She huffed out a breath and retracted her hand. "Do I look like someone who would leave a fake bomb?"

"No—but I have no experience with people who leave fake bombs. I don't know what they look like."

She tucked her purse under her arm and hiked up her chin again. "This is not a discussion I intend to have in the middle of a restaurant. If you want our friendship to continue, I'll expect an apology. Otherwise, I won't be here next Monday."

With that, she spun on her heel and stalked to the door.

Doug didn't follow.

Unfortunately.

That meant he was unconvinced about her innocence. Unsure whether to trust the woman he'd been mentoring for the past eight months.

This setback was past aggravating. It was downright disturbing.

She pushed through the door, into cloying air thick with humidity.

After all the months she'd spent currying Doug's favor with mild flirting and ego strokes, pinning her radio future on him, how could he distance himself from her? Aside from Wednesday's ill-advised call, she'd done nothing to deserve his distrust.

Nothing that he could prove, at least.

Tightening her grip on her purse, she trekked toward her car.

Maybe he'd come around, call her to apologize, beg her to keep their lunch date next Monday.

But what if he didn't? What if, instead of caving to the

temptation to spend time with her . . . and perhaps share more than lunch . . . he cut her off? Continued to doubt her innocence?

Would he take his suspicions to the police?

And if he did, what would that do to her career—and her ambitions?

Despite the warmth in the air, a cold chill raced through her.

Gritting her teeth, she shook it off.

Even if Doug did mention his misgivings to the case detective—and the police decided to investigate—their efforts would come to nothing. If there was any evidence to be found for any of the incidents that had occurred with Eve, it would have surfaced by now.

There was no reason to worry.

She was safe—and so were her ambitions.

Knock, knock.

At the hard rapping on her back door, Eve jerked away from the floor buffer she'd just turned off in the living room and swiveled toward the kitchen.

Calm down, Eve. If someone was up to no good, they wouldn't be knocking on your door.

Gulping a steadying breath, she stripped off her dust mask and ducked around the plastic barrier taped over the opening to the foyer that was supposed to contain the mess. Heart still hammering, she hurried toward the back of the house.

As she approached the door and her neighbor waved at her through the window, her pulse slowed.

After wiping her hands on her jean cutoffs, she unlocked and opened the door. "Hi, Olivia. I'd invite you in, but the house is a dust bowl." She slipped outside.

"My." The woman gave her a once-over. "Have you been cleaning out your attic?"

"Worse. Refinishing floors. A job not for the faint of heart, let me tell you."

"I don't mean to interrupt such an ambitious enterprise—but I baked chocolate chip pecan cookies and brought you a few." The woman lifted a plate covered with plastic wrap. "They came out of the oven ten minutes ago."

"Wow." Eve took the home-baked goodies and breathed in the scent seeping through the plastic. "These smell delicious. You're going to spoil me."

Olivia waved the comment aside. "An occasional sweet-tooth indulgence never spoiled anyone."

"In that case—I'll eat one . . . or two . . . or three." She grinned. "If I get us each a soda, would you sit with me for a few minutes while I take a break and put a dent in these?" She indicated the plate.

"I'd be delighted. The only item on my afternoon schedule is a few soaps, and I'd much rather visit with my famous neighbor."

Eve snorted. "Hardly famous."

"But you're getting there. You keep at it, you'll be up there with that Russ Limbo everyone talks about."

Not likely—but it was a kind sentiment . . . even if Olivia wouldn't know Rush Limbaugh from the current teenage heartthrob. The woman was much more conversant about vintage movies than current events.

"Thanks."

"You're welcome." Olivia patted her arm. "I may be old, but I can recognize talent."

"Have a seat while I get those sodas."

Eve returned to the kitchen, fixed their drinks, and rejoined her neighbor at the patio table.

"True confession—I stole one of your cookies." Olivia flashed a guilty smile as she accepted a soda.

"You can't steal cookies you baked." Eve bit into one and closed her eyes, letting the gooey chocolate dissolve on her tongue. "Bliss."

"I'm glad you like them. What with all the recent excitement in your life, I decided comfort food was in order."

"I agree—and these fit the bill."

"I keep hoping the police will find whoever is behind the unfortunate incidents. Have they made any strides at all?"

"None they've shared with me."

The woman exhaled. "I'm sorry to hear that. I noticed that nice-looking young detective leaving your house Saturday night and I hoped there'd been a break in the case."

"No." Eve took another bite of cookie. How to explain Brent's visit? If she told her neighbor about the incident in the school parking lot, Olivia would worry more. "He was here to follow up on a few details." True—except the details were about the latest attack.

"Oh." Olivia's face fell. "That's disappointing."

"I know they're working hard to find the culprit—but in the meantime, I'm hoping he'll get tired of the game and my life will return to normal."

"I wonder if that's already happened? It *has* been six days since that call to the station."

"True." Eve picked up another cookie and changed the subject. "These are delicious."

"I'm glad you like them, my dear. Best of all, you don't have to worry about how many you eat. Hard as you work, you'll burn those calories off in a jiffy."

"I wish."

"No wishing necessary. It's true. You're refinishing floors, for heaven's sake." She shook her head. "In my day, women didn't tackle such jobs. Not that we couldn't have, mind you—but letting a man do the heavy work does have its advantages." She winked.

"I see your point." But having someone to work *with* her, side by side, on projects like this would be even more appealing. Especially someone with dark brown eyes . . . warm, firm lips . . . and character stamped on every contour of his face.

"Besides, all your running around keeps you in shape too. Going to the radio station at the crack of dawn, riding your bike, taking those spanning classes, your frequent speaking engagements." She exhaled. "I don't know how you keep all those balls in the air."

"There are days I don't either." Eve took a third cookie.

"You gave a speech last weekend, didn't you? At an outdoor event—a rally, I believe?"

"No, that's a week from Saturday. Last weekend was the PTA talk."

"Oh yes. I remember now. The next event is a picnic for politicians . . . or is it young entrepreneurs . . . or veterans?"

"All of the above, I expect." She washed down the remains of her last cookie. "It's the annual barbecue for a Young Republicans group. The members fall into all those categories."

"You are one busy lady."

"I love my work—and I like doing my part to protect the values that built this country."

Olivia nodded. "It's important to stand up for what you believe—no matter the risk."

"I agree."

"Well . . ." The older woman pushed herself to her feet. "I should be off. You have to get back to your floor job."

"And prepare for tomorrow's radio program." She rose too. "Thank you again for the cookies. I can assure you they won't last long."

"I'll whip up another batch soon. Don't work too hard." Olivia patted her arm and crossed the deck.

"Would you like an extra arm to lean on while you go down the steps?" Eve knew the answer before her spry neighbor responded.

"I'm fine." She started down. "The doctor's after me to use a cane, but I'm resisting. These legs may not be as strong as they once were, but they get me where I have to go without any propping up."

Eve waited until Olivia crossed the lawn and disappeared onto her patio, then wandered back inside, locking the door behind her.

Quiet descended.

Too much quiet.

It was a shame she didn't have an excuse to call Brent for an update.

But he'd left one on her voicemail yesterday, while her cell was stowed in a locker during spinning class—and it had been both detailed and concise. The CSU tech had found a few dark hairs clumped beside her car, and Brent had promised to call her if they yielded any useful information. He hadn't asked about the status of the tire situation, nor offered to drive her to the school parking lot to retrieve her car, so she'd hitched a ride in the mechanic's truck.

Sighing, she set the plate of cookies on the counter and tossed the two empty soft drink cans into the recycle bin.

Why, oh why, had he called during her class?

Eve trudged back to the living room, slipped on the dust mask, and flipped the switch on the buffer.

But her mind wasn't on the task at hand. It was busy trying to manufacture a reason to call Brent.

Could she fill him in on her conversation yesterday with the security firm he'd recommended, perhaps? Was that a sufficient excuse?

No.

Give it up, Eve.

Grasping the handle on the buffer, she resumed the tedious chore of moving the piece of equipment from side to side, following the grain. The old finish turned to powder beneath it, making it easy to see where to move next.

Too bad the course to follow with Brent wasn't as obvious.

Nevertheless, the basics were clear.

If he wanted to talk with her, he'd call—and if he got her

voicemail again, he'd ask her to return the call rather than leave a message.

He hadn't yet done that.

So . . . she should wait. Give him breathing room after their conversation on Saturday night. If he was running scared, a woman who was too forward could send him fleeing the opposite direction.

Or maybe her impromptu kiss had already done that.

The drone of the buffer masked her huff as the machine continued to smooth out the rough spots in the wood and remove the layers of protective finish.

It was a shame there wasn't a buffer for the soul—and the heart.

Other than love, of course.

But love carried risk. It required taking a leap into the unknown and a willingness to fail—and fall.

For a person like Brent, whose experience with love—or the lack of love—was disastrous, that risk could be too formidable.

Not the happiest thought she'd had today—and it stuck with her for the remainder of the job.

Once all the bad junk had been stripped off the wood, she shut off the buffer, leaving the mask over her nose as dust motes swirled around the room.

There were two tactics she could employ to convince Brent to take another chance on love.

The first involved a follow-up phone call—after a reasonable interval—if he didn't get in touch with her. That step was a given. The only challenge was deciding what constituted a reasonable interval.

The second tactic involved prayer. Also a given—and one she intended to launch immediately.

Because cutting through all the garbage that was preventing him from dipping his toes into romance again could very well take a miracle.

13

THE EVE REILLY STORY had dried up.

Buzz skimmed the Wednesday *Post* headlines again, flipping through the pages.

Nothing.

There hadn't been a single mention of it in the paper—or on the news—since the phone call to the station a week ago . . . and that had only merited a one-paragraph follow-up. Apparently she'd weathered the storms of the past ten days and was staying the course.

Some people had a knack for escaping danger unscathed.

For a while, anyway.

But if blows continued to rain down on them, eventually one would hit its target and their luck would run out.

"Aren't we the cerebral one."

At the taunt from Suds, he closed the paper and tucked it between the insulated food carrier and the tree supporting his back. "I decided to improve my mind as well as feed my stomach during lunch break."

Suds snorted and waved toward the paper. "There's nothing but bad news in there. I get enough of that in real life. Give me Candy Crush any day." He lifted his cell.

"Video games will turn your brain to mush."

"Me and the hundred million other people who play it."

No wonder the world was in such a mess. Didn't anyone worry about important issues anymore? Like politicians controlling people's lives. The oppression of capitalism. The evil inherent in authority.

Not to mention the people who promoted a society where big government, getting rich, and institutions of authority were not only accepted but encouraged.

People like Eve Reilly.

He swallowed past his distaste.

Unthinking morons like Suds and Crip were slaves and they didn't even know it—because they'd rather play Candy Crush than fight for their rights . . . and their freedom.

Idiots like them got what they deserved.

But he wasn't an idiot—and the status quo wasn't acceptable. That's why—

"Hey." Suds stared at him. "What's with you? You've got a weird look on your face."

He clenched his fist but relaxed his features. "I'm thinking about the screen porch we're going to tackle this afternoon. It's going to be a bear to paint, with all that lattice."

Suds watched him for a few moments, then shrugged. "At least it's not a hundred degrees in the shade anymore. Crip lucked out pulling that pool house job in Ladue, though. His gig is air-conditioned—and the owner buys the crew those froufrou frozen drinks from Starbucks every afternoon."

"Sweet."

"No kidding." He shoved his phone back in his pocket. "You ready to hit it again?"

"Yeah." Buzz pushed himself to his feet. "Let me put my stuff in the truck and I'll join you in a minute."

"See ya there."

Suds strolled toward the back of the house, whistling one of those stupid songs with asinine lyrics that were the rage.

After he disappeared around the corner, Buzz picked up the insulated carrier and newspaper from the spot he'd claimed in the side yard and headed for the truck in the driveway. Compared to the estate where Crip was working, this neighborhood was low end.

Not that he begrudged his high school acquaintance a plum job. Ever since that varsity football injury had left him with a limp—and a politically incorrect nickname—he'd had more than his share of challenges.

Buzz tossed the paper and carrier in the truck and swiped the sleeve of his T-shirt over his forehead, anger roiling anew in his gut. No one should have to sweat in this heat to put food on the table and a roof over their head while the fat cats sat on piles of money and pulled the strings on the puppets who did all the real work.

Unless more people were enlightened, though, nothing would change.

Nor would it change if personalities like Eve Reilly, with her bully pulpit, kept convincing the masses that the structure of this country, and the capitalistic society championed by those in power, was worth defending.

"Hey, Buzz." Suds waved at him from the corner of the house. "Grab the electric screwdriver."

"Okay." He turned back to the truck and rummaged for the tool.

Four more hours until he could chill out in his apartment.

It felt like a lifetime.

But he'd survive.

Because he had more to look forward to than a cold beer and another round of Candy Crush.

He had plans to make.

"Yes!" Brent pumped a fist in the air.

"Must be good news."

As the male voice spoke behind him, he swiveled around in his desk chair at headquarters.

Colin Flynn leaned a shoulder against the door frame. "Either you just secured a hot date or there's been a positive development with one of your cases."

At the mention of a hot date, an image of Eve flashed through his mind.

If only.

But the detective colleague he shared an office with had nailed his reaction with his second guess.

"My euphoria is case related."

"Congrats from a work standpoint. My condolences on the social front." Colin strolled in and dropped into the chair at his desk. "What case?"

"Eve Reilly."

"Yeah?" He leaned forward, interest sparking in his eyes. "I was beginning to think that was destined for the deep freeze."

"Me too. But CSU came through for me at the car scene."

"What did they find?"

"A small clump of dark hair containing a few strands with roots."

"Aha. You got a DNA match in CODIS."

"No." The FBI database hadn't yielded anything. "But I got a hit in the DOD DNA Registry."

"Department of Defense." Colin leaned back and linked his fingers over his stomach. "So your guy is military—or ex-military."

"Ex."

"Any previous lower-level run-ins with law enforcement?"

"That's what I intend to find out." A major crime would have yielded a match in CODIS—but that didn't mean their man was 100 percent clean.

"If you want any help tracking down leads, let me know." He pulled out his cell and scanned the screen. "I have to take this."

As Colin angled away, Brent hunkered down and refocused on his computer. With a name and a few other identifying details in hand, it should be easy to gather additional data.

Thirty minutes later, his pulse picked up and he leaned closer to the screen he'd pulled up a minute ago.

How about that?

His suspect wasn't merely a disenfranchised listener. He had a link to Eve.

Meaning he must have a personal ax to grind.

And now that they had a name, it was possible Eve could shed some light on the motivation.

He eased back in his chair.

A phone call would suffice for professional purposes—but he wanted to see her, even if he still had cold feet after everything he'd shared on Saturday night.

He didn't have to stay long, though. He *wouldn't* stay long. As soon as he passed on the news, he'd get out of there.

But seeing her face when she learned her troubles were almost over would be the highlight of his day.

Get real, Lange. The highlight of your day will be seeing her face, period.

Yeah, yeah.

He stood abruptly, and Colin looked over at him, one eyebrow raised.

Ignoring his colleague, he picked up his cell and made a fast exit. He might be able to hide the truth from his coworkers, but he couldn't hide it from himself.

Eve Reilly, with her sparkling eyes and sharp wit and innate intelligence, had him flummoxed. And there didn't seem to be a thing he could do about it.

As for what that meant for the future—who knew?

For now, he was going to quash his misgivings, pay the lady a visit—and worry about tomorrow when the new day dawned.

———————

"Eve! I didn't think you'd still be here." Meg emerged from the showers in the locker room, running her fingers through her still-damp hair.

Eve slid her phone into her gym bag. "I didn't plan to be. I got caught up checking messages."

"I hear you—but I'm glad I have a chance to say thanks again for carving out an hour to introduce me to spinning."

"I'm happy the session worked with your schedule." Eve slung her gym bag over her shoulder and appraised the other woman. "Don't be surprised if you're sore tomorrow."

"I followed your advice and paced myself—but I won't mind a few sore muscles. It was invigorating to get real exercise."

Eve fished out her keys. "I hope the showers here weren't too bad. It's a challenge for the staff to keep up with the turnover. That's why I always wait until I get home to clean up."

"They were fine. I have to grocery shop, and I didn't want to run off the other customers." She waved her hand in front of her face and laughed.

Eve chuckled too—but it was doubtful that errand was Meg's prime motive for showering at the fitness club. Despite the fact he carved out a bowling night for himself, from all the comments Meg had dropped about her husband, he didn't approve of her having a life separate from him. It was possible she didn't want any indications in the house that she'd met a friend for an unapproved activity—like evidence of an oddly timed shower.

What a way to live.

Meg deserved better.

But until her high school acquaintance realized that for herself, the status quo would continue.

Eve shifted her bag into a more comfortable position. All

she could do was leave Meg with a standing invitation. "I have to shower too. ASAP. If you ever want to join me again for a session, let me know."

"Thanks, I will." Meg picked up the small tote that held her shorts, T-shirt, and tennis shoes. "See you at the station on Friday."

"I'll be there."

As Meg walked away, Eve's ringtone gave a muffled rendition of her signature song from inside her bag.

She pulled it out, read the name on the screen—and her heart missed a beat.

Brent was calling her!

Now she wouldn't have to manufacture an excuse to call *him*.

"Hi." She put the phone to her ear and claimed a quiet corner of the locker room.

He returned her greeting. "Am I interrupting anything?"

"No. I finished a spinning class about ten minutes ago."

"Are you going home from there?"

"That was the plan. Why?"

"I have an update I'd like to share—in person."

"On the case?"

"Yes."

She bit back the question that sprang to her lips. If she asked too much on the phone, he could end up relaying all his news—eliminating the need for a visit.

Patience would be a virtue in this situation.

"I could be there in fifteen minutes."

"Give me thirty. I have to wrap up a few loose ends at the office."

Perfect. She'd have a chance to jump in the shower once she got home.

"That's fine. I was going to pick up a salad at Panera. If you don't already have dinner plans, I'd be happy to order food for you too."

Silence on the line.

Well, shoot. She'd been too forward. Again.

If this kept up, she was going to scare this man away before—

"I don't have any plans. Or I didn't, until now. But let me get the food."

He wanted to buy their dinner? Like this was a sort of . . . date?

Don't get your hopes up, Eve. Assume he's just being polite and wants to save you a stop.

"That would be great, if you don't mind. I'll reimburse you later."

"Don't worry about it. Consider this repayment for two pieces of fabulous carrot cake. What would you like me to order for you?"

He didn't want to be reimbursed.

That could be a positive sign—but it would be safer to withhold judgment until he arrived and she appraised the situation up close and personal.

Once she gave him her order and hung up, she zoomed home as fast as she could without incurring the wrath of any patrol officers eager to hand out speeding tickets.

In twenty minutes flat, she was out of the shower and pacing the hall, waiting for him.

By the time he rang the bell precisely half an hour after their phone conversation, she'd had ten minutes to get all hot and bothered.

Sheesh.

At this rate, she'd need another shower.

Fluffing her hair, she took a deep breath . . . peered through the peephole to confirm the identity of her visitor . . . and opened the door.

He gave her a swift head-to-toe—and the quick glint of appreciation in his eyes put her doubts to rest. Brent might be here on business, but he was glad to have an excuse to see her.

Maybe she hadn't scared him off after all.

"Come on in." She stepped back and waved him through the door. "As you can see, the living room floors have been stripped. That accounts for the dust motes floating through the air and coating every available surface. I've kept them under control in the kitchen—sort of. I'd suggest we move there as fast as possible."

"I'm right behind you."

She led him back, shaking her head at the surface of the table as they approached. "I wiped this down ten minutes ago. So much for the plastic shield in the doorway that was supposed to keep the dust in the living room. Give me a sec." She retreated to the sink, retrieved a dishcloth, and dispensed with the new layer of fine powder.

He claimed one of the chairs and set the bag on the table, along with their drinks. "Do you want to eat first or hear my news?"

"News first—unless you ordered a hot item that will get cold."

"Nope. I got a sandwich." He removed the lemonade she'd ordered from the tray and set it in front of her.

"No coffee tonight?" She indicated the large, clear cup of amber liquid he put in his own place.

"After spending several hours questioning a suspect in an apartment building with temperatures approaching sauna level, I was in the mood for iced tea. The plain version, not mango."

"I wish I could convince Grace to settle for that. It would be much less expensive." She sat and pulled the paper off her straw. "Tell me you have good news."

"I consider it good."

Curious answer.

"You mean I won't?"

"I'm not certain." He stuck his straw through the opening

in the lid and took a drink. "We were able to identify the person whose hair our CSU tech found beside your car."

"How can that be anything but good news?"

"The person has an indirect connection to you."

She squinted. "You mean he's more than a listener?"

"He may not be a listener at all—but he's married to someone who works on your program at the station. Steve Jackson."

Eve's jaw dropped.

Meg's husband was the person who'd been plotting against her? Planting fake bombs, calling in during the program with exposés about her past, slashing her tires?

"Are you certain?"

"DNA databases are pretty accurate."

"Does he have a criminal background?" Somehow that wouldn't surprise her.

"Nothing serious, as far as I can tell. We made the connection through the military DNA database."

"So he's a vet."

"Yes. What do you know about him?"

"Very little." She relayed the few pieces of information Meg had shared with her.

"Have you met him?"

"Yes. Twice."

"What did you think?"

"I hate to pass judgment on someone I've only seen twice, at work-related gatherings."

"I hear you. But you seem to have excellent instincts. I'm after impressions, not facts."

She played with her straw. "We didn't talk long. He was cool. Abrupt. I got the feeling he didn't want to be at the events. He was also short with Meg, which I found offensive." Eve explained the connection between her and the administrative assistant. "Those meetings, and a few comments from

Meg, gave me the impression he's selfish and thinks the world should revolve around him."

"Any idea why he'd target you?"

"No. I mean, I don't think he's crazy about Meg working at the station, but I can't believe anyone would go to such extremes for something like that." She exhaled. "This is going to devastate Meg. I know you have a DNA match—but are you sure he's the one who's been doing all this?"

"My gut says yes—but I can't definitely prove it . . . yet. The hair is circumstantial evidence. However, it seems too much of a stretch that it would just happen to be beside your car on the night the tires were slashed. On the other hand, if he has an alibi for that evening, we're sunk."

"Have you questioned him yet?"

"No. I've been getting a court order to access his cell records and digging into his background first. I also wanted to get your read on him."

Eve rested her elbow on the table and propped her chin in her palm. "Much as I want this to be over, I hate for him to be your man—for Meg's sake. And while I'm not discounting your instincts, I suspect he'll have an alibi for Saturday night. Meg says they stick close on weekends. Plus, on the day the fake bomb was left, he was probably at work."

"We don't know when the package was put on your porch. He could have slipped away from his job over his lunch hour."

"True—but it feels like a stretch. I can't imagine anyone would take that kind of risk because he's mad about his wife's job."

"Depends how controlling he is. From what you've told me, he wants Meg at his beck and call. If your radio program folds—or you quit—the job goes away."

Eve grimaced. "That's sick."

"We don't always deal with rational people in my business. And some of the most irrational know how to present a normal face to the world."

"So what are you going to do?"

"Keep digging into his background—and find out if he has alibis for the incidents in question."

"If he *is* the guilty party, Meg's clueless. She's as honest as they come."

His lips thinned into a taut line. "Love can make people behave in . . . surprising ways."

Was he thinking about his bad experience with Karen? The one he hadn't shared over carrot cake and coffee?

Perhaps . . . but this wasn't the time to delve into that.

"Well, bad as I feel for Meg if your evidence nails Steve, I'm glad this may be winding down for a bunch of reasons— including the health of my bank account. I got the Phoenix rate sheet and about had a heart attack. Forking out those big bucks would have been painful."

Twin grooves creased Brent's brow. "We're not home free yet. As long as the perpetrator is out there, so is the danger."

A shiver rolled through her. "Does that mean you think I should still hire Phoenix?"

"I know it's a big expense." His frown deepened, and he rubbed the back of his neck. "If you can hunker down here for the next couple of days, I'll arrange to have the patrol officer in the area do a few walk-arounds outside during each shift. I'll also check with Sarge on available resources to keep Jackson under surveillance. I know you have the radio program on Friday, but I'd be happy to escort you to and from the station. By the weekend, this may be over."

Brent was willing to play bodyguard on his own time?

Her spirits rose.

"You do realize I leave the house at five-fifteen on program days."

"I assumed you got an early start. I can sleep in on Saturday."

"I don't know . . ." She studied him. Was he simply being

kind . . . or was there a deeper meaning behind his concern? And could she find out? "I appreciate the offer, but I don't want to impose."

He captured her gaze. Held it. "Trust me. I'll sleep better if I know you're safe."

The intensity in his eyes sizzled through her, short-circuiting her lungs.

Even if the left side of his brain didn't want to have anything to do with romance, the right side was sending different signals to his heart.

She'd wanted confirmation that his motivation was more than friendly concern—and boy, did she have it.

Breathe, Eve.

She forced her lungs to inflate and nodded. "Okay. I can hang around here until the next show. I'm giving a speech a week from Saturday, and I have to prep anyway."

"Good. And keep—" His voice rasped, and he cleared his throat. Tried again. "Keep tonight's discussion under wraps until we know more about Jackson's culpability."

"Got it."

After a moment, he looked away—with obvious difficulty. "Let's eat." He pulled out her salad and set it in front of her.

She opened the disposable container and poured her dressing over the greens, shooting Brent a sidelong glance. The diligent attention he was giving his meal suggested he was either hungry or anxious to be on his way.

And if it was the latter, that was fine—now that she had the answer to the question that had plagued her since Saturday night.

She hadn't scared him off. He might be running scared, but he wasn't running away.

That was the best news she'd had all day.

Make that all week.

Except for the fact that the case appeared to be almost solved.

Maybe, if all went well, the danger would be gone by the weekend, as Brent had suggested.

Besides, if Steve was the culprit, once he realized the police were on to him, he'd be crazy to do anything else to implicate himself.

And with Brent and the police watching her back, she'd be safe until this wrapped up.

There was no need for further worry.

The danger was over.

14

"YOUR GUY IS NO BOY SCOUT." Colin swiveled around in his chair as Brent entered their office.

Thank goodness his colleague had followed through on his promise to help with the case. Digging up Jackson's background had been a slower slog than he'd expected.

"What've you got?" Brent propped a hip on his desk.

"Did you know he'd been married before?"

That was a new piece of information.

"No." But since he'd been focusing on current events while Colin researched the man's history, it wasn't surprising his coworker had been the one to uncover that fact.

"Uh-huh. In Texas. Four years ago. Six months later, his wife filed for divorce and took out a restraining order against him."

Brent let out a soft whistle and folded his arms. "I wonder if his current wife knows about that?" Not likely, if what Eve had said about Meg being a straight arrow was accurate. A woman with principles wouldn't hook up with a guy like Steve if she knew his background.

Then again, love could make people behave in uncharacteristic ways—as he'd told Eve.

"His wife would have to answer that question." Colin leaned

back and crossed an ankle over a knee. "I have more. Before he lived in Texas, Jackson called Seattle home. There was a restraining order against him there too."

"Another wife?"

"Not that I can see. Must have been a girlfriend. Both orders were for alleged abuse and stalking."

"What a prince."

"More like a frog."

"Eve would agree with you on that."

"Eve?" Colin hitched up one side of his mouth. "We're on a first-name basis, are we?"

"I didn't see any point in formalities." Brent resisted the urge to tug at his collar. Why did the office suddenly feel stuffy?

Colin rocked back in his chair, watching him. "She's a very attractive woman. Single too."

His coworker was on to him—and denying the obvious would give him more ammunition.

"I noticed." He kept his tone casual.

"Any eligible man would be crazy not to."

"You're not eligible. What would your bride say about you ogling another woman?"

"Trish has no worries. She's the only woman for me and she knows it. Besides, I was appreciating, not ogling. Any guy would have to be blind not to recognize Eve Reilly's attributes."

"She does have a fine mind and an engaging personality."

Colin grinned. "I'm sure she does—among other worthy qualities. You should investigate them all."

How had this conversation degenerated into a discussion about his personal life?

He had to get them back on track.

"Do you have anything else?"

"On Ms. Reilly—or your suspect?" Humor lurked behind Colin's question.

"The latter."

"I talked with one of the detectives in Texas who had a couple of run-ins with your guy relating to the restraining order. His personal assessment was less than favorable." He pulled out his cell, scanned the screen, and put it back in his pocket. "What did you find?"

"The cell records were of marginal use. They did confirm he's been in the area for the past two weeks, but the origination point of the calls during the times in question aren't precise."

Colin snorted. "Tell me about it. All you get on those reports is a cell tower location—and switching centers can route even consecutive calls to different places. In a congested urban area like this, the best you can do is place a subject within a several-square-mile range."

"And triangulation with GPS only works during a live call—or if we ask the cell provider to ping a phone periodically to track movements. I've got surveillance on Jackson for a day or two, but I may have to resort to pinging after that if we don't have a resolution."

"So let me rephrase my earlier question. Did you dig up any *helpful* information?"

"Yeah. I paid Jackson's boss a visit. He confirmed our guy was on the job the day the bomb was left at Eve's—except for the half hour he disappeared on lunch break. The job was in Kirkwood."

Colin pursed his lips. "That would put him—what? Eight to ten minutes from Eve Reilly's place?"

"Right."

"I wonder if anyone can vouch for his whereabouts during the missing half hour?"

"That's one of the questions I plan to ask him—especially

since his boss said his typical lunch routine is to hang around and play with his cell."

"Suspicious."

"But not incriminating." Brent rose from the corner of his desk and settled into his chair. "I asked the boss to keep our conversation confidential."

"You think he will?"

"Yeah. He didn't come across as a huge fan of Jackson."

"Did he offer anything else?"

"He said Jackson shows up and does the job, so no complaints on the work side. But he's overheard him making demeaning remarks about his wife to his coworkers—and bragging about his, shall we say, extracurricular activities—which didn't endear him to the man."

"He's cheating on his wife?"

"His cell records would suggest that. There are frequent calls to a waitress named Candy Norris who works at a local bar."

"What a loser." Colin snorted his disgust. "However . . . planting a fake bomb, slashing tires, and issuing threats just to get his wife back under his thumb on the home front seems excessive."

"Eve agrees with you. But we've got his DNA at her car."

"I know—and that can't be coincidence. Everything points to him." Colin shrugged. "Maybe the guy's just arrogant. Thinks he's smart enough to put one over on law enforcement. Some criminals are convinced they're invincible and get bolder and bolder . . . until they get caught."

"That could be the case here."

"But if he *is* your guy, how would he know about the history that caller brought up on the radio program?"

"He may have run into someone who knew Eve back in her teaching days. The wife of the jerk she dated told at least a few people what happened."

Colin laced his fingers over his stomach. "We have more questions than answers at this stage."

"Agreed. That's why I'm going to go talk to him. Want to come along?"

"Sure. It could be interesting—and the intimidation factor of two-on-one won't hurt."

"That did occur to me."

"I'm meeting Trish for dinner after we're finished, so I'll join you at the house. I've got the address."

"Sounds good."

Five minutes later, after attending to his own messages and riffling through a stack of papers in his inbox, Brent left the office behind.

And tried to tamp down his disquiet.

New as he was to the detective ranks, he'd been around the law enforcement block often enough to develop accurate instincts—and those instincts said Jackson was guilty.

Yet something felt . . . off.

Frowning, he exited the building and lengthened his stride toward his car.

Maybe his uneasiness would dissipate after he talked to the man. Jackson could let a key piece of information slip that would lead to solid, admissible evidence.

The very thing needed to take this case forward.

Because other than that tiny clump of hair, they had nothing. The crime scenes were clean and there were no witnesses. There was no absolute proof Steve Jackson was their man.

Without that, he could walk.

Meaning Eve's life could still be in danger.

―――――――――

"That's odd." Meg stopped as she passed the front window and peered outside.

Steve took a long pull from his beer and continued toward

his recliner. If he ignored her, maybe she'd shut up. After working in the heat for eight hours, he wanted to cool off and veg—not listen to his wife's inane chatter.

"I wonder why that detective who's working on Eve's case would be in front of our house?"

The swig of brew he'd swallowed lodged in his windpipe, and Steve started coughing.

Meg was beside him in an instant, her voice dripping with concern. "Are you all right, honey?"

"Fine." He choked out the response and sped toward the window as he tried to catch his breath.

But the sight outside froze his lungs, cutting off his air supply.

Two tall guys in jackets and ties were talking on the sidewalk in front of his house.

If one of them *was* the investigator on Eve's case, this visit was bad news.

Very bad.

"Are you certain that's the detective?" He threw the question over his shoulder as he watched the men.

"Yes." Meg joined him. "He's the one on the left. He came to the station to review the threatening notes I pulled from Eve's social media and the letters she gets from listeners. I saw him up close."

Steve bit back a curse—but a second later it slipped out as the two men started up the walk toward the front door.

What was going on?

"Steve—what's wrong?" Meg edged closer to him, trepidation etched on her features.

"Nothing."

He hoped.

It was possible they were here to talk to Meg. She'd been involved in the case from the beginning.

Yet it was doubtful his wife was the person they'd come to see.

And if she wasn't, he wanted her out of here until he heard what they had to say and came up with a plan to deal with it.

The two men stepped up onto the porch.

He angled toward Meg. "Could they be here to talk to you about the case?"

"I doubt it. If they wanted to ask me any questions, they could do it at the station. Or call me." She wrinkled her brow. "But why else would they come here?"

"I guess we'll find out." The doorbell rang, and he gripped her arm as she turned to answer it. "If they're here to see me, I want you to leave the house. Make an excuse. You have to go to the grocery store, pick up dry cleaning. Anything."

"Why?" The grooves on her forehead deepened.

The bell chimed again.

"Just do it. I'll explain later." He tightened his grip and glared at her.

"O-okay." She looked scared now.

He could relate.

But he couldn't let these two men sniff one hint of fear. He had to act polite, cooperative—and clueless.

"Answer it." He released her with a slight shove.

She stumbled back . . . caught her balance . . . and hurried to the door.

Beer in hand, he sat in his recliner and forced himself to take deep breaths.

After a brief murmur of voices, Meg reappeared in the doorway to the living room, the two men behind her. "Steve, these are detectives from St. Louis County. They'd like to talk with you."

He blinked, feigning surprise, and stood. "Detectives?"

The two men stepped around Meg, who seemed rooted to the spot, and approached him, extending their hands as they introduced themselves.

He returned the gesture, apologizing for his damp, cold palm and attributing it to the sweaty beer can.

A lie—but they wouldn't know that.

"Make yourselves comfortable." He motioned to the couch and side chair. "Does my wife have to stay? She has errands to run tonight."

The one named Lange spoke. "No."

He pivoted to Meg so she alone could see that the grim set of his face was at odds with his pleasant tone. "You don't have to hang around, honey. I don't want to disrupt your evening plans."

"Well . . ." She twisted her hands together, and he glowered at her. "In that case, I'll take care of my errands." She nodded toward the two men, who remained standing.

They waited until she left the room to take seats.

Nice manners.

The cop he'd tangled with in Texas could take a few lessons from these guys.

Yet as he reclaimed his recliner and assessed the two men across from him, their probing gazes and the controlled, coiled tension emanating from them suggested there was steel beneath their veneer of politeness.

Messing with these guys could be tricky.

A bead of sweat popped out on his forehead, and the other detective—Flynn—homed in on it.

"Are you guys hot?" He swiped the drop away. No sense pretending he wasn't sweating. "We turn the thermostat up during the day while we're at work, and Meg must have forgotten to reset it when she got home."

"I'm fine." Lange leaned back, his posture relaxed, as if this was nothing more than a friendly visit.

But his sharp eyes said otherwise.

"Let me check it anyway." He set his can on the side table. "I'll be back in half a minute."

Leaving the two detectives behind, he fled to the hall, moved the thermostat three degrees lower than usual, flexed his fingers, and rotated his shoulders.

He had to loosen up. If these guys possessed one iota of incriminating evidence, they wouldn't be wasting time on a casual chat. They'd be reading him his rights. Whatever they'd found to bring them to his doorstep wasn't usable in court.

Everything was fine. There was no reason to panic.

Pasting on a smile, he rejoined them. "It should cool down in a few minutes. Now tell me how I can help you."

"I'm the lead detective on the Eve Reilly case." Lange pulled out a notebook. "I'd like to ask you a few questions related to that."

His mouth flattened. "May I ask why?"

"We're following up on several pieces of information. One of them led us to you."

"Which one?"

Lange ignored him. "Could you tell us where you were last Saturday evening?"

They'd linked him to the tire slashing.

But how?

"Why do you want to know?" Unless he knew what they had on him, he wouldn't be able to come up with a viable defense.

Lange offered him a smile that contained no trace of humor. "I'll answer your question if you answer mine."

Checkmate.

Steve picked up his beer and took a sip of the tepid brew. Refusing to answer would add to the suspicions these two already had. But he couldn't tell them the whole truth, either. There were gaps in the timing between his activities.

If they'd run his credit card history, they'd found the gas receipt from that night, when he'd filled his tank while he was out. If they hadn't, they would eventually. Lying about that would be crazy.

His skin began to itch, and he scratched his arm. "I was here, with Meg. I did run out for a few minutes to fill up my car at the station down the street, but that was it."

Not true . . . and Candy would lie for him, tell these cops whatever he asked her to . . . but bringing her into the discussion would cause all kinds of garbage to hit the fan on the home front if Meg found out.

Meg would also lie for him about Saturday night if he pushed her—but that shouldn't be necessary. A wife didn't have to testify against her husband. And he'd tell her that later tonight, in case one of these guys cornered her away from the house and began asking questions.

The lead detective never broke eye contact with him. "Can you tell us where you were on your lunch hour on Friday, August 24?"

The day of the fake bomb incident.

He was definitely in their sights.

And he still didn't know why.

"I'll be happy to—but you haven't answered *my* question yet. Why do you want to know? Am I a suspect in this case?"

"Should you be?"

"Of course not! Why would you think that?"

"We found a small clump of your hair next to Eve Reilly's car on Saturday night."

Shock reverberated through him—but he managed to keep his alarm from showing.

Careful, Jackson. That incident never made the news, and Meg hasn't mentioned it. You don't know about it.

He scratched his arm again and gave them a look he hoped came across as confused. "At the gas station?"

The two men exchanged a glance he couldn't decipher.

"Let's not play games, Mr. Jackson." This from Flynn.

"I don't know what you're talking about."

His baseball cap should have been sufficient protection that

193

night—and it would have been if he hadn't scraped his head on the doorframe and lost the cap in the process.

He'd checked, though—and there'd been no evidence of that tiny mishap.

Who'd have thought a few stray strands of dark hair would be noticed on black asphalt—or even still be there by the time Eve came out?

"Then explain how your hair ended up in the parking lot at the middle school where Ms. Reilly was giving a speech." Lange rejoined the conversation.

Keep playing dumb, Jackson. You can explain this.

"I was on a painting job at a middle school last week." He named it. The flyer on the bulletin board in the lobby was what had tipped him off to Eve's speech. "Is that the one you mean?"

The two guys traded another look. It wasn't any easier to read—but his legitimate explanation had to throw a major fly in their ointment.

"You can verify that with my boss if you want." It couldn't hurt to keep trying to be helpful.

"You haven't told us where you were on August 24 during your lunch hour." Lange dropped the pleasant pretense.

"I went to Subway to get a sandwich. Do you want to see my credit card receipt?"

"Which Subway?"

"The one in Maplewood." The opposite direction from Eve's house.

Giving his card to one of his coworkers and asking him to pick up a sandwich while the man ran home over lunch to let his dog out had been inspired. He'd never expected to need the alibi—but covering all your bases was smart.

Lange closed his notebook. "We appreciate your time."

"Always glad to help out law enforcement."

"Not in Texas—or Washington."

Another film of sweat broke out on his upper lip.

They'd dug into his background.

But that's what cops did.

Everything they'd found had been history, however. It had nothing to do with his current life—or the Eve Reilly situation.

"I've made a new start. My record is clean."

The detective pocketed his notebook. "We'll be in touch if we have any other questions."

Without waiting for a response, the two men walked toward the door without offering to shake his hand again.

He followed them, twisted the knob, and let them out in silence.

After he secured the lock, he moved to the window and watched from the side as they retraced their steps down the walk.

They paused for less than a minute to talk at the end of the sidewalk, then peeled off toward their separate cars. They couldn't have covered much ground beyond acknowledging they'd run into a dead end.

Yet they could continue digging tomorrow.

Steve returned to the living room and dropped into his chair.

No matter how much they dug, though, he should be safe. The hair was a mistake—but that was his only one.

Nevertheless, it was important that Meg keep her mouth shut about his absence last Saturday night if those detectives happened to speak with her.

An instruction he would pass on as soon as she got home.

She'd have questions, but a little fast talking and a healthy dose of affection would put those to rest. Meg was all about keeping the waters at home smooth—and she was a sucker for a little smooching.

Yeah, she'd be easy to keep in line.

And once the detectives realized they had nothing worthwhile to pursue, they'd let this go—and he'd be home free.

15

THE DOORBELL RANG on Friday morning at precisely five-fifteen, and Eve smiled.

Punctuality joined the list of Brent's many other attributes.

As she entered the small foyer, she ran her fingers through her hair. Rising in what felt like the middle of the night wasn't her favorite part of the radio gig—but being chauffeured by a handsome man made the pre-dawn jangle of the alarm much more palatable.

She pulled open the door and gave Brent's crisp white shirt, silk tie, tailored jacket, and dress slacks a fast sweep. The more formal attire suited him, but she'd be willing to bet he'd exchange it in a heartbeat for jeans and a T-shirt.

Which also suited him.

"Morning." He smiled at her, fine lines crinkling at the corners of his eyes.

"You look chipper for such an early hour." She smoothed a hand down the tunic that hit her leggings mid-thigh and motioned him in.

"Law enforcement isn't a nine-to-five gig." He entered, his gaze heating up as he discreetly surveyed the casual attire that was one of the perks of a job where her audience never saw her. "I learned long ago to function on less-than-optimal amounts of sleep."

"Well, I hope you turned in early last night to compensate for the long day ahead."

"That was my plan, but I got called to a crime scene on my way home. I didn't hit the sheets until after midnight."

"Ouch." She winced. "You should have left me a text message and cancelled this morning. I could have driven myself."

"Not an option." His tone brooked no arguments. "Are you ready to go?"

"Yes—as soon as I grab our coffee. Give me a sec."

She hurried to the kitchen to retrieve the two insulated travel mugs she'd prepared, then rejoined him in the foyer. "At this hour, I figured we could both use a caffeine infusion."

"I was going to pilfer coffee at the station, but your java is far superior to the stuff in your break room." He took the offering she held out.

"That's a low bar. There are days you could stick a spoon upright in the station sludge." She picked up the tote bag that held her notes for today's program. "I'm all set."

He followed her outside, waited while she locked the door, and stayed close as they walked to his car. For security purposes—or were there other, more personal motives?

Perhaps both, if she'd been reading his signals correctly.

Once she was buckled into the passenger seat, he circled around the hood to the driver's side.

She waited to speak until he started the engine. "I want to thank you for sending the patrol officers around yesterday. They did several circuits of the house over the course of the day and evening."

"I know. I checked." He slid his mug into the cup holder, flipped on his headlights, and pulled away from the curb. "I was going to call you last night with an update on the case, but it was too late by the time I had a free minute."

"Did you end up talking to Steve?"

"Yes—after he got home from work."

"Does he have alibis?"

"It appears so."

The note of caution in his inflection put her on alert. "But you're not buying them."

"Let's say I'm not convinced they're legit, given his background."

She listened in growing horror as he filled her in on the man's history—and when he got to the part about the protection orders, her lungs locked. "Poor Meg. She'll be devastated if she finds out."

"She'll find out." There was a hardness in his voice she hadn't heard before. "I'm planning to hang around the station during your program and talk to her as soon as she arrives."

"You're going to tell her about Steve's past?"

"Yes."

"Why?"

"Because if she's the straight shooter you think she is, she'll want to know she's been duped. And she'll also want to protect a friend—you—and see justice done."

"But she's his wife."

"I know—and she doesn't have to tell me a thing. After our visit last night, he may have told her not to. But even if she won't help our case, she deserves to know the character of the man she married. Don't you agree?"

Eve stared through the front windshield into the darkness, gripping her mug.

Did she?

Sharing information that would hurt someone and change their world forever . . . that would destroy their dreams . . . seemed harsh.

Yet did masking the truth do anyone any favors?

She could feel Brent scrutinizing her as she tried to organize her thoughts. "In theory, I do. I'm just concerned about what this will do to Meg. She pinned all her hopes on Steve, built her future around this marriage, and if it goes away . . . she could fold." Eve exhaled. "I realize that may seem melodramatic, but being disillusioned about someone you love . . . maybe losing them . . . could shatter some people."

"I know."

At the subtle anguish in his quiet response, she squinted at him. The car was too dark to distinguish his features, and his face was in profile, but his rigid posture spoke volumes.

He was speaking from personal experience. Thinking about Karen, no doubt.

Dare she ask a few questions?

She stroked a thumb over the smooth aluminum of the insulated mug, the cool exterior masking the heat within, as she mulled over that option.

It was possible he'd feel safe revealing a few tidbits under the cover of darkness, where she wouldn't be able to read his eyes or discern his expressions. Yet much as she wanted to know why Brent had written off romance, she ought to let him choose the timing for that explanation.

Why not respond with a comment that allowed him to decide whether he wanted to share details or move on to another topic?

"I expect you deal with difficult situations on a regular basis."

"Yeah, I do. Disillusioning Meg will be one of them. I've seen someone shatter when a romance goes south, and it's not pretty."

O-kay.

That sounded like an opening to her.

Eve readjusted her seat belt and angled toward him. "Are you talking about Karen?"

He groped for his mug. Took a sip. "Yes."

"Whatever happened must have been traumatic." A simple yes would suffice if he didn't want to expound on the subject—but why would he bring it up unless he'd decided to tell her the story?

"It was—for both of us." He signaled for another turn.

He didn't pick up the account as he accelerated, and she risked another question that wasn't too probing. "When did this happen?"

"We broke up three years ago."

She waited—but he offered nothing more.

Hmm.

Brent could be one of those guys who had to be taken by the hand and led through emotion-centered discussions that pushed them beyond their comfort level.

Fine. She was up to the challenge.

"I take it the relationship was serious?"

"Yes—but also a bit of a whirlwind." He executed another turn. "We met at a Christmas party a mutual friend was hosting, and by Valentine's Day she was beginning to drop hints about a proposal."

"Wow. That is fast." And from what she'd observed, not this man's style.

"Too fast. I knew that in my head, but falling for someone can short-circuit your common sense. I did convince her we should give it another month or two before we took such an important step, and she agreed. In my mind, I was thinking of an Easter proposal. But we didn't make it that far."

Given the previous hints he'd dropped, it hadn't been a simple breakup—if such a thing existed. Whatever had gone wrong in that relationship, the man beside her must be carrying around a boatload of guilt if he'd written off romance forever.

"Do you want to tell me what happened?"

"The truth? No. It's hard to revisit a bad scene. The only

person who knows the whole story is Adam, and we don't talk much about it anymore."

Her spirits plummeted. If Brent had shared the painful episode with no one but his best friend from childhood, there wasn't much chance—

"But I'd like to tell it to you too—so you'll understand why I've shied away from romance." Waves of tension rolled off him as he felt around for the cup holder and fitted his mug into it.

"I'd like to hear it." And hopefully find a way to convince him there was room in his life for love.

Despite the shadows in the car, she could see his throat work as he swallowed. "I'll try to spare you as many of the gory details as possible—but three weeks before Easter, while I was on a routine traffic stop, I was critically injured by a drunk driver who slammed into me."

Eve gasped. Critically injured meant he could have died.

The mere thought of that sent a chill through her.

Yet it was obvious the vibrant man beside her had made a remarkable recovery.

She touched his arm, the gesture involuntary. As if her subconscious required physical confirmation he'd survived. "What sort of injuries did you have?"

"Broken leg, shattered pelvis, fractured wrist, ruptured spleen, and head injuries. I was in a coma for six days."

Her stomach bottomed out. That was far worse than she'd expected.

"But you recovered and went on with your life." That was the most important fact.

"Yes—after months of rehab. For weeks, the doctors weren't sure I'd ever walk normally again."

"Oh, Brent. I can't begin to imagine trying to cope with all that."

"Neither could Karen."

They passed under a streetlight as his comment hung in the air between them, and Eve studied the flat, rigid line of his mouth, the deep grooves denting his forehead.

"Did she . . . walk out on you?" What else could his comment mean?

The car passed back into darkness, leaving his features in shadows. "No."

Not what she'd expected.

"So what happened?" If he'd told her this much, that direct question shouldn't scare him away.

"When I came out of my coma, she was a basket case." A slight quiver disrupted his previous steady, flat delivery. "Adam told me she'd spent every minute she wasn't at work by my side, and it showed. She was pale and stressed and had already lost several pounds."

"In other words, she loved you deeply and was devoted to you." Eve frowned, trying to grasp the problem. "Was that bad?"

"No—but her stress never went away, despite my faster-than-expected recovery."

She was still missing the issue. "Explain that."

He let out a slow breath and hung a right onto the entry ramp for I-64 east, toward downtown. "She had concerns about a host of potential complications. Whether I would ever walk without assistance again. How we'd manage if I couldn't. Would medical expenses overwhelm us? Would it be fair to bring children into a marriage with a disabled parent? Most of all she worried about how she'd live with the uncertainties of my job. Of not knowing every day when I left for work if I'd come home that night."

All of those worries were legit. Anyone would have similar questions and qualms in that situation.

What wasn't he telling her?

"Those concerns seem valid to me." She worked hard to keep her tone conversational rather than critical.

"They were—but her anxiety was excessive. She ended up resorting to pills to help her get through the day. This was a woman who had a responsible job, juggled multiple balls without missing a beat, and always had her act together."

"Resorted to pills as in . . . addiction?"

"Yeah."

Okay. That could freak a guy out.

But there was more. He hadn't yet told her the key problem.

"I can see where that would be disconcerting for you. Did she get any professional assistance—counseling—to help her cope?"

"No. She told me it wasn't necessary. In the end, as I continued to improve, she did calm down a bit and eased back on the pills as much as she could. But she also gave me an ultimatum."

This was the missing piece—and Eve could guess how it had played out. Brent wasn't the type of guy to succumb to threats or demands.

"What was it?"

"She wanted me to get out of law enforcement. Find a less dangerous job where my skills would be useful. She suggested I join the security department of a large company, or work for a home protection firm."

Eve wrinkled her nose—likely the same reaction Brent had had. Passive jobs like that wouldn't suit the man sitting in the car beside her. Nor would they be the best use of his years of street experience.

But it wasn't hard to understand why a woman who'd watched the man she loved almost die would deliver such an ultimatum.

He looked over at her. "You're thinking I should have caved."

"I don't know if caved is the right term. Maybe there was a way to compromise."

"Maybe there was—but at the time, I couldn't come up

with one." He flexed his fingers on the wheel, as if he was trying to restore circulation.

"Did you consider quitting County?"

"No." His answer held a hint of sadness—and disgust. "I'm ashamed to say our relationship wasn't important enough to me to make that kind of sacrifice. But it should have been. Karen had worried herself sick about me. Literally. And I'd been planning to propose. Yet I wasn't willing to give up my job to keep her."

"How did she handle that?"

"Not well. She said I was cold. Unfeeling. That from the beginning, I'd shut her out, kept a piece of myself locked away from her. That I didn't know how to recognize love—or return it. That my heart had atrophied. That she felt sorry for any woman in the future who fell for me. Then she walked out."

Eve cringed.

What a terrible situation.

A woman who'd fallen apart at the end of a romance, and a man who'd emerged with serious scars—and less confidence than ever in his ability to form attachments.

It was a lose-lose situation.

But Karen's biting indictment of Brent wasn't entirely deserved. He may have been deprived of emotional sustenance as a child—and he might have had trouble opening his heart to his almost-fiancée—but from what she'd seen in their brief relationship, he wasn't cold or unfeeling. Nor had his heart atrophied. He was more than capable of recognizing and expressing love.

The challenge was how to convince him of that.

She touched his arm, and a muscle contracted beneath her fingers. "Did you ever consider there may have been another explanation for what went wrong? That your feelings for Karen may not have been as deep as you thought they were?"

He kept his focus on the road. "Yes. But that felt more like an excuse for my shortcomings than a rational justification for my choice." A beat passed. "Or it did—until I met you."

The air whooshed out of her lungs. His meaning *seemed* clear—but what if she was jumping to conclusions?

"Um . . ." She fiddled with the edge of her seat belt, straining to read his expression in the dim light. "I'm not certain I—"

"I meant exactly what you thought I meant." He shot her a quick glance. "I believed what I felt for Karen was love—but in hindsight, I realize it was more superficial than that. It was hormones rather than heartstrings. She was a fine person—but she wasn't the one for me. No woman is."

She blinked.

What?

Hadn't he just said—more or less—that his feelings for her went a lot deeper than the feelings he'd had for Karen?

"Wait . . . back up. Did I miss something?"

"No." He sighed. "You interpreted my first comment correctly. My feelings for you, even at this early stage, are deeper than they were for Karen. But that doesn't mean I'm husband material. A woman deserves a man who's comfortable expressing feelings. I was only able to handle this discussion today because I could hide in the dark while we talked. That's the reality."

So her theory had been correct. He viewed the dim car as a safe place for sharing touchy-feely information.

"But we did talk, no matter the environment. That's what counts. And while you may be uncomfortable with emotional discussions, the evidence suggests you have feelings—and a warm, caring heart."

"It's a moot point anyway."

Another curveball.

"What do you mean?"

"My emotional aptitude isn't the only issue. After I saw what my injury did to someone strong and capable like Karen, I realized it wouldn't be fair to subject another woman to that kind of pressure. If Karen could fold, anyone could—and I couldn't live with myself if I had to watch someone I care about go through that again."

"Does that mean you've shut the door to romance?"

"Yes."

"But that's . . . that's crazy!" The words popped out before she could stop them, and she clapped a hand over her mouth. This wasn't her radio program, where she spouted off uncensored opinions on topics of the day. This was an interpersonal relationship with a man who required kid-glove handling on topics of the heart.

"Sorry." She touched his arm again. "I didn't mean to come off so . . ."

"Honest?" A touch of humor lurked in his voice. "Your candor is one of the qualities I lo . . . like about you. If I didn't know otherwise, I'd think you and Adam had talked."

Thank goodness he hadn't taken offense at her less-than-tactful pronouncement.

"He agrees with me?"

"Yes. And he tends to be far more direct than you were about his opinions. During our last discussion on the subject, he told me I was nuts."

Kudos to his buddy. Sometimes friends—or sisters—could rush in where angels feared to tread.

"Why don't you listen to him? He's your best friend."

"I take everything he says in the romance department with a grain of salt. Since he met Rebecca—and married her six months ago—he views the world through rose-colored glasses and sees happy endings around every corner."

"Not a bad attitude."

"But not realistic. You and I both know from our professions that's not how the world is."

206

"The parts we control can be, if we work at it." They were approaching the exit for the radio station—and their situation was still in limbo.

They needed a resolution before they parted.

"What time does Meg get to work?" He flipped on his blinker.

"Her official workday begins at eight, but I think she often arrives by seven-thirty."

"That will give me a chance to get a bagel at the coffee shop on the corner and deal with email."

He appeared ready to move on to a new subject—but she wasn't.

"Brent." She waited until he looked at her. "I understand your concerns. But I don't agree with your self-assessment. As for subjecting someone to the stresses your job entails—I could take the same position, given all that's been happening in my life these past two weeks."

"Your situation is temporary." He swung onto the exit ramp that was empty in this prelude to rush hour.

"Given the strong emotions I sometimes stir up in my audience, it could happen again. If I followed your philosophy, I should write off romance too."

He guided the car down the deserted streets, toward the parking garage at the station. "That's different. You don't carry a gun and deal with the dregs of society every day."

"Not carrying a gun makes me *more* vulnerable—as Cate has reminded me ad nauseam. So I guess it wouldn't be fair for me to put a guy through that kind of stress either."

Brent pulled into the well-lit parking garage, giving her a clearer view of his face.

His brow was furrowed.

She locked her lips, letting him digest her comments.

Only after he swung into a vacant space and killed the engine did he give her his full attention, his demeanor somber.

"I get what you're trying to do, Eve—and I appreciate it. What you say is logical, and if I hadn't had such a bad experience with Karen, I might agree that my position is extreme. I might even buy your argument that with the right woman, I could dredge up the emotions I buried years ago and take a chance on love. But those are two big strikes to overcome."

"I won't dispute that. I'll just remind you that the game's not over until the third strike. So I choose to believe there's hope for you. For us."

Another car pulled into the garage, the headlights illuminating the interior of his car and putting them in a spotlight.

"We should go inside. Sitting around in parking garages isn't the best idea under any circumstances—less so in yours. I'll get your door."

Eve started to protest, but he was already out of the car.

By the time she picked up her tote bag, stowed their empty travel mugs, and unlatched the door, he was there to pull it open.

"I think we should talk more about this." She waited while he closed her door and set the locks.

"At the moment, my priority is finding the person who's disrupting your life. Let's get inside." He took her arm and urged her toward the door, his professional demeanor back in place as he scanned their surroundings.

The discussion was over for today.

And he was correct about maintaining perspective. Closing the case had to be their top priority for the immediate future.

But once the threat hovering over her was contained, there were other important issues that had to be addressed.

If Brent was reluctant to revisit this discussion . . . if he required convincing that his emotions were up to the task and his heart was ready for romance . . . she was just the woman to tackle the job.

For now, though, she'd let him close out this case. With Steve in the crosshairs, it shouldn't take long. In fact, if all went well, by next week this chapter of her life could be history.

Because once Steve was out of the picture, there would be no more looking over her shoulder or worrying about danger lurking in the shadows.

———

Al — FRI., SEPT. 7, 7:52 A.M.

Been quiet. Status?

Dan — FRI., SEPT. 7, 7:54 A.M.

Too quiet. Need another incident. Will handle.

Al — FRI., SEPT. 7, 7:54 A.M.

What about main event?

Dan — FRI., SEPT. 7, 7:55 A.M.

Instructions to follow. Keep next weekend open.

Al — FRI., SEPT. 7, 7:56 A.M.

Part of other event?

Dan — FRI., SEPT. 7, 7:56 A.M.

Yes.

Al FRI., SEPT. 7, 7:57 A.M.

Smart.

Dan FRI., SEPT. 7, 7:57 A.M.

Why I'm paid the big bucks. ☺

Al FRI., SEPT. 7, 7:58 A.M.

Standing by to make ER history.

16

MS. JACKSON . . . may I speak with you for a few minutes?"

As the familiar male voice addressed her, Meg jolted to a stop and swiveled around, pulse hammering. Steve had been right. The detective on Eve's case had, indeed, sought her out at the office.

What a way to end the week.

Somehow she managed to call up the facsimile of a smile. "Good morning, Detective Lange. I have to let my boss know I'm here and see if he wants me to handle any urgent matters."

"I've already spoken with him. He said he didn't mind if you were delayed for a few minutes."

The man had covered all the bases.

But Steve had told her not to talk with anyone from law enforcement.

"I, uh, have a ton of work to do."

"This won't take long."

She shifted her weight. Squeezed the strap of her purse. "Steve doesn't . . . he prefers I not talk with you."

"Why is that?" The detective's tone remained cordial.

"He said he already answered all your questions."

"We always like to get several perspectives. I won't detain you long."

Other arriving staffers cast curious looks their way as they skirted past in the hall, and her cheeks warmed. The middle of a busy corridor wasn't the best place to have this discussion.

"Can we talk somewhere else?"

"I've staked out the conference room." He motioned behind him.

Without responding, she walked past him and entered the room.

He followed her in and shut the door.

"I can't tell you anything more than Steve already has." She clutched her purse to her chest. "This is a waste of time for both of us."

"That's possible—but I can spare a few minutes, and a brief chat shouldn't eat into your day too much." His posture was open and affable as he motioned toward the table.

Short of being rude—and further raising his suspicions— what choice did she have?

Besides, as long as she was careful, what harm could there be in a brief conversation?

"Fine." Legs stiff, she crossed to the table and sank into a chair, setting her purse in front of her.

"Would you like coffee?" He indicated the pot. "It's not the best brew I've ever had, but it does contain a generous amount of caffeine." He offered her an engaging grin.

"No thanks. I'm not a coffee drinker."

The detective pulled out the chair beside her, angled it her direction, and sat, his posture relaxed. Friendly. Approachable.

He and his partner had been polite at the house last night too. Not many men these days displayed the small courtesies, like standing in a woman's presence. Including her husband.

"If you change your mind about a beverage, let me know.

I'll be happy to get you a soda if you prefer." He pulled out a notebook, his demeanor pleasant.

"Thank you. I'm fine."

She scrutinized him, trying to reconcile this well-mannered, accommodating man with the negative picture Steve had painted of him after she'd returned from her "errands" last night.

Failed.

Either Brent Lange was an excellent actor, or her husband hadn't presented a truthful portrait of him and his partner.

On the other hand, the detective may not have been as cordial to Steve if he suspected him of harassing Eve. As if her husband would ever do such a thing. Steve had his faults, but he wasn't a criminal, no matter what this man thought.

So she'd listen to what he had to say—and be careful in her replies. As Steve had reminded her, a wife didn't have to talk to law enforcement about her spouse.

"Did your husband explain the nature of my visit to your house last night?" Detective Lange's manner remained genial.

"Yes."

"Were you surprised?"

"More like shocked. Trying to link my husband to the problems Eve has been having is . . . it's ludicrous."

"Did he tell you we found his DNA last Saturday close to her car at a middle school?"

"Yes. He assumed there must have been another incident. But he had a job at that school earlier in the week."

"So he told us."

"It's true."

"I'm not disputing that. Were you aware that Ms. Reilly's tires were slashed that evening, and a threatening note was left in her car?"

Meg's heart skipped a beat. "No."

"Your husband's DNA was found within inches of her car door."

That was kind of a weird coincidence.

As if he'd read her mind, Lange continued. "Don't you think the odds of that are minuscule?"

She straightened her shoulders. "He *was* working at that facility. It could happen."

Lange crossed an ankle over a knee. "Where was your husband that night?"

Steve had said they might ask that if they cornered her.

"Mostly at home, other than a quick trip to get gas."

Except he'd been gone far longer than it took to fill up his tank at the corner station. A sudden urge to take a drive and clear his mind from the clutter of the week was how he'd explained his absence to her—but the police wouldn't consider that a valid alibi. She had to verify his presence at the house.

Any woman would do as much for her husband.

"How quick?"

The detective wasn't giving up—and while his tone was smooth as ever, his eyes were sharp. Probing.

"I didn't time his absence."

"An estimate would do. Ten minutes . . . an hour . . . two hours?"

She clenched her fingers together in her lap. "I don't mean to be rude, but Steve said I'm not required to talk with you."

"That's true. However . . . since Eve is an old friend, I hoped you'd be willing to help us find who's been targeting her."

"Of course I am. But it's not Steve."

Lange watched her for a moment, then flipped open his notebook. "Do you know a woman by the name of Candy Norris?"

If the left-field query was intended to throw her, it succeeded.

"No." She'd remember a name like Candy. "Why?"

214

"Your husband calls her on a regular basis. Has he bought you any jewelry lately?"

She twisted the combination wedding/engagement band with the line of diamond chips on top that adorned her finger. The only jewelry he'd ever given her.

"No. Why?"

"According to his credit card report, he's made three purchases over the past year at a local jewelry store."

A cold knot began to form in her stomach.

Why was Steve frequenting a jewelry store? Did those purchases have anything to do with this Candy woman the detective had mentioned?

Except . . . jewelry stores did sell other items, like watch batteries. And they did repairs and appraisals and—

"He bought an emerald ring, a diamond tennis bracelet, and a woman's gold necklace."

As the detective ticked off her husband's purchases, the knot in her stomach tightened and the air whooshed from her lungs. Steve had been buying women's jewelry. And given how Lange had framed his questions, he suspected it was for Candy.

But . . . but Steve wouldn't do that to her. They'd only been married eighteen months. They'd taken vows. Why would he wed her if he wanted to play around?

Simple. He likes to control people—and you're easy to manipulate.

No.

She smothered the taunting voice in her head.

That wasn't true.

Steve would have an explanation for the purchases. For his calls to Candy. They could be grief related, even. A coping mechanism. From the beginning, he'd admitted that the loss of his first wife had been devastating. You had to cut people whose hearts had been broken a little slack.

Didn't you?

"In case you're wondering who Candy is, she works in a local bar." The detective named it.

The burger joint Steve visited on occasion with his buddies. Never with her.

Tentacles of suspicion began to slither through her, as insidious as the calories that crept onto her hips and undermined her good intentions to lose weight.

"Who do you think the jewelry was for, Ms. Jackson?"

The bagel she'd scarfed down this morning after dragging herself out of bed hardened into a lump.

While his question came across as casual, it was obvious this man had already reached his own conclusion about the answer.

But it couldn't be true. Not after last night. Not after all the things she and Steve had done into the wee hours. It had been as if they were back on their honeymoon. Operating on fumes today was a small price to pay for that romantic interlude.

The detective watched her, waiting for her to comment.

She had to defend Steve—at least until she talked with him.

"I know what you're implying." Her interlaced fingers began to throb, and she loosened the pressure on her knuckles. "But you're wrong. About that, and about his involvement in the situation with Eve. Why would he want to hurt her?"

"How does he feel about your job here?"

She blinked. "What?"

"Is he supportive of your career?"

Why would this man ask that?

Unless . . . had she let a comment or two slip about Steve's reservations during one of her chats with Eve at the station or at the spinning class? Had Eve mentioned that to the detective?

"It's a temporary job, until we have a family. He and I discussed it."

That didn't answer the question—and the slight narrowing of the man's eyes indicated he knew that.

But what did this have to do with anything?

He spoke as if he'd heard her silent question. "If Eve goes away, so does her show. And your job."

When his implication sank in, Meg's jaw dropped.

He thought Steve would try to ruin Eve's career just to get his wife to stay home?

That was absurd.

Wasn't it?

She massaged her temple as she tried to sort through all the information and insinuations that had been zipping around this room during the past few minutes.

"Detective Lange, I appreciate that you're trying to do your job. But Steve would never be involved in anything illegal. He may still be working through all the issues associated with his loss, but he—"

"What loss?"

"The death of his first wife. You knew about that, didn't you?"

It was impossible to interpret his expression. Not surprise, exactly—but it was clear he hadn't known about Steve's first marriage.

That was odd. This guy struck her as the type who did his homework.

He studied her for a moment. Let out a breath. "His first wife isn't dead. They divorced two years ago—after she got a protection order on him for abuse."

Meg heard the words. Understood them. But they were as difficult to make sense of as an algebra equation.

Before she could process this new information, Lange dropped another bombshell.

"His previous girlfriend also took out a protection order on him."

Steve had been in two abusive relationships.

His wife hadn't died.

The marriage he'd described as blissful had been the polar opposite.

Why had he lied to her?

And if he'd lied to her about all that . . . could she believe *anything* he'd told her?

Mind spinning, she lurched to her feet, gripping the edge of the table to steady herself. "I have to . . . to get to work." Her response echoed in her ears as if it came from a great distance.

The detective rose too, and a business card appeared in her field of vision. "If you want to add to your story—or change anything—you can reach me at this number. Night or day."

After a tiny hesitation, she took the small rectangle and stumbled toward the door.

The detective beat her to it. He twisted the knob and pulled it open.

Somehow she made it to the ladies room before she lost her breakfast.

Leaning against the wall of the stall, stomach quivering as she hovered over the toilet, Meg tried to digest all she'd learned in the past fifteen minutes.

Maybe . . . maybe there was an explanation for everything. Steve may have been afraid that if he told her the truth about his past, she wouldn't have wanted anything to do with him. It was possible Candy was nothing more than a friend. The jewelry purchases could have a simple explanation too. His friends might have asked him to put gifts on his credit card to keep the purchases hidden so they could surprise their wives. Some guys were thoughtful like that. The hair on the parking lot could also be coincidence.

But that was a lot of maybes and might haves and could be's.

Too many.

Meg pulled out a length of toilet paper and wiped her mouth, but bitterness clung to her tongue—and her heart.

It appeared she'd been a fool.

The very word her parents had used when she'd told them she was going to marry Steve.

Someone came into the ladies room, and Meg straightened up. She should get back to her desk. Focus on her job. She had eight hours to decide what to do about the situation at home. And if she needed more time than that, she'd figure out how to buy some.

She wadded up the soiled tissue and tossed it in the toilet bowl, flushing away the evidence of her bout of nausea.

Nausea.

She watched the water swirl in the bowl.

That could work, considering how Steve had walked a wide circle around her during the morning sickness phase of her pregnancy. Even a hint of the stench of vomit made him queasy—and she knew how to produce that, thanks to the battle she'd once waged with bulimia.

If necessary, that tactic could give her breathing space to discover the truth about Steve.

Because if he'd done everything the detective claimed, she'd rather stick a finger down her throat than let Steve lay another finger on her body.

That hadn't been fun.

Brent exhaled and propped a shoulder against the conference room wall. Watching someone crumble never was—even if they were a virtual stranger.

But his job was to nail the bad guys, and sometimes the innocent people who got sucked into their orbit crashed and burned too.

That wasn't the fate he wished on Meg.

God willing, she'd survive this. And in the long run she'd be better off without that user. It was even possible that once she thought through everything, she'd be willing to admit her husband had been gone far longer than was necessary for a fill-up at the corner gas station. If they could poke a few holes in his—

"Knock knock." Eve stuck her head around the half-open door. "May I come in?"

"Sure." He pushed off from the wall.

She entered and closed the door behind her. "I caught a glimpse of Meg in the hall. She looked bad."

"I know."

"You don't look too hot yourself."

He conjured up a smile. "Gee, thanks for the ego boost."

"That's not what I meant." She surveyed him and sighed. "I don't envy you this part of your job."

"Goes with the territory."

"Did she tell you anything helpful?"

"Helpful as in giving us ammunition to nail her husband, no. But after she digests everything—and has a talk with Jackson—she may reconsider. You ready to go home?"

"I can get a cab if there's somewhere you have to be."

"I'll drop you off en route."

She didn't protest.

He followed her out the door, into the elevator, and to his car.

Not until they were buckled in and pulling out of the parking space did she speak. "What happens next with the case?"

"We continue to dig. I'm going to talk with a few of Jackson's coworkers, keep the heat on. We also have eyes on him periodically—and we're not trying to be covert about that. I want him to think we're watching him 24/7. That should keep him from trying anything else until we get definitive evidence against him."

Unfortunately, the man had covered his tracks well. Finding evidence could be a matter of *if*, not *when*. A possible outcome he wasn't yet ready to admit to Eve.

"Does that mean I can go about my business as usual and forget about hiring Phoenix?"

"Do you have a busy weekend scheduled?"

"If you mean will I be running around doing errands, no. I plan to finish the floor in the living room. That will keep me housebound other than going to church on Sunday."

"Don't bother to call Phoenix, then. I'd offer to take you to services, but the youth group from my church has its annual weekend campout, and I always volunteer."

"That should be fun."

He hiked up one side of his mouth. "Depends on how you define fun. Watching over a group of ten-to-twelve-year-old boys for thirty-six hours is a challenge. Many of them have never spent a night in the woods. We've had more than a few freak out during a coyote howlfest at midnight."

"I can imagine."

"So tell me about today's program. I was only able to listen to bits and pieces. Any unusual calls?"

She glanced at him as he maneuvered the car out of the garage and headed toward the highway.

Uh-oh.

Unless he was misinterpreting the vibes, she was debating whether to reintroduce the subject they'd discussed during the drive down in the dark.

Please don't, Eve. I'm not up for that after talking to Meg.

As if she'd heard his silent plea, she launched into an account of the exchange she'd had with one caller who was convinced the American Revolution had been about slavery, not taxes.

By the time he asked several questions and they shared a few chuckles over the more bizarre calls that had come in, he was pulling into her driveway.

"I'll walk you to your door."

He set the brake and circled the car, giving the neighborhood a quick scan. All appeared to be quiet.

As they followed the path to her porch, he took her arm—and when she smiled up at him, his heart did a strange flip-flop.

Funny.

Since Karen's scathing assessment after their breakup, he'd been convinced he wasn't up to the job of being a husband. Women needed emotional connections, sharing at the deepest levels, and that had never been his strong suit. How could it be, after the upbringing he'd had?

Karen had never complained much about his reticence until the end, though. Perhaps she'd thought that in time she could change him. And perhaps she could have.

But with Eve, it was already different. In the space of two weeks, he'd shared more about his past than he'd ever revealed to Karen—which was telling.

It also supported Eve's theory that he had it in him to open up . . . with the right woman.

That didn't solve the other problem, however.

He stepped back while she fitted the key in her lock, keeping tabs on their surroundings.

It had been a good try on her part to suggest their jobs had similarities, that if she abided by his rules she'd never marry either. Yet that was a stretch. Once they got past this traumatic incident in her life, there wasn't likely to be a repeat. It was an anomaly, even for a high-profile career like hers.

The danger in his job, on the other hand, would last forever. While detectives weren't as vulnerable as first responders, no street job in law enforcement was without risk.

Was it possible, though, that because of all she was going through now, Eve would be better equipped than most women to understand and handle the psychological pressures that came with the risks of his job?

That question continued to loop through his mind as he said goodbye, waited until the lock clicked on the other side of the door, then returned to his car.

It was certainly a possibility worth pondering this weekend in the few spare minutes he'd have between bandaging cut fingers, putting salve on minor burns suffered while toasting s'mores, and comforting kids who'd never spent a night in the arms of Mother Nature.

Nor could it hurt to send a few prayers heavenward. Not asking for a specific outcome—he believed the line in the Lord's Prayer that said thy will be done—but for guidance to make a wise decision . . . and the fortitude to follow through.

Wherever that might lead.

17

SOMETHING WAS WRONG.

Steve closed the door from the garage and sniffed as he entered the kitchen. No savory aromas greeted him.

He checked the stove. Nothing was simmering on the burners.

Frowning, he swiveled toward the table. It wasn't set.

But Meg's car was in the alley.

The niggle of unease that had plagued him all day morphed into gut-knotting dread. Maybe his calls and texts today hadn't gone unanswered because she was too busy to respond. Maybe the cops had gotten to her.

Muttering a curse, he tossed his keys on the table and stalked to the living room. Empty.

He tried the bedroom next. Also empty . . . but the covers were thrown back on the bed.

The toilet flushed, and a few seconds later Meg exited the bathroom, dressed in a ratty tee and baggy shorts, clutching a towel.

He furrowed his brow. "What's going on?"

"I wish I knew." She circled around the far side of the bed and slid under the covers. "I've been throwing up."

He retreated a step. Blood, he could handle. Puke? No way.

Another reason he'd never been thrilled about having a bunch of rug rats cluttering up his life. Kids were always throwing up.

"So, uh, I guess I'm on my own for dinner." He eased toward the door.

"Sorry."

The sentiment was appropriate. Her tone wasn't.

He stopped. Squinted at her. "What's wrong?"

She punched two pillows into position and leaned back, watching him. "Detective Lange stopped by."

His pulse picked up. "You didn't talk to him, did you?"

"He did most of the talking."

"About what?"

"Candy . . . jewelry purchases . . . restraining orders."

He bit back another oath, mind racing. What could he say to mitigate the damage the cop had done? He needed his wife in his corner for the immediate future.

Meg scrutinized him in silence, fingers kneading the towel draped across her lap, her expression wary. Yet a touch of hope glimmered in the depths of her eyes.

She didn't want to believe all the incriminating information the detective had dumped on her.

That was a positive sign.

But unless he smoothed this over fast, he could lose her.

"Whatever he told you is a bunch of garbage." He crossed the room, trying to rein in his gag reflex. One whiff of vomit, though, and they'd both be leaning over the toilet.

As he sat on the bed and lifted a hand to touch her cheek, she recoiled and lost a few more shades of color. "Don't jiggle the mattress. My stomach won't be able to take it."

He jerked his hand back and froze. "I'll be careful."

"Who's Candy?"

Answer her questions fast, Jackson, or she'll realize you're making up most of this as you go along.

"A waitress at the bar I always go to. She's been having issues with her boyfriend, and she calls once in a while if she wants a sympathetic ear."

"What about the jewelry?" Meg locked onto his gaze.

His brain began cranking at warp speed. The detective could have given her details about his purchases. He had to mention all three items. "I bought two pieces for you. One for your birthday, one for Christmas. The third piece was for a buddy to give his girlfriend. He couldn't figure out what to get her, so I picked it out for him and he paid me back."

She plucked at a loop on the terry-cloth fabric. "Why did you lie to me about your first wife?"

"Because I was ashamed." He heaved a sigh that stopped just shy of being overly theatrical. "I wanted a new start with a good woman, and I didn't think you'd have anything to do with me if I told you my real history. In hindsight, I can see that was a mistake."

Several beats passed as she studied him. "They think you're behind the threats Eve's been getting."

"I know. It's crazy."

"Your DNA was next to her car in the parking lot."

"Coincidence." He had to stick with that story. It was the only innocent explanation—and while implausible, it was possible.

Meg swallowed, and her eyes began to shimmer. "I want to believe you." The admission came out in a whisper.

Yes!

Once again he leaned over. Stroked her cheek. "I'm telling you the truth, babe."

She didn't respond.

He scooted closer to her. "Why don't I lay here for a while with you? Later, if you feel up to it, I could show you how much I love—"

All at once, she clapped the towel to her mouth, scooted

off the opposite side of the bed, and dashed for the bathroom.

Seconds later the sounds of retching came from behind the closed door.

His own stomach heaving, Steve hightailed it out of the room and down the hall, where he could no longer hear his wife upchucking.

In the kitchen, he braced his hands on the edge of the sink and took slow, deep breaths until his nausea passed.

He had to get out of here. Find a distraction.

Like Candy.

But paying the curvaceous waitress a visit while he was on law enforcement's radar would be reckless. For all he knew, they were watching his every move. A car with dark windows had been on his tail during most of his drive home.

Spending the evening with a sick wife, however—especially one who wasn't up to providing him with an evening meal . . . or satisfying his other appetites—held no appeal.

Why not grab a burger somewhere and see if any of the guys from work wanted to bowl a few games? If he was lucky, by the time he returned, the worst of Meg's bug would be over.

He picked up his keys from the table, jiggling them as he looked toward the hall. Had he convinced her he was telling the truth? That none of the detective's allegations had any basis in reality? Or was she weighing his explanations even now, trying to decide who to believe?

Impossible to know. For once, his transparent, needy wife had been difficult to read.

But the cops had no hard proof to tie him to any of the threats made to Eve. Soon, they'd leave him alone and the case would go cold.

As long as he forked out the dough to buy Meg jewelry and kept a low profile with Candy for a while, he could smooth out the waters in his marriage. The setup on the home front was too sweet to muck up. What was not to like about a wife who cooked, cleaned, handled chores, did his bidding, and shared his bed?

Spirits rising, he tossed the keys in the air . . . caught them . . . and strolled toward the door to the garage. This would all turn out fine. Meg was easy to influence, and the cops were at a dead end.

He had this under control.

The first coat of finish was done.

Yay!

Eve swiped the back of her hand over her forehead and surveyed the gleaming hardwood floor in the living room. Not a bad end to the week. One more coat tomorrow, and by next Saturday she could begin putting all her furniture back where it belonged.

At a sudden, loud rumble from beneath her rib cage, she twisted her wrist.

Good grief. Was it seven-thirty already? No wonder her stomach was sending out distress signals. For a woman who rose long before the sun, this was way past the dinner hour.

A salad from Panera would be the perfect meal—but she'd promised Brent she'd stay close to the house . . . and home delivery would take too long.

Eve blew out a breath.

An omelet would have to do. Any other hot meal would require more energy than she could muster after all her hours of labor.

But once she finished the final coat on the floor tomorrow, she'd dig out her recipe for—

The doorbell chimed—and her heart skipped a beat.

She wasn't expecting company, and Brent was out of town.

Pulse accelerating, she crept across the tiny foyer to the front door and peered through the peephole.

On the other side, Cate and Grace were making goofy faces at her.

What on earth?

She undid the bolt, twisted the handle, and pulled the door wide.

In unison, her two sisters did a double take.

Cate recovered first. "The Martians have landed."

"I was thinking more creature from the Green Lagoon." Grace gave her mask, safety goggles, long-handled roller, and booties a sweep.

"Cute." Eve pulled off her mask and motioned them in. "Welcome to my world—if you can stand the smell."

Cate sniffed . . . wrinkled her nose . . . and nudged Grace. "We may want to rethink this."

"Not a chance. After driving for close to two hours, I'm not leaving without a short visit, at least." Her youngest sibling marched in, a brown bag in her hand.

"The smell shouldn't linger long. I used a water-based finish." Eve set the roller in a bucket. "But we can sit on the deck."

"That'll work." Cate entered.

"Give me a few minutes to ditch this garb and clean up. Help yourself to drinks while you wait. Hey." She snagged Cate's arm as her older sister started toward the kitchen. "I thought you were undercover."

"Job's done. Can't you tell by this?" She swept a hand down her usual off-duty attire of jeans and tank top.

"Yeah—and that outfit is a vast improvement over the all-black number you had on last visit."

"I agree."

"You nail the bad guys?"

"Yep." Cate continued down the hall and disappeared into the kitchen.

"I didn't get any more out of her either." Grace shrugged and lifted the bag. "I brought you gumbo for dinner tomorrow from the Cajun place you like near my house."

"How about dinner *tonight*? I haven't eaten yet." She took the bag and lifted it to her nose. Inhaled. "Bliss."

"I'll nuke it while you clean up. It's been in a cooler."

"With gumbo as an incentive, that won't take long."

Six minutes later, she found Grace monitoring the microwave and sipping her iced tea. Outside, Cate had already claimed a chair and put her feet up on the railing, legs crossed at the ankles, head thrown back to catch the last rays of sun.

"She looks tired—but more relaxed than the last visit." Eve motioned outside and picked up the glass of soda one of her sisters had poured for her.

"I agree." Grace pulled the gumbo out of the microwave. "I brought corn bread too." She indicated another container on the counter.

Eve began to salivate as she took out a piece. "You're a keeper."

"Remember that the next time we have a disagreement."

"What? Us, disagree?" She grinned at Grace as she took a huge bite of the crumbly yellow square.

"Now and then. Come on. If we don't join Cate soon, she may doze off on us." Grace picked up the bowl of gumbo and moved toward the door.

Eve got there first and pushed it open.

"I was beginning to think you guys had succumbed to the fumes." Cate kept her face angled toward the sun.

"Didn't anyone ever tell you that ultraviolet radiation is harmful to your skin?" Eve took a seat at the table.

"I need the warmth and light right now, okay?"

Eve looked at Grace, who arched an eyebrow.

"Does that mean the undercover gig was tough?" Eve kept her tone conversational.

"It wasn't easy—and it definitely isn't my thing. Straight detective duty for me from now on."

"Want to tell us about it?" Grace plunked a chair halfway between her sisters.

"Nope."

"I guess that ends that discussion, huh?" Grace prodded their big sister's leg with her toe.

Cate didn't respond.

Eve knew better than to push. Once Cate clammed up on a subject, she was as hard to pry open as the humidity-laden windows in this fixer-upper of a house.

"So . . ." Eve ate a spoonful of the gumbo, savoring the spicy flavor. "What brings you two to my doorstep unannounced. Again."

"Do we have to have an invitation?" Grace's eyebrow peaked.

"No—but you usually call first."

"This was a spur-of-the-moment decision. After Cate and I compared notes by phone, we decided we wanted an in-person update on your situation."

"I've been texting you."

"We want details, girl." Grace took a sip of her iced tea. "'Suspect identified and being checked out' doesn't cut it. Who is this guy and what's his beef?"

"I bet Cate's already reviewed a full dossier on the case." Eve spoke around a mouthful of food, mangling her pronunciation. But her sisters had been through this drill often enough to interpret her gibberish.

"Not this go-round." Cate angled toward them. "I just wrapped up my case two hours ago. I barely had time to go home and change before Grace swung by to pick me up. Spill."

"Fine." Eve washed down a mouthful of gumbo and gave them a topline.

"In other words, this guy is mad about his wife working, so

he decided to launch a terror attack and destroy your career?" Grace stared at her.

"That's the theory in a nutshell. Problem is, there's no solid evidence yet to back it up."

"You mean he's still on the loose?" Grace began to bristle.

"Calm down. Brent says they'll make sure he knows he's being watched, and there isn't much chance he'll try anything else once he realizes he's on their radar."

"Brent says that, huh?" Grace's forehead smoothed out and one corner of her mouth twitched.

It was all Eve could do not to roll her eyes.

"Surveillance won't last long—and it will be spotty. We don't have the budget for that." Cate frowned, tapping a finger on the arm of her chair.

"We're hoping this will be over soon."

"It won't be unless more evidence surfaces."

"Aren't you the optimist." Eve made a face at Cate.

"Realist." There was no humor in her sister's demeanor. "I don't like this."

"Chill. I trust Brent. If he says I don't have too much to worry about at the moment, I believe him."

"Let's talk about Brent." A glint of amusement sparked in Grace's hazel irises.

"Let's not." Eve went back to eating.

"Why not?" This from Cate.

"There's nothing to talk about. He's not in the market for a relationship."

"How do you know?" Grace leaned toward her.

"He told me."

"Why did that subject come up?" Cate leaned in too.

Eve stopped eating. "What is this, the third degree?"

"We're just asking a few questions."

"A rose by any other name . . ." Eve waved her spoon at them.

Grace glanced at Cate. "If they were discussing such a personal subject, I'm betting he kissed her."

Eve almost choked on a piece of shrimp.

"I told you." Grace raised her arms in triumph, palms up.

Eve guzzled water as Cate pinned her with a laser look.

"For the record"—Eve paused again to cough—"he did not kiss me."

It had been the other way around—not a detail her sisters had to know.

"I should hope not. That would be totally unprofessional." Cate folded her arms, lips compressed into a thin line.

"Well, poop." Grace sank back in her chair. "You should spread some of that passion you generate for your professional life to a more personal . . . outlet."

"That could happen one of these days." Maybe soon, if Brent got with the program.

"You're not getting any younger, you know."

Eve snorted. "Neither are you . . . or Cate."

Her older sibling held up her hands. "Hey . . . leave me out of this discussion. I have no time for romance."

"Who does?" Grace exhaled. "But don't you both . . . I mean, once in a while when you're alone at night . . . or you see a couple walking arm in arm in the park . . . or you hear a great tune and get in the mood to dance . . . don't you ever wish the right guy would come along?"

"I do." Eve scraped the last of the gumbo from the bottom of the bowl. There was no harm admitting that—especially since she had a suspicion *her* right guy had already put in an appearance.

"Not me. I'm happy with the status quo." Cate slipped on her sunglasses, even though the golden orb had dropped below the tree line. "After work, I can go home, shut the door on the world, and leave my responsibilities on the other side. I don't have to worry about anyone else."

"But there's nobody to worry about *you*, either—except us and Dad." Grace drained her iced tea. "I'm kind of tired of the solo act."

"So go find yourself a boyfriend." Cate crushed her empty can in her fingers, the crinkle of the aluminum adding a discordant note to the measured evensong of the cicadas.

"Easier said than done. I work with dead people, remember."

Cate snickered. "I can see where that could be a problem."

"Plus, guys tend to be freaked out by my profession."

"You could always date a mortician."

"Ha-ha."

"I bet the right guy for you is out there somewhere." Eve touched her sister's hand. "And you have us to keep you company tonight. How long are you staying?"

"Only until morning. I have reports to write tomorrow, and Cate's heading out of town for a few days."

Eve turned to her older sister. "Where are you going?"

"My usual chill-out spot."

"Cuivre River State Park?"

"Yep. A campsite above the lake has my name on it."

"Well . . . as long as we're all together tonight, how about a game of Scrabble here on the deck? I'll make popcorn later."

"The perfect antidote to a busy week. I'm in." Grace moved her chair to the table.

"Me too." Cate scooted over too.

Eve popped in the final bite of corn bread and stood. "I'll be back as soon as I unearth the game from the guest room that's crammed full of my living room furniture."

"Don't hurry. It feels good to sit and veg." Cate settled back in her chair.

After picking up her empty bowl and brushing a few crumbs off the table, Eve retreated inside to scrounge up the game they'd enjoyed since they were old enough to spell. Sometimes the competition was cutthroat—but information had been shared, advice sought, and memories relived over the Scrabble board. Tonight would be no different.

Except she wasn't talking anymore about Brent, no matter how much her sisters probed—for two reasons.

First, it might go nowhere, and second, the two of them had other priorities for the immediate future.

Yet as she wiggled through the furniture in the guest room in search of the game, the threats that had dominated her life these past two weeks receded. After all, they had a credible suspect under surveillance, Brent was working the case hard, and everything had been quiet for several days.

Conclusion? This disturbing chapter in her life was winding down.

And now that her world was settling back onto its axis, what else could possibly happen to disrupt it—or resurrect the danger?

18

DOUG SHUT OFF THE ENGINE of his car but stayed behind the wheel as the garage door rumbled down behind him, snuffing out the Saturday afternoon sun.

The potent scent of the lilies in the extravagant bouquet on the passenger seat swirled around him, churning his stomach.

Maybe this was a mistake.

What if she thought the gesture was silly? Or worse, suspicious. That he was bringing her flowers because he owed her an apology.

Although in truth, he did. Wasn't the romantic notion he'd dreamed up as he'd lain awake in bed last night prompted by guilt? Maybe the rift between them wasn't entirely his fault, but a large portion of it was.

And he didn't want to lose her.

Drawing in a deep breath, Doug picked up the bouquet, slid out from behind the wheel, and went in search of his wife.

He found her in the laundry room, makeup free, hair uncombed, dressed in her oldest sweats as she pulled a load of clothes from the dryer and turned to dump it on the folding table.

She jerked when she spotted him standing in the doorway, and a few of his T-shirts landed in a heap on the floor as one hand fluttered to her chest. "Doug! I thought you were going to be at the office most of the—" Her gaze flicked to the bouquet he was gripping . . . then moved back to his face, her expression morphing from startled to uncertain.

"That was the original plan . . . but I got to thinking about—" He swallowed. Cleared his throat. Shifted his weight. "About us, and how much fun we used to have—and how I miss those early days. They seem like . . . they feel like another life sometimes."

She hugged the armful of laundry tighter to her chest, one of his handkerchiefs drifting to the floor to join the jumbled T-shirts. "To me too."

"So I was thinking . . . why not try to build in more time for us? Leave our responsibilities behind for a few hours every week and focus on all the things that brought us together in the first place." His heart was thumping as hard as it used to during his high school track meets, his respiration just as choppy.

Moisture filled her eyes, and she released an unsteady breath. "Why now?"

Because he'd come too close to throwing away all the years he'd invested in building a life with this woman he'd vowed to love and honor as long as he lived. And that had scared him.

But the impetus for his epiphany was irrelevant. What mattered was that it had happened. That he'd regained his senses before he made a mistake he'd have regretted until his dying day.

So he searched for other words.

"I don't like how we've drifted apart—and I was afraid if that continued, we'd end up on opposite shores, with a huge gulf between us that couldn't be bridged." He exhaled. "I'd like to try and recapture a bit of our dating days, when we were young and carefree . . . and the center of each other's world."

"I'd like that too." She sighed, and her shoulders slumped. "But we're different people now. Life moves on. Circumstances change."

"I know. And along the way, our love got buried under bills and aging parents and health issues and teenage angst and work pressures and deadlines and a thousand other distractions. I'd like to put it back on top of our priority list."

She regarded him for a long moment, still clutching the pile of clothes. "Can I ask you a question?"

A nuance in her tone put him on alert, and he braced. "Yes."

"Did you have an affair?"

His lungs locked. "What?"

"It's a simple question."

No, it wasn't. There was nothing simple about it. But it did deserve a direct—and immediate—answer.

"No! Why would you . . . what have I done to make you think that?" Other than his lunches with Carolyn, he'd never spent one-on-one time with another woman since the day he'd met Alison.

She set the pile of clothes on the table, her throat working. "I don't know. It's just that you've grown . . . distant. When we *are* together, it's so . . . mechanical. And all we ever talk about are schedules and chores and obligations. I thought you might have . . ." She tucked her hair behind her ear and picked a piece of lint off her shorts. "I mean, I know there are beautiful women out there, and I don't have the figure I had twenty years ago . . ." Her voice caught.

"Alison." He closed the distance between them, set the flowers on the folding table beside the clothes, and took her hands. "You were—and are—a beautiful woman. But I didn't marry you for your physical beauty. I married you for the beauty inside—and despite the curves and challenges life has thrown us, I've never stopped loving you."

She searched his face. "I love you too. I always have. But I didn't know how to fix what was broken—or even how to bring it up." She tucked the crown of her head into the curve of his neck and wrapped her arms around him, a familiar, tender posture he'd once savored but had too long taken for granted.

While adrenaline and testosterone provided fleeting moments of excitement, nothing beat the contentment of quiet affection in a relationship built on trust and history.

Thank God he'd realized that before he'd started down a path that would have destroyed what mattered most to him.

"Well, let's work on it together, okay?" He brushed his lips over her forehead and handed her the flowers. "Beginning with this—and dinner tonight at Tony's. I reserved a table for seven."

Her eyebrows rose. "That could break the bank."

"We can afford a splurge on occasion. One of the outcomes of having a fair number of working years under your belt— along with a few extra pounds." He patted his midsection.

"You look perfect to me." She smiled up at him, with all the sweetness he remembered from their long-ago dating days.

"Thank you for seeing me through rose-colored glasses." He leaned down and kissed her. A real kiss, not his usual token lip-brush that was more perfunctory than passionate. "Now why don't you go do whatever you have to do to get ready for tonight while I fold the laundry? What else is on your to-do list this afternoon?"

"Other than putting those flowers in water—nothing that can't wait until tomorrow." Her gaze locked onto his. "You know, I haven't used our Jacuzzi in ages. It seems like a waste of water for one person."

His pulse picked up as he caught her drift. "I think you should indulge."

"I could be a while. Is there anything else we should . . . discuss?"

"Let me consider that while I fold the laundry and take care of the flowers. I'll come find you after I'm done."

"I'll leave the door open." Smiling, she nudged him with her hip and padded barefoot down the hall, throwing him a wink over her shoulder.

A slow grin tugged up the corners of his mouth. Alison's

flirty behavior did far more to fuel his libido than Carolyn's suggestive touches and innuendoes.

Yet he'd come dangerously close to falling under the news-woman's spell. Of succumbing to temptation.

His lips flattened. If the situation with Eve hadn't occurred, who knew how this would have ended?

At least that was one positive outcome from all the trauma.

Plus, he no longer had to worry about whether Carolyn was involved, as he'd feared. The detective had put that concern to rest yesterday with the news that a suspect was under in-vestigation. She was aggressive and ambitious, but she wasn't a criminal.

She was also on her own going forward if she wanted to pursue a career as a radio show host.

Doug dived into the laundry, folding at warp speed.

Come Monday, he'd send her one final text—for closure, so there was no misunderstanding about his position.

And now that he was confident she'd had nothing to do with Eve's problems, he could end that chapter in his life with no lingering doubts or regrets.

———

"Come on, Meg . . . if you felt well enough to go to church, you ought to be able to handle a little cuddling."

As Steve gave her an engaging grin, Meg dropped her purse on the kitchen table. She'd managed to keep him at arm's length since Friday night, but she couldn't feign sickness forever.

Yet reconciling the information Detective Lange had offered with everything she'd believed about Steve was proving difficult.

Who was she supposed to trust?

She bit her lip and studied the man across from her.

If the police had sufficient evidence to charge him, he wouldn't be in their kitchen this morning. He'd be in jail. Or out on bail. And he *had* been sweet to her yesterday—in his own way. Yes, he'd kept his distance to avoid any stench of vomit, but he'd bought her a carryout dinner. High-carb, of course—but it was the thought that counted, right?

Still . . . she wasn't ready to cuddle—or go where that would lead. If he'd targeted Eve or fooled around with Candy, that was a game changer. So until she knew for sure, she had to keep her distance, no matter how hard he pushed.

"I'm not up to it, Steve. Going to church wore me out."

His good humor faded. "So you have time and energy for God, but not your husband."

Guilt pressed in on her, but she pushed it aside. For once in her life, she had to stay strong. If she'd been wrong about Steve . . . if he'd used her . . . sticking her head in the sand was stupid. "Give me another day or two."

His eye twitched, and a muscle clenched in his jaw. "Fine." He shoved his hand into his pocket and pulled out his keys.

"Where are you going?"

"What do you care?" He brushed past her none too gently as he stomped toward the door.

"I care."

"Yeah." He paused on the threshold. "How much?"

"What does that mean?"

His lip curled. "Do you care enough to cuddle for a while?"

She fought back a wave of nausea—this one for real. He was measuring her love by whether she'd bend to his will. Do something she was less in the mood than ever to do. Let him control her.

Was that all their relationship was to him? A power play?

"Well?" He glared at her.

She could feel the color draining from her face.

He frowned. "Are you going to puke again?"

"Maybe." She groped for the back of a chair to steady herself.

Disgust contorted his features. "I'm out of here."

With that, he swiveled away and pushed through the door,

slamming it behind him. Less than thirty seconds later, the garage door rumbled up . . . then down.

He was gone.

Legs quivering, Meg sank into the chair and dropped her head in her hands.

Now what?

If she walked out on him and he was innocent, her marriage would be over—along with the life she'd dreamed of.

But it's been more dream than reality anyway, Meg. You have to accept that. Admit you made a mistake.

A sob caught in her throat, and her vision misted. That was the harsh truth, and she couldn't ignore it any longer. Even without the recent developments, Steve hadn't been the Prince Charming she'd imagined him to be during their courtship.

Far from it.

Her husband was selfish and domineering and manipulative, with a mean streak a mile wide that he hid beneath a veneer of charm when it served his purposes.

No wonder his first wife had divorced him.

Yet how did you reconcile divorce with a till-death-do-us-part vow?

Meg lifted her head and pushed her hair back, staring at the dark clouds gathering outside the kitchen window.

If the detective was wrong about his allegations, might Steve be willing to work on their relationship? Get counseling, perhaps?

That's a pipe dream, Meg. He's not the type to admit he has issues.

The same persistent voice that had warned her eighteen months ago to proceed with caution in this marriage once again offered a prophet-of-doom pronouncement.

Yet this go-round, she wasn't going to ignore it.

Yes, she'd mention her idea to Steve. Give him a chance to work through this with her—assuming he wasn't behind the threats to Eve. That was only fair.

But if he said no? If he refused to change his behavior? This marriage was over.

"Hey, Mom."

Sara Allen double-checked the Tupperware inventory in her trunk as her son spoke. "What?"

"There's the delivery guy I saw the day you picked me up from school and we went to drop off the stuff you sold at that party."

"Uh-huh." Sara did another count of the small containers that could keep two pounds of brown sugar fresh. Always an easy sell at parties, once she demonstrated her personal piece of Tupperware filled with still-soft two-year-old sugar. If she was one container short, she'd have to schedule another trip—and who had time for that?

"He's not wearing a uniform today either."

"Uh-huh."

"How come he didn't wear a uniform at that house? Or drive a truck with the company name on it? Our FedEx guy always does."

"What?" Yes! There it was. The small piece of Tupperware was tucked behind the grocery bags she carried for her trips to Aldi.

"That guy over there. How come he didn't have a truck with FedEx on it?"

She pulled her head out of the recesses of her trunk and turned her attention to Jeremy. At nine years old, her son was a constant font of questions. And he noticed everything, from the color on the outside of flower petals to the number of holes in a button.

Definitely not a skill he'd inherited from her.

"What guy are you talking about?"

"Over there." He pointed to a tall man who was striding

243

toward a vehicle in the fast-food parking lot, a bag with arches on the side in one hand and a large paper cup in the other.

"Why do you think he's a delivery guy?"

"'Cause of that package he left at the house across the street."

"What house? Which street? When?" She shut the trunk. This quick stop for a milkshake to reward Jeremy for sitting in the car half of Sunday afternoon while she delivered Tupperware was taking too long. They had to get rolling.

"You know. That day you picked me up from school at lunchtime and you stopped to deliver an order. 'Member?"

"Yes." That had been two weeks ago Friday. The first week of school, when dismissal had been at noon. Hard to forget that day, since the neighborhood where she'd made the delivery had been on the news that evening, thanks to a fake bomb someone had planted on the doorstep of a radio celebrity.

A fake bomb that had been inside a FedEx package.

Sara froze.

Was it possible . . . could her son have seen the guy who'd left it? Last she'd heard, the police didn't have any suspects.

She squinted after the man, who was approaching a Grand Cherokee. He appeared to be a normal guy. Nothing about him sent up any red flags.

"Mom." Jeremy tugged on her arm. "Don't all those guys drive a truck with FedEx on the side? And aren't they 'sposed to wear a uniform?"

"Uh . . . yeah. I think so." She peered at the license plate. Fumbled for a pen and scrap of paper in her purse. Jotted down the numbers and letters while the guy backed out.

As he drove past, he gave them a quick glance.

She bent her head and pretended to search her purse for her keys.

Jeremy slurped up his shake through the straw, gawking at the car.

"Jeremy—don't watch him."

"Why not?"

"Just don't, okay? Get in the car."

For once he complied without further questions or argument.

She slid behind the wheel, locked the doors, and slipped on her sunglasses, following the progress of the guy in the SUV as he swung onto the main drag with a screech of tires and a heavy foot on the gas.

Now what?

She stuck the key into the ignition, watching until the Cherokee disappeared into the traffic.

"How come we're not moving?" Jeremy continued to suck on his drink.

"Honey . . ." She angled toward him and looked over her shoulder. "Are you sure that's the same man you saw the day I was delivering Tupperware?"

"Uh-huh."

"How do you know? Did you see his face?"

"Uh-huh. He was wearing a baseball cap and sunglasses, but I think a bee was buzzing around him, 'cause he took them off for a minute and swatted the cap through the air. I saw him when he turned toward me. What I noticed most though was how he walked."

"What do you mean?"

"He kind of steps lighter on one foot. Like Dad did last year after he broke his toe. Didn't you notice that?"

"No." She'd hardly noticed her husband's limp, let alone a stranger's.

However . . . if the man's off-kilter gait had been obvious, she'd have spotted it. Whatever abnormality Jeremy had picked up must be very subtle.

"So how come he wasn't wearing a regular uniform that day? I mean, his clothes kind of looked like a uniform, but they weren't. Like, there was no company name on his shirt. And why didn't he have a truck?"

She could think of one answer—but if she shared her suspicions with the police, what were the chances they'd take the comments of a nine-year-old seriously, even if she vouched for his powers of observation and attention to detail?

And did she want to put him through what might be a traumatic experience?

Yet if his testimony could help the police find the lunatic who was planting fake bombs, wasn't it worth the risk?

She rubbed her forehead and sighed.

"Mom? What's wrong?"

At her son's uncertain question, she smoothed out her brow and put the car in gear. "Nothing, honey. Let's get these deliveries done so we can go to the park with Dad this afternoon after he gets home from his meeting at church."

"Yes!"

She caught his exuberant fist pump in the rearview mirror, smiling as she pulled out of the parking spot.

But as soon she left the fast-food restaurant behind, the corners of her mouth leveled out. She had a serious decision to make—but she wasn't making it alone. John needed to weigh in as soon as he got home from his meeting.

And if they both agreed their son's story was credible, their Sunday could end up including a visit from the police.

Yawning, Eve pressed the automatic door opener on her garage and edged around her car toward the lawnmower.

After hours of physical labor on the living room floor, cutting the grass didn't hold much appeal—especially with temperatures hovering around ninety. But thanks to all the rain they'd had last week, her lawn was past due for a haircut.

The job shouldn't take long, though. An hour, tops. By

five-thirty, she'd be done with the chore and have the rest of the evening free. She could kick back with a soda on the deck and relax.

And who knew? It was possible Brent would call. He ought to be back from his camping trip by then.

In fact . . . maybe he'd join her if she asked.

Now wouldn't that be a great cap-off for the weekend?

Grinning, she wheeled the mower out onto the driveway and pulled the cord. Two tries later, it roared to life, and she aimed it toward the grass.

As she walked along behind the self-propelled machine, she scanned the neighborhood. Quiet, as usual. The older folks tended to hibernate if the temperature climbed above eighty-five, and kids today would rather play on their computers or smartphones than indulge their imaginations with outdoor games of make-believe.

Hmm.

Not a bad topic for one of her shows.

She circled the garage. Tired as she was, it would be wise to begin in the back. If she got the hardest part of the job done first, she ought to be able to muster up her flagging energy for the easier home stretch.

Tooling along the property line, she surveyed the adjacent yards. Just as quiet as the front. No neighbors visible . . . yet a faint whiff of barbecue suggested someone had fired up a grill.

That would be an appealing Sunday dinner—but barbecuing for one never seemed worth the trouble.

Those steaks in her freezer weren't improving with age, though. And she'd wiped down the patio furniture an hour ago, deadheaded and watered the flowers in her container garden around the railing, cleaned up the stray kernels of popcorn that had spilled during the Scrabble game with her sisters. It would be a lovely spot for dinner.

Lovelier still, of course, if she was sharing the meal with—

Her step faltered.

Why was a piece of paper attached to the railing of the deck steps? It hadn't been there an hour ago. She'd have noticed it while she was cleaning up.

Slowly she released the control bar on the mower—and silence descended, save for the chatter of a squirrel in the oak tree that shaded the deck.

Pulse accelerating, Eve circled around the mower and crossed to the railing.

A single, folded sheet was thumbtacked to the cedar upright supporting the handrail.

Could it be another message from her tormentor?

Her gut said yes.

But . . . how was that possible?

Unless . . . had Steve eluded whoever was assigned to watch him—or done this in between County surveillance gigs? After all, both Brent and Cate had admitted they couldn't watch him 24/7.

On the other hand, her intuition could be wrong, given how she was jumping at shadows these days, looking for danger around every corner. It was possible the note had nothing to do with the threats. What if it was from a neighbor—Olivia, or Ernie's owners? If that was the case, raising a false alarm would cause unnecessary angst.

Why not check it out herself first? In light of past experience, there wouldn't be any fingerprints anyway. Steve had been careful all along—and he had more incentive now than ever to be extra diligent.

Eve scrubbed her palm on her shorts and worked out the thumbtack with a fingernail. Pulled it free and opened the note.

It was short and to the point.

It was also time to call Brent.

19

Tell your sisters to watch their backs. Don't expect that detective to keep you—or them—safe. If you want this to end, shut up. Now.

Brent reread the note Eve had handed him the instant he walked in the door. Looked at her.

Her arms were folded tight against her chest, and her fair skin had paled, calling attention to the few, faint freckles on her nose that weren't usually detectable.

The latest incident had shaken her.

And he wasn't any too steady, either—especially after the phone calls he'd placed on the heels of his conversation with her while he was driving back to St. Louis.

"Let's sit somewhere."

"I'd offer the living room, but as you can see, it remains furnitureless." She motioned toward the empty space as she walked toward the back of the house.

"Floor turned out great, though."

"Thanks." She indicated the fridge as she entered the kitchen. "Do you want anything to drink? Or a killer brownie made by my eighty-one-year-old neighbor? She may be totally clueless about technology and prefer soaps to heavy discussions about social issues, but she sure knows how to use an oven."

Eve's uncharacteristic chatter was more evidence her nerves had kicked in.

"No thanks."

She continued to the table, perching on one of the bar-height chairs as he dropped the note into an evidence envelope and claimed the seat next to her. "Always prepared, I see."

"Goes with the territory. I keep a few of these in my personal car for emergencies." He ran his hand over the scruff on his chin. "Sorry about this, by the way. I don't shave on these camping trips, and rather than detour to the house after your call, I drove straight here."

"No problem. The bad-boy stubble is intriguing on a good-guy face." She attempted a smile, but the corners of her mouth quivered. "So what's going on? Did you find out if your people have had Steve under surveillance?"

"On and off—but not for the past two hours."

She exhaled. "So he could have put that on my porch." She touched the evidence bag.

"No, he couldn't. He's been in the emergency room for several hours. Car accident."

Eve stared at him. "But I . . . I don't understand. I thought he was . . . isn't he our guy? I mean, you found his DNA in the parking lot. Doesn't that incriminate him?"

"Circumstantial evidence isn't all that helpful, unless there's a preponderance of it. Even then, it's iffy. A competent defense attorney would dismiss it. But I'd bet my bank account he was the slasher."

"Yet he isn't responsible for that." She waved her hand toward the note. "So where does this leave us?"

Nowhere good.

However . . . Eve was already spooked. He'd have to ease into the theory he'd been formulating since the hospital con-

firmed Steve's presence—one that had solidified after he read
the note resting on the table between them.

"It leaves us with a new possibility."

She squinted at him. "I'm not going to like this, am I?"

"No—and neither do I. But we have to consider the facts
and follow them to their logical conclusion."

"Which is?"

"Let's back up first. Based on the window between straight-
ening up your deck and finding the note, Steve couldn't have
left it. It's possible he has an accomplice—but my take on his
personality is that he operates solo. That means this note is
from someone unconnected to him."

He waited, giving her a chance to reach the same conclusion he had.

After a few beats, her eyes widened. "That must mean . . .
could *two* people be targeting me?"

"I'd say that's a credible theory—more so in light of the
written communication you've received. The two notes we
think Steve left are short. One had a misspelling. This is much
longer and the spelling is correct. Also—the one left the night
of the tire slashing said it was the final warning. Why leave
any more messages?"

Eve lost a few more shades of color. "So Steve may not be
behind all the incidents that happened before today."

"Or he could have been—and someone with another ob-
jective is seizing the opportunity to coast in under the radar,
wreak havoc . . . and let him take the fall."

"Wonderful." She tucked her hair behind her ear, inhaled,
and linked her fingers on the table. "Let's switch gears for a
minute and talk about the threat to my sisters. That's never
come up before. And why did this person mention you?"

"I'm assuming he's been monitoring your activities. Watching your house. He's seen me coming and going, and you said
your sisters visit on a regular basis."

Dismay tightened her features. "It was hard enough dealing with the idea that someone was after me, but if I'm also endangering my sisters . . ." Her voice trailed off.

"Let them know about the note. From what I've seen and heard of Cate, she can take care of herself—and your other sister isn't in town."

"She also carries a gun."

"Two points in her favor. She won't be the most convenient target—if this person even follows through on the threat."

Eve lifted one hand and massaged her temples. "Can this get any more complicated?"

Yeah, it could. But why bring that up unless—

His phone began to vibrate, and he pulled it off his belt. Frowned at the screen.

Sarge wouldn't be calling him on a Sunday evening unless they were short of personnel at a major crime scene.

"Give me a minute." He rose, walking away as he spoke.

"Don't hurry on my account. I could use a few minutes to absorb this latest curveball."

He put the phone to his ear and retreated to the foyer as he greeted Sarge—and prepared to beg off an assignment for tonight. The situation with Eve required his immediate and full-time attention. While there was no question Steve had broken the law, the challenge was gathering sufficient evidence to book him.

But the possible involvement of a third party put a whole new spin on this—and added an exponential degree of risk.

Meaning Eve was back in the bull's-eye.

This was getting old.

As the low rumble of Brent's voice drifted into the kitchen from the foyer, Eve stood.

Neither of them might want a soft drink, but she had to

expend some of the restless energy coursing through her—and sitting here waiting for him to return wasn't doing the job.

She should also warn Cate and Grace ASAP in case this guy followed through on his latest threat. Brent could be correct in his assumption that neither of them were at as much risk as she was, but until they nailed her nemesis, she wasn't going to be able to shake her worry.

As she set their drinks on the table, Brent returned, his expression difficult to read.

"Trouble?" She pushed his soda toward him.

He picked it up and took a long swallow. But he didn't sit. "A new development. It seems we may have an eyewitness to the fake bomb delivery."

A surge of hope buoyed her spirits. "That's fantastic news!"

"If it pans out. He's nine."

"Children aren't credible witnesses?"

"Not under the age of seven, usually. Older than that? Depends on the child. This one's closer to ten, which helps." He finished the drink in a couple of long gulps and set the can back on the table. "I'm going to call a colleague of mine, see if he's free for an hour to go along on the interview. I want a second read on whatever we hear. And I have to swing by the office first to prep. Walk me to the door?"

She followed him to the foyer. "I guess this means I'll have to go back into red-alert mode."

"Yes." He paused, his hand on the knob. "I'll swing by and take you to work again tomorrow."

"I can't keep asking you to get up at the crack of dawn to chauffeur me to the station."

"You didn't ask. I offered. If this continues to drag on, we'll regroup and you can think about hiring Phoenix. But I don't want you to break the bank until there's no other option. Seem reasonable?"

"To me, yes. I'm not certain it's a fair deal for you."

"It's more than fair. I'll sleep sounder knowing I'll have your back while you're out and about. You'd actually be doing me a favor." He flashed her a quick grin.

The corners of her lips rose. "When you put it like that . . ."

"Lock up. I'll call you after the interview, assuming we can pull this off tonight. Otherwise, expect me bright and early tomorrow morning."

She caught his gaze. Held it. "Thank you."

His brown eyes warmed, like molten, rich chocolate. "It's my pleasure."

He hesitated for a moment—then took a step back, exited, and followed her walk to the street.

Eve closed the door but remained by the sidelight, watching as he circled the cul-de-sac and drove away. Only after his taillights disappeared did she wander back to the kitchen to face the task at the top of her priority list.

Calling her sisters.

She scrunched up her nose. This was *not* going to be fun.

Aside from the fact that she was worried about *them*, they were both going to morph into uber-protective mode and fixate on the danger to *her*. Cate would push her again to get a concealed carry permit, and Grace would feel compelled to make more long drives into town from her rural digs.

But she already had protection, in the form of a very competent, very handsome detective.

Nevertheless, this case needed to get solved fast so everyone could return to their normal life.

Eve unplugged her cell from the charging cord, sat back at the table, and sighed.

Normal.

That sure sounded appealing about now. Fake bombs and old scandals and slashed tires and threatening notes were the pits.

Yet as she speed-dialed Cate, she had a sinking feeling there was another chapter or two left to play out in the living nightmare that had become her life.

———

"Sorry for the Sunday night callout." Brent locked his car as he joined Colin in front of the Allen house.

"Not a problem. Trish and I finished dinner while you ran to the office. Besides, she's used to this drill."

Brent pocketed his keys. Despite his usual walk-a-wide-circle-around-personal-territory philosophy with colleagues, this was too perfect an opportunity to pass up. "How does she handle the danger of your job?" He kept his tone casual.

"She prays a lot." One side of Colin's mouth rose.

The blow-off answer told him nothing. But that was what you got when you nosed into other people's business.

"You ready to do this?" He nodded toward the house and took a step.

Colin grabbed his arm. "Hey."

Brent turned back. His colleague's humor had evaporated.

"I was more than half serious with that answer. Trish has always relied on prayer. But she also knows I never take unnecessary risks, and that I'm well trained and experienced at this job. She factors all that in. Does she still worry? Yes. On the flip side, I worry about her too. The school where she teaches is in a risky area. In the end, though, you have to let people do what they're called to do and put the rest in God's hands. Once you manage that, life is much less stressful."

That was the longest speech Colin had ever made in his presence—and it seemed to come from the heart.

"Thank you."

"Hey . . . anything to help smooth the path of romance." He winked.

Brent wasn't touching that comment. "You ready?"

"Yeah. But you may want to get rid of the blood." Colin tapped the left side of his own jaw.

"I must have cut myself shaving at the office. I was in a hurry." He fished out a handkerchief and scrubbed at the spot.

"I thought you kept an electric razor there."

"I do."

"In that case, how—"

"Don't ask. Let's do this." He stuffed his handkerchief back in his pocket. No way was he admitting he'd been so distracted since getting Eve's call almost three hours ago that he'd shaved against the grain.

In all his years of law enforcement, that had never, ever happened—and the significance wasn't lost on him.

But he didn't have time to deal with the implications.

A guy who appeared to be in his late thirties answered the door seconds after they pressed the bell.

"John Allen?" Brent held out his hand.

"Yes."

He did the introductions. "Thanks for your call. Every lead is appreciated."

"Happy to help." He lowered his volume. "Jeremy knows you're coming, and he's pumped about the idea of meeting a real-life detective—or two." He encompassed Colin with that comment.

Excellent.

A kid who was excited was more apt to offer useful information than one who was nervous.

"You didn't tell him why we're interested in the man he saw, did you?"

"No. I understood your rationale for wanting to get his input without referencing a particular case. Please . . . come in." He pulled the door wide. "Jeremy and my wife are waiting for you in there." He indicated an archway off the foyer.

Brent crossed to the threshold, Colin on his heels.

A thirtysomething woman rose from the sofa, and the young boy beside her leaped to his feet, eyes dancing with excitement.

Brent repeated the introductions, ending with the nine-year-old. He bent down and held out his hand. "Very nice to meet you, Jeremy."

The boy shook his hand. Did the same with Colin.

"Why don't we all sit?" John moved to the couch.

Brent took a seat beside the sofa, leaving Jeremy bookended by his parents. Colin claimed a side chair that would allow him to observe but was close enough for him to jump in if he chose.

"Jeremy, your mom told us you saw a man today who may be someone we want to question. Can you tell us why you noticed him?"

"Sure." The boy proceeded to repeat the story his mother had relayed during the conference call she and her husband had placed to him two hours ago, ending with the comment about the man's gait—a distinctive identifying characteristic that would be gold in any investigation . . . if it was accurate.

In this case it was, according to one of the detectives he'd spoken with who'd done a shift tailing Jackson. He was the only one who'd noted the very slight hitch in the man's walk—making this kid more observant than most of the highly trained surveillance experts who'd been on the job.

And there was an explanation for Jackson's gait.

After Jeremy's mother had passed on her son's observation, it hadn't taken long to dig into Jackson's background and discover a football injury to his ankle that had ended his high school varsity career but wasn't otherwise debilitating.

"What did the man do that day after he left the FedEx box?" Brent kept his posture relaxed and open.

"He looked around—kinda like he was worried someone was watching him—then walked real fast back down the street, right past our car. But he didn't see me, 'cause I was in the backseat. I thought it was weird he didn't have a truck. I was gonna ask my mom when she got back, but she was talking on her phone and I forgot about it—until I saw the guy again. Did he do something bad?"

"That's what we're trying to find out." Brent opened his small portfolio and extracted the five headshots he'd printed off—including one of Steve. He spread them on the coffee table. "Are any of these people the man you saw at the house that day, and in the parking lot this afternoon?"

The boy wiggled to the edge of the couch and gave the photos a fast sweep. "That one." He pointed at Jackson's photo.

Brent glanced at the boy's mother.

"That's the man we saw today," she confirmed.

The boy leaned closer to study the image. "See how his eyebrows are kinda crooked? I noticed that about him too." He leaned back again. "And I saw stuff that's not in the picture. Like, the day he walked by the car, after he left the box? He was sweating real bad. And he kept scratching his arm. I thought he had a mosquito bite, but it was more than that 'cause he kept doing it."

Brent looked at Colin. That was the same behavior they'd noticed while they'd questioned Jackson.

This was one perceptive kid.

"I think we can wrap up for today. Thank you for your time—and a special thanks to you, Jeremy. People like you help us do our jobs." He took out three cards and handed one to each of the family members. "If we have any other questions, we'll be in touch. And feel free to call if you remember anything else that could be useful."

The boy fingered the card. "I never met a real-life detective before. Can I tell my friends about this?"

"Yes—but why don't you wait until we close this case? For now, it's best if only insiders know what's going on, and we always ask our important sources to cooperate. Can you keep a secret?"

Jeremy's chest puffed out. "Yeah. I'm good with secrets."

"Perfect." Brent rose, and Colin followed his lead.

They said their goodbyes at the door and retraced their steps down the walk.

"Sorry to pull you out on a Sunday night, but I wanted a second opinion on the boy's credibility." Brent dug out his keys.

"Very high, in my opinion. That is one sharp kid. He didn't miss a trick. We could use more like him in our ranks."

"That was my take too—and the timing of his sighting the day of the bomb threat coincides with Jackson's lunch break."

"So what's next?"

"Another conversation with Jackson—and I'll get a warrant for his arrest in the works. I'm also going to talk with any of his coworkers who were on the job the day of the bomb scare. It wouldn't hurt to touch base with Candy, either. That guy has guilt written all over him." Brent shifted into the shade.

"I agree. I'm sold that he's our man for the fake bomb and tire-slashing incidents—but I'm still not convinced he'd have the resources to find the old dirt on Eve Reilly. I also doubt he had anything to do with today's note. We know he couldn't have delivered it personally, and I agree with you he isn't the type to work with a partner on a scheme like this."

"Which brings me back to the theory that someone is using all the threats against Eve as a cover for their own agenda."

"I see where you're coming from with that—but you realize it puts us back at square one. Makes this a whole new investigation."

"Yeah." Brent stopped by the hood of his car and shook his head. "And here I thought we were about to wrap this up."

"You do have one advantage."

"What?"

"This third party made a mistake. They didn't know we

had a suspect in our sights. If they had, they wouldn't have sent that note. So they've outed themselves. It's just a matter of figuring out their identity and their plan."

"Right. Piece of cake." Brent expelled a breath.

One side of Colin's mouth twitched. "There is one other positive spin to this. You'll have a war story about your first case no one will ever be able to match."

"I'd give up bragging rights in a heartbeat to keep Eve safe."

Colin's momentary humor vanished. "I hear you. Been there, done that. I came within an inch of losing Trish during *her* case. Hang in. We'll get this figured out. See you at the office tomorrow." With a wave, he returned to his car.

Brent opened his door, slid behind the wheel, and started the engine.

First priority? Get an update on Jackson's condition, see if he was able to handle an interview. With all the evidence they'd compiled, it was possible the man would cave.

A long shot, but it could happen.

Yet a huge question remained.

Who else was targeting Eve—and why?

Dan SUN., SEPT. 9, 8:35 P.M.

Ready to go. Pick up plans at place discussed.

Al SUN., SEPT. 9, 8:36 P.M.

2night?

Dan SUN., SEPT. 9, 8:36 P.M.

Yes.

Al   SUN., SEPT. 9, 8:37 P.M.

Heading out now.

Dan   SUN., SEPT. 9, 8:37 P.M.

Good luck—and ditch phone.

Al   SUN., SEPT. 9, 8:38 P.M.

Will do. All power to everyone.

20

He wasn't going to show for their Monday lunch.

Biting back a curse, Carolyn watched the minute hand on her watch flick to 11:45, then finished off the glass of wine she'd ordered at the bar.

Doug must have been serious about that kiss-off text he'd sent her early this morning. But her placating follow-up note, her plea for one more lunch to talk through his decision, should have smoothed out the waters. It would have worked with any other man.

Yet the mentor on whom she'd pinned all her hopes hadn't succumbed to her charm this go-round.

So much for all the groundwork she'd laid, the months she'd spent cultivating a relationship with the man she'd been certain would eventually open doors for her in radio.

But why had he walked away? How had her acting skills failed her?

She crossed her legs and watched the new arrivals push through the door, as an eager Doug used to do. Yes, she'd been a mite too aggressive when Eve's spot had been in jeopardy, but they could have gotten past that.

There was more to this breakup than her faux pas.

She tapped her nails on the bar.

Maybe Doug still suspected her of inside knowledge about the on-air phone call Eve had received.

Maybe he even thought she was involved in the other incidents.

If he did, was he thinking about going to the authorities with his suspicions? Could that inclination be behind his sudden case of cold feet about their relationship?

"Would you like another glass of wine?" The bartender lifted her empty stem.

What she'd like and what she was going to have were two different things.

"No." She dug out her wallet and set a ten on the counter. No more alcohol for her today. Her task this afternoon required a clear head.

Thank goodness she had an interview scheduled for that article on South Side carjackings and wasn't expected back at the office. A quick phone call could delay the meeting for an hour and a half while she took care of other, more pressing personal business.

She left the restaurant, heading for her car rather than the office.

Eighteen minutes later, she pulled into her condo.

The material on Eve was well hidden, but the cops would tear the place apart if Doug managed to convince them she was a suspect and they secured a search warrant. Best to dispose of it ASAP. It had served its purpose—though the outcome hadn't been close to what she'd envisioned.

Carolyn bolted the door behind her and hurried to the kitchen. Riffled through the boxed dinners stacked in her freezer. Pulled out the chicken tetrazzini.

After working her fingernail under the re-glued flap, she eased it open and removed the notes she'd stored inside, plus the contact information for the wife of the man who'd led Eve on. A real nutcase . . . but more than happy to dish about her husband's wayward eye with a sympathetic listener during their "chance" meeting at a charitable event.

That was one of the beauties of being a reporter. You knew how to delve into people's backgrounds, find connections, locate sources, search for dirt. And if you dug deep enough, you usually found it—or something that could be spun to suggest dirt.

Not that it had helped her in this case.

She tossed the empty package in her recycle container and moved to her home office. One by one, she fed the sheets into her shredder.

That task completed, she dumped the minced remnants from the bin into a plastic grocery bag, tied the top, and re-trieved her purse. All she had to do was dispose of this in a trash can at a fast-food place en route to her interview. The burner phone loaded with the voice-altering software had been discarded days ago. No one would ever be the wiser about the source of that call.

And after work tonight, she'd shift focus.

St. Louis had never been her first choice as a home base, but you went where the job openings were. With all the experi-ence she'd gained here, however, she could ditch this town in a heartbeat. It wasn't the best market for journalists anyway. Only her promising affiliation with Doug had kept her here.

But there were glitzier cities where she could thrive, bigger fish to cozy up to who could help boost her career to the next level. And her resume was going to be crossing their desks within forty-eight hours. She didn't need Doug Whitney to pave the way, or Eve Reilly's slot to open up, in order to get her chance.

All she needed was the right connection—and somewhere out there, he was waiting to fall under Carolyn Matthews's spell.

———————————————

The detective was here.

Meg scrambled to her feet as Brent Lange, accompanied by the colleague who'd come with him to their house, entered Steve's hospital room. A shaft of midmorning light peeking through the canted blinds whited out her vision, and she shaded her eyes.

"Good morning." After directing that greeting toward her, Detective Lange transferred his attention to her husband, who was propped up with several pillows while his cast-enclosed left ankle rested on another pillow, a white bandage covering the gash on his forehead.

Steve glowered at him. "What do you want now?"

"We have a few more questions."

"I don't feel like answering them."

"Nevertheless, we intend to ask them. We can do that here, this morning—or we can reconvene at the station after you're released this afternoon."

"I'm not talking to you again until I get an attorney. This is harassment."

"Questioning a suspect isn't harassment."

"So now I'm a suspect?"

"You've been one all along. The difference today is that we have a witness who saw you leave the package at Eve Reilly's house—and a warrant for your arrest is in process."

Meg's stomach dropped to her toes. So much for all her prayers last night that the allegations about Steve were wrong.

Her husband's complexion grew more pasty. "You're bluffing. You don't have a witness."

"Yes, we do. He came forward yesterday, and his testimony is credible."

Meg's legs began to shake, and she sank back into the chair she'd occupied most of the night.

"I also spoke with a few of your coworkers this morning." The other detective joined the conversation. Colin something. "Including the guy who picked up lunch for you at a Subway near his house the day of the bomb incident. Which leaves you unaccounted for during that hour."

"And I touched base with Candy." Detective Lange sent her a brief glance. There was no missing the sympathy that flared in his eyes for a nanosecond before he turned back to her husband. "She confirmed you'd spent an hour with her the night of the tire slashing—but there's a significant gap between the time you gassed up and your arrival at her place."

Meg stared at Steve.

He'd lied about the waitress too.

As if sensing her scrutiny, he looked over at her. "Why don't you go get a cup of coffee?"

It wasn't a request.

But thanks to his injury, he was in no position to make her do anything.

Nor would he be ever again.

"I'm staying."

He glared at her, but she straightened in her seat—even though she felt like curling into a ball and sobbing. Because all at once, her course was clear.

When the detectives left, she would too—and she wasn't coming back.

"Let me tell you how this is going to play out." Detective Lange moved to the foot of the bed and folded his arms. "As soon as you're released, we'll be booking you on multiple counts."

"That's crazy! Everything you have is circumstantial—and witnesses aren't always reliable."

"This one is credible."

Steve's lips thinned. "I'm not talking anymore without a lawyer."

266

"Your choice. But if you cooperate, you improve your chance of a plea bargain. Keep that in mind."

After glancing her direction, the two men disappeared out the door.

Meg stood, drawing Steve's attention again. Beneath his veneer of bravado, he looked scared—and she almost felt sorry for him.

Almost.

But he'd brought this on himself. On them.

She picked up her purse and clenched the strap to steady her shaking fingers. "We're done."

"You're leaving me?"

"Yes."

"What about those vows we took?"

"I don't think the 'for worse' part includes deception, cheating, manipulation, and law-breaking."

"The evidence they have won't hold up in court."

"So you're admitting you threatened Eve? Left the fake bomb, slashed her tires?"

"I'm not admitting anything."

"What about Candy?"

He studied her for a moment. Shrugged. "I made a mistake, okay? But she doesn't mean anything to me. And they can't put me in jail for having a fling. That's not a crime."

Despite the rays of sun warming her back as she faced him, a cold chill rippled through her. "No—but it's a sin."

He snorted. "Don't get all religious on me. You're not perfect either, you know."

"I know—and you've reminded me of that on a regular basis for the past eighteen months. But I would never, ever cheat on you. Or do anything illegal—or immoral." She crossed to the door, hoping her shaky legs would support her.

"So that's it? You're going to walk out on an injured husband in his hour of crisis?"

"You wouldn't be injured if you hadn't been driving reck-lessly. I heard the officers talking in the ER after they brought you in. This"—she swept a hand over the bed—"and every-thing else is your fault. Not mine. My lawyer will be in touch."

As soon as she hired one.

Turning her back, Meg walked out the door.

But once she reached the hall, she leaned against the wall and tried to shift her numb brain into gear.

Besides finding an attorney, she had to pack up her belong-ings and get out of the house before Steve was released from the hospital. Thank heaven she had a job, and money to pay for an apartment until whatever lawyer she found could sort through the mess and divvy up the assets.

What a sad end to the fairy tale life she'd envisioned.

Her vision misted, and she sniffed. She should have known this wouldn't end well.

Nothing in her life had ever been a fairy tale.

"Are you okay?"

At the question, she blinked and straightened up. One of the nurses had stopped beside her, faint furrows denting her brow.

Okay?

Not even close.

But she couldn't admit that to a stranger.

"Yes. Just . . . um . . . thinking about everything that has to get done."

The woman offered her a sympathetic nod. "I hear you. Ill-ness and accidents can overwhelm families. If you need any assistance, our social services department can recommend several resources."

"I appreciate that, but I'll be fine."

Meg waited until the woman walked away. Then, straight-ening her shoulders and lifting her chin, she continued down the hall toward the elevator.

She *would* be fine. This setback wasn't going to destroy her. She wouldn't let it.

Maybe she wasn't as smart or pretty or dynamic as Eve Reilly, but watching her high school acquaintance in action these past few months—and especially during the recent trauma—had been inspiring.

If you approached life with a can-do attitude, stuck with your principles, and stood up for yourself and what you believed in, life could be good.

Beginning today, she was going to follow in Eve's footsteps.

And thanks to the radio station job, she had the financial wherewithal to walk away from Steve—and find her own happy ending.

Eve stood on tiptoe and felt around on the top shelf of her kitchen cabinet. Huffed out a breath.

Where had she put that box of little-used spices? Her dolmathes wouldn't be the same without the distinctive hint of dill that gave her mother's recipe its extra zing.

Between a blog post that was fighting her every step of the way, an air conditioner that was making odd noises, and now a key spice gone missing, this Tuesday had been a bust.

She stretched further—only to jerk back as the pulsing beat of "I Won't Back Down" erupted from her cell on the counter.

Sweet mercy!

Grabbing the edge of the cabinet to steady herself, she coaxed her lungs to kick back in. If Brent and his cohorts didn't wrap up this case soon, her nerves would be shot.

She picked up the phone, skimmed the screen, and greeted Grace.

"Am I interrupting anything?" Her sister seemed a tad distracted.

"No. I'm on a spice search."

"A what?"

"Spice search. I'm trying to find my dill for Mom's dol-mathes recipe. I haven't made that one in a while, and I thought I'd whip up a batch for us when you and Cate come to dinner tomorrow."

Two seconds ticked by. "I didn't know we were invited for dinner tomorrow."

"You weren't. But I talked to Cate earlier, and she mentioned she might drop by. She also said you were going to be in town for a forensic seminar. Rather than have you two show up with food in hand again, I decided to feed *you* this visit."

"Is your detective going to be there too?" Her sister was fully engaged in the conversation now.

"No. Why would he be?"

"Well, he's doing chauffeur duty for you. It would be a hospitable gesture to invite him to join us."

And subject him to the third degree from her sisters?

Not a chance.

"Considerate of you to think of that—but plan on a three-some. So what's up?"

As if she had to ask.

Her two sisters had been tag-teaming phone calls since she'd told them on Sunday about the twist her case had taken. While neither had seemed concerned about the threat to themselves, they had *not* been thrilled to hear that there could be a second person targeting her.

But two calls a day from each of them?

Overkill.

Now another in-person visit.

Much as she loved them, they had their own lives—and impinging on their free time wasn't fair.

"I had kind of a gruesome case today—but I doubt you want to hear about it." Humor lurked in Grace's inflection.

Eve put her hand on her stomach. "Gruesome is more than sufficient detail. Anything else going on?"

"Nope. How is it on your end?" Her sister's casual tone didn't fool her one bit.

"If you're asking whether I've received any more communication from my harasser, the answer is no."

"Any updates from your detective since we last talked?"

"He isn't my detective." Yet. "And I promised during our last chat to let you know if there were any developments. That was a mere seven hours ago, by the way."

"I know—but I like to hear your voice. You have an issue with that?"

Eve leaned back against the counter. "No. But you and Cate have full plates. You don't have to keep checking in with me. I'm in excellent hands." She cringed. Poor choice of words.

"In a literal or rhetorical sense?"

Of course her sister would home in on her faux pas.

"Very funny."

"I'm serious. Cate texted me a photo of Brent Lange. Whoa! Hot guys like him never enter my orbit—not that I'd want to replicate your meeting strategy, you understand. There have to be easier . . . oops. Call coming in. I have to take this."

"Go. I'm fine. I'll see you tomorrow. Come hungry."

"Never a problem. Watch your back."

The line went dead.

Eve set her cell back on the counter and went in search of the stepladder to chase down the elusive dill. It had probably gotten pushed to the back of the cabinet.

But her mind wasn't on cooking. It was on her sister's suggestion that she invite Brent to join them.

Too bad Cate and Grace were so nosey. If she did ask him to dinner, they wouldn't give him a moment's peace the whole evening.

As soon as this nightmare was over, though, he was going

to be first on her guest list. She'd make her killer moussaka—and she would *not* invite her sisters.

Brent could very well drag his feet about accepting her invitation, given his conviction that he wasn't romance material. But nothing could be further from the truth.

And proving that to him was going to be her number one goal the instant the person or persons intent on wreaking havoc in her world were safely behind bars.

21

YOU DON'T LOOK like a happy camper on this bright, beautiful Thursday."

Brent leaned back in his desk chair and scowled as Colin entered. "Jackson lawyered up—and clammed up. He's out on bail."

"Who'd he hire?"

When Brent shared the name of the attorney, Colin groaned. "He doesn't play nice."

"I know. I ran into him while testifying during a few trials. With this case, he'll discredit all the circumstantial evidence in the first ten minutes—and I hate to think what he'll do to Jeremy's testimony if the boy ends up on the stand. Assuming we get that far."

Colin sat. "He'll do his best to punch holes in it, that's a given. But on the bright side, Jackson can't evade the reckless driving charge. There are too many witnesses."

"His wife also walked out on him. He did let that slip during our interview here, before his attorney shut him down."

"So there's some justice, at least."

"Not the kind I'm after."

"May I offer a suggestion?" Colin linked his fingers over his stomach. "For all intents and purposes, the threat from Jackson is over. He'd have to be a lunatic to try anything else—as I'm sure his lawyer has counseled him. Step back and let the prosecutor try to get a conviction. In your shoes, I'd focus my energy on finding out who wrote the last note to Eve. Did your canvass of the neighborhood turn up anything?"

"No. None of the neighbors saw anyone suspicious on Sunday afternoon." Brent stood and began to pace.

"It could have been a one-off perpetrated by a sicko who got a vicarious thrill by tagging on to the string of threats. Eve may never hear from him again."

Colin's theory was plausible. Copycat crimes weren't uncommon, and there were people who jumped into the fray simply to get a taste of the action.

But that wasn't what was going on here.

Someone else was targeting Eve—and it wasn't for fun and games. The danger was real . . . and getting closer with every hour that ticked by. He could feel it in his bones.

"You're not buying that theory, are you?" Colin tapped his index fingers together, watching him.

"It's possible—but my gut is telling me to be on red alert."

"Then go with your gut. If you're wrong, worst outcome is you get a few gray hairs. If you're right, you'll be more prepared to handle whatever's coming."

"Problem is, I don't know where to go from here." It killed him to admit that, but it was the truth—and Colin wasn't the type to rib him about being a rookie. "The note came back clean from the lab, no one saw the person who left it, and the threat is too vague to address."

"Those are the negatives. On the plus side, the note was left four days ago and nothing else has happened, correct? No one's bothered Eve or her sisters or you?"

"No—but that doesn't mean they won't. And I don't want to sit around waiting for this guy's next move."

"You may not be. Did you see the memo Sarge sent out an hour ago?"

"No."

"Check your email. There could be trouble brewing at a political event this weekend. FBI intel says that anti-government Antifa factions may turn out in force. Groups from several states are apparently planning to crash the venue to demonstrate and disrupt. County is going to have a large uniformed police presence."

"How are we involved?" Brent sat again. Most situations of this type were handled by patrol officers, not detectives.

"We're on standby in case the situation goes south and extra hands are needed to investigate."

"When is this happening?"

"Saturday."

"Where?"

Colin named the county park. "Knowing how those groups operate, this could get dangerous. You may want to read the memo and the backup material, just in case."

"Yeah." Brent swiveled toward his desk. "But Antifa is a known quantity. They're easy to identify if they go black bloc, with those dark hoods and masks—and that attire is also a tip-off to prepare for violence. I'd rather deal with them than this shadowy figure targeting Eve, whose appearance and methods are a mystery."

"I agree with you in principle—but I clashed with Antifa folks once. It wasn't pretty. Let's hope they're content to carry signs and chant slogans, and that they leave the black garb at home."

"I hear you."

"You still on chauffeur duty for Eve?"

"Through tomorrow. We'll have to regroup after that. Phoenix is a possibility for security."

"Excellent resource. Also pricey."

"That's why I've tried to pick up the slack while the case was hot."

Colin booted up his laptop. "Maybe something will break in the next couple of days."

"I hope so."

Brent opened his email to read the memo from Sarge about the Antifa situation—but his mind kept wandering to Eve. As far as he could see, given the lack of clues to follow on this latest threat, it would take another incident to generate new leads that could help them identify the most recent note writer.

But much as he wanted a break in the case, the prospect of another episode that could put Eve in the line of fire curdled his stomach.

It was possible, as Colin had suggested, that whoever was behind the latest note was nothing more than a thrill seeker. Someone who'd fade away once the press sniffed out the news that Jackson was a serious person of interest in the case.

Much as he wished that was how this would play out, however, every instinct in his body was screaming that another incident was about to happen.

And that this one could be deadly.

"Hey, Buzz, you wanna stop in at Bubba's for a beer?" Suds took off his painter's cap and wiped the sleeve of his T-shirt across his forehead as they walked toward the company truck. "A cold one—or two—would hit the spot after working in an oven all day. It's not supposed to be this hot in September."

"Can't tonight." Buzz stopped at the truck and set down the drop cloths he'd been carrying. He had more important things to do than spend an hour guzzling beer with a moron.

"Hot date?" Suds grinned as he repositioned the eight-foot ladder he was lugging and slid it into the truck.

"Nope. Errands to run."

"Can't they wait? Crip and most of the other guys will be there."

Not a selling point.

"Drink one for me." He loaded up the empty paint cans, and Suds gave him a hand with the tarps. Driving his own wheels to the job site today had been a smart choice.

"You'll miss out on the fun—and the babes." Suds waggled his eyebrows.

Buzz tried not to grimace. "Maybe next time."

"Your loss."

Hardly.

"I'll see you tomorrow."

"Yeah. If we're lucky, we'll finish up here early. I wouldn't mind getting a jump on the weekend."

Neither would he.

But while Suds probably had more party plans in mind, he had important work to do.

All at once, his fingers began to tingle—and Buzz froze. What was with the sudden case of nerves? He was prepared for the task ahead. Everything would be fine.

He took a calming breath and deposited the last of his painting paraphernalia in the truck. "Enjoy your beer."

"Count on it." Suds smacked his lips.

With a lift of his hand, Buzz hurried to his car, slid behind the wheel, and headed home.

Although his stomach began growling as he parked in front of his apartment and ascended the stairs to his second-floor unit, food could wait.

A final gear inspection was his top priority this evening. Everything should be in order, but in case he'd missed an item, it would be helpful to identify it tonight. Running around tomorrow after work to handle a last-minute equipment glitch would be distracting. He wanted nothing on his mind after tonight but the big event.

Buzz dropped his lunch pail on the counter in the kitchen, continued to his bedroom, and pulled out his list. One by one, he laid the items on the bed, ending with the black hood that had seen its share of marches and demonstrations.

But never had it been as critical as it would be this weekend.

He gave the clothing and equipment one final survey. Double-checked it against his list. Nodded. Come Saturday, he'd be ready to roll.

Now he could relax for the evening. Eat dinner, take a shower, read.

And while his high school acquaintances were wasting their weekend with babes and booze, he'd be making an important contribution to the cause. One he'd never get credit for—but that was okay. The hood would keep him out of jail so he could continue the good fight.

Besides, this wasn't about one man's glory. It was about securing power for everyone.

He strolled toward the kitchen, a hum of excitement thrumming through his veins. One person would know what he'd done, though—and if he pulled this off, more responsibilities would come his way. More chances to contribute on a large scale. All he had to do was show up, stay cool, and wait for the perfect moment.

Ten seconds later, in the chaos that followed, he'd disappear into the crowd.

And there would be one less voice proclaiming the greatness of America's corrupt social, economic, and political system.

―――――――

"Thanks for being such a trouper all week." Eve glanced at Brent as he swung the car onto her cul-de-sac. "Getting up at the crack of dawn isn't for the fainthearted."

"It wasn't an issue. I've put in a fair number of odd hours

during my career." He slowed as he approached her driveway. "Now that Friday's here, let's talk about the weekend."

Drat.

She'd been hoping he wouldn't ask about her plans. Her Saturday schedule wasn't going to thrill him—and she was done imposing on him for bodyguard duty. But there was no avoiding his question.

"I'm giving a speech tomorrow."

He frowned. "Why didn't I know about this until now?"

"Because it's no big deal. Everything's been normal all week. Whoever left that last note must have decided not to take any further action—and as you told me yourself, Steve won't try anything else or his lawyer will have a fit. I feel perfectly safe."

A bit of a stretch . . . but she wasn't going to walk around in fear either. She had a life to live—and commitments to keep.

"Tell me about the speech. Who, what, when, where, why." He pulled into her driveway and set the brake.

"Wow. You got very official on me all of a sudden." She grinned and nudged him with her elbow.

He didn't smile back. "Just give me the details."

"Fine." In staccato fashion, she rattled off the particulars about the Young Republicans event and her keynote address.

A muscle clenched in Brent's jaw, and he closed his eyes. "That is *not* what I wanted to hear."

"Why? What's going on?"

He looked at her. "Did you know there could be an Antifa presence at that gathering?"

"Yes. The president of the group called to tell me he'd been alerted to that possibility. I wasn't thrilled, but he said they were beefing up security. They're even sending a car for me. They'll whisk me in, I'll do my thing, they'll whisk me out. Piece of cake. Otherwise I would have called Phoenix."

Brent's taut features said he wasn't buying her assurance—

and his next comment told her why. "County is gearing up for trouble."

Despite a sudden kink in her stomach, she did her best to maintain a placid expression. "What kind of trouble?"

"We don't know. But that's a volatile, unpredictable group. There will be a large law enforcement presence."

"As a precaution, right? There haven't been real threats of disruption, have there?"

"Antifa doesn't always tip its hand. FBI intel suggests quite a few of the groups aligned with the movement have encouraged members from our region to attend. It's being touted on their websites and message boards. What will happen after they all convene is anyone's guess." The twin furrows on his brow deepened. "Have you ever had any direct contact through your show or on your blog with anyone who's identified themselves as a member?"

"No—but many of my critics could fall into that camp. I stand for everything they abhor. Left to their own devices, they'd abolish the government and Constitution, which they believe are inherently racist. They'd do away with capitalism because they think it enslaves people. And they're convinced our political system is fundamentally corrupt."

"They're also not afraid to engage in violence or property destruction to achieve their goals—and some have no compunction about killing people who defend the system. They think of it as self-defense for the world. That's why the FBI classifies their activities as domestic terrorism."

"I understand all that."

"Yet you didn't think it was important to mention to me that you were speaking at an event where they may have a strong presence?"

"The president of the group has me covered—and I'm not going to hijack your weekend. You've already gone above and beyond with my case."

His eyes narrowed. "What time is the speech?"

"One o'clock."

"When are they picking you up?"

"Ten. There's a private meet and greet at eleven, followed by lunch, then the speech. I should be home by two-thirty."

"I'll join the motorcade. I'd say cancel the car, but let's leave it in case I get called in."

Her heart warmed—but her independent streak reared its head. "Brent, I don't want you to—"

"Eve." He killed the engine and turned to her. "Humor me. Other than an early run with Adam, my Saturday is open. If I'm not with you, I'll be at home worrying."

After a beat, she sighed. How could she refuse after that admission? "Fine. I accept—if you'll let me treat you to Starbucks afterward."

"Not necessary."

"I'll be in the mood for a Frappuccino, and I hate to drink alone."

He cocked his head. "Is it a deal breaker on me riding shotgun if I turn down your invitation?"

"Yes."

One side of his mouth twitched. "You drive a hard bargain."

"Seems like a fair arrangement to me—I get a bodyguard, we both get a treat. Are you in?"

"Yeah. I'm in." He pulled his key out of the ignition. "I also have another piece of news for you. During your program I got word the story's about to break on Jackson. His attorney tried to contain it as long as he could, but the news hounds sniffed it out. Headquarters got a call this morning from two media outlets to confirm. A brief written statement will be released within the hour."

"There's no downside to that, is there?"

"Not from your standpoint. In fact, there may be an upside. This may deter your latest harasser. If he was coasting on Jackson's coattails, trying to get a vicarious thrill, that gig is up. He knows if he strikes again we'll be searching for another suspect."

"I'll take that as a very positive way to end the week. And it would also suggest there's less justification than ever for you to spend your Saturday afternoon listening to a boring speech. The danger may be past." She released her seat belt.

"May be isn't good enough. I'm not letting my guard down until I have definitive proof this is over. Sit tight while I get your door."

He slid out of the car without waiting for her to respond. After giving the neighborhood a practiced sweep while he circled the Taurus, he pulled her door open.

Eve joined him on the pavement. "I could get used to this curb service."

"Anytime." He hitched up one corner of his mouth and took her arm as they walked to her door. "What's on your calendar for the rest of the day?"

"Catch up on my blog, practice my speech, do a load of laundry." She felt around in her purse for her keys.

"So you're not venturing out anywhere?"

"No."

He waited while she opened her door. "I'll call you tonight."

"I'd like that." She dropped her key back in her purse but didn't enter. Now that her case appeared to be waning, why postpone her dinner-for-two invitation? "I'm planning to make moussaka next weekend. Assuming all remains quiet, will you join me? It's my mom's recipe, and she was a fantastic cook."

Despite the obvious conflict in his eyes, his tone was definitive. "We've already had this discussion. I'm not the best guy for you, Eve. For any woman."

"I disagree. You may believe that's true, but—"

He reached past her, twisted the knob, and pushed the door open.

Her alarm began beeping.

"If you don't shut that off fast, you'll have a patrol car barreling down your street."

She expelled a breath. "I can't believe you did that. This conversation isn't over, you know."

"It is for today."

"Chicken."

"Sticks and stones . . ." He gave her a gentle push toward the house. "I'll talk to you later."

Making no attempt to hide her annoyance, she swiveled around, shut the door in his face, and scurried toward the kitchen.

She disarmed the alarm with four seconds to spare and dashed back to the front door. Only Brent's taillights were visible in the distance.

Well, shoot. Getting the man to talk about their relationship was going to be a challenge.

But challenges had never daunted Eve Reilly. So over their Frappuccinos after her speech tomorrow, she'd tackle this one head-on.

Because after almost a week of normalcy, she'd be willing to bet that whoever had put her in his sights last weekend would cease and desist once the suspicions about Steve became public knowledge—if he hadn't already.

After all, as Brent had noted, why would someone who was using Steve as a cover continue to bother her knowing that would put them on law enforcement's radar? Only a person with a far more sinister intent than Meg's husband had had would risk exposure by persisting in his harassment.

And the odds of that had to be small.

Didn't they?

Al   FRI., SEPT. 14, 12:10 P.M.

Did u c news re Jackson?

Dan   FRI., SEPT. 14, 12:11 P.M.

Yes. Following story.

Al   FRI., SEPT. 14, 12:11 P.M.

We waited 2 long.

Dan   FRI., SEPT. 14, 12:12 P.M.

No. Working on plan. U will b covered.

Al   FRI., SEPT. 14, 12:12 P.M.

How?

Al   FRI., SEPT. 14, 12:15 P.M.

U there?

Al   FRI., SEPT. 14, 12:18 P.M.

U still there?

Dan   FRI., SEPT. 14, 12:20 P.M.

Will make sure Jackson has no alibi. Carry on as planned.

22

YOU GOT THE SHORT STRAW for this one too, I see."
As Colin greeted him, Brent finished signing the crime
scene log, ducked under the police tape, and joined his colleague in front of the abandoned warehouse. "Yeah—and a
murder investigation wasn't in my Friday afternoon plans."

"I doubt it was in his, either." Colin hooked a thumb toward
the tarp-covered body visible a few yards inside the door.

Right.

Perspective check.

"What do we know?"

"Only what the responding officer observed."

Brent listened as Colin filled him in, sifting through the
facts. "Could be a drug deal gone bad."

"Has all the earmarks. We'll know more after Hank weighs
in." He motioned to a Crime Scene Unit van executing a fast
left into the parking lot with a slight screech of tires.

"How do you know that's Hank?" Brent squinted at the
windshield, but the glare hid the driver's identity.

"He's a lousy driver. Always takes his corners too sharp.
He also waits until the last second to hit the brakes."

As if on cue, a squeal pierced the air as the van came to an
abrupt halt.

285

A few moments later Hank exited the vehicle, marched over, and gave them both a visual frisk. "You two didn't mess with my scene, did you?"

"Wouldn't think of it." Colin folded his arms, his tone mild.

"Right." The CSU tech snorted, his unruly gray hair flapping in the breeze. As Brent transferred his weight from one foot to the other, Hank turned his attention to him. "Do I know you?"

"Brent Lange." He held out his hand. "Detective now, but patrol for most of my career."

"Knew I'd seen you around." He gave him a firm shake. "In case Colin didn't fill you in, I don't like interlopers at my crime scenes."

The man was living up to his reputation as brusque, eccentric—and territorial.

"Understood."

"You can look, but don't touch."

"Got it."

"Good." Hank gave the scene a sweep. "Lacey here yet?"

"No." Colin jumped back in. "Sarge said she was tied up at another scene but should be here within the hour."

"Can't do much around the body until the medical examiner's office weighs in." Hank shouldered past them, grumbling under his breath.

Colin watched the tech disappear into the warehouse and rolled his eyes. "Talk about a curmudgeon."

"I only saw him from a distance as a patrol officer—but I heard he was top-notch at his job."

"He is. That's why we all put up with him." Colin tipped his head. "You look tired. That crack-of-dawn chauffeur gig must be catching up with you. Any new leads?"

"No."

"You pulled a tough one for your first case. But you did meet Eve." The corners of Colin's lips rose.

286

Brent jammed his hand in his pocket. How was he supposed to respond to that loaded comment? Yes, he was glad he'd met her—but despite her confidence that he could be the kind of man she wanted . . . and her assurance she could handle the dangers of his job . . . he was nowhere close to convinced moving forward would be in her best interest.

"Hey." Colin's amusement vanished. "Sorry. I must have read too much into the situation."

Why not be honest with his colleague? Colin had opened up to him not long ago—and he could use all the guidance he could get.

"No, you didn't. Your take is spot-on. There are just some . . . issues."

"Other than the danger-on-the-job one we talked about?"

"Yeah."

"You want my advice? Don't overthink it or create complications where they don't exist. If you like the woman, go with your gut. Or, as my wife would more genteelly put it, follow your heart." He motioned toward the warehouse. "Let's do a walk-through."

It took Brent a second to switch gears. "Will Hank be okay with that?"

Colin grinned. "No. But we'll put on booties and gloves and keep our distance." He struck off for the building.

Brent fell in behind him. The crime scene deserved his full attention until they were done with their assessment.

But after that, he'd have to give Colin's advice serious deliberation. Eve was sure to bring up the subject again tomorrow over their cold drinks, and he couldn't keep putting her off.

In the interim, though, a few prayers for guidance—like a definitive sign from above—wouldn't hurt. Because with every encounter, her appeal grew . . . and the thought of letting her go was getting harder and harder to stomach.

Meaning he had to come to a reasoned decision soon, before the left side of his brain shut down.

An imminent possibility if he continued to fall for the lovely radio personality at his current breakneck pace.

Life stunk.

Steve eased his recliner back and stared at the ceiling.

His broken ankle was aching.

Meg had cleared out, so there was no one to wait on him.

His high-priced attorney wasn't making any guarantees about getting him off the hook, thanks to a stupid nine-year-old witness. The man had already broached the idea of a plea bargain.

And Candy had dumped him.

As Friday nights went, this one sucked.

He didn't even have much food in the house. A can of soup would have to suffice for dinner—unless he ordered a takeout pizza. That wasn't—

The landline began to ring.

He started to struggle to his feet. Stopped. Why answer? Everyone important had his cell number.

Sinking back in the chair, he picked up his phone from the table beside him, scrolled through for the pizza joint's number, and placed his order as the landline went silent.

Fifteen minutes later, it rang again.

He ignored it.

Fifteen minutes after that, as he heaved himself to his feet to answer the door for the pizza delivery, it trilled a third time.

Weird.

Someone must really want to talk to him.

He paid the delivery guy, clumped into the kitchen, and rummaged around in the fridge for a beer. That supply was running low too. He'd have to go to the grocery store tomorrow and restock. That chore wouldn't be fun with this cast, but—

The landline rang again.

Muttering a curse, he limped to the wall, snatched the phone off the hook, and snapped out a greeting.

"Steve Jackson?"

The deep voice was muffled, as if someone was speaking through several layers of cloth.

"Yeah. Who is this?"

"You have legal difficulties. I have information that can help you."

He studied the cracked pane of glass in the back window that Meg had been after him for weeks to fix. "Who is this?"

"That's not important. But what I have may keep you out of jail."

Was this for real—or someone's idea of a sick joke?

"What do you have?"

"I'll give it to you tomorrow."

Steve frowned. The whole tenor of this call felt . . . off. Maybe the press coverage was bringing out a bunch of nutcases—or people who were up to no good. The last thing he needed was more problems.

"Why don't I give you my lawyer's—"

"No." The caller's tone sharpened. "I'm not dealing with anyone but you. If you don't want my information, fine."

Steve leaned against the counter, taking his weight off his bum ankle, mind racing.

Was it possible this person *did* have a nugget that would help his defense? It wasn't as if he was innocent—but the case was circumstantial except for the kid, and his lawyer ought to be able to undermine a nine-year-old's credibility. However, it wouldn't hurt to have a piece of tangible evidence that further chipped away at the prosecution's claims.

"Fine. You can come by whenever—"

"No. We have to meet at a neutral place. No witnesses. I'll give you directions." The caller began spewing out instructions.

"Whoa! I have to write this down. Give me a minute to get a pen and paper."

"Hurry. I'm not staying on the line long."

Steve moved as fast as he could to the bill drawer and pulled out a blank envelope and a pen. "Ready."

He jotted as the stranger talked—but red flags began popping up as the location sank in. "That's way off the beaten path."

"It's safe."

Steve doodled a bull's-eye on the envelope. He was liking this setup less and less. "Why are you doing this?"

"Let's just say I'm returning a favor. Be there tomorrow at one o'clock. Tell no one about our meeting, come alone, and don't be late. I'm not waiting around. Stay in your car until I drop the envelope and drive off."

The line went dead.

Slowly Steve replaced the handset in the cradle. Reread the directions he'd written down.

Was it safe to go alone to such an isolated spot?

Did this person actually have useful information, or was this a scam?

Had he ever done a favor for someone who would feel compelled to repay him? And if so, where had they gotten whatever information they had?

Stymied, he limped over to the table, sat down in front of his cooling pizza, and popped the tab on his beer.

Could this be a trap?

He took a long pull on his beer as he mulled that over.

Nah. He was being paranoid. Who would target him? He didn't have any enemies.

Well . . . okay, a few. His ex-wife and ex-girlfriend weren't his biggest fans, but they were far away. Candy was annoyed with him, but she'd find a new guy fast. And Meg didn't have the guts to do him any physical harm.

So what did he have to lose by showing up? He'd stay in his car, with the doors locked, and if anything seemed the slightest bit suspicious, he'd be out of there.

His attorney wouldn't approve of such a mysterious, clandestine rendezvous, of course—but it wasn't the lawyer's butt on the line. If the meeting was a bust, he never had to know about it. If, on the other hand, it produced a useful piece of information, he'd be happy to have it.

Steve flipped open the pizza box and picked up a slice. He didn't have to decide this minute whether to show up or not. Why not sleep on it, see if any concerns came to mind overnight?

And if they didn't, at one o'clock tomorrow he'd be sitting locked tight in his car, cellphone in hand on the off chance he ran into trouble, waiting by an abandoned railroad bridge in far west St. Louis County.

That was odd.

Juggling the plate with two homemade cinnamon rolls in one hand, Eve twisted her other wrist to confirm the time.

No, she wasn't too early. Olivia had said she always rose at dawn, and it was eight-thirty. Nor would the woman have gone somewhere at this hour. She never ventured out on the roads before nine or ten—or after dark. One of her concessions to advancing age, as she'd confided the day she'd come over with a plate of cookies to welcome her new neighbor.

A return gesture to thank the woman for her many kindnesses was long overdue—but how was she supposed to deliver it when Olivia wasn't answering the door?

Eve caught her lower lip between her teeth. Could her

neighbor be sick . . . or injured? Was that why she wasn't responding to the knock?

She set the rolls on a patio chair and peered into a window, cupping her hands around her face. The kitchen was dark, the counter clear, the coffeepot empty. As if no one had yet ventured into the room this morning for food or drink.

A niggle of unease skittered up her spine.

Something was definitely wrong.

She dug out her cell. Punched in Olivia's number. Waited while the phone rang . . . then rolled to voicemail.

Her alarm ratcheted up another notch.

Too bad they hadn't exchanged keys in case of emergency.

But the older woman had dismissed that suggestion, saying she'd told the police where a spare key was hidden on the property should there ever be a crisis.

Like maybe today.

Trouble was, there was no way to know for certain whether her neighbor required assistance or was sleeping soundly.

Eve swiveled around and surveyed the yard. If she could figure out where the key was, she wouldn't have to raise what might be a false alarm.

But after ten minutes of fruitless searching, she threw in the towel. If Olivia did need help, every minute she wasted could compound whatever was wrong. She'd have to call the local police, explain the situation, and ask them to send an officer.

After one final knock went unanswered, she summoned help.

Less than five minutes later, a police cruiser swung onto the cul-de-sac sans sirens—as she'd requested. This neighborhood had had enough excitement over the past three weeks. Why wake everyone up on a Saturday morning?

The car stopped in front, and the same officer who'd escorted her to safety the day of the bomb scare emerged. He followed the walk to where she waited by the front door.

"Morning, ma'am. I'm Officer Clark. You have concerns about your neighbor?"

"Yes." She repeated what she'd told the dispatcher by phone. "There's supposed to be a key hidden around the house somewhere. Olivia said she'd left that information with the local police."

His brow puckered. "Not to my knowledge. Give me a minute." He pulled out his cell and retreated a few yards, speaking in low tones.

He finished his call fast and returned to her. "We can't find any record of a key location for this address, although we do have that information on file for a number of residents. You've tried the doors?"

"Yes. And the windows." The task had kept her occupied while she waited for help to arrive.

He scanned the front door. "Let's go around back."

She led him to the rear, stepping aside as he examined the door and frame.

"This shouldn't be difficult to open. The homes in this area don't tend to have very secure doors. You may want to back up."

As she complied, the officer angled sideways and kicked with his heel below the lock. With a splintering clatter, the door swung open and smashed against the wall.

"Wait here." The officer entered the kitchen.

Eve clamped her hands on her hips as he disappeared into the hall.

Wait?

Not her forte.

Tamping down the urge to follow him in, she paced the small back porch.

One minute passed.

Two.

Three.

Four.

Why was a walk-through of the small house taking—

She halted as the faint wail of a siren keened through the quiet Saturday morning. It was coming their direction.

Had the officer summoned an ambulance?

Ignoring his orders to stay outside, Eve entered the house.

A male voice was speaking, but the volume was too low to distinguish the words.

She moved toward it.

"Try to stay calm, ma'am. The paramedics will be here within a few minutes."

Her pulse stuttered. Olivia *did* have a medical emergency!

Eve picked up her pace, following the voice to the living room.

In the corner that led to the hall, Olivia lay on the floor beside a closed door. She was pushing at the officer with her left hand, as if she wanted him to leave, while her other arm lay limp on the carpet, a key beside it. One side of her face was contorted, and the syllables coming out of her mouth were garbled.

Classic stroke symptoms.

Eve's heart sank.

Fighting back tears, she crossed to the woman and dropped down next to her. If the officer didn't like her being here, tough. "It's Eve, Olivia. Don't worry about anything. I'll watch out for you."

The woman's gaze shifted to her, the emotion in her glazed eyes difficult to read. And the string of mangled words she uttered was incomprehensible.

"Does she have any family we can contact?"

At the officer's question, Eve shook her head. "None that I know of. She's a widow, and she told me once she didn't have children. I've never heard her mention any family other than her husband, Nathaniel. I think she's been alone since he died twenty years ago."

The sirens outside were louder now, and the officer glanced toward the street. The ambulance must have turned on to the cul-de-sac.

"Can you stay with her while I open the front door?"

"Of course."

The man left her alone with her neighbor and disappeared into the small foyer.

Eve took the older woman's hand in a comforting clasp. "The paramedics are here, Olivia. They'll take you to the hospital and you'll get the best of care."

The reassurance had no effect on her neighbor's agitation. She continued to thrash weakly on one side and mumble muddled words.

Eve's throat tightened again. It must be awful to be helpless and have no one in the world to call upon for assistance.

But if—no, when—Olivia recovered, she wouldn't be alone. None of the Reillys were wired to walk away from a friend in need. A fact she'd relay as soon as her neighbor was calmer and able to think more rationally.

In the background a door opened, and a muted conversation took place. Seconds later, two paramedics entered the room.

Eve gave Olivia's hand a final squeeze and relinquished her position to the professionals.

As the paramedics went to work, the officer motioned her into the kitchen.

Her cell began to vibrate, but she ignored it as she joined him. This was more important.

The man stopped beside the kitchen table and pulled out a notebook. "You said she has no family as far as you know. Are you aware of any church affiliation, or a close friend who could be a proxy for her or have power of attorney?"

"No. I'm sorry. I only met Olivia about three months ago, after I bought the house next door."

"Does she have a cellphone?"

"The old flip kind, not a smartphone. She carries it for emergencies. She told me once she had no idea how to do anything with it but place a call. I doubt there are any contacts stored in it that would help you."

"We'll check anyway. Do you know if she's close with any of the other neighbors?"

"Not that I'm aware of. I mean, she's friendly to everyone and shares her baking talents with all of us, but I've never picked up that anyone is more than a casual acquaintance."

"I'll see if I can find any useful information in the house."

"Would you like me to help?"

"I'll ask for backup if necessary. It may be as simple as going through her purse. Let me get your contact information in case we have any questions."

The man must have forgotten about their earlier meeting during the bomb scare.

She recited her name, address, and cellphone number.

"Thanks." The officer jotted it all down. "I remembered the name, but this saves me hunting up the address and phone."

So he did recall their previous encounter.

"If I can offer any further assistance, don't hesitate to call." She leaned sideways and called out to the paramedics. "What hospital will you be taking her to?"

One of the technicians responded.

"If you're thinking about following her there, that may be a wasted effort." Officer Clark spoke as if he'd read her mind. "Unless you're next of kin or have power of attorney, no one will tell you anything."

That was true.

Yet sending Olivia off alone didn't feel right.

On the other hand, she had a speech to give.

Eve blew out a breath. "I hate for no one to be there for her, but I do have another commitment."

"I'd be happy to let you know who ends up being responsible for her decisions, if that helps." The officer put away his notebook.

"That would be great. Thank you."

"Let me walk you to the door."

It was only a few feet away—but the man must be following protocol. With the owner incapacitated, law enforcement would probably be responsible for safeguarding the house.

He led her to the back door, and she eyed the splintered jamb around the lock as she passed.

Good luck securing that.

Not her problem—though it wouldn't hurt to drop by later and make certain someone had taken care of this.

But for the next few hours, she had to keep the Young Republicans event top of mind—even if worry over Olivia would be nipping at the edges of her concentration.

She picked up the plate of cinnamon rolls and headed for home, pulling out her cell to see who'd called a few minutes ago, while she was in the house.

Brent—and he'd left a message. One bright spot in her day, at least.

She smiled as she put the phone to her ear . . . but her lips flatlined as she listened.

"Eve, I'm sorry to bail on you, but I got pulled into a double homicide early this morning and I expect to be here for hours." She had to strain to hear him against the backdrop of sirens and a cacophony of voices and other noises. "I'll do my best to get to the park for your speech, but I can't guarantee it. Please be careful. If I don't make it to the event, I'll call you later."

Sighing, she silenced her phone and shoved it back in her pocket. Why leave it on? Brent wouldn't be calling, and she wanted no interruptions during her appearance.

Back in her kitchen, she set the plate of rolls on the counter, said a quick prayer for Olivia, and retreated to her office.

She had exactly one hour to review her speech and transform herself into Eve Reilly, glam radio personality. Coiffed hair, sophisticated makeup, chic clothing . . . the whole nine yards.

She wrinkled her nose. The least favorite part of her job.

Thank heaven she didn't have to worry about glamour while she was behind the mic in the studio. If she did, the gig would hold far less appeal. As it was, she could put all her energy into what mattered—content, not image.

But all her primping would be worth it if Brent was able to join her later for the speech—and a trip to Starbucks.

Before the day ended, however, she'd swing by the hospital. Perhaps by then Olivia would be allowed visitors. You didn't have to be family or have power of attorney to hold someone's hand and offer a bit of comfort.

Focusing on someone else's needs might also help her deal with the insidious fear she hadn't been able to shake. While she'd reassured Brent that fear had diminished, her instincts continued to warn her danger was nearby, waiting to pounce.

And until law enforcement was certain the threat was over, she intended to keep looking over her shoulder and preparing for the worst.

23

WE'RE READY TO TRANSPORT. Did you find any contact information?" As the paramedics stood, one of them called the question over his shoulder.

"No." Officer Clark shook his head. "I went through her purse. Nothing in the wallet but credit cards, driver's license, library card—the usual." Nor had the cell he'd found been helpful. Eve Reilly had been correct. It was ancient technology. A password hadn't even been required to pull up the contacts list—which had been blank.

The other paramedic angled toward him and locked onto his gaze. "The hospital will want that information fast. Decisions may have to be made."

In other words, the homeowner was in bad shape, and dramatic measures could be necessary in the near future to keep her alive.

Or not, depending on her medical directive—if she had one.

"A colleague's on the way. We'll see if we can find anything more."

"Call the hospital ASAP if you do."

"Understood."

As the paramedics wheeled her out, the older woman

continued to mumble. Her eyes were glassy, yet a hint of panic lurked in their depths. Despite her obvious disorientation, on a peripheral level she seemed to realize the gravity of her situation.

Clark followed them to the porch. As they started down the walk, another patrol car pulled up outside.

Perfect timing.

These days, you wanted witnesses and backup if you poked around a private residence without the express permission of the owner—and you better have an ironclad reason for doing so. Like a life-and-death emergency.

In this case, there shouldn't be any issue. Exigent circumstances would allow them to do a quick walk-through of the house and look for contact information.

But he wanted someone else on hand who would verify they'd restricted their search to the bare necessity.

Gabe Ramirez emerged from the patrol car and walked toward him, veering around the paramedics as they continued down the front walk toward the ambulance.

"What's up?"

Clark briefed him. "Let's keep it simple and straightforward. We'll stick together and tackle a room at a time."

"Works for me."

They began in the bedroom. But after a quick pass through drawers and closets yielded nothing, they moved on to the kitchen.

Also a bust.

"Let's try the spare bedroom, then the living room." Clark took the lead down the hall.

"You notice something kind of weird about this house?" Ramirez fell in behind him.

"Like what?"

"Everything is super organized. There isn't even a junk drawer in the kitchen."

Clark snorted. "Just because some people's homes are less than orderly—not mentioning any names here—that doesn't mean everyone's is."

"Very funny. You try containing clutter in a household with five kids under the age of twelve."

"No thanks."

"You know . . . you don't have to come to dinner anymore if the bedlam at our place is too much for you."

"For your wife's cooking, I can live with a little chaos. Her tamales are to die for. And she's great with the kids. If patience is a virtue, she's the poster child."

"No kidding. I married a saint. And that's another odd thing about this place. There's nothing personal anywhere. Not a single family photo."

Clark entered the pristine back bedroom and motioned for his colleague to take the far side while he concentrated on the area near the door. "Her neighbor said she doesn't have any family."

"Yeah, but unless she was an orphan, she must have had one in the past. Parents, aunts, uncles, cousins. There isn't a single picture in this house."

Now that he mentioned it . . .

"I'll grant you that's a bit unusual." He began pulling out the drawers in the dresser.

Every one was empty—but the woman did live alone, and she obviously didn't accumulate many odds and ends that required storage.

"Was she ever married?" Ramirez opened the closet door, and Clark gave the space a quick inspection.

Empty too.

"Yes. According to the neighbor, she's a widow."

"Then why aren't there any photos of her husband around the place?"

"Maybe they remind her of her loss and make her sad."

"Maybe." Ramirez didn't seem convinced. "You want to try the living room?"

"Yeah. There's nothing in here that will help us."

As they retraced their steps down the hall, his colleague bent near the spot where the woman had fallen and retrieved a key from the floor. "What's this for?"

"No idea. I noticed it earlier but didn't bother to pick it up."

Ramirez set it on a credenza. "Let's check out the living room."

They worked the space, each taking half again.

Nothing useful surfaced.

"I don't get this." Clark fisted his hands on his hips. "No address book, no names, no legal documents—nothing."

"Like I said . . . weird." Ramirez motioned toward the door near the hall. "That must lead to the basement. You want to rummage around down there?"

"We could do a quick pass—but if it's like the rest of the house, it'll be a dead end."

He descended to the mostly unfinished space. Other than a washer and dryer, the lower level was empty except for the usual heating and air conditioning equipment.

"There may be contact information in there." Ramirez motioned toward a drywalled area in the far corner. "Some people keep records in filing cabinets in their basement."

"Why would she do that? The unused bedroom and empty closet upstairs could accommodate that kind of storage."

"You have any other ideas? There's nowhere else to look."

"True." He crossed the concrete floor. Twisted the knob on the door to the space.

Locked.

"Huh." Ramirez moved beside him. "Could be she keeps her valuables in there."

"How many valuables could a woman living in a neighborhood like this have?"

"You might be surprised. Ever hear of a book called *The Millionaire Next Door*?"

"No."

"My sister told me about it. The premise is that most millionaires in this country are simple, hardworking people who've saved their money, invested well, and lead a modest, unpretentious life. People like your next door neighbor." He shrugged. "Just saying."

"That doesn't help us find any contact information for Olivia Macie."

"It could be in here." Ramirez tapped the door. "But I don't want to break in without an okay from Sarge."

Except . . .

"We may not have to." Clark headed back to the stairs. "That key we found on the floor? It's possible she was holding it when she went down. And she was close to the basement door."

"Worth a try."

Clark took the steps two at a time, retrieved the key, and rejoined Ramirez.

His DIY colleague was down on his haunches, examining the base of the uprights. "You know . . . on a first pass, this room appears to be thrown together—but that's deceptive. The construction is solid, and the door is steel."

"Which would support your theory that she stores valuables in here." Clark fitted the key in the lock and turned it. "Let's see if that includes emergency contact information."

He twisted the knob and pushed the door open.

Ramirez followed him into the room. Stopped. "Whoa. I didn't expect this."

No kidding.

Clark walked over to the desk. Gave it a scan. Blinked. Repeated the process.

"Are you seeing what I'm seeing?" Ramirez spoke from behind him.

"Yeah." Clark pulled out his radio. "And this is way beyond our pay grade. We're handing it off to the higher-ups. Now. Let's get out of here."

Ramirez didn't argue.

And as they ascended the stairs . . . as he connected with headquarters . . . as he gave the closed door to Olivia Macie's basement room a final perusal, Clark expelled a breath.

A millionaire living next door was one thing.

But he'd be willing to bet no one in this quiet suburban neighborhood had a clue what was going on in the cellar of the amiable older woman who baked them cookies and shared their cul-de-sac.

"How did we manage to pull two back-to-back homicides?" Brent stripped off his latex gloves and tossed them in a trash can outside the upscale house that had become a crime scene.

"Rookies tend to get the weekend and late-night assignments." Colin dispatched his gloves too.

"That explains my presence—not yours."

"They pair novices with experienced detectives. That would be me." His colleague gave him a one-sided grin. "Since we worked the scene last night together, I'm assuming the powers that be decided to team us up for this one too."

"Sorry to ruin your Saturday."

"No sweat. It's not the first weekend I've worked, and it won't be the last. I'm sure this wasn't in your plans, either."

Far from it.

Brent glanced at his watch. Ten-fifty.

He should be with Eve right now at her speaking gig.

Colin studied him. "Big plans this morning?"

"I had a run scheduled with a buddy—and I was also supposed to go with Eve to a speaking engagement today. She's the keynote—"

His phone began to vibrate, and he pulled it off his belt. Skimmed the screen. "Sarge."

"Checking up on us. Want a water?" Colin motioned toward a cooler someone had brought to the scene of what they were beginning to think was a murder/suicide instead of a double homicide.

"Yeah. Thanks." Brent put the cell to his ear. "Lange."

"You guys at a stopping point at the scene?"

Typical Sarge. No greeting, just straight to business.

"No. We have two or three more hours of processing— minimum."

Sarge grunted. "I was afraid of that. I'm sending in replacements. I need you and Colin elsewhere."

Brent frowned. He might be new to the ranks, but as far as he knew, pulling detectives off a scene not long after they'd been assigned wasn't standard protocol.

"What's up?"

"We had a trauma call this morning for Eve Reilly's neighbor. Apparent stroke. But the responding officers found more than a medical emergency after they started looking for next-of-kin contact information."

As Sarge filled him in, Brent understood why he was being tapped for this assignment. And by the time the rapid-fire download wound down, his nerves were wound *up*.

Tight.

"I'm sending Colin with you. He has experience that may be useful. Your replacements should be there in the next few minutes. As soon as you bring them up to speed, head over to Olivia Macie's. Assess the situation and let me know if I should start the gears grinding for a warrant."

"Roger."

Brent slid the phone back onto his belt and joined Colin. The other detective handed him a water. "What's up?"

"We're being reassigned."

Colin's eyebrows peaked. "In the middle of a scene investigation?"

"Yeah."

As he briefed him, his associate's demeanor grew more and more serious. "I'm not liking the sound of this."

"Neither am I. The proximity and access are suspicious." He motioned to the street in front, where another detective was pulling up. "Our first replacement is here. Let's bring him up to speed and get out of here."

"I'm with you."

Before the new arrival was barely out of his car, they'd cornered him.

Ten minutes later, Brent was jogging to his vehicle.

Maybe the equipment and material the officers had found in Olivia's house wasn't as serious as the men suspected. Both were recent academy graduates. It was possible they were reading too much into what they'd seen.

That's why Sarge was sending him and Colin over there to evaluate the situation.

But if the officers weren't overreacting . . . if there was a darker side to the sweet older woman Eve had risked her life to protect the day of the bomb scare . . . they had to figure out how and why she was involved in the efforts to silence the woman who was fast staking a claim to his heart.

And since Olivia wasn't able to talk to them, they'd have to hope the clues they needed to piece together this puzzle would be waiting for them inside the small house she called home.

Organizations that planned private events in public places were asking for trouble.

But it made this job easier.

Buzz drove past the lot at the back entrance to the park,

near the small museum, and gave it a sweep. The spots were already filling up—but most of the 250 or so official attendees were probably parked near the main entrance on the other side of the park.

His group, however, was gathering back here. Dan had said that as many as two or three hundred like-minded souls could show up.

He continued down the road to the small upscale mall a mile away, where parking was plentiful. After slipping on his shades and helmet, he slid out of the car and reached into the backseat to retrieve the small saddlebag containing his black slacks, black hoodie, and scarf.

As he removed his bike from the rack on the back of his car, he gave the parking lot a casual perusal.

No one was paying any attention to him.

And why should they? This mall was on a popular biking route, and the Starbucks a few doors down was a favorite spot to take a break and rehydrate. In his cycling gear, he was just another weekend warrior.

Buzz took off down the two-lane road, back toward the park. As the bike trail began to parallel the road, he zipped over to it and continued toward the spot in the wooded section he'd found last week during his scouting trip. The small, densely shrubbed area was a perfect place to hide his bike and don the black pants and hoodie over his biking gear.

And after his job was finished, all he had to do was wend his way back here and become a biker again. With the massive congestion in the park on Saturdays—weddings, family reunions, picnics, joggers, bikers, equestrians, the activities at the rec center . . . not to mention the chaos he'd soon cause—he should have no problem melting into the melee and slipping away.

Still, despite all the careful planning, it would be a relief to have this over. The job had to be done—and it was an honor to be trusted with the task—but crossing a major moral line like this was a bit . . . unnerving.

Even if it was necessary for the cause.

He pulled on his hoodie, shoved the scarf into his slacks, and quashed the tiny trace of doubt niggling at his conscience. This mission required his full focus.

Squaring his shoulders, he jogged down the path toward the parking lot where everyone had been instructed to gather.

As he emerged from the woods, he gave the area a slow survey. It wasn't hard to pick out the Antifa folks. They were all dressed like him. In black. Not the most common color choice for a day in the park when temperatures were expected to approach eighty—but it was a free country.

Or so the other side said.

At least there was no law against black clothing. Yet.

Brown tones were also in evidence—thanks to the large police presence.

A typical intimidation tactic.

Settling his shades more firmly on his nose, Buzz strolled over to a small group of black-clad people congregated on the asphalt.

His people.

While he didn't know their names, they were all fighting for the same cause.

They welcomed him as he drew close, and he blended into the group as one of the guys began giving them a rundown on the plan for the day and passed out a few signs emblazoned with the slogan "Down With Government Oppression."

Similar small groups were coalescing elsewhere in the lot, forcing the cops to spread out in order to keep tabs on everyone.

Smart tactic.

Plus, while large gatherings required a permit, small clusters were legal. That's why they weren't going to join together until the speeches began and they were ready to do what they'd come to do.

Demonstrate and disrupt.

Or that's what most of these people were here to do.

His assignment, however, was much, much bigger—but only he and Dan knew about that.

Buzz touched the bulge in his pocket where his Glock rested, loaded and ready to do its job. As he was ready to do his.

"—the ten-minute mark, we'll start marching toward the stage and chanting. Keep the volume loud, to drown out the speaker. And stay bunched together. We want a large block of black to heighten the impact."

Buzz tuned back in to the guy issuing quiet instructions to the small huddle of people around him.

"As we get close to the stage, one lucky person in each group gets to hurl one of these." He pulled out a smoke cartridge and discreetly displayed it. "This will emit smoke for three minutes and add to the impact without causing any harm. Do I have a volunteer?"

A woman stepped forward, and he passed the cartridge to her, keeping it out of sight of the cops. She tucked it under her hoodie.

"When I raise my hand, let it fly. Everyone put your hoods up before we leave here, and cover the bottom of your faces with your scarves. Got it?"

At the nods of assent, Buzz exhaled. Everything was playing out just as Dan had said in the instructions he'd picked up, right down to the smoke that would intensify the confusion as the shots rang out—and make it more difficult to locate their source.

While Antifa's loose conglomeration of independent groups lacked a central authority, a few people—like Dan—had their finger on the pulse of the movement and knew how to rally the different factions when a statement needed to be made.

Today they were going to make a big one.

Far bigger than anyone here but him realized.

And it would happen in—Buzz twisted his wrist—one hour and thirty-five minutes. During the march and chant their temporary leader had mentioned. In all that noise and confusion, he should have ample opportunity to slip on his latex gloves as they got close to Eve Reilly—and if the Antifa people were loud enough, his several back-to-back shots wouldn't even register at first.

The instant he fired his last round, he'd drop the gun, dive into the throng, and escape through the bedlam as first responders rushed the stage and the Antifa people scattered.

As soon as he was safe in the woods, the lighter in his pocket would melt the gloves. Back at his bike, it wouldn't take more than forty-five seconds to shed his black attire, stow it in the saddlebag, and continue his ride—in the opposite direction of all the excitement. The clothes could be disposed of in the dumpster behind the mall.

He had it all planned, down to the tiniest detail—and his dry runs had been flawless.

Given all his preparation, the real deal shouldn't be any different.

And after all was said and done, there would be one less high-profile person undermining their cause.

It was a brilliant plan—with him as the linchpin.

A surge of pride swept over him, and his resolve hardened. He would do this, and do it well.

Best of all, he would walk away, ready to continue the fight. The police may have identified Eve Reilly's harasser sooner than expected, jeopardizing the cover they'd counted on to mask Antifa involvement, but Dan had a plan to deflect suspicion to Jackson. Had said so in their last text exchange.

There was nothing to worry about as long as he did his part.

Fingers twitching, Buzz again ran his hand over the outlines of the Glock and took a steadying breath.

Soon, baby.

Soon.

24

TWO STEPS into Olivia's basement office, Brent came to an abrupt halt. No wonder the patrol officers had sent for reinforcements.

A high-end laptop in screensaver mode was open on the desk, a large monitor beside it. Three burner phones were lined up on the faux wood surface, within reaching distance of the swivel chair. A tablet next to the phones was filled with notations in some sort of shorthand. Four filing cabinets lined one wall. A flat-screen TV was tuned to CNN, the sound muted. An oversized map of the United States filled a significant portion of another wall, pins with colored heads stuck in various cities around the country.

"Wow." It was all he could manage.

"Yeah." Colin completed his own three-sixty perusal. "This place looks like command central. Who *is* this woman?"

"I have no idea—but she's not the sweet, tech-challenged senior citizen Eve thinks she is." He motioned toward several photos lying on the desk. "Those are pretty clear evidence that this space isn't being used to manage investments or run an eBay business."

"Yeah." Colin moved toward the shots that featured black bloc protestors in full demonstration mode, then motioned toward a faded, framed photo on the desk of a twentysome-thing jeans-clad guy sporting a full beard and mustache, with a bandanna tied around his long hair. "I wonder who that is?"

"No idea." Brent scanned the image. The man was holding a hand-lettered placard that said "Stop the War." In the crowd behind him, similarly dressed young people were toting signs referencing Vietnam. "But if we can ID him, that could answer a lot of questions." He pulled out his cell and snapped a photo of the framed picture. "We need a warrant."

"Not happening without grounds. We can't search some-one's house or open an investigation because of an affiliation with Antifa. That isn't illegal. There has to be evidence of a crime, threat of force, or violence."

"I know that." Unfortunately. "But if Olivia is as deep into Antifa as those photos suggest, she has reason to hate Eve based on ideology—and many of the zealots affiliated with that movement have no compunction about the use of violence to achieve their ends."

"I hear you. But it's not illegal to support organizations involved in protest activities. Our hands are tied unless their actions turn violent."

"There have already been threats and violence against Eve."

"Perpetrated by Steve Jackson, per your young witness."

"I can only link him to two of the four incidents—and the most recent one occurred while he was out of commission at the hospital. Who had easier access to leave that last note Eve found than her neighbor?"

"But to what end?"

"She may have seen the bomb scare and related incidents as an opportunity for someone in the group to silence Eve without taking the fall for it. As a chance to pin it on someone else." Brent raked his fingers through his hair. "We have to get that warrant."

Colin eyed the stacks of material on the desk. "I don't

disagree—but unless we can find a direct connection between Olivia and Eve, no judge will—" He frowned. Leaned closer to one of the stacks. "I think we may have our link. Look at this."

Brent joined him. It took a few seconds to identify the location of the aerial photo—but the instant he did, his stomach bottomed out. "That's the park where the Young Republicans group is holding its picnic . . . and where Eve is speaking. Check out the time at the top." He pointed to a handwritten notation of 1:00 p.m. "That's when her speech starts."

"That could be enough to get us our warrant."

It better be.

Because every instinct in his body was blaring a red alert.

"Why don't you call Sarge about the warrant while I try to reach Eve—and see if he'll put security on her."

"You got it." Colin pulled out his phone.

Brent thumbed in her number. "Tell him she's scheduled to speak at one o'clock. And County should give someone from the Republican group a heads-up that they may have to alter their scheduled programming. Alert him I also sent that photo I took. Facial recognition software may be able to flag someone in the database."

"It's an old photo." Colin gave it a doubtful scrutiny.

"Can't hurt to try."

"I'm on it."

While Colin exited the room to place his call, Brent punched in Eve's number.

After four rings, it rolled to voicemail.

He tried texting her.

No response.

She was probably tied up at the meet and greet, shaking hands. Her phone must be on silent mode.

Brent blew out a breath.

Headquarters would get through to someone on site, and given the large police presence at the picnic there shouldn't be an issue assigning a security detail to her for the duration of the event.

But he wanted to talk to her.

Scratch that.

He wanted to *be* there with her.

The officers assigned to her would do their best, but they didn't have a vested interest in keeping her safe. Their blood wouldn't run cold at the mere thought she could be in danger. Fear wouldn't twist their stomachs into a knot. Their pulse wouldn't pound like a jackhammer or—

Wait.

Brent squinted at the aerial shot on Olivia's desk and massaged his temple.

Would a man whose heart was atrophied experience all those emotions?

No.

Meaning Eve had been right during their discussion a week ago. There wasn't a thing wrong with his heart.

And despite his concerns about subjecting a woman he loved to the risks and rigors of his job, maybe Adam's take on that score was correct. Maybe not all women would cave in the face of crisis, as Karen had.

As for Colin's more recent advice—to stop overthinking the issue, let people do what they were called to do and put the rest in God's hands—that was also astute.

The communication piece might still be a stumbling block—but he could work on that. He *would* work on that. Finding the words to tell Eve how he felt shouldn't be an insurmountable challenge if he could let go of the fear.

Too bad it had taken a crisis for him to arrive at that insight.

But assuming they could foil whatever plans had been cooked up in this basement command center, he wasn't letting another day pass without—

"Sarge is going to work this hard." Colin strode back into the room. "You talk to Eve?"

He had to forcibly shift gears. "No. She must have turned off her cell during the appearance."

"Not a problem. Sarge is assigning several of the on-site patrol officers to stick with her. He's also got people digging into Olivia's background. We should do the same while we wait for the all clear to dive in here."

"Does Sarge think there will be any issue with the warrant?"

"Not in view of the link between Eve and Olivia, the tactical setup here—including the map of the park—and the threats Eve's been receiving. Plus, there could be a public safety issue with today's event."

"Okay."

But it wasn't. Not really.

Though his job demanded he stay here, he wanted to be with Eve.

Now.

"I also asked Sarge to have one of the officers there tell Eve to give you a call if you hadn't gotten through." Colin gave him a one-sided grin.

"Thanks."

"Happy to do it. Did you bring your laptop?"

"Yeah. It's in the car."

"Mine too. Let's grab them and see what we can unearth on Olivia Macie. We can use our phones as a hotspot."

With a clipped nod, Brent followed him out.

Waiting for confirmation that a warrant was in process was beyond frustrating.

But in the interim, perhaps they could pull some data on Olivia that would explain why a brownie-baking, soap-opera-watching senior would be running what appeared to be an Antifa command center in her basement.

"Ms. Reilly . . . may I spirit you away for lunch?"

At the touch on her arm, Eve excused herself from the conversation she was having with one of the Young Republicans during the meet and greet and swiveled toward the president of the group. "Of course."

In truth, though, eating before a major speech was never her preference—less so with news vans parked nearby. The flutter of nerves in her stomach was a definite appetite killer.

Strange how she was perfectly comfortable spouting off to tens of thousands of people from a studio, but in front of a couple hundred warm bodies she always had to fight a slight but unnerving case of stage fright.

The man motioned her toward the tent that had been erected to protect the sound equipment for the speeches in case of inclement weather, and she arched an eyebrow. The sun was shining, and the food was set up near the picnic pavilions, where she assumed they'd all be eating lunch.

He took her arm, leaning closer as they walked. "I've just been alerted that law enforcement is ratcheting up security. The officer in charge asked us to gather in the tent for a briefing."

Her pulse faltered. This was exactly what Brent had feared would happen.

As they approached the tent, two uniformed officers lowered the sides in one corner near a table, then circled around to the outside and assumed sentry duty. Two other officers took up positions inside but facing away from the table.

All four directions were being covered.

Whatever was going on must be big.

Eve took a deep breath as she sank into a chair at the table, where two other members of the organization's board were already seated.

Another police officer—this one higher ranking, if she was reading his uniform insignia correctly—joined them.

"Lieutenant Anderson." He extended his hand to each of them and claimed a chair. "I want to bring you up to speed on the situation here."

Eve listened as the man described the growing Antifa presence in a nearby parking lot—and mentioned new intel that suggested the protestors could have more planned than mere marching.

"What kind of intel?" The president of the group narrowed his eyes.

"I'm not at liberty to discuss that. We're waiting for a warrant to give us the green light to search a suspicious area. It was a chance discovery that raises the threat level here significantly."

"Are you suggesting we shut the event down?"

"That's your call—but I would advise that, at a minimum, you delay your afternoon program while we bring in additional officers and continue to assess the intel coming in. We'll also put tighter security on your keynote speaker in the interim."

Now it was Eve's turn to furrow her brow. Was the Antifa presence here related to her—and the threats she'd been receiving?

"We don't want to put anyone in danger—our speakers, the audience, or any of the innocent people in the park." The president glanced at his fellow board members, who nodded their agreement. "If we have to shut this down, we will."

"But then the Antifa people win." Eve's blood began to boil, as it always did when she was confronted with efforts to undermine the free speech that was a foundation of American society. "I can live with shouting and picketing, if that's all we're talking about. Or are you thinking this could get violent?"

"Unknown." The lieutenant folded his hands on the table. "Most of the Antifa folks claim they prefer peaceful protests— but we've all seen how these kinds of situations can degenerate. As I said, delaying the program would be wise at this point, until we know more."

"We can do that," the president confirmed.

"I'll have the officers circulate in the crowd and make that announcement quietly. Let's try to keep Antifa off balance as long as we can. We should have new information soon that will give us further direction."

"That's fine with us." Again, the president checked with the other board members, who murmured their assent.

The lieutenant rose. "Ms. Reilly, I was instructed to have you call Detective Lange. I understand you have his number."

"Yes." She stood too.

"May I ask that you remain here for the time being? I'm sure these folks would be happy to give you privacy."

The president and his cohorts took the cue and stood at once. "We'll mingle too and help spread the word among our members. And Ms. Reilly—given the circumstances, we fully understand if you choose to withdraw from the speaker lineup."

Not in her plans—unless the situation deteriorated further.

"Let's play it by ear for now."

She sat again, pulled out her cell, and turned it back on as the corner of the tent emptied—except for the four officers forming a perimeter around her.

Brent answered on the first ring—and his greeting did nothing to reassure her.

"Are you okay?"

"Fine. We just had a briefing from a lieutenant—such as it was. He just alluded to an increased threat level and asked the organizers to delay the program. I also have armed, uniformed officers stationed in close proximity. What's going on?"

"Are you sitting down?"

"Yes."

"We're beginning to think Olivia Macie is the second person who had you in their sights."

Eve's jaw dropped. "Wait. Repeat that."

"You heard me correctly. Your neighbor appears to be a strong person of interest."

She stared at the shadows of the officers on the other side of the tent flaps as Brent filled her in on what they'd found in her neighbor's basement.

But the connection wasn't computing.

Olivia . . . Antifa?

Bizarre.

She waited to speak until he finished. "I'm reeling."

"So are we. While we were in her office, we found a framed photo of a young man that appears to be from the midsixties, early seventies. It was taken at a Vietnam War protest. Did she by chance ever mention anyone from her past who had been important to her?"

"No. She never mentioned anyone, period. I don't think she had a family, other than her husband—and he died twenty years ago."

"That's what I figured, in view of what you told the responding officer this morning. We're waiting for word that the warrant's a go to dig in here. Has your speech been delayed?"

"Yes."

"Good. Stick close to your armed guards until we know more—unless you're willing to cancel the speech?"

"I'd rather not unless you uncover a tangible threat. It's the keynote address. Besides, backing down to intimidation tactics goes against my grain. These groups spout free speech, yet they do their best to shut down voices that don't agree with them. It doesn't make sense."

"I think their tactics fall under the any-means-to-an-end philosophy—whether those means are logical or not. Keep your phone on. As soon as I know more, I'll give you a call."

"Thanks."

Several seconds of silence ticked by—but Brent made no attempt to sever the connection.

Curious.

Eve waited him out.

"Listen . . . as soon as this situation is resolved, we have to talk."

Not what she'd expected—and it was impossible to tell from his tone whether his comment was good news or bad.

"About us?"

"Yes." A voice spoke in the background on Brent's end. "I have to go. We have tons of work to do in a very short time. Be careful, and I'll call you soon."

The temptation to ask a few follow-up questions was strong—but the man was super busy. She'd have to wait.

"No worries. I'm fine." She managed to maintain an upbeat inflection. "Go do your job."

As the line went dead, however—and she canvassed the four police officers assigned to keep her safe—a new spate of nerves kicked in. They were guarding her as a result of evidence the police had found in Olivia's basement.

But why would such a sweet woman be involved with an anarchist group like Antifa? And how could someone who'd been so nice and thoughtful in person be masterminding a plot against the neighbor she'd welcomed with open arms?

Was the image Olivia presented to the world nothing more than a façade? A cover for nefarious activities?

The whole notion was surreal.

Yet it must have serious credence if the police were on full alert and a security detail had been assigned to her.

Eve drew in a lungful of air. Slowly let it out. Sitting around waiting for news wasn't going to calm her. Keeping busy would.

But doing what?

Jiggling her foot, she watched the board members circulate through the picnickers outside the tent as they passed the word about the security alert. Expressions ranged from startled to solemn to nervous.

Understandable.

It was one thing to read about Antifa and activist gatherings on the news. It was another thing entirely to be in the midst of one.

She pulled out her cell and opened her browser. Brent and his colleagues would have access to much more detailed intel on Olivia than she could pull up by surfing the net—but a search would keep her occupied.

And while she was browsing, it wouldn't hurt to say a few prayers that Brent's team would get a warrant fast and find answers before the Antifa crowd waiting nearby got impatient with the delay in the afternoon program and decided to forge ahead with its mission.

Whatever that was.

25

I F THIS WAS SUPPOSED to be a joke, he wasn't laughing.

Steve clamped his lips together, surveyed the desolate area around the abandoned railway bridge, and glowered at the digital clock on the dashboard of his rental car.

One-ten.

Apparently he'd been lured here under false pretenses.

Given that the anonymous caller who'd promised to meet him with helpful evidence had threatened to leave if he wasn't here precisely at one, the odds were no one was going to come forward with a silver bullet to help him beat the rap hanging over his head.

As the truth hollowed out his stomach, he watched a vulture circle above the corroded bridge and let out a slow breath.

Could Meg have done this, out of spite?

No. Much as she might hate him, it wasn't in her nature to be mean to anyone.

So who had called him, dangling a carrot he couldn't resist?

The answer eluded him.

But whoever had devised this prank could be concealed nearby, watching him. Laughing at the desperate man who'd fallen for a mean-spirited trick.

Anger began to churn in his gut, and he squeezed the steering wheel until his knuckles whitened. No one made a fool of Steve Jackson.

No one.

Muttering a curse, he twisted the key in the ignition. Put the car in gear. Executed a quick U-turn, spewing gravel into the tall weeds rimming the deserted road. He was out of here.

And if he ever found out who had orchestrated this waste-of-time Saturday outing, they'd find out why his ex had nicknamed him Steve the Smasher.

Something was wrong.

Beads of sweat that had nothing to do with the rising air temperature broke out on Buzz's forehead. Swiping them away with the sleeve of his hoodie, he gave the parking lot another once-over.

More police had shown up, cars attempting to enter were being turned away—and the Antifa demonstration was getting further and further behind schedule.

He checked his watch again. One-twelve.

At this moment, the black bloc groups should be marching and chanting and infiltrating the Republican gathering as they approached the stage where Eve Reilly was speaking. His finger should be on the trigger, ready to dispatch the bullets that would take her out.

Instead, the Antifa crowd was milling around—and becoming restless.

Buzz searched the throng for the guy who'd been their group leader. There. Off to the side, conferring with another group leader.

Buzz headed toward them. He needed answers—and he couldn't text Dan. His burner phone was history.

As he approached the two men, it was obvious they were as concerned as he was about the change in schedule.

However . . . the delay had far more serious consequences for him than anyone else. If necessary, the group could switch gears, crash the Republican party later in the day, with or without the speeches. While the impact wouldn't be as dramatic, nor their efforts as disruptive, they would still make the news—and further the overall mission of the movement.

But to complete *his* mission, he needed access to Eve Reilly and the camouflage of the black-clad group.

He also needed whatever cover Dan had arranged to deflect guilt to someone else—and timing was everything for that. If they got too much off schedule, that cover might not hold.

The two men stopped conversing as he approached.

"Hey." He tried not to let his nerves show. "Everybody's wondering what's going on."

"So are we." His group leader furrowed his brow. "The speeches have been delayed. We've been trying to reach our contact person for direction, but we're not getting any response."

Were they talking about Dan?

Very possible.

And if so, it was strange that communication with the organizer of this gathering had shut down. Dan above all knew how critical today's rally was.

But he couldn't say that, or reveal his own contact with the person who'd coordinated this protest from behind the scenes. Only the two of them knew about today's other mission.

Whatever the glitch, though, he had to find a way to get to Eve Reilly.

Because unless it became absolutely impossible to pull off, he wasn't leaving the park until he silenced her forever.

> Warrant approved and in process. OK to search. Computer tech en route. Possible matches to photo attached.

Brent finished reading Sarge's email and looked over at Colin, who was concentrating on his computer screen at Olivia's kitchen table. "Sarge says the search is a go."

"Good. We're getting nowhere online. How is it possible there are no database or Google references for a person in the twenty-first century? It's like Olivia Macie lives in a cave."

"The cookie-baking Olivia Macie that Eve knows does in terms of the internet. I'm thinking she uses another name for her illicit activities." He relayed the rest of Sarge's message and opened the photos, tipping his cell so his colleague could see the screen too.

"That's him." Colin pointed to one of the images.

"I agree." He touched it and read the brief bio that came up, pulling out the pertinent facts.

Peter Arnold. Prominent SDS activist. Killed in violent confrontation during a protest in 1964.

"What's SDS?" Colin frowned at the screen.

Brent's fingers were already flying over the keys, searching for that answer. He clicked on the first hit. "Students for a Democratic Society. The group was a critic of the US political system, big business, economic inequality, racial discrimination—and a host of other things. A memo from the FBI in 1969 called it an organization dedicated to the destruction of American society and Western democratic traditions and ideals."

"Sounds like Antifa."

"Doesn't it, though?" Brent typed in Peter Arnold and quickly scanned his bio. "Whoa. Get this. Arnold married a woman named Olivia Wallace in 1961."

"I assume that's our Olivia. But she told Eve her husband died twenty years ago—and the names don't match."

"There could have been a second marriage. The patrol of-ficer who responded to the emergency call this morning told me Eve said Olivia was married to a guy named Nathaniel."

"Try pairing the names for a search."

Brent resumed typing. "The uncommon last name should help keep this manageable." He scrolled through the hits that popped up. Clicked on one that seemed promising. "She mar-ried her second husband in 1970. Nathaniel Macie was quite a bit older than her. They were together until he died in 2000 after a debilitating battle with Parkinson's disease."

"Was he also a radical?"

"No. A prominent banker."

"Huh." Colin arched an eyebrow. "She went over to the dark side—or at least that's what her old activist cohorts would say."

"The evidence downstairs would suggest she didn't stay there."

Colin rose. "Let's dive in and—"

Ding dong.

"Must be the computer tech Sarge is sending." Brent stood too.

"I'll let him in and meet you downstairs."

They parted in the hall, and Brent clattered back down the stairs. Now that the tech was here, they could dig into the woman's computer. That might yield gold. And the texts and call history on the burner phones would also be valu-able.

Unless everything was password protected and their tech guru couldn't get them into the devices fast.

And fast was key. The Antifa fanatics at the park could lose patience any second.

However, Eve should be safe—unless she and the powers that be in the Republican organization decided to proceed with the afternoon programming.

A shudder rippled through him as a litany of potential consequences strobed through his mind.

But without hard evidence to suggest there was a plot directed specifically against her, she wasn't the type to back down in the face of pressure. She would stick with her principles, even if that put her at risk.

And all along he'd been afraid *his* job would freak *her* out. How ironic.

Colin joined him in the basement, followed by a jeans-clad guy who could pass for a teenager.

"Sam Harris." The new arrival held out his hand.

Brent returned the shake and introduced himself.

"Colin already gave me the highlights." The younger man pulled on a pair of latex gloves and moved to the computer. Touched a key. The screensaver vanished, and an email program appeared on the screen, a half-composed note front and center.

"That was easy." He grinned at them. "Even you guys could have hacked into this one." He opened the full header and examined the gobbledygook that came up. "She's using a remailer to preserve her anonymity. Maybe more than one. No surprise there. You want to look at this email account while I check out the cells?" He picked up one of the phones.

"Yes." Brent crossed to the computer and dropped into the chair. Colin joined him as they both donned gloves and read the partially composed, cryptic email.

It didn't appear to have anything to do with today's event or Eve. A date in October was referenced. Olivia must have been working on a future Antifa gathering.

"Notice the From line." Colin indicated the spot. "She goes by the name Dan."

"I wonder why?"

"Could be an acronym for the Direct Action Network." Sam spoke without taking his focus off the cell he was examining.

Brent glanced at Colin, who shrugged.

He pulled out his cell and typed in the name of the organization. Tapped on the first hit. Skimmed a few lines.

It fit.

"How'd you make that connection?" He swiveled toward Sam.

The other man stopped fiddling with the cell. "In grad school we had an exercise that involved hacking into communiques about the World Trade Organization protests twenty-some years ago. That was a DAN-coordinated event. Given the Antifa angle of this investigation, I connected the dots."

"Impressive." Colin folded his arms. "You ever think about being a detective?"

"Not my cup of tea. I'd rather solve puzzles that have logical solutions"—he lifted the phone—"than deal with irrational people."

Hard to argue with that answer.

As Sam went back to the phone, Brent fed Colin the Wikipedia highlights. "DAN was a collection of anti-authoritarian anarchist groups. It fell apart in 2002—but a bunch of the key people went on to play active roles in regional and national mobilizations of independent affinity groups in the Antifa movement."

"From the setup down here, Olivia could be one of those. It has all the earmarks of a command center." Colin gave the room another sweep. "Maybe after her banker husband died, she returned to her anarchist roots."

"You guys want to take a look at this cell?" Sam held it up. "As far as I can tell, it was never used for calls, only texts—and only with one person. The last one was yesterday."

"Yeah." Brent took it from him, and Sam moved on to the next phone.

Colin leaned over his shoulder to see the screen. "Who's Al?"

"Any ideas?" Brent directed the question to Sam.

"Sorry." One side of the computer tech's mouth rose. "You're on your own with that one."

"Scroll down." Colin motioned to the screen. "We can worry about who Al is later."

Brent complied . . . but sucked in a breath when Jackson's name popped up.

"I see it too." Creases scored Colin's brow. "Another link between Olivia and Eve. Your theory about a third party slipping in on Jackson's coattails just got legs."

Brent's heart missed a beat as he zipped through the exchange from September 7. "Look at the reference to next weekend . . . and making ER history. That has to refer to today's event—and Eve." He continued to scroll through the texts.

"Stop." Colin leaned closer. "Another reference on September 1, to ER being gone in two weeks."

"Al must be the hit man."

Meaning he was at today's event, preparing to carry out his assignment.

"Forget later. We have to identify this guy *now*." Colin's tone was grim.

Brent handed him the cell. "You work on that—and call Sarge. I want Eve out of that park ASAP. If they can make it happen before I arrive, fine. But with sirens and lights, I can be on site in ten minutes—and if she's still there, I'll light a fire under whoever's in charge."

"Go for it."

He took the stairs two at a time, pulled out his cell, and raced through the house. Sarge would be all over this—but Eve needed to hear about the danger from him.

And that danger had just increased exponentially.

Jackson may have threatened to silence Eve, but it was questionable whether the man would ever have followed through.

Olivia and the guy named Al, however, were deadly serious in *their* intent to silence her.

They wouldn't succeed today—not if he could help it—nor would they in the future. From the prognosis Sarge had relayed, Olivia was out of the picture. Since she appeared to be calling the shots, that should eliminate the threat.

Once they found Al.

And they would. Whatever it took.

Because keeping Eve safe was his top priority.

For her sake—and his.

At the sudden vibration in her hand as she paced the confined area within the tent, Eve jolted to a stop. Fumbled the cell. Grabbed it as it plummeted toward the ground.

Mercy.

Between the armed guards surrounding her and learning that her kindhearted neighbor was involved with a radical anarchist group, every nerve in her body was vibrating. If this kept up, she'd be a basket case before the day was over.

Thank goodness Brent was calling with an update, as he'd promised.

Instead of returning her greeting, he got straight to business. "Are the guards sticking close?"

"Yes."

"Stay near them. We think you're being targeted at this event."

Her stomach bottomed out. "Targeted how?"

"Unknown. But the intent is deadly."

She groped for the edge of the table and sank back into her chair, stomach churning as she tried to digest that news. "Olivia wanted to kill me?"

"It appears so. Does the name Al ring any bells?"

"No. Why?"

"We found a text exchange between the two of them. Since the name she used was fake, we assume the other one is too. It could be a male or a female." His last sentence was muffled.

"Where are you?"

"Getting into my car at Olivia's. I'm heading your way with lights and sirens. I should be there in ten minutes, but my boss has been notified about the new developments and they may move you to a secure place or even take you out of the park before I get there."

An engine started in the background, and she clutched the phone. "I'd rather wait for you."

"If they can get you out faster, go. I'll catch up with you. And please . . . don't take any chances. I have plans for us, and if anything happened to you . . ." His voice hoarsened, and he cleared his throat. "Just be careful."

Despite the cold fear snaking through her, a surge of tenderness warmed her heart. "I will."

The call ended with the sudden, piercing wail of a siren and the revving of an engine from Brent's end.

Eve slowly tucked the phone into her purse and surveyed the subdued picnickers who were clustered in small groups, talking in low tones. All traces of their earlier revelry had vanished. The crowd had also thinned.

Who could blame people for leaving, given what the lieutenant had said?

But intimidation tactics had the opposite effect on her—as they did with Cate and Grace. The Reilly women were a strong bunch. Sometimes headstrong.

And this could be one of those times.

As the lieutenant started toward her through the crowd—no doubt coming to pass on the news Brent had already shared—Eve shored up her resolve. Brent wanted her safe—and away from this park. She wanted that too.

But would running eliminate the threat? Would this Al

person give up if today was a bust—or would he or she be more determined than ever to carry out their mission?

If they were, this nightmare was going to drag on. And that was unacceptable. After sticking close to home as much as she could and operating on high alert in public for three long weeks, one fact was crystal clear.

Living in fear stunk.

She had to put this chapter of her life behind her and begin a new one with the man racing toward the park at this very moment.

But how to turn that page sooner rather than later?

As the lieutenant approached, an idea began to percolate in her mind. It was a bit audacious—and carried a certain amount of risk—but it could end this now. Today.

Brent, however, wouldn't like it. At all.

She rose when the lieutenant entered the tent, weighing the pros and cons of the plan forming in her mind. Details would have to be worked out so as few people as possible were at risk, but it had potential.

The challenge was convincing law enforcement—and one detective in particular—to consider it.

Especially since running away and hiding would be a whole lot safer for her.

26

SOMEONE MUST HAVE alerted the cops that Eve Reilly was a target.

From his position behind a tree in the wooded area on the far fringe of the picnic site, Buzz surveyed the scene through his dark-tinted sunglasses. The bulk of the crowd was milling around the picnic pavilions—but she was in a tent, surrounded by uniformed officers.

As he watched, more cops lowered the remaining flaps, hiding her from view. Unless they'd gotten wind of the plan Dan had concocted, they wouldn't be taking all those precautions to keep her out of the public eye.

He muttered a curse. This was not how today was supposed to play out.

With the speech already thirty-five minutes behind schedule, whatever cover Dan had arranged to shift suspicion away from him wouldn't last much longer. In fact, it might already be toast. Everything had been scheduled on the assumption that the Republican group would follow its agenda for the afternoon.

So what was he supposed to do now?

Buzz squinted at the tent, mind racing.

Could he somehow still make this work? Come up with

an alternate strategy that would allow him to complete his mission?

Maybe. Unlike his high school chums, he was inventive. Creative. Smart.

If he could pull this off despite the change in plans, Dan would be impressed—and perhaps entrust him with other high-profile assignments. Carrying signs and marching against oppression was fine, but he was capable of doing more. Much more.

And taking out Eve Reilly despite the challenges he faced would help him going forward. Perhaps Dan would even involve him in the planning for future events.

Not that being in charge was important, of course. Hierarchies were inherently undemocratic. Organizations should be horizontal.

Nevertheless . . . someone had to arrange and manage events like this, and he was more prepared than—

A movement behind him caught his eye, and he swiveled away from the tent.

The black bloc folks who'd been infiltrating the woods during the delay, trying to catch a glimpse of what was going on at the picnic site, were drifting back toward the parking area.

Someone must have finally taken charge or gotten direction on how to proceed.

That would be a positive development.

He checked the tent again, where cops were stationed every few yards around the perimeter.

An idea began to take shape in his mind.

Having Eve on stage—and clueless about the planned attack—was ideal, but isolating her could also work to his advantage . . . if he could convince the small-group Antifa leaders his proposal had merit.

He followed his fellow protestors back to the lot, formulating his spiel as clusters of people drew close to their leaders to hear the low-pitched updates.

"From what we're observing, the organizers and cops think the keynote speaker should have extra protection. She's been secured in a tent." The thirtysomething guy who was in charge of his group pulled up his hood and shifted away from the cop loitering a few yards away. "We assume that's why they've delayed her speech. Worst case, they could cancel it. We're of a mind to proceed with the march, but we want to hear your thoughts."

Buzz let a few people speak first. No one had any alternate ideas, and the consensus seemed to be to proceed with that approach given how far many of them had traveled to take part in the protest.

"I have another suggestion." Buzz pulled up his own hood. "I think we're missing an opportunity here. Eve Reilly stands for everything we hate. I have to believe, given the original plan, that our gathering was designed to call attention to the disparity between her view and ours—and the danger she poses to our cause thanks to her wide platform."

Nods of assent gave him the confidence to continue—and as he outlined the tactic he'd come up with for the group to home in on her, they grew more vigorous.

"I like your idea." The leader glanced around at the other groups. "And we have to make it happen fast. She could leave the park at any moment. Let me touch base with the others. If everyone's in agreement, we'll head over there ASAP. Be prepared to move. And you"—he indicated the woman with the smoke emitter—"watch for my signal as we get close."

Buzz faded back, avoiding the quiet conversation taking place in his group. He didn't have to say anything else. His idea had been well-received by everyone, and the other groups would likely fall in line.

This wasn't as perfect as the original plan, but it would

give him the access and black bloc anonymity necessary to carry out his mission.

And before this day was over, if all went as he hoped, he'd make history—by making Eve Reilly history.

"No way." Brent folded his arms tight against his chest and gave Eve his sternest look. The one that never failed to intimidate even hardened street criminals.

It had been bad enough to arrive on site and find she'd refused to leave until the two of them talked, but her idea to smoke out Al was short-circuiting his lungs.

Unfortunately, his intimidation tactic didn't work with the woman standing toe-to-toe with him.

"Brent . . . be reasonable."

"I am being reasonable." He scanned the officers, who'd withdrawn a few yards to give them privacy while they conversed, and dropped his voice. "Eve, I know you want this solved. I do too. And I promise you, we'll work relentlessly to identify and find Al."

"But Al is here today. With my plan, we don't have to wait. We just force his or her hand and end this now."

"No. It's too dangerous. Your plan could get you killed."

"Not if precautions are taken. Put several officers around me, give me a bulletproof vest like all of them are wearing, and I'll be fine."

Appealing to her own safety wasn't working.

Time to switch tactics.

"Other people could be hurt or killed."

"That's why I suggested a buffer area between me and the Republican group during the speech. This Al can't be toting a rifle in the Antifa crowd. Everyone would notice it. So he or she must have a pistol or a knife. They'll have to get close for either to be effective. If someone darts from the crowd toward me, your people should have more than sufficient opportunity to take them down."

"We don't know that Al is part of the black bloc group. This person could be a hired sniper—and a proficient marksman can hit the T-zone"—he traced a line with his none-too-steady index finger between her eyes and down her nose—"from very far away."

She swallowed. "You think Antifa hires snipers?"

"Never underestimate the enemy."

Her brow knitted . . . and then she shook her head. "No. If they're somehow trying to pin this on Steve, we know he isn't a sniper. It's someone in the group hiding under cover of black attire and the crowd."

No surprise that she'd found the flaw in his logic, but it had been worth a try. Because he really hated to resort to the easy solution—asking the president of the Young Republican group to cancel the remainder of the event as a matter of public safety. The man had been amenable to that suggestion earlier, according to the lieutenant hovering near the entrance to the tent. It was a viable option.

But he'd rather not pull rank on Eve. That kind of high-handed tactic could undermine their relationship. Best case, she'd come to terms with the situation on her own and decide to walk away. After that, they could have her out of the park in—

"We've got movement at the perimeter."

As one of the officers at the edge of the tent relayed that terse observation, the lieutenant joined them. "We have to leave. The Antifa folks are heading this direction."

Brent gritted his teeth. The time for talk—and negotiation—was over. If Eve hated him for taking control, he'd have to live with the consequences.

At least she'd be alive.

"What's the plan?"

"Officers are asking everyone attending the event to vacate the site as fast as possible. Most of them are parked nearby and shouldn't have any issue getting to their cars."

Over the man's shoulder, Brent watched the crowd begin to stream toward the parking area as black-clad figures appeared from several directions in the distance and surged toward the picnic area.

Further debate with Eve about her harebrained scheme to flush out Al would be pointless.

Al was coming to them on his or her own.

Pulse skyrocketing, he took Eve's arm. "We have to get Ms. Reilly out."

"A cruiser is waiting in the parking lot." The lieutenant waved over the officers on security duty, who closed in around them. "Let's move."

He took the lead, while Brent stayed close to Eve as the officers tightened the circle around them and set a fast pace toward the lot.

In four minutes, they should be safe.

But four minutes was an eternity in a volatile situation—and much could go wrong.

So until they were in the car, on the road, and speeding away, the danger remained.

And at this juncture, all he could do was pray they'd make it to safety.

―――――――

They'd waited too long.

Eve was getting away!

Buzz glared at the small cluster of officers bunched around her as they left the tent and hustled her toward the parking lot—and the large contingent of uniformed officers between her entourage and the encroaching black bloc force.

His fellow Antifa supporters, who'd split up to come in

from different directions, continued to march toward the picnic site, but with their target on the move, no one seemed sure what to do.

"Follow the speaker!" He called out the command and ducked low, leaving his group behind to work his way into a cluster closer to Eve.

It was time to hurl those smoke cartridges and create chaos, slow down her exit.

As if they'd read his mind, the group leaders began lifting their hands.

Within seconds, smoke began to swirl through the air.

Yes!

He had three minutes to carry out his mission.

"Hurry! Close in on the speaker, keep her from leaving!" He grabbed the arms of the two people closest to him. "Link up!"

They did as he instructed, while a dozen people managed to muscle past the police and block off access to the patrol car waiting for her.

The cluster of officers around her stopped. Unholstered their weapons.

Not good.

Dan had assured him he'd be able to complete his task and get out before the confrontation turned nasty—but no one had expected a leak would alert the cops that Eve could be at risk or the heightened police presence.

Should he give up? Abort his mission?

No.

He was too close to back off.

Around him, the chanting was growing louder, and the anger swirling through the air was almost tangible as police began to tussle with several of the more aggressive protestors.

Buzz flexed his fingers, his respiration quickening. Pointing his gun at someone other than Eve today hadn't been part of the plan, but if that's what it took to get to her—so be it.

Because whoever came between him and his target—or him and escape—was fair game.

———

She should have agreed to go when the lieutenant asked her to leave the picnic after Brent's phone call. Had she done so, she wouldn't be watching dark smoke billow in the sky above her, nor would she be putting others in danger.

If anyone got hurt today, it would be her fault.

As Eve grappled with guilt and regret, the officers around her halted their forward momentum and closed ranks.

At the abrupt stop, she stumbled.

Brent's grip on her arm tightened, steadying her, and she rose on tiptoe to try and see what was going on.

"Watch your head!" Brent snapped out the order and tugged her back down as the angry shouts and loud chanting around them grew louder.

"Is it too late to say I'm sorry?" She looked up at him.

"We can discuss it later." His razor-sharp gaze was focused on the black-clad crowd that was getting closer and closer, the grim line of his mouth and every taut angle of his face screaming red alert.

"Why did we stop?"

"No access to the car. We're surrounded."

He retrieved his own weapon—and her heart rate rocketed to warp speed. Would it really come down to a shoot-out?

She clenched her fingers and tried to keep breathing.

"Brent." She had to raise her volume to be heard above the shouting and chanting that continued to crescendo as the Antifa contingent advanced. "Do they have weapons?"

"Unknown. That's why ours are out."

"You won't shoot unless they do, though—right?"

"That's the general rule, especially in today's world. St. Louis police can't afford to be in the news again."

True. Disputes about discrimination or race relations or anarchy or a dozen other lightning-rod issues could rip a community apart—as she'd often discussed on her program when covering current events.

But she'd never expected to be in the middle of one.

Thank God there were men and women who were willing to put their life on the line every day to keep citizens safe, despite the constraints and lawsuits and vilification that had become part of a career in law enforcement.

If she got out of this alive, that was going to be the topic of her next broadcast. *If* being the operative word, given the mob scene around her.

The truth was, there was a high probability this wasn't going to end without someone being seriously injured—or worse.

Including her.

He had sixty seconds left until the smoke emitters ran out of juice—and Eve Reilly was still twenty yards away.

But the surging crowd was gaining ground, and the police were on overload trying to deal with the belligerent protestors, the noise, the smoke, and the media that had rushed into the fray.

He was going to be able to do this.

A rush of exhilaration coursed through him, and he pushed the black-clad guys ahead of him toward Eve.

"Surround her!"

As he yelled the battle cry, he dove into another cluster of shouting protestors that was also closing in on Eve.

The stars had aligned at last.

Around him, the strident voices were loud, the smoke was creating a screen, and there were a sufficient number of similarly dressed black bloc people to provide anonymity.

He slid his hand into his pocket.

Clamped his fingers around the handle of the pistol.

Took a deep breath.

This was it.

In less than thirty seconds, he'd take out the cop blocking his view of Eve—and then with a fast pop . . . pop . . . pop . . . fire the next bullets into her. He'd drop the gun, dive back into the teeming mass of people as chaos reigned, and disappear.

It was as good as done.

27

THIS WAS A NIGHTMARE.

Heart pounding, Brent did a rapid three-sixty sweep.

The protestors had broken through the police lines on two sides, and other breaches appeared to be imminent.

A loud cry went up on his right, and he swung that direction.

Tear gas had been deployed.

He winced.

There may have been no other recourse, given the deteriorating state of affairs, but getting a faceful of oleoresin capsicum would only make a confrontational crowd more hostile.

"Taser! Taser! Taser!"

The shouted alert by an officer on his left was followed by the crack of the discharge.

It sounded like a gunshot.

Screams erupted from all directions.

The chaos worsened as about half of the protestors scattered while the rest pushed harder against the uniformed human barricade with enraged shouts and curses.

This was as volatile and dangerous as any situation he'd encountered in all his years as a street cop.

But his precarious position wasn't what jacked his pulse

into the stratosphere. Personal risk came with the job. He could handle that.

The risk to Eve?

Not so much.

"We have to keep moving." As he spoke, he urged the cop ahead of him to press on toward the patrol car. Hunkering down wasn't going to protect them if more of the protestors broke through the barrier.

The officer in the lead started forward again.

Eve's grip on his arm tightened, and he gave her a fast assessment.

Face white. Eyes too big. Lips quivering.

She was scared out of her mind.

He could relate. This crowd was beyond hostile.

But reinforcements had to be on the way. Someone would have called this in to dispatch by now, alerted headquarters that the simmering conditions had exploded. The already large law enforcement presence would soon swell and they'd regain control—if the officers on site could hold off the crowd that long.

"Taser! Taser! Taser!" Another warning shout . . . followed by the sharp crack of a second shot.

More screams added to the pandemonium.

The small entourage around Eve stopped again, and Brent scrutinized the area ahead.

A half dozen or more hooded activists were barreling toward them.

"Back off!" The officer in front shouted the command and yanked out his pepper spray.

Not the best tactical weapon, given the direction of the wind. If the OC blew back at them, they'd be—

A rock sailed past his head, and Brent ducked, folding Eve beneath him.

Ugly didn't begin to describe the scene.

And with a hundred feet separating them from the squad car, it could get a lot uglier.

He was almost there.

Buzz pulled out his subcompact Glock and tucked it against his hoodie, barrel aimed at the ground as his feet pounded the pavement in rhythm with his pounding pulse.

All around him black-hooded figures were breaking through the uniformed human barricade and shouting the slogan of the day—Less Power, Less Politics, More People—and waving signs with the same message.

The noise level was rising, and the Tasers that had been fired had conditioned everyone in the area to the bang of a gun. A few more shots would get little attention.

Perfect.

He tucked himself into the middle of the group racing toward Eve Reilly.

The protestors around him planned to block her path—but he would do much, much more.

In T-minus ten seconds and counting.

A bead of sweat slid down Eve's forehead as Brent remained bent over her, forcing her to lean forward.

It was hard to breathe in the close huddle of bodies.

Or maybe fear was paralyzing her lungs.

Whatever.

She had to have air.

Lifting her head as high as she could, she tried to inhale a few wisps.

No go. There was zero ventilation in these claustrophobic quarters.

Black spots began to flicker in her field of vision—but just when she thought she was going to pass out for lack of oxygen, the bodies around her shifted, and a slight opening let in a puff of fresh air.

Thank you, Lord!

She leaned toward it and filled her lungs. Started to repeat the process.

Froze.

One of the hooded protestors running toward them was holding a gun against his chest!

An instant later, he was gone, lost in a sea of black.

She stared at the spot.

Had she imagined that? Was her crushing fear creating danger where there was none?

Or had her tiny window to the outside world, which framed that one protestor to the exclusion of all else, given her a spotlighted view no one else had?

All at once the guy was back in sight, charging to the front of the group.

She gasped.

Her imagination wasn't playing tricks on her.

He had a gun.

"Brent!" She tried to shout a warning, but it was lost in the cacophony around her.

The man swung the gun toward the cop in front of her.

"No!" With superhuman strength, she broke free of Brent's hold and shoved the officer shielding her with as much force as she could muster.

Under normal circumstances, her willowy frame wouldn't have had much impact on a muscled six-foot-tall guy who was in full-alert mode, but a push from behind hadn't been on his radar—and adrenaline was known to impart superpowers in life-and-death circumstances.

This situation qualified.

No one was going to die because of her.

As Eve thrust the cop aside, she pointed and shouted. "Gun!"

A sharp report echoed through the crowd.

She jerked back.

Frowned.

Had someone shoved her?

Another crack snapped through the air.

This one, however, was more muffled. Fainter. In fact, all the noise around her began to fade.

How odd.

And why did her legs suddenly feel weak and—

All at once, a searing pain sucked her into a vortex, and she slumped toward the ground.

Had she been . . . shot?

Maybe.

Because the last image that registered as the world around her faded was the ashen face of the man she'd hoped would play a starring role in a future that now might never be.

No!

As Eve sagged against him, Brent holstered his Sig and swept her into his arms, his gaze riveted on the round, ragged—and widening—red stain on the right side of her abdomen.

Despite all their efforts to protect her, Al had bested them.

But he wasn't going to win.

Lord, please don't let him win!

"Ms. Reilly's been shot! Close ranks!" As he barked out the order, the cops around him complied while the other officers in the vicinity became more aggressive, driving the crowd back with every available means short of using bullets.

Thank God.

They had to regain control here.

"Let's get her back to the tent, away from this mess." The

lieutenant muscled in and spoke in his ear, motioning for nearby officers to accompany them as he hustled the group toward the protective canopy.

Brent followed him, trying not to jostle Eve. She was breathing, but her complexion had lost every vestige of color.

Once inside the tent, he gently set her on the ground and knelt beside her.

Her eyelids fluttered. "Brent?"

At her barely-there whisper, he leaned close. "I'm here, Eve." He took her cold hand. "Hang in. Help is coming."

She didn't respond.

On her other side, the officer she'd shoved aside dropped down beside her. "I'm also an EMT." He rolled her a bit to the left. "It was a through and through. Pretty straight trajectory. That's a plus."

Meaning the bullet probably hadn't ricocheted too much off bones or organs and left a ton of unseen damage in its wake.

"What can I do?" Brent had to force the strained question past the constriction in his throat.

"We have to put pressure on the wounds, front and back. Sterile pads would be ideal, but whatever we can muster will suffice." The man lifted Eve's wrist and pressed two fingers to her radial artery.

Brent fumbled with the buttons on his shirt and ripped it off. Folded the fabric and tucked it under Eve, against the exit wound.

One of the other officers handed him a stack of paper napkins.

He pressed those against the smaller entrance site and exerted pressure, sandwiching the two wounds.

In the background, multiple sirens pierced the air.

Please let the ambulance be one of them!

One of the other officers started to elevate her legs, but the EMT waved him off, keeping his attention on his watch. "Not with an abdominal injury."

The man backed away.

Brent watched the rapid, shallow rise and fall of her chest. Shock was setting in.

Across from him, the officer raised his head. "For the record, she saved my life. I didn't see the guy with the gun—but he was aiming for me. She must have spotted him, then shoved me out of the way."

The pressure in Brent's throat intensified. That sounded like Eve. She was the kind of woman who cared passionately about others, who would rather take a bullet than put someone else at risk.

The kind of woman any guy with half a brain would want to pursue.

And if God gave him another chance to test the waters of romance, he intended to paddle with both oars toward the copper-haired radio personality who'd breathed new life into a heart that had long lain dormant.

Was that Cate's voice . . . and Grace's?

Eve strained to hear the hushed conversation taking place just out of earshot.

Yes, it was them—but why were they hovering nearby while she was sleeping?

She shifted—but gasped as pain knifed through her right side.

The voices fell silent.

Had she been dreaming them?

And why did every muscle in her body ache?

Did her discomfort have anything to do with the strange dream she'd—

"Eve?" Someone smoothed the hair back from her forehead with gentle fingers. "Can you hear me?"

Grace again.

She forced her sluggish eyelids open.

Grace stood above her, features fuzzy—but clearly worried. On her other side, Cate gave her an appraising inspection.

Why were they—

Oh!

A swirl of memories engulfed her.

The belligerent crowd.

The guy with the gun.

The intense burning sensation.

Brent's strong arms and ravaged face as she fell.

Brent!

He'd been close to the shooter too—and at least one more shot had been fired after the one she took.

Panic squeezed her heart.

"Where's Brent?"

"Hey." Cate gave an indignant sniff. "What are we, chopped liver?"

"And here I came racing in from outstate to see you." Grace affected an insulted tone, but the squeeze of her fingers and her quick wink communicated affection rather than offense. "I could have gotten a speeding ticket."

"I would have taken care of it for you, given the circumstances."

"I know." Grace smirked at Cate.

"Where's Brent?" Eve tightened her grip on Grace's fingers.

"Hey. Chill." Grace motioned toward the door with her free hand. "He's in the hall, taking another call. But for most of the time since you were brought up here, he's been within touching distance of your bed."

"So he's not h-hurt?"

"No."

Thank you, God.

"Did anyone else get injured?"

Grace motioned toward Cate.

Her older sister picked up the narrative. "Minor damage for the most part. What you'd expect when a large crowd gets unruly. The lowlife who went after you is the only one with serious damage, courtesy of two gunshot wounds inflicted by law enforcement. It's fifty-fifty whether he makes it." Cate's expression hardened. "Right or wrong, I'm not wasting any prayers for recovery on his behalf."

"Me neither." Grace squeezed her fingers again. "You're the one I care about."

"But I'll be okay, right?"

"Only by the grace of God." Cate blinked away the out-of-character sheen in her eyes.

Uh-oh.

Eve braced for bad news.

"You're scaring her, Cate." Grace sent their eldest sibling a chiding look, then refocused on her. "Yes, you'll be fine. The bullet clipped your liver and cracked a rib but didn't hit any other major organs and there was no vascular damage. The liver laceration was grade III, and those don't require surgery. However, there *is* bleeding, so they'll be monitoring that until it stops. You'll also be on bed rest for a while to avoid any more tearing and to prevent further blood loss. Did I cover it all?" She checked with Cate.

"Other than the entry and exit wounds. They cleaned them up and bandaged them. Those scars will be the only visible signs of today's trauma. If the bullet had entered—or traveled—a couple of inches to the right, we'd be having a different conversation. Or not."

In other words, she could have died.

A shiver ran through her.

Cate drew closer and laid a hand on her shoulder, gentling her voice. "It's okay, Evie. Take a deep breath."

Evie.

Her big sister hadn't called her that since the day she broke up with her first high school crush and was certain the world had ended.

Eve managed to summon up a smile. "It hurts too much."

"A cracked rib can do that to you." Grace adjusted the sheet over her. "But it will heal."

"What time is it?"

Cate twisted her wrist. "A few minutes after six."

Eve did the math. "So I've been in a fog for hours?"

"I think they pumped you full of narcotics while you were in the ER."

She wrinkled her nose. "I don't want any more of those."

"You may feel differently once the painkillers in your bloodstream wear off." Grace gave her a stern look. "You don't have to suffer, you know. That's what drugs are for."

"I'll keep that in mind." Especially since every movement hurt.

But she didn't want narcotics.

All she needed was a brown-eyed detective by her side.

Her gaze strayed to the door.

"He'll be back as soon as he gets off the phone, if his pattern holds." Cate folded her arms, and one side of her mouth rose. "In the meantime, you'll have to put up with us."

She transferred her attention back to her sisters. "Not a hardship." She reached for both their hands. "I love you guys."

"Mutual, I'm sure."

Eve's lips twitched. Leave it to Cate to resort to their old game of responding with lines from the classic movies they'd watched over and over again while growing up. Mushy wasn't her sister's forte, even if her heart was gold.

"*White Christmas*. And I'm sorry to put you guys through this."

Never one to be left out, the baby of the family chimed in. "Love means never having to say you're sorry."

"*Love Story*—and you guys are nuts."

"But we're *your* nuts. One for all, all for one." Grace grinned. "However—we're not opposed to swelling the ranks." She flicked a glance toward the hall.

Eve didn't respond—but it was good to know her sisters were on board with the program.

Because unless today's drama had given Brent a lethal case of cold feet, from now on her number one priority was getting to know him better—and perhaps, if all went well, adding a fourth Musketeer to her family circle in the not-too-distant future.

Brent dropped more coins into the vending machine, punched a button, and waited for the soft drink can to clunk down the chute.

Come on, Colin. Return my call.

His cell began to vibrate as he retrieved the can of Diet Sprite.

Finally.

He set the soda beside the bottle of Lipton mango iced tea on the table beside him.

"What do you have?" He snapped out the question without bothering to greet his colleague.

"Hello to you too." Was that a touch of annoyance under Colin's dry humor?

"Sorry." He wiped a hand down his face. "I hate not being in the thick of the investigation, but I don't want to leave until I talk to Eve."

"Understood. Been there, done that. How's Al, aka Michael Alan Lander?"

"Critical. They're saying fifty/fifty. Olivia didn't make it. What's the story on Lander?"

"We're still digging. He and Eve went to the same high school but were in different classes. After living in California for a while, he came back here two years ago. Not married. Works as a house painter."

"What's his connection to Antifa?"

"Evidence in his apartment suggests he's been involved in the movement since his days in California. Unless Eve can shed some light on why he may have a personal grudge against her, my take is that he was a zealot who somehow caught Olivia's eye, and she tapped him for today's assignment."

"Did you find out anything else about her?"

"Some. The Battle of Seattle material in her file cabinets— along with attached handwritten notes—indicates she took part in the 1999 World Trade Organization protests . . . in which the Direct Action Network played a major role. That's the earliest indication we've found of radical activities after her first husband was killed."

"I wonder if that event reignited the fire in her, and once her second husband died she dived back into anti-government protest mode in a more behind-the-scenes role."

"Could be. Once a rebel, always a rebel."

"But why would she marry a banker and live a quiet life for more than three decades?"

"Maybe she didn't. It's possible she was dabbling in anarchist activities on the QT all along. The files in her office or on her computer may confirm that. Or not. At this point it doesn't much matter."

True.

"Keep me in the loop, okay?" Brent glanced toward the door to Eve's room.

"You got it."

Brent pressed the end button, slid the phone back onto

his belt under the bilious green scrub top he'd scrounged up to replace his bloodstained shirt, and picked up the drinks. With Eve's sisters hanging around, he might have to defer the discussion he wanted to have with her.

But Cate and Grace had to go home and sleep sometime.

If necessary, he'd wait them out.

Because he wasn't leaving without saying what he wanted to say.

He strode down the hall, shouldered the door open—and stopped as three pairs of eyes swung his direction.

Only one set, however, stayed on his radar.

Eve's beautiful jade-green irises were focused on him—bright, alert . . . and filled with warmth and tenderness.

His breath hitched.

"Are those for us?"

Somewhere in the recesses of his consciousness, the amused question registered, and he dragged his gaze away from Eve.

Cate was pointing at the drinks he was holding.

"Oh. Yeah." He handed her the Diet Sprite and passed the tea to Grace. "They didn't have your brand. Sorry."

"I'll suffer. Thank you." She lifted it toward him in a toast.

"A man who fetches drinks for the sisters." Cate grinned at him, then gave Eve a thumbs-up. "Grace—I think this is our cue to leave. We can rustle up dinner and come back later."

"Works for me." Grace bent and kissed Eve's forehead. "Take care of yourself while we're gone—although I think we're leaving you in good hands."

Cate squeezed Eve's fingers. "Call if you need anything your friend here can't supply. As if." She snickered.

The two sisters made a quick exit.

As the door shut behind them, Brent walked toward the bed.

"Hi." A slight flush bloomed on Eve's cheeks as he approached her. "I've been waiting for you to—"

He leaned down, covered her lips with his—and discovered that the trite cliché was true.

Time stopped.

A minute later . . . an hour . . . who knew? . . . he backed off a few inches.

Eve stared up at him. "Wow."

That didn't come close to describing his reaction.

"Yeah." The hoarse response was all he could manage while trying to convince his lungs to kick back in.

Her hand found his, and she gripped it. Tight. "Does that mean what I think it does?"

"Uh-huh."

Joy chased away any lingering shadows on her face. "Epic, as the younger crowd would say. But I could use a little more convincing." She tugged him closer.

He resisted. Despite the temptation to dive back in, he had a speech to give. "Hold on a sec. I want to clarify a few things."

After studying him for a moment, she folded her hands on the white sheet that outlined her slim form. "Fine. As long as you're not about to give me the I-like-you-a-lot-but-this-will-never-work-and-that-was-a-goodbye-kiss speech."

He hitched up one side of his mouth at her blunt, to-the-point comment. No pussyfooting around with this woman. "A couple of weeks ago, that's where I was." He sat on the bed beside her, careful not to jostle the mattress. She seemed alert and in high spirits, but she had to be hurting. "However, I've had a change of heart. Emphasis on heart."

She tipped her head. "What does that mean?"

"It means your assessment was on the mark. My heart wasn't atrophied. It was sleeping. Waiting for the right woman to come along and nudge it awake. Kind of like in Cinderella."

She grinned. "Wrong fairy tale. The prince awakens Sleep-ing Beauty with a kiss. Cinderella was more proactive."

"Then I think our story is the best of two fairy tales."

"Nice take." She touched his hand. "Does that mean you've made peace with your worry about the risks of your profession, and the effect they could have on a significant other?"

"Having just lived through that scenario—in reverse—I've realized that as scary as risks can be, strong people aren't freaked out by them. They do what has to be done to support and protect the one they lo . . . they care about. I'd put you in the strong camp."

"I'm liking the sound of this."

"Good." He took a deep breath—and took the plunge. "I know we only met three weeks ago . . . and my previous rela-tionship notwithstanding, I'm not usually the impulsive type . . . but from the day our paths crossed, I felt a spark with you that I've never felt with anyone else. Unless I'm misreading your signals, you feel it too. So I'd like to propose that we spend the next few weeks . . . or months . . . seeing where that spark leads. What do you say?"

"Sign me up. Starting now." She urged him close again.

This time he didn't balk.

Except as he leaned down, the door to her room opened and a nurse entered.

He rested his forehead against hers and groaned.

"Talk about rotten timing." Eve muttered the comment close to his ear.

"I have to check your dressings." The woman looked at the two of them, and her eyes began to twinkle. "But I'll work fast."

Brent eased his hand out of Eve's and stood. "I'll wait in the hall."

"Don't go far." She touched her lips with her fingertips

and blew a kiss his direction, sending a jolt of testosterone hurtling through him.

"Never."

And as he left the room and took up a position in the hall across from her door, that was a promise he intended to keep not just today, but every single day for the rest of his life.

EPILOGUE

C AN YOU BELIEVE this view is real? Don't you feel like you've stepped into a fairy tale?" From their perch on top of a vineyard-covered Tuscan hill, Eve straddled the frame of her bike and rested her hands on the grips.

Brent gave the scene a sweep. The newly green grapevines, silvery olive groves, fields of vibrant red poppies, and—clinging to a distant hillside—a cobblestone-paved village were, indeed, charming.

But no more charming than the woman sharing this journey with him.

He smiled at his bride beside him. "I feel like that every day."

She turned toward him, the sun glinting in her copper-colored hair as she removed her helmet. "I was talking about this idyllic place. It's like a storybook."

"The place is only the backdrop for the book. You're the star of my story."

And what an amazing story it was.

Who would have believed eight short months ago—when he'd been convinced love wasn't in the cards for him and he'd end up spending the rest of his life alone—that he'd be here today, honeymooning in these ancient hills with a woman who filled his life with sunshine and laughter?

Pressure built in his throat as gratitude welled up inside him.

Her eyes softened. "Have I told you lately that I love you?"

"No. It's been at least two hours."

"I'll let actions speak louder than words." She leaned over and kissed him.

Thoroughly.

Only after a passing car offered a quick honk of encouragement and the driver shouted *"Viva amore!"* did she back off with a soft flush.

"Whoops. I keep forgetting there are other people in the world—and you may take that as a compliment." The corners of her mouth rose, and she traced a finger along the line of his jaw.

"I shall." He captured her hand in his. "But if you keep that up, I'll be tempted to thank you in ways not suitable for public consumption."

She waggled her eyebrows. "In that case—why don't we find a nice, secluded spot to enjoy the picnic lunch the inn packed?"

"Secluded is perfect—and I *am* hungry." He winked at her.

"You've turned into a real flirt, you know that?"

"Complaining?"

"Nope." She gave a saucy toss of her head and mounted her bike. "First one who finds a spot for a picnic gets a prize."

Pushing off, she pedaled down the road.

Brent gave her a head start, more for his benefit than hers. What a joy to watch her so happy and carefree and healthy after all she'd been through. It had taken months for her stamina to recover after the shooting—and she still struggled with nightmares, as he'd learned this past week.

But Olivia was gone, along with the basement control center that had launched countless attacks nationwide—and while the infamous Al had recovered from his wounds, he was facing a very long prison sentence.

That threat was over.

As for any new challenges that lay ahead—he'd be by her side through those too.

A spot he intended to occupy all the days of his life.

For the Scripture passage read at their wedding summed up his feelings to a T. The value of a worthy wife was far beyond jewels.

And as he pushed off to follow her toward a line of tall, stately poplars in the distance, he gave thanks for the unexpected happy ending that had graced his life and filled all the dark places with the light of love.

"Do you want another grape?" Eve dangled a cluster in front of her husband.

Husband.

Still hard to believe, even though they were halfway through their two-week honeymoon.

How on earth had she lucked out and found a guy like Brent?

Or maybe luck had nothing to do with it. Maybe a greater hand had been at work.

"Nope." He stretched out on his side beside her, propped himself up with his elbow on the picnic blanket, and played with her hair. "I want my prize. I found this spot, didn't I?" He swept a hand around them.

She felt around in the picnic basket, withdrew a biscotti, and held it up.

"Uh-uh. I want something softer and sweeter."

She reached for the basket again. "I think there's a piece of that pine nut cake you liked at dinner last—"

He grabbed her hand. "I can think of a much better prize."

A tingle of excitement spiraled through her at the ardor in his eyes. "Like what?"

"Like this." He brushed her hair aside, leaned close, and pressed a kiss behind her ear.

Whew.

"You do realize . . ." Her voice squeaked, and she cleared her throat. "You do realize we're outside. Anyone could happen by and find us in a clinch."

"So? This is Italy. You heard the man a few minutes ago. *Viva amore.* I think the locals would approve of a few passionate kisses in a romantic setting like this." He nuzzled her neck again.

Eve checked out their picnic spot. They were surrounded by the ruins of an old stone barn, nothing but open fields of bobbing poppies around them over the low walls that remained and a cloudless, cobalt-blue sky overhead. There hadn't been a single house on the dirt track that had led to this hilltop, which boasted a stunning view.

She shifted toward him. "I'm in." She snuggled closer to him. "For the record, I wouldn't let just any guy talk me into heavy-duty kissing in public."

"I should hope not."

She gave him a playful swat. "I mean it would take a very special man to convince me to be this bold." She touched his cheek and softened her voice. "Someone I'd trust with my life—and my heart."

A sudden, faint sheen shimmered in Brent's eyes. "I wish I had your skill with words."

"Your words are fine—and your actions are eloquent."

"You're being kind."

"Nope. Honest."

"Trust me, I know my limitations—and I'm not great with words. That's your forte. I'm always afraid I'll disappoint you."

His earnestness tightened her throat. "You could never disappoint me."

"You'll tell me if I'm not communicating enough, right?"

It was the same concern he'd raised on numerous occasions—and she offered the same reassurance.

"I promise. But that works both ways. If there's anything I can do to be a better wife, you have to promise to tell me too."

"You're perfect exactly as you are."

"No one's perfect."

"You're perfect for me."

"That's how I feel about you."

And it was true. Brent may have closed off his heart for most of his life—and he might be new at the relationship game—but he was a fast learner.

Most important of all, he tried his best every single day to make her happy, and he loved her with every fiber of his being.

What more could a woman ask?

"So about that prize . . ." He skimmed his hand down her side, pausing at the curve of her waist.

She held out her arms. "Come here."

He didn't hesitate.

Lowering his mouth to hers, he showed her with each move, each touch, each tender caress, how much he loved her.

Eve sighed into his kiss, memorizing every nuance of this enchanted moment.

The lark trilling its sweet song from the bough of a nearby olive tree.

The soft brush of the gentle breeze.

The sun smiling down from the heavens, dispensing warmth and light.

The scent of wild thyme drifting through the air, imparting tranquility and contentment.

And most of all, the special man who'd pledged his love forever and brought her to this magical place.

Not every day of their life together would be this perfect, of course. Their Tuscan idyll was the stuff dreams were made of.

Yet it wasn't a dream. It was real. As real as the vows they'd recited before God a week ago.

And as long as she lived, she would hold the memories of these days in her heart to measure the world against. A reminder that with Brent by her side, happiness was never more than a touch away.

For in his arms, surrounded by his love and cherished for exactly who she was, she'd found a rare treasure.

A preview of paradise here on earth.

Keep reading for a sneak peek of
Blackberry Beach–
the newest book in the
HOPE HARBOR SERIES
by Irene Hannon!

THE MYSTERY WOMAN WAS BACK.

Zach Garrett poured the steamed milk into the coffee mixture, creating his signature swirl pattern with the froth—all the while keeping tabs on the female customer who'd paused inside the door of The Perfect Blend, dripping umbrella in hand.

As she had on her first visit two days ago, the lady appeared to be debating whether to stay or bolt.

Wiping the nozzle on the espresso machine, he assessed her. Early to midthirties, near as he could tell given the over-sized dark sunglasses that hid most of her features. A curious wardrobe addition, given the unseasonable heavy rain that had been drenching Hope Harbor for the past seventy-two hours.

He handed the latte to the waiting customer and angled toward his Monday/Wednesday/Friday assistant barista. "Bren, you waited on her Monday, didn't you?" He indicated the slender woman with the dark, shoulder-length blunt-cut hair who continued to hover on the threshold.

Bren spared her a quick once-over as she finished grinding another batch of the top-quality Arabica beans he sourced from a fair-trade roaster in Portland. "Yeah."

"Do you remember what she ordered?"

"Small skinny vanilla latte."

"Did you get a name?"

"Nope. I asked, but she said she'd wait for her order at the pick-up counter."

In other words, the woman wanted to remain anonymous. Also curious.

While it was possible she was one of the many visitors who dropped into their picturesque town for a few days during the summer months, his gut said otherwise.

And since his people instincts had served him well in his previous profession, there was no reason to discount them now.

So who was she—and what was she doing in Hope Harbor? Only one way to find out.

"I'll take care of her."

"That works. I've already got customers." Bren inclined her head toward the couple waiting for their pound of ground coffee.

Zach called up his friendliest smile and ambled down to the end of the serving counter. "Let me guess—a small skinny vanilla latte."

The woman did a double take . . . took a step back . . . and gave the shop a quick, nervous scan. As if she was scoping out potential threats.

No worries on that score. There was nothing in The Perfect Blend to raise alarm bells. While several of the tables tucked against the walls and cozied up around the freestanding fireplace in the center were occupied, no one was paying any attention to the new arrival. The customers were all reading newspapers, absorbed in books, or chatting as they enjoyed their drinks and pastries in the Wi-Fi-free environment.

The door behind the woman opened again, nudging her aside.

Charley Lopez entered, his trademark Ducks cap secured beneath the hood of a dripping slicker.

"Sorry, ma'am." His teeth flashed white against his rich brown skin as he touched the brim of the cap, pushed the hood back to reveal his gray ponytail . . . and gave her an intent look. "I didn't mean to bump you."

"No problem." She dipped her chin and moved aside, putting some distance between them. As if his perusal had spiked her nerves.

"Are you coming in or going out?" Charley maintained his hold on the half-open door.

"Coming in." Zach answered for her. "I'm betting she's in the mood for a skinny vanilla latte."

"Excellent choice." Charley closed the door.

"Bren will handle your order as soon as she finishes with her customers, Charley." Zach kept his attention on the stranger.

"No hurry." The taco-making artist who'd called Hope Harbor home for as long as anyone could remember moseyed toward the counter. "I doubt I'll have much business at the stand, thanks to our odd weather. August is usually one of the driest months on the Oregon coast."

"Any day is a perfect day for a Charley's fish taco." Zach flashed him a grin.

"I may steal that line. It'd be a great marketing slogan."

"As if you need one. Your food speaks for itself—and from what I've observed, word of mouth generates plenty of business."

"That it does." He winked, then directed his next comment to the woman. "If you haven't visited my truck yet, it's on the wharf. Next to the gazebo."

"I may stop by."

"Please do. First order for newcomers is always on the house." He continued toward Bren.

Zach frowned. Everyone in town knew about Charley's

welcome gift of a free lunch for new residents . . . but this woman hadn't moved to Hope Harbor.

Had she?

What did Charley know that he didn't?

She edged toward the exit, and Zach shifted gears. He could pick the town sage's brain later. In the meantime, why not try to ferret out a few facts himself?

Unless his skittish customer disappeared out the door first.

He hiked up the corners of his mouth again. "One small skinny vanilla latte coming up—unless you want a different drink today?"

Hesitating, she gave the room one more survey . . . then slid her umbrella into the stand by the door. "No. That's fine."

She was staying.

First hurdle cleared.

"Can I have a name for the order?" He picked up a cup and a pen.

Silence.

He arched his eyebrows at her.

"Uh . . . Kat. With a K." She eased away, toward a deserted table in the far corner.

Second hurdle cleared.

"Got it." He jotted the name. "I'll have this ready in a couple of minutes."

She nodded and continued to the table—out of conversation range.

Blast.

Thwarted at the third hurdle.

He wasn't going to find out anything else about her.

But what did it matter? Just because he was beginning to crave feminine companionship—and the pool of eligible women in town was limited—didn't mean he should get any ideas about the first single, attractive woman who walked in.

Yeah, yeah, he'd noticed the empty fourth finger on her left hand.

He mixed the espresso and vanilla syrup together, positioned the steam nozzle below the surface of the milk until the liquid bubbled, then dipped deeper to create a whirlpool motion.

Charley wandered over while Bren prepared his café de olla, watching as Zach poured the milk into the espresso mixture, holding back the foam with a spoon to create a stylized K on top of the drink. "Beautiful. You have an artistic touch."

"Nothing like yours." He set the empty frothing pitcher aside and reached for a lid as he signaled to the woman in the corner. "I wish my coffee sold for a fraction of what your paintings bring in."

"Life shouldn't be all about making money. My stand isn't a gold mine, but I enjoy creating tacos as much as I enjoy painting. Customers for both can feel the love I put into my work. Like they can feel the love you have for this shop. It seeps into your pores the instant you cross the threshold. A person would have to be über stressed not to find peace and relaxation in this wireless zone."

The very ambiance he'd hoped to create when he'd opened a year and a half ago.

"You just made my day."

"That's what it's all about, isn't it?" Charley motioned toward the foam art. "Why don't you show that to your customer? Brighten *her* day."

Not a bad idea. Perhaps it would elicit a few words from her—or initiate a conversation.

He set the cup on the counter as she approached and offered her his most engaging grin. The one that usually turned female heads. "Your personalized skinny vanilla latte."

Lips flat, she gave his handiwork no more than a fleeting

perusal, extracted a five dollar bill from her wallet, and set it on the counter. "Keep the change."

Not only was the lady immune to his charm, she wasn't planning to linger.

Fighting back an irrational surge of disappointment, Zach put the lid on the drink and picked up the money. "Enjoy."

"Thanks." She hurried toward the door, pulled her umbrella out of the stand, and disappeared into the gray shroud hanging over the town.

"I think my attempt to brighten her day was a bust." He folded his arms as the rain pummeled the picture window.

"Oh, I don't know. Sometimes the simplest gestures of kindness can touch a heart in unseen ways."

He didn't try to hide his skepticism. "Assuming there's a heart to touch. The lady didn't exude much warmth."

"She may be hiding it behind a protective wall. Could be she's dealing with a boatload of heavy stuff. That can dampen a person's sociability."

Zach's antennas perked up. "You know anything about her?"

"Nothing much—though she seems familiar." He squinted after her. Shook his head. "It'll come to me. Anyway, I spotted her on the wharf Monday, sipping a brew from your fine establishment. She was sitting alone on a bench during one of the few monsoon-free interludes we've had this week. I got gloomy vibes. Like she was troubled—and could use a friend."

Zach wasn't about to question the veracity of Charley's intuition. The man was legendary in these parts for his uncanny insights and his ability to discern more than people willingly divulged.

Present company included.

How Charley had realized there was an unresolved issue in his past was beyond him. He'd never talked about it to anyone. But the man's astute comments, while generic, were too relevant to be random.

In fact, on more than one occasion he'd been tempted to get Charley's take on his situation.

Yet as far as he could see, there was no solution to the impasse short of returning to his former world and toeing the line—and that wasn't happening. The new life he'd built these past two and a half years suited him, and now that he was settled in Hope Harbor, he was more convinced than ever his decision to walk away had been the right one.

"You still with me, Zach?" Charley's lips tipped up.

"Yeah." He refocused. "You think she's a visitor?"

"I'd classify her more as a seeker."

What did that mean?

Before he could ask, Bren appeared at his elbow. "Here you go, Charley." She popped a cinnamon stick into his drink, snapped on a lid, and handed the cup over the counter.

"Thanks. It's a treat to have authentic Mexican coffee available here in our little town."

"We aim to please." The door opened again to admit what appeared to be a family of tourists, and Zach lifted his hand in welcome. "Everyone must be in the mood for coffee today."

"Count your blessings." Charley raised his cup in salute. "I'm off to the taco stand."

"I'll try to send a few customers your direction."

"Always appreciated. Maybe Kat will stop by."

"You know her last name?" He kept tabs on the newcomers as they perused his menu board and examined the offerings in the pastry case.

"No. But I may find out if she visits the stand. Or she might come back here again and you can take another crack at breaching that wall she's put up. See you soon." He strolled toward the door.

The new customers began to pepper him with questions about the pastry selection, but as he answered, the image of the mystery woman sitting alone on a bench at the wharf—

and Charley's comment that she could use a friend—remained front and center in his mind.

If she *was* dealing with a bunch of garbage, he ought to cut her some slack for her lack of sociability today. Been there, done that—and it was a bad place to be.

Yet thanks to grit, determination . . . and the kind people of Hope Harbor, who'd welcomed him into the community he now called home . . . he'd survived.

Hard to say if the woman hiding behind the dark shades had similar fortitude . . . and if she was merely passing through, he'd never find out.

But if she stuck around awhile, perhaps in Hope Harbor she'd discover a resolution to the thorny issues Charley seemed to think might be plaguing her.

AUTHOR'S NOTE

A S I WRAP UP my fifty-ninth novel, I'm grateful for all those who've supported and encouraged me throughout my career—and for the many sources who've lent their time and expertise to help me get the factual details right.

For this book, I want to single out FBI veteran Tom Becker, one of my first law enforcement sources when I branched into suspense in 2009 after writing contemporary romance for many years. At the time we met, Tom had moved on to a second career as a police chief after retiring from the Bureau. Since then, he has graciously and promptly gone above and beyond to answer my often complicated questions. I couldn't write credible stories without the input of professionals in law enforcement, and Tom has always brought unique insights because of his dual background at both the national and local level. He's now retired from his police chief career, but he continues to assist me whenever I reach out to him—and he was my key law enforcement source for *Point of Danger*. Thank you, Tom, for all you've done through the years to help me write the best possible books. Words can't express my gratitude.

I also want to thank my husband, Tom, for his steadfast

love and encouragement; my mom and dad, Dorothy (now cheering me on from heaven) and James Hannon—my original fan club; the readers who buy my books, many of whom have become Facebook friends; and the talented, professional team at Revell, including Dwight Baker, Kristin Kornoelje, Jennifer Leep, Michele Misiak, Karen Steele, and Gayle Raymer.

Looking ahead, in April 2021 I'll take you back to my charming Oregon seaside town of Hope Harbor, where hearts heal . . . and love blooms. In *Blackberry Beach*, you'll meet former executive Zach Garrett, who runs the local coffee shop, and a woman who comes to town incognito in search of answers . . . and winds up as Zach's neighbor. The girl next door captures his heart . . . but will she only be a temporary resident?

And next October, watch for Book 2 of the Triple Threat series, when Cate goes undercover at an exclusive girls school . . . only to run into an old flame who threatens to disrupt her case—and her heart.

Irene Hannon is the bestselling, award-winning author of more than fifty contemporary romance and romantic suspense novels. She is also a three-time winner of the RITA award—the "Oscar" of romance fiction—from Romance Writers of America and is a member of that organization's elite Hall of Fame.

Her many other awards include National Readers' Choice, Daphne du Maurier, Retailers' Choice, Booksellers' Best, Carol, and Reviewers' Choice from RT *Book Reviews* magazine, which also honored her with a Career Achievement award for her entire body of work. In addition, she is a two-time Christy award finalist.

Millions of her books have been sold worldwide, and her novels have been translated into multiple languages.

Irene, who holds a BA in psychology and an MA in journalism, juggled two careers for many years until she gave up her executive corporate communications position with a Fortune 500 company to write full-time. She is happy to say she has no regrets.

A trained vocalist, Irene has sung the leading role in numerous community musical theater productions and is also a soloist at her church. She and her husband enjoy traveling, long hikes, Saturday mornings at their favorite coffee shop, and spending time with family. They make their home in Missouri.

To learn more about Irene and her books, visit www.irene hannon.com. She posts on Twitter and Instagram, but is most active on Facebook, where she loves to chat with readers.

DANGER LURKS AROUND
EVERY CORNER